DOVE'S NEST

The Atkinson Saga
Book Three

Mollie Hardwick

SAPERE
BOOKS

DOVE'S NEST

Published by Sapere Books.

24 Trafalgar Road, Ilkley, LS29 8HH

saperebooks.com

ISBN:

CHAPTER ONE

Dove Atkinson was satisfied with the dining table. The silver shone, the napery was a brilliant white, the flower holder in the centre was filled with early roses gracefully arranged. Each of the five napkins had been folded into an intricate fan shape. It was really very gratifying to have a capable housekeeper and maids who obeyed her, without Dove being put to the necessity of speaking to them herself. She was much better at dealing with awkward people and situations than she had once been, but it was still not in her nature to be harsh.

The three wall mirrors under three cut-glass girandoles, twinkling diamonds in the light of their candles, reflected three images of Dove, each a graceful figure in an evening gown of soft rose pink, the wide hooped skirt many-flounced, the bodice as low-cut as decency permitted and fashion dictated in this year of 1854, revealing an expanse of white shoulder and quite a lot of white bosom. Bosoms were admired and proudly displayed in these days when maternity, fecund and virtuous, was personified by Queen Victoria, already the mother of eight at the age of thirty-five. Dove was forty, but looked years younger. Most women appeared dumpy, as the Queen did, in their billowing skirts; Dove had kept her slenderness and girlish air through four pregnancies. The pale gold hair was paler now, almost silver-gilt, but still held its lustre, drawn primly back from a centre parting and gathered into a chignon half hidden by an evening cap of half lace, half silk flowers. And her large, soft eyes of darkest hazel were as meltingly beautiful as when they had first charmed her husband, Joe.

Dearest Joe. How lucky she was to be married to a man so kind, tender and faithful, who adored her still after so many years of marriage. It seemed almost no time, so happy their life had been, since he had brought her to this house, their home ever since: a gracious house, plainly built of grey stone a hundred years before, its round-bayed front softened now with a veil of ivy. Through the windows Dove looked out to trees and lawns, fresh green in the dress of late spring, carefully tended by gardeners. Yes, it had mellowed. Fifteen years really had passed, since she had come here as a young wife, pregnant with her first-born, Edwin, and the stone lions guarding the porch had seemed to welcome her.

'The Lion House,' she had said, stroking the stone manes.

Dreaming, she let her mind rove back through time. Herself at sixteen, already deep in love with her cousin Joe, the red-haired young idealist who had set out to reform conditions in cotton factories, and in the course of doing so had saddled himself with a most unsuitable wife. What a blessing that Dove's lawyer father, Ephraim Atkinson, had managed to obtain that almost unheard-of thing, a divorce, for Joe, setting him free to marry the cousin he loved.

Her twin sister Belle, beautiful, passionate and wilful, the family rebel; once infatuated with her father's friend Will Raven, a man three times her age, then head over heels in love with the dashing merchant sailor George Dilworth, now her husband. Dove shook her head. She would never be quite easy in her mind about that marriage. Worrying over Belle and her stormy life had helped to kill their mother. Now Ephraim lived with his sister-in-law, Mary's spinster sister Margaret, in the tall grey house in the grey northern town of Lancaster, that crouched beneath its frowning castle.

Some of the handsome appointments of this dining room had come from that house, Dove's birthplace. Atkinson portraits, Atkinson furniture made of the mahogany brought up the River Lune to Lancaster from the West Indies, Cuba, Honduras, and made up by the firm of Gillow; Atkinson crests on Atkinson silver, all bestowed on Joe and Dove by Ephraim. 'We shan't be holding many banquets, I expect,' he had said half-ruefully; and Joe had accepted, though he could afford furnishings of his own, many times over. Now the long dining room of the Lancaster house was empty and shut, the two ageing inhabitants of the house living modestly in their separate workplaces, Ephraim in his study among his law-books, Margaret in the parlour she had made into quite a library with books of her own; among them books she had written, for she was a popular and successful novelist whose historical romances had a host of eager readers, mostly female.

'Madam?' Dove came back to reality with a start at the voice of her housekeeper, Mrs Skerritt. 'Will the gentlemen be long now, do you think, madam? Cook was wondering about the roast.'

Dove smiled. 'Yes, I know how particular she is about her beef. I should think they'll be here any time now — unless Mr Atkinson has got quite carried away in demonstrating the beauties of his model estate.'

'I shouldn't wonder. Gentlemen don't think about such things as meals being on time, it seems to me.' Mrs Skerritt sniffed, glancing at the mantelpiece clock, a pretty marble affair with a Grecian damsel reclining on top of it.

Dove went to a window. 'I thought I heard the gate. Oh, good, they're here now. Tell Cook, will you?' Three figures, dark clad and top-hatted, were advancing up the drive between the lawns. Dove quickly patted her hair and twitched at the lace of her bodice. Voices in the hall as hats and coats were taken by a maid, the door opening, the three of them in the dining room.

Joe went to her and kissed her cheek, as he always did after even a brief parting. Forty-five years had only slightly stooped his shoulders and put a scatter of grey in his dark auburn hair — red pepper and salt, Dove called it. His face was a pleasant rather than a handsome one: the strong Atkinson nose, the chin less marked, a look of kindliness about the eyes and mouth.

'My dear. We're not too late for your arrangements, I hope?'

'Not at all — it's just on six. Did you enjoy your visit, Mr Dickens?'

The novelist smiled, his great beaming smile that lit the strange eyes, once so bright but now hooded under drooping lids, tired, tired. The whole face was tired, lined with worry and ill health and overwork. He was only forty-two, looking ten years more. A goatee beard and drooping moustache veiled the sensual mouth; the once luxurious brown hair was thinning. *Tortured, driven by a fiend,* Dove thought. *Poor man, so famous and so unhappy.*

'A revelation, Mrs Atkinson. Everything I hoped for when I revisited Preston, and didn't find.'

She turned to the third member of the party. 'Basil, you look tired. Tramping all over that familiar ground again? But I expect you enjoyed it.'

'I always do. It's a matter of pride with me, as it is with Joe.' Basil Absalom, Joe's works and estate manager, was younger than any of them, a slight, tall figure who conveyed a touch of the exotic in his loosely knotted neckerchief of yellow and the length of his dark curling hair, longer than Dickens's, falling in careless profusion on his shoulders. He was Jewish in every feature: the large dark melancholy eyes, sallow complexion and full lips, the long sensitive hands of the artistic Jew; yet his brain was as acute as that of any financier. Without him Joe's factory and workers' settlement would never have flourished, Dove knew well. They had a little conspiracy of two between them. All Joe's practical ideas were encouraged by his wife and his manager. His impractical ones met with respectful treatment, but somehow, in the course of discussion, got thrown out. Sometimes importunate people would come to Joe's office or the house with hard-luck stories: a brood of children to feed, ill health, family misfortune. Occasionally they asked for work. More often they wanted money, clothing, baskets of food; but most of all money. Basil and Dove could spot them at a glance, and ask the right questions.

'Have you worked for Atkinsons before? Any references? Who is your doctor?' Discreet enquiries would be made, particularly at the Cock, the tavern in the square which was the only place to drink in the village. If the supplicant was well known there his suit was doomed. Neither Joe nor his two lieutenants supported the popular teetotal movement wholly; ales and wine were freely served at Lion House, nobody grudged the working man his pint at the end of the day. But when the pint grew to several and led to weeping wives with blackened eyes and children starved of food and bare of foot, the case was altered. There were plenty of earnest reformers around the cotton towns to wag admonitory fingers and sing cautionary hymns.

'Oh! stand back in godly terror,
When temptation's joys begin;
'Tis such wily maze of error,
Few get out who once get in.

'Shun the dram that can but darken
When its vapour gleam has fled;
Reason says, and ye must harken —
Lessened drink means doubled bread.'

Over the years Basil and Dove had grown sharp-eyed and adamant. Joe, they knew too well, was soft with people if they were allowed to get at him. Between them, and without being harsh, they guarded him from importunity. Mrs Atkinson's gazelle eyes and the soft tones of Mr Absalom were misleading to scroungers, who went away from their doors disappointed. He never knew that they had called.

Cook's beef was everything that could have been wished, the vegetables tender, new-picked from the kitchen garden. Basil ate very moderately, even though the meal had been tactfully planned not to contravene Jewish dietary laws. He looked seldom at his plate, often at his hostess. It was a mixed pleasure to dine at Lion House, sharing her with Joe and any guests who might be there. More than anything he treasured their meetings to talk over estate matters, the schools, the library, the local events they planned together. She had a good clear brain for accounts and economies; it would have surprised the childhood teachers who had neglected such subjects in favour of the piano and needlework. It was part of her charm for Basil, a bonus added to the looks, the voice and manner, that charmed him wholly and had so far kept him from marriage with many eligible young ladies of his own faith.

He watched her, easy and happy at the head of her own table, a rose in its midsummer perfection. Dickens, who missed nothing, watched him while rhapsodising on Joe's estate, the little world he had built for his workers.

'I never in my life saw anything so perfect. Sometimes, heaven knows, one despairs of ideals and idealists. I went back to Preston recently, as I think I told you. I heard there was something like a model establishment there, but I found it a nasty place, like Manchester and Wolverhampton. Filthy streets, filthy dwellings, children with dead eyes. No attention paid to the Ten Hours Bill; everything for Mammon, nothing for God. Hateful, hateful. Such conditions led me to begin *Hard Times*. I half wish I could change my scheme now to show your principles in action, but too much has been written already — my poor Stephen Blackpool is doomed not to know such a place as Deansbury.'

Joe looked pleased. 'I must say I'm proud of the way it has turned out. The library and schools were always part of my original concept, and the lecture hall — but the houses are far better than I'd ever imagined. I had a really capital man to design for me, and of course the basic idea came from Prince Albert's model cottages...'

Dove, who had heard it all before, looked bright and expectant. Dickens wore the air of rapt attention to what his host was saying which made him so popular with those who talked a great deal; and Basil watched the play of candleshine mingled with the sunset light from the windows on the smooth wings of Dove's hair. Joe was fairly launched on his hobby-horse; how the squalid conditions of labourers' houses, hardly allowing of common decency, had outraged him long ago, and how he had studied to build cottages which would give them privacy, adequate room for living, eating, sleeping, dry foundations, good ventilation, even aspects facing the sun to promote health and save coals.

'The sun, now there's a thought,' said Dickens, who had never paid very much attention to that heavenly body in his writings.

'People draw their blinds against it,' Joe said earnestly. 'Mothers swathe their children up to keep their young skin from its contamination. Women wear enormous, ridiculous hats — no, I know you don't, my dear — to stop it ruining their hair. Yet we need it — all living things need it. When we ran about naked in our primal state it kept us alive. And so the living-parlours of my cottages receive it as long as it shines, one window at the front and one at the back to see its rising and setting, and all their gardens are fertile. I love to ride by and see them in bloom.'

'May I ask what rent they pay?' Dickens asked.

'Certainly — one shilling and threepence a week.'

Dickens reflected that if the workers could afford such a rent they must be uncommonly well paid. Once more he regretted that there was no way in which he could fit a benevolent factory owner, modelled on Joe Atkinson, into *Hard Times*. As his bright glance flashed between the others at the table, and his quick answers and comments gave the impression that he was wholly intent on and enthralled by their company, part of his mind was constructing just such a situation and set of characters: the mild, earnest reformer, the happy employees, as nauseatingly pious as his readers would expect, the mistress of the establishment — he considered Dove in that light, and rejected her. She was no doubt most capable in real life, but he would have to stick to one of his usual models, a sweet sickly little woman with nothing below the waist but her crinoline. That was what his public was used to, and what he liked himself — or thought he did, for his views on women were hopelessly mixed up. Delicate, clinging burr-like to her man, yet as ruthlessly efficient as himself in running her home, that was the perfect woman: an angel of purity with a bunch of housekeeping keys jingling beside her tiny frilled apron. No, Mrs Atkinson was not his type — too old, for one thing, beautiful as she was. He preferred them under the age of twenty, and virgins at that. There was an air about her which suggested that it was her husband who clung to her rather than she to him; and for one of his good fictitious women she was very frivolously dressed. At her age, and she must be all of thirty-five, a matronly cap would be more suitable than that butterfly confection on her hair.

Besides, she was unconventional. She called her husband Joe, not Mr Atkinson, as ladies of the middle class usually did; and once she addressed him as 'Dearest', which for some reason Dickens found offensive. He decided that northern women were probably a race apart. But the other person at the table obviously found her most attractive. Jewish, and unmarried, something that had emerged in conversation: Dickens had come in for a lot of indignant criticism for making Fagin such an out-and-out villain. He would have to correct that, some day, with a portrait of a Jew who was almost unbearably saintly... He studied Basil for hints on this, but instead began to weave a plot about a factory owner whose life was made wretched by the supposed infatuation of his wife for another man; should it all turn out to be a misunderstanding, with a rapturous reconciliation at the end, or should the guilty pair fly together, and the wife be found dying in a state of abject repentance and social ostracism?

'More pudding, Mr Dickens?' Dove asked, breaking the momentary, unforgivable wandering of his mind. He refused gracefully. He ate and drank very moderately, she noticed, for all his famous descriptions of feasting. They moved into the drawing room to take tea and talk of generalities; the outbreak of war in the Crimea, Britain and France allied with each other to defend little Turkey, the reputedly villainous character of the Czar of Russia.

'Nobody had ever heard of the Crimea before all this started,' Joe said. 'We're very badly informed about foreign parts in this country. I got someone to talk to my workers about it, but I doubt if they understood one word in ten.'

'Is it true,' Dove asked, 'that the French consulted the spirit of Napoleon by means of a planchette? I wonder what sort of answers they got?'

'A great deal of twaddle, one would expect,' said Dickens. 'Table-rappers get what they deserve — silly answers to silly questions.'

'Oh, don't you believe in spirits, Mr Dickens?' Dove's tone was innocent, though she knew perfectly well the novelist's denunciation of the new craze, spiritualism, in flat contradiction to his own glorious, savoured ghost stories.

'In blessed spirits above us, Mrs Atkinson. In the sweet spirits of little children, hovering about the Christmas firesides they once clustered around. But in the kind of spirits which descend on drawing rooms to bang tambourines and impart news about the celestial doings of Julius Caesar and Mary Queen of Scots I cannot and never shall believe.'

'Perhaps not. No one does any table-rapping round here. But we do have a ghost in the family, don't we, Joe? Oh, come, you believe in her as much as I do. She was my Uncle Jesse's grandmother, and she came back to tell his wife, Aunt Eleanor, something that … well, it was quite remarkable. Aunt told me about it not all that long ago — when she supposed I was old enough, I imagine.'

Dickens's face was avid with longing to hear the story. He was a man torn apart, in love with the supernormal, forced into materialism. It was a dichotomy almost as strong as his revulsion from mature, normal women. Dove knew he would not ask her for details of the ghost, but wanted very much to hear them.

'Well,' she said, 'like the ghosts in your stories, she was very picturesque and very antique. A little old lady in the dress of the middle of last century, with high powdered hair and a panniered dress and beauty spots. She was rather indistinct, but Aunt recognised her at once from a meeting many years before. And what she said — don't worry, dearest, I'm not going to give away any family secrets — could only have been known to somebody *not of this world...*'

To her guest's disappointment, a knock at the door came to interrupt. There entered what at first sight seemed to be a young man, then resolved itself into a boy, a strapping tall youth with a fresh complexion and a mane of light hair in startling contrast to dark eyes. He was unmistakably the son of Joe and Dove, and yet very positively himself, forthright and stalwart.

'Mother? May we come in? You said we might, about now.'

'Indeed, Edwin. Bring your sisters in. We can't let Mr Dickens go without giving you the privilege of being introduced to him.'

They filed in and were introduced, Edwin with a very correct bow, the two younger sisters behind him with bobbed curtseys. They were obviously twins, tall like their brother, and well grown for their thirteen years. Like him they were strikingly good-looking. Their hair was an unusual caramel colour, like dark brown honey, their eyes a lighter hazel, the shade of their father's, their skin dazzlingly fair, the whole appearance suggesting Scandinavia rather than Lancashire.

Dove introduced the children formally: Edwin, Maybelle and Marigold. 'But I'm always called May,' that twin volunteered. 'Maybelle sounds so sissy.' She was noticeably different in character from her sister, more lively and humorous, her mouth merry and her eyes meeting the stranger's in flirtatious challenge. Marigold's face was still, almost expressionless, but for a faint smile of greeting; it had the dollish, waxen prettiness of a face in the *Book of Beauty*.

To Dickens she was perfection. A child, yet almost woman-high, innocence personified. Instinctively he held out his arms to her, but she ran to Basil and clung by his side.

'She's shy,' her sister explained hastily. 'Don't mind her, she'll come round.' Their mother shot her a glance — was it reproof or warning?

Basil said, 'Marigold's my girl, aren't you, pet?' stroking the barley-sugar ringlets. Dickens felt a pang of envy, even when May plumped herself down on a box-stool at his feet and embarked on a flood of chatter: she had read some of his books and thought Mr Pickwick and his friends frightfully funny (he noticed that her parents allowed her slang to pass without comment) but Oliver Twist was in her opinion a complete muff — she much preferred the Artful Dodger. As for Little Nell, it had not seemed to her at all sad when Nell died, she was such a soft thing and not anything like a real girl.

'May, you talk too much,' her father said, sternly for him. 'Mr Dickens has children of his own, and knows a good deal more about them than you do. Remember your manners.'

'Well, she *was* —' May began, but stopped, meeting her mother's eye.

'I'm sorry you don't like my Nell,' Dickens said, smiling. 'She happens to be a very great favourite of mine. I think your sister here might have sat for Nell's picture, if she had been old enough when I wrote the book.'

May made a comic face. 'Oh! Why her and not me? We look exactly the same. Still, I'm glad you don't think I look such a cake as Nell.'

Edwin broke in with an elder brother's authority. 'Don't be so jolly rude, May, you know Mother and Father don't like it. I'm sorry, sir,' he added to Dickens. 'She speaks out of turn sometimes and I have to squash her. But I say, may I ask you one thing? I've always wondered what Little Nell actually died of?'

Dickens stared, disconcerted. Not one of the multitude who had wept over his child heroine's premature decease had asked him such a question.

'What she...? Well, Master Edwin, of fatigue, and exposure to the elements, and under-nourishment, I suppose, after her long, weary travels.'

'But none of those would necessarily kill her, would they? I mean, she was only about my age, or a bit more than the twins', and none of us would be killed off by a lot of walking and not much to eat, because we're healthy to begin with, and so was she — there's something about her red cheeks early on in the story.' Edwin's mother was making signs to him, but he disregarded them, pressing on with an enthusiast's zeal. 'Of course, if she caught a consumption that would be different, but you don't say anywhere that she had a cough. Did she?'

Dickens laughed. 'I don't believe she did. Come here, Edwin.' He stroked the boy's hair back from the high intelligent brow with a fatherly hand. 'I'll let you into a little secret. Poor Nell died because she had to, in order to be remembered as the noble creature she was. I cried a good deal myself when I killed her, but I knew that both she and I must suffer if she was to win the heart of the nation — as she did. There, does that satisfy you?'

'Well … people don't die of nothing, that's the trouble.'

'You seem very well informed about disease. I doubt if my own boys would have thought of putting such a question to me.'

Edwin's face brightened. 'I intend to be a doctor, sir, that's why.'

'Edwin,' Joe said, 'I doubt if Mr Dickens wants to hear about your ambitions. And you're far too young to make up your mind.' It was his dream that Edwin would follow him into factory management, carrying on the work he had started into a better, more humane age.

'Oh, Father, I'm not,' Edwin said earnestly. 'I was top of class in Natural Science and Physics last week, and I shall be again this week with luck. I go to Manchester Grammar School now, Mr Dickens, and I intend to go on to Owens College, or perhaps the Edinburgh School of Medicine.'

'If you work hard and persevere you will go as high and as far as you wish,' Dickens said gravely. He was always impressing this maxim on his own elder boys, who grieved him by a deplorable lack of application, a preference for play above work, and a tendency to squander their pocket money that reminded him all too sharply of his own father, the original of Micawber. 'Work, work, that's the answer, Edwin.'

'Yes, sir. I'll remember.'

Dove firmly brought the grown-ups back into the conversation. She was not pleased with Edwin or May, but they had been promised half an hour of the celebrity's company, and exactly half an hour they should have. Dickens talked with animation and his own peculiar wit, making them all laugh; all except Marigold. Now and again his gaze rested on her, sitting beside Basil, who had drawn up a small chair for her. She said not a word, occupying herself with dressing and undressing a tiny peg doll, her shining head bent. What otherworldly thoughts were going through that angelic head, Dickens wondered? Her brother and sister were all animation, May openly flirting, Edwin talking with an authoritative air beyond his years, but Marigold seemed to care nothing for the presence of one who was perhaps the most famous and popular man in England.

A little piqued, and intensely intrigued, he asked, 'Has Marigold not a word for me?' His kind, coaxing voice always drew children to him, but Marigold stayed mute. May uttered a curious sound, something between a chirp and a whistle, as if attracting the attention of a bird or a pet.

Then Marigold looked up and gave him a smile, a sweet, blank smile.

'Come, children, quickly,' Dove said, 'upstairs you go. No, May, no extra time allowed. Yes, you may see Mr Dickens in the morning if he takes his breakfast before you go to school, but I shall certainly *not* call him.' There were goodnights, a handshake for Edwin, a kiss for May, and another dropped lightly on top of Marigold's head, for she did not raise her face to him. Dove watched, frowning slightly.

There was no more talk of the children after they had retired. But in their own bedroom Dove, unpinning her hair, said over her shoulder to her husband, 'He noticed, of course.'

'Do you think so?'

'Sure of it But too tactful to say anything. I was glad of that. I hate it so when they make a sympathetic fuss. May talked a great deal too much and was altogether too pert, but I think she did it to protect her sister, so that he wouldn't notice.'

Joe nodded. 'I thought it best to let her and Edwin carry the conversation.' He heard Dove sigh wearily, and went to lay his hand on her shoulder. 'We can't hide her, love.'

'I know. It's best for her to be in company. It may ... brighten her, in time.'

'Yes. There's always hope of that, as she grows...'

But each knew the other had very little hope. Marigold's brain had not developed with her body, and at thirteen she had the mind of a child of four. Affectionate, biddable, capable of doing very easy tasks, she could neither write nor read and was impossible to teach. With strangers she was not so much shy as withdrawn into some dream-world of her own. People talked of her as 'simple'; there was no other word. Everybody loved Marigold. She had all the appeal of a young kitten, a sweet temper and a touching dependence on others. Her twin sister adored her and would have fought tigers for her. But Dove was thankful that the child she had conceived after the twins had miscarried, and that when Marigold's condition was obvious Joe had wisely, without consulting his wife, acquired the knowledge that would protect her from further pregnancies. Birth control was to the Victorians a shocking thing, flying in the face of religion and morality. Joe and Dove cared nothing for such opinions, and were deeply thankful that their sophisticated uncle, Jesse Bradshaw, had been able to impart his own knowledge to Joe.

Dove finished plaiting her hair. Joe saw her face in the mirror, her eyes still shadowed with trouble.

'What is it, love? Don't think any more about Dickens having ... noticed. He's the kindest, most compassionate of men.'

She swung round. 'It isn't that, Joe, it's the way he looked at her — as if she were a woman. Other men are going to look at her like that. What if…? She'll need so much protection. I never thought of it before, but I see it now.'

'Don't think about it at all. Years will pass before any such thing could happen, and then — it would have to be explained. Besides, there *may* be an improvement in her; who knows what time will do? Perhaps her cousins' visit will help.'

'Yes.' Dove tied the strings of her lace nightcap under her chin. The mirror showed her three faint frown lines etched in her forehead: one for each of her children.

CHAPTER TWO

Laurence Dilworth put his fingers in his ears to shut out the sound of the voices downstairs. For a few minutes he would have a respite from them: his mother's, shrill and tear-filled, his father's, an angry growl sometimes rising to a shout. The subject of their quarrels was always the same — his father's going away to sea, leaving his wife behind, and her conviction of his unfaithfulness when he was abroad.

Lying in bed, stopping his ears, he wished that his father were not an officer in a merchant ship, and lived at home like other fathers. He wished his mother had the serene strength of her sister, Aunt Dove. He wished he had brothers and sisters. He wished, at this particular moment, that the long school holiday were ending, instead of just beginning. He was fifteen, a nervous, sensitive boy, made more so by being used as the rope in a tug-of-war between his parents. He loved his handsome, curly-haired father, but had no desire to go to sea with him. At sea he would not have his books, or the familiar streets of Lancaster, the romantic castle, the glowing beauty of St Mary's Priory Church, where he could spend hours looking about him, thinking of times past and of the wonder of the human spirit. Sometimes he would sit there, the only person in the church, looking from the carven choir stalls to the five-light east window. Before the altar there his grandfather Ephraim Atkinson had been married. Now grandmother Mary lay in the churchyard near the south door, among older generations of the family. Would he, Laurence, lie there one day — soon, perhaps? He rather wished he might. He pictured his parents coming into his bedroom one morning to find him dead, a peaceful sculptured figure like someone on an old tomb. Peace.

He took his fingers from his ears; the attitude was too uncomfortable. The voices were still going on below.

'Very well — take him. It's not enough for you that I should have to live here day in, day out, without a husband. Go on, take my son too — perhaps you'll be happy then.' Violent sobs.

'How the devil can I take him? He doesn't want to go, and I won't force the lad. Besides, his education ain't finished yet. Do be reasonable, Belle.'

'Reasonable? Haven't I been reasonable all these years, managing as best I could with you away? Haven't I put up with all your callousness?'

'*Callousness?* Dammit, Belle, when have I ever said an unkind word to you except when you bait me like this?'

An indistinct murmur, then, 'Those women…'

'Oh, God, what women? Have you ever seen me so much as look at another woman?'

'It's not what I've seen, but what I know.'

'If you know, let's have some evidence! Locks of hair, fond letters, found when you've gone rooting through my pockets and my sea chests? Let's have these women's names, shall we, so that I know 'em as well…'

On and on went the voices. Laurence could not have said how he knew, but instinct told him that his father was lying — that he had other women when he was abroad. Lancaster had its ladies of the night; everyone knew about them. Other boys at school had enlightened him about the commerce between men and women. All grown men, it seemed, wanted the kind of thing such women provided, which was not supposed to be provided by their wives. So Mama had no real reason to be angry, if she didn't...

It was all so difficult to fathom, and he was weary. Sleep overcame him.

It was a relief when, some days later, George Dilworth went back to sea, bound for Honduras. Laurence thought it odd that though his mother raged so at being left, she seemed to lead a very gay and social life when his father was away. There was a fair number of sea-wives in Lancaster, and George had many relations in the sail-making trade. Day after day Laurence would see his mother come downstairs dressed to the nines — very frivolously, for a lady of forty years — with her hair, still golden, in spaniel-ear clusters framing her face, a tiny silk bonnet perched right on the back of her head, and an elegant long flounced jacket instead of an enveloping matronly shawl. She was still very pretty, though not so pretty as Aunt Dove, Laurence thought, because her mouth was thinner and turned down, and her dark hazel eyes flashed with temper on very small provocation.

One evening, Laurence had come home from a friend's house in Castle Park and walked unthinkingly into the parlour to see his mother and a gentleman together on the sofa. The gentleman seemed to be lying almost on top of Mama, whose skirts were wildly dishevelled, and both were obviously startled, not to say shocked, by Laurence's entrance. There was a flurry of movement and a cry from Mama, and the gentleman said something fierce under his breath, before the boy hastily retreated, shutting the door behind him. He hardly related what he had seen to the things his schoolfellows had told him. It was not possible. Mama was a wife, and wives didn't do such things, with anybody. But he was shaken and disturbed.

Next day Mama was very cool, as though nothing had happened. The incident was not mentioned. As they began their midday meal she said, 'Oh, and by the way. You are to go on a visit to Aunt Dove and Uncle Joe.'

'I am?' He was amazed, delighted. 'But — has Aunt Dove written, Mama?'

'Not recently, but the invitation is open. She'll be pleased to see you. The children are on holiday, and it will do you good to have some company. Besides, I hear the cholera is spreading in Skerton and the streets round the quays. Of all diseases I dread that one for you, Laurence. I had it myself when I was a girl and it nearly killed me.' She shuddered. 'I'd prefer you to be out of town until it dies down.' *And out of my way,* was her thought, but innocent Laurence saw no connection with what he had witnessed the night before. Eagerly he looked forward to the holiday, the company of Edwin and May and gentle Marigold, and the aunt and uncle who were so much more calm and settled than his own parents.

It was an added delight to know that Grandfather would be taking him to Manchester, and that they were to call at Downham and pick up another cousin. Lucy Bradshaw was the adopted daughter of his uncle Jesse and aunt Eleanor, who lived in great state at Eagle Hall. She was the same age as Laurence and Edwin, who had met her only a few times but wished she lived nearer, they had got on so well. Downham was far south-east of Lancaster, almost halfway to Manchester.

The morning came for his departure. He had looked out of the window a hundred times before Grandfather's double brougham rounded the corner and stopped before the tall narrow house, and Grandfather's tall figure, now a little stooped, descended. Laurence ran out to welcome him.

'Grandfather! Ain't it exciting, though!'

Ephraim held the boy in his arms for a moment. He was deeply fond of this only child of his wayward daughter Belle. Nobody knew better than he how turbulent was her life with her husband, and how Laurence suffered from the strife between them. Belle should have married an older, steady man — someone who would have kept her in order and given her more children to keep her quiet, instead of the roving adventurer George. Ephraim thought wistfully of his old friend Will Raven, who had courted Belle long years ago. Will had been twice Belle's age or more, but they had loved each other, Ephraim was sure. Then circumstances had come between them; now Will, an old man, looked after his antique shop in Kendal. Did he ever think of his one-time sweetheart, and was he lonely, as Belle in her way was lonely?

Ephraim put Laurence from him and surveyed the pale, oval face, the large eyes and straight fair hair. What a lot of blond locks there were among these children; what had become of the Atkinson brown?

'Well, young man,' he said, 'you look as if you could do with a holiday. Are your bags packed?'

Laurence was off almost before he had finished speaking. Ephraim went inside, to find Belle trimming a bonnet. They talked, waiting for Laurence to come down, Belle not overjoyed to be visited by her father, though she kissed his cheek dutifully. He noticed that she smelt strongly of a violet scent he disliked, and that her eyebrows seemed darker than they had been. The room was full of trophies George had brought back for her: a parrot — which had never talked, but bit anyone who went near it except Belle — exotic shells with deep pink hearts, a picture made out of feathers, an African head, a stuffed tropical fish.

'How is Aunt Margaret?' Belle asked.

'Troubled with rheumatism nowadays — doesn't get out much — but bobbish, bobbish. Why don't you call on her sometimes? We haven't seen you since Christmas.'

'I don't like to disturb her at her writing.'

'Nonsense. She loves company round her. As for writing, she does too much of it for the good of her eyes. But her three-volume novels bring in a good deal of money.'

'I suppose so.'

Laurence's footsteps were heard running downstairs. 'That boy's very thin,' Ephraim said. 'Arms and legs like drumsticks. And when did he last have a new jacket and trousers? The ones he has on are inches too short for him.'

'Oh, Papa, why do you worry so?' Belle's voice was peevish. 'You've no idea how fast he grows. I don't have unlimited money, you know.'

'You seem to be dressmaking for yourself — can't you make clothes for him?'

'That's *quite* different. Laurence is quite all right, Papa — don't trouble yourself.'

Laurence put his head round the door. 'I'm quite ready now, Grandfather.' In the hall, Ephraim noticed that two modest bags were the extent of Laurence's luggage. No gun, no fishing rod. The luggage was soon loaded into the brougham to join Ephraim's, farewells were said, and they were off. Belle did not watch them out of sight, but went into the house as soon as the brougham began to move.

Laurence's face had lost its paleness for an excited glow. 'I say, Grandfather, this is jolly!' he said. 'When shall we get there?'

'By evening, I expect, unless we meet with an accident. It's a beautiful drive — don't you remember it? Perhaps you were too young, last time. We go through the Trough of Bowland, grand country. Come and sit next to me, facing the way we're going — you'll see more that way.'

The drive was all Ephraim had hoped, calm and pleasant, through a sunny countryside. Downham Village was as pretty as ever, a charming hamlet of grey-gold stone houses and a Norman church, a stream running placidly under the old bridge, Pendle Hill above. Laurence was deeply happy. It was good to travel and good to arrive, and here they were at Eagle Hall.

Long ago the house set in beautiful grounds and gardens had been a near-ruin: mediaeval stone and Tudor brick crumbling with time and neglect, decay eroding its timbers, the garden creeping in on the house to smother it. Then the brothers Jesse and Shem Bradshaw had come, for it had been bequeathed to Jesse by his grandmother, old Lucetta, and with Bradshaw money it had been restored to its past glories, and more. Jesse's wife Eleanor loved it passionately. It was she who had furnished it in the old graceful style, yet with modern comforts. A domestic wing which had once been something of an eyesore had been demolished and rebuilt, Ephraim noted, and now was a handsome affair with large windows wreathed by a purple clematis, and a fashionable turret on top. When a lady was the wife of a flourishing Tory politician with an inherited fortune, she could build what she liked.

As the brougham stopped in the drive she came running out. Tall, slender to the point of gauntness, she was as quick and lithe in her sixties as she had been as a girl, and her hair was the kind that managed to look only extremely fair, not white. Her greeting to Ephraim was sincerely warm. She, his dead wife's sister, knew that he had always spoken up for her in the years when she and Mary had been estranged.

'Ephraim, how delightful to see you. And Laurence, so much grown!' They were being bustled in, the coachman following with the luggage. Laurence gasped at the splendour of Eagle Hall's interior, oak panels, marble statues in niches, dark oil paintings of people in rich silks and satins.

But someone was coming down the staircase: a girl of his own age, slightly taller than himself, in a full-skirted dress of golden brown. Her hair was brown, too, a rich nutty shade, shining in the light from the window behind her, falling in smooth tresses on her firm young bosom. Laurence remembered her face vividly, but it was older now than last time he had seen it; a squarish face, wide across the cheekbones, the blue eyes candid beneath dark, slightly heavy brows, the nose classically straight, the mouth firm and well formed, unlike the popular rosebud.

'Well, Laurence.' She gave him her hand, like a boy, to shake. 'How are you? Gracious! How tall you are.'

'Not as tall as you,' he murmured, suddenly shy, and was then afraid he might have offended her, but she laughed.

'I know, I'm growing into a regular maypole, Mama says, but I don't mind. There's room for all shapes and sizes, I suppose. Have you had a good journey? Uncle, you must be tired — come and have some tea.'

Ephraim was indeed tired from the journey, Laurence from his half-sleepless night. It was restful to be in this beautiful house, with its soothing atmosphere and smooth service from placid-looking maids. Sitting by the fire in the evening, in the old dark-panelled Tudor room upstairs which was Eleanor's favourite, Laurence found himself yawning again and again, to his annoyance, and able to say very little in answer to his aunt's bright chatter. Lucy was sewing; the action of her arm and fingers had a hypnotic effect on him. He would have liked to talk to her, but a strange shyness seemed to come over him in waves.

Later in the evening Uncle Jesse appeared, a stout John Bullish figure and a red amiable face. He clapped Laurence on the shoulder, shook hands with Ephraim, touched his wife's hair lightly, but swept Lucy up in his arms and held her there. 'And how's my girl spent the day, then? Is she happy to have her cousin here?'

'Very happy, Papa.'

'Still going to leave me, though, for foreign parts?'

'Manchester is hardly foreign parts. I'm sure Aunt Dove will have you to stay, too, if you feel inclined.'

'No chance of that till the recess, worse luck. I shall just have to miss you, shan't I?' He put her down, but beckoned her to move her chair nearer his, and, talking animatedly to Ephraim of the attitude of the country to the Crimean business, glanced very often at her down-bent head, sometimes throwing in a remark that made her lift her face and smile. Laurence saw, when she did this the first time, a strong likeness between her and Uncle Jesse. It was nothing to do with their features, but a trick of expression. Then he remembered that there was no kinship of blood between them; Lucy was the orphaned child of one of Jesse's constituents, adopted by Jesse and Eleanor soon after her birth.

But Ephraim, the only person besides Joe and Dove to know the secret, saw the love in Jesse's eyes as he looked at his daughter, born to him by a poor maid-servant who had died giving her birth.

Two days after their arrival Ephraim and Laurence left Eagle House for Manchester, Lucy with them. She refused to take her maid, saying that Aunt Dove had plenty of servants, and that she was perfectly capable of seeing to her own clothes and toilette. Laurence admired this, and the fluency with which she chatted on the journey, seeming to know about all kinds of things which had not entered his sphere of knowledge. It occurred to him for the first time that the masters at school spent most of lesson times instructing the boys in ancient history, ancient languages, ancient sciences, without a glance at what was going on in the modern world. Lucy, it seemed, had a governess who taught her French and German, not merely Latin, and read newspapers with her, so that she knew of such matters as Baron Haussmann's redesigning of Paris, the new public aquarium in Regent's Park, London, and a picture just exhibited at the Royal Academy called *The Awakened Conscience* which had very much startled art lovers.

Ephraim was amused. 'And why is it so startling, pray?'

'Well,' said Lucy composedly, 'it shows what I suppose most people don't think of — that nobody can be past reclamation provided that they listen to their inmost heart.'

'What an original thought. I wish it had occurred to some of my clients in the dock. And how does it do this, pray?'

'Oh, very strikingly, Uncle. A young fallen woman is sitting on her seducer's lap at a piano when a cadence of the music she is playing recalls to her memories of her innocent home. She leaps up, and the artist makes it clear from her expression that she will never go back to the old way of life. Mademoiselle showed me a print of it — I thought it very good indeed.'

'Did you, now.' Ephraim regarded Lucy with respect, but forebore to ask the questions he would like to have asked about young ladies' education in this year of 1854. Laurence would certainly not have been able to follow such a discussion, and was looking uncomfortable enough as it was.

The croquet lawn of the Lion House was starred with human flowers in flowing dresses and light sporting clothes, round straw hats and streaming curls. The Atkinson children and their cousins had been joined by the families of neighbours. Squeals and laughter came up to the open window where Dove and her father were watching, Basil Absalom standing a little behind them.

'How they enjoy themselves,' Dove said. 'Of course, May's cheating, and Laurence knows it but wouldn't dare challenge her. I saw her kick a ball through the hoop with her foot, naughty girl. Edwin pulls her hair for that sort of thing.'

'Lucy has no need to cheat,' said Ephraim. 'She plays excellently. She does everything excellently. I don't wonder Jesse is proud of her. But — how curious, this had not struck me before — there are the children playing croquet, and this is Sunday.'

'So it is. What of it, Papa?'

'Only that when you and Belle were children nobody played games on a Sunday. I suppose times are changing.'

'Oh, many of the workpeople would think it very shocking, I'm sure. But as we don't have to ask them we don't concern ourselves with their views.'

Basil smiled. 'The rules are changing, not the times.'

A shade of annoyance crossed Dove's face. 'All very well to say that, but I don't understand you entirely, Basil. Here you are, a sensible, level-headed person and entirely one of us, yet you won't eat meat and drink milk at the same time, or eat oysters with anything... A person should be above rules if they make no sense. You know perfectly well that all those things about food apply to Israel in goodness knows what year, something BC, and were made up to suit a hot climate, which we certainly haven't. There!'

This is certainly May's mother speaking, not my gentle Dove, thought Ephraim, and for some reason he felt superfluous there at the window with them. Quietly he withdrew. Someone was sitting on a chair in the corridor outside, a small figure in a short white frock and frilled pantalettes. She looked up as he approached, and he saw there were tears on her cheeks.

'Marigold, pet! What is it? Why are you not playing with the others?'

'A boy shouted,' she said almost inaudibly.

'At you? Shame on him. Come here.' He scooped her up into his arms, feeling her weight but enduring it gladly, and carried her to a settle, where he placed her on his knee. She put her arms round his neck, clinging to him wordlessly. Dove had said nothing to him about her fears for Marigold's future, nor had he formulated them for himself, but he sensed that for all the love her family could give her, this flawed child would need more protection than perhaps any of them guessed.

'What shall we do? Shall we go to the schoolroom, so that you can show me your pictures?' She nodded. 'Come along, then.' Her hand in his, they went to the room on the same floor which had been set aside for the children's lessons when they were all little. But both May and Edwin went to school now, had done for years, May to a small academy kept by a bluestocking lady of strong views; and it had soon become sadly obvious that no schooling would help Marigold. Among the bookshelves, desks and easels, she searched eagerly until she found what she was looking for: a volume of fashions, from which she was cutting out figures very neatly and colouring them with water-paint: ladies, children with tops and hoops, gentlemen in correct morning and evening attire. Her little plump hands were skilled in the manipulation of scissors and brush. Ephraim saw that she had assembled a cast of characters in a theatre which was three sides of a box. Murmuring, she grouped and posed them; he saw that she was playing out a drama in her mind, sometimes smiling, sometimes frowning, giving the figures names. 'Ella.' 'James.' 'Mary.'

'Have you seen the pantomime, Marigold?' He was suddenly desperate to make her speak properly. She nodded, but that was not enough. 'No, you must tell me. Where did you see it — where did Papa and Mama take you?'

She thought. 'Man-ches-ter.'

'Good. And who did you like best in the pantomime?'

Surprisingly, she sketched a graceful dancing attitude, her skirts held wide, a foot pointed. 'The pretty lady.'

My God, she can *talk, if one only takes the trouble.* 'Not the clown?'

'No. Silly man — not kind. To the poor goose.'

'No, he isn't, is he. But it's only his fun, you know, the goose doesn't mind greatly. The goose is the clown's pet, when he's at home. Does Marigold have a pet?'

She smiled radiantly. 'Yes. Granfa come and see.' She almost pulled him down to the kitchens, where, by the wide grate where a fire burnt night and day, a blanket-lined box held five tiny kittens of assorted colours, tumbling in play and mimic fight. Marigold knelt by them and lifted the squirming, squealing bundles of fur, one by one, to her cheek, whispering to them, kissing the small heads with the pink-lined ears. Their squealing lessened as she held them, and the baby mouths nuzzled her. Ephraim saw that the mother cat was watching from nearby, thoughtfully licking her paws and grooming her whiskers, not apparently disturbed by the handling of her infants. His grandchild was closer to nature and animals than ordinary folk, blessed in her very deficiency. Watching, he was thankful.

The croquet was still in progress, the two at the window still watching, though they could not have described what was happening in the game. Basil was very close to Dove, not touching her.

'Why are you so angry with me? Do you want to change me?'

'Of course not.'

'I think you do. Why?'

She shrugged. 'So that you should be more sensible, I suppose.'

'If I were to change,' he said very deliberately, 'I should need to have a great prize held before me. Can you guess what it is?'

Dove turned her head away. 'No.'

'I think you can. Yourself. Dove, I'd give my life to you. Not by taking it, like a fool, but by becoming something other than I am. It would be the hardest thing in the world to do, but I'd do it, for you. What do you say?'

She faced him now. 'How can you talk so, Basil? What about Joe? What about your loyalty to him — and mine? How can you say such things in his own house? I'm ashamed of you. To take advantage... Dear Joe, who's always treated you like a friend rather than a manager. You don't deserve to hold a position of trust.'

Her colour was high, her eyes bright, but she did not move away from him. He held her gaze with his own.

'One thing you haven't said: "I hate you, go away." *Do* you hate me — so presumptuous, so disloyal?'

'You know I don't. How ridiculous you are this afternoon!'

He looked out of the window. 'Yes. Such a beautiful afternoon, warm and green and gold, an afternoon for love;

and you smell of hayfields and hawthorn, and we're both still young, wasting our time, pretending to be sober old people... I shouldn't have said what I did. But time is so short, life is so short, and tomorrow I shall be back at my desk and you pouring out tea for Joe and giving orders to Mrs Skerritt, and everything will be quite respectable again. Shall I go, then?'

It was not herself, surely, who said 'No,' and put out a hand towards him. As though he had touched a spring of some Pandora's box, a host of fantastic emotions were flying about her. She was conscious as she had never been before of his dark looks, the alluring quality of his voice and his nearness to her. Basil, her friend, her ally, almost her employee, who had been there so long, unnoticed, now turned to someone different, dangerous, exciting. There was no way in which she could compare this new feeling for him with what she felt for Joe. Joe was her husband, safe, reliable, kind and fond, and yet ... they were cousins again now, rather than lovers; alike in so much — inheritance, experience, memory — and whatever fire had been between them had gently died down. *I must be honest and not run away,* she told herself, and turned to him.

'Basil, you should not have said what you did, and I should not have listened. But it's been said now, and I must tell you that I feel as you do. I'm very surprised at myself, but I do. There is simply nothing to be done about it, you must realise that. We must never speak of it again, either of us. It's simply the folly of a moment.'

'Yes,' he said, not moving. Then, as though the cord uniting them tightened, they were drawn together in an embrace more passionate than any Dove had known, matron and mother as she was. The fire that had died between her and Joe was kindled and blazed between her and Basil, consuming them in its wild flames. In that moment she would have yielded anything, everything to him, but he almost flung her away and strode out of the room. She heard his footsteps running down the oak stairs as she sank into a chair, shaking, her hands to her burning cheeks, feeling her face branded with his kisses, the touch of his hands still on her.

Down on the lawn the young people were crowding together under the cedar tree; the maids were bringing tea out. She breathed deeply, trying to calm herself before she must go down and appear just as usual.

'Seems hardly decent, to me, having a ball with our poor soldiers going to fight in that place Sevastopol, or whatever they call it,' observed Susan, the Atkinsons' head parlour-maid, watching the supper tables being laid in the dining room.

'Do them no harm,' returned Mrs Skerritt, 'and be a nice way to see Miss Lucy and Master Laurence off tomorrow. No, Peggy, not there — that table's wanted for the ice bucket. And you haven't brought half enough plates. There's thirty guests, you know.'

Susan sniffed. 'What Mistress wants asking them from the estate, I don't know. Caps me, that does, when there must be plenty of young folk their own sort round Deansbury.'

'Don't you let Mr Atkinson hear you talking like that,' the housekeeper returned severely. 'It's his notion, and he knows what's best. The servant's as good as the master in this house, and you be thankful for it.'

The ballroom had been built on to the older part of the Lion House in Regency times. It was a high, pleasant room with a bay window wall and a moulded ceiling, supported by two Doric columns. Tonight it was filled with young people, dancing to the music of a small band of musicians on a dais at one end of the room. Gamely they sawed, piped and plucked away at quadrille, schottische, Mazurka and even waltz, though it was noticeable that a number of girls from the estate left the floor and perched self-consciously on the sitting-out chairs when its alluring strains began.

Dove pointed them out to Ephraim. 'Their mothers have told them they mustn't because it's abandoned.'

'In my day it was certainly thought so — positively wicked, indeed. It would never have been danced in a respectable assembly when you and Belle were girls. But I should have thought people were more broad-minded nowadays.'

'Unfortunately, no, Uncle,' Joe said. 'There's a lot of Puritan prejudice left over. I do try to educate them, but it's very difficult for a man to address women on these matters, and the women are the diehards, I'm afraid. You don't happen to know any very progressive lady who would come and give them a talk on "Morals in our Time"?' Joe asked earnestly.

Ephraim's mouth twitched. 'I wish I did. Your Aunt Margaret would be well qualified, but I doubt if she would fancy the lecture platform.'

A set of the Lancers was in progress. Both Edwin and Laurence had positioned themselves near Lucy, and partnered her as often as possible. She gave exactly the same attention to them as to the other young males who took her hand. Her dance card contained Edwin's and Laurence's names — three dances apiece and no favours shown, though Edwin had tried strong-minded charm on her to get more, and Laurence's pleading eyes had besought her to protect him from the strange girls who made him desperately shy.

May danced like a sunbeam. Good-naturedly she helped out clumsy youths who knew the steps very little or not at all, enduring cheerfully their large feet treading on her own or on the hem-flounce of her yellow dress. They were fun to flirt with, clumsy or not, sometimes more fun than the boys of her own class. She could say outrageous things to them and get a laugh, listen to their dialect and make them laugh in turn with her imitation. Dove watched her, thinking that in a very few years May would need watching very carefully indeed.

And Marigold danced. Her brain and body were uncoordinated in many things, but in this they were perfectly together. She learned steps by watching them once, moved with light effortless grace, barely touching her partner's arm or hand, not speaking except to say 'Thank you' at the end of a dance, smiling remotely; so a fairy might dance and smile. The boys were a little afraid of her, the girls stared. Ephraim's eyes followed her, fond and troubled.

To Dove he said, 'I suppose you wouldn't let me take her back with me? I would care for her so well, and … would she not be more peaceful among older people? Sometimes I feel all this is distracting to her.'

Dove shook her head. 'She needs other children, Papa. And she loves her twin. I know how much that counts, remembering me and Belle. But thank you.'

'May I have this dance?' Basil was before her, holding out a hand to her. She had carefully avoided being alone with him since the incident at the window. It had been madness, and it must not be repeated.

'Oh, my dancing days are over,' she answered lightly. 'Elderly matrons shouldn't make fools of themselves in public.'

Joe, sitting next to her, overheard. 'What rubbish, my dear! As if you weren't as light on your feet now as ever you were. Go out with Basil, and show the lasses what dancing is.'

There was nothing she could do but take Basil's hand and move out on to the floor with him. It was a waltz, languorous, smooth-flowing, intimate as was no other dance. For the first time she realised why it was thought immoral. She was acutely conscious of Basil as a man, aware of his arm round her, their hands clasped, his warmth and nearness, the intensity of his eyes, trying to draw hers to his face.

At last she said, 'Don't.'

'Don't what? Dance with you? I can hardly lead you back before the music stops.'

'I know that. I mean don't look so at me. How can you, with Joe watching?'

'He doesn't notice. Oh, Dove, be kind to me.'

Mercifully, the musicians played out their final chords. Dove went back to her seat, hurrying ahead of him. May was there, talking animatedly to her father. She looked up brightly.

'You didn't say "thank you", Mama.'

'Didn't I?' Dove refused to meet Basil's amused glance. 'Thank you,' she said in a very final tone.

CHAPTER THREE

Whistling, Edwin strode across Edinburgh's North Bridge towards the Canongate. The wind was sharply exhilarating to his face, bringing the fresh colour up in it, and sending his thick fair hair flying. He was used to being told that he looked like a young lion. One of his father's mild jokes was that his mother must have been strongly affected before his birth by the stone beasts that guarded their front door. As Edwin passed a group of girls, their bonnets swerved round simultaneously to look after him. He was used to that, too.

Twenty years old, and the world before him. He had got his own way about his choice of profession, as he did about most things. Before he left the grammar school his father had summoned him for a last appeal.

'I've worked very hard for the mill and the estate, Edwin. Who is to look after it when I'm gone? It's a great inheritance for you. Prince Albert himself has called it one of the finest establishments in the country. Could you not consider…?'

'No, Father. I want to be a doctor.'

'You could study in your spare time, as a hobby. That would give you all the more knowledge for the welfare of the workers. Come now — I know your powers of application. It would be no effort for you to combine management with the study of this enthusiasm of yours.'

'One can't be an amateur doctor, Father. How could I go round dosing people with my own mixtures, when the medicos do it for a living — and after a jolly expensive training, at that. Yes, it *is* expensive, and I'm sorry about that, but you can afford it, can't you? And I promise I won't hang round failing exams year after year. Besides, I want to be a surgeon, not just a doctor, and one can hardly learn that in one's spare time.'

Joe smiled. 'It would be difficult, certainly. Oh, Edwin ... I had so hoped you'd follow me. If it weren't for what I remember of my own youth I'd go on fighting you.'

'What was that?'

'By the time I was twenty-one I'd made up my mind to devote myself to the reform of factory conditions. I thought I could partly do it by engineering improvements. I was wrong about that, but not about other ideals of mind — ideals I've carried out here. But your grandfather had very different ideas for me. He had no son, and I was almost like a son to him, though I was only a nephew — he wanted me to follow him into the law. And I knew it was impossible. So I had to hold out against him, as you have done against me. Very well; the game is yours.'

Edwin's cheeks glowed. 'Oh, thank you, Father!' He had known the game would be his, but it was so much pleasanter to conquer without bloodshed. He and Joe shook hands; Joe never mentioned his disappointment again.

For two years Edwin attended the newly formed Owens College in Manchester. It was small, having its headquarters in a house in Quay Street that had once been the home of the great Richard Cobden. He studied general science, chemistry and anatomy, as well as advanced mathematics, which to him were child's play. It was all too easy, and it seemed to be getting him nowhere. He obtained permission to walk the wards of Manchester Infirmary, set in the pleasant open land of Piccadilly. The sights he saw there were often sad and terrible, encouraging him by their very unpleasantness and the inadequate nursing they received to know all there was to be known about the treatment of such cases. He walked round the mean streets, where thousands lived in indescribable filth, often in cellars, and almost every person he met was deformed or stunted by rickets, bone disease or chronic illness.

The life of his womenfolk was made a misery by Edwin's private studies. If a bird were lying dead in the garden, or a cat shot by a boy's air gun, the corpse would find its way into the shed he used for his experiments. Once he went so far as to convey a dead frog into the house; the weather was wintry, the large scullery nice and warm. He was working comfortably with knife and magnifying glass at the table when Marigold came in and saw what he was doing.

'Edwin! Don't! Oh, please!'

He looked up. 'It's all right, dear. It's quite dead — it can't feel anything.'

But large tears were already rolling down her cheeks, and she was on her way to her mother, sobbing. Edwin received the telling-off of his life, not only for upsetting Marigold's tender heart but for defiling a clean table with such horrible work. 'I know all about that shed, of course,' Dove went on, 'and the fire you light in it for some unspeakable experiment or other, which is a very great danger to the house — and I know about the cemetery where you bury your victims, because May went to get snowdrops from near there and saw one of the graves. Really, Edwin, your ways are horrible!'

'But they aren't victims, Mother — I never kill anything, truly! I only want to see what they've died of, and how they're made. You can't think how interesting it is…'

'No, I can't,' Dove snapped. 'It's quite disgusting. Laurence would never behave so.'

'Laurence is a muff.'

'He's a dear, good boy — you'd do well to take a leaf out of his book.'

'Coom on, Moom, don't you luv us, then?' Edwin assumed a coarse version of the local accent and put his arm round his mother's small waist; he was already much taller than she. She gave in and laughed, as she always did, in the end.

Edwin had progressed since then to real, human subjects. Dissatisfied with what Manchester had to offer he had transferred to Edinburgh, the home of medical studies. At twenty, he was established at the medical school, attending lectures at the Royal College of Surgeons, familiar with its grisly museum and that of the Royal College of Physicians, and frequently in attendance on doctors and surgeons at the Royal Infirmary. Not a romantic young man, Edinburgh's colourful history interested him not at all, except for the body-snatching activities, some thirty years earlier, of Burke and Hare in the service of Dr Robert Knox, the anatomist, still alive and flourishing. He discoursed on them to his relatives at Eagle Hall, calling there on his way home at the end of his second term at the university.

'The victims were almost always smothered when they were drunk,' he told his audience, Jesse and Eleanor Bradshaw and Lucy. 'Lured into some low spot, filled up to the eyes with liquor, then done for. It's not all that easy to smother a full-grown party, but Burke and Hare managed it between them. I must say they were a highly organised pair.'

'But not very comfortable in the eyes of the law or decent citizens,' Jesse said.

'Oh, I don't know, Uncle. The victims weren't exactly decent citizens themselves, were they? Common prostitutes, down-and-outers. No use to anyone, really.'

Lucy looked up from the sewing in her lap. She had put few stitches in during Edwin's description of resurrectionists and their ways. 'Don't you think it wrong to take life, then?'

'Well ... not if humanity benefits.'

Lucy's large, clear eyes dwelt thoughtfully on Edwin, and under her gaze he felt himself diminish to a boastful small boy trying to impress his elders. There was no need for her to say anything. She was his own age in years, far older in character. Somewhere in one of the Edinburgh museums there were a pair of caryatids holding up a ceiling, or appearing to do so, on the palms of their strong hands and the tops of their noble heads, stone eyes staring straight before them, classic features calm, stone draperies slipping from large comely breasts. It was ridiculous that Lucy should make him think of these impassive creatures, but she did; it was something to do with the air of wisdom she had, and her invariable honesty. One couldn't imagine a caryatid telling a fib. In deference to that level gaze, he would say no more about body-snatchers, as he had been going to do, but Lucy pressed the point.

'Would you think it justified if the victims were alive and in pain when Dr Knox dissected them?'

'Good heavens, Lucy, what a mind you have! No, of course not.'

'Then you don't take part in experiments on animals?'

Edwin looked uncomfortable, and Eleanor put her hands to her ears, saying, 'Do be quiet, both of you — talk about something else, pray.'

But Edwin answered, 'Yes, I do — there's no choice. If you mean do I enjoy them, no. Some of the fellows do, and I can't swallow that. But you get cads everywhere, even in medicine. And there's no other way of finding out about the circulation, the nervous system, all that. Don't come down hard on me, Lucy. I see you think it wrong, but I can't help it.'

Jesse, who knew his daughter better than the others did, said, 'Perhaps you'll get a movement going to stop such experiments one day, my dear. We've had no private bills brought up in the House about it lately.'

'Yes,' she said levelly, 'I expect I will.'

'What about anaesthesia?' Eleanor enquired. 'I thought it quite splendid of the Queen to let Dr Snow administer it to her at Prince Leopold's birth, and so successfully. Why should we women have to suffer without reason? All for a lot of silly old men babbling about bringing forth children in sorrow. I should like to think Lucy's children would be produced in complete comfort.'

'If I decide to have any, they will be,' Lucy said.

The men regarded her with admiration, Edwin with a certain awe. He knew perfectly well from his brief time as a medical student that there were ways and means of not distributing unwanted offspring all over the Canongate and the Lawnmarket, while at the same time enjoying what female talent the town had to offer, but it was hardly a proper subject for a young lady. He admired her all the more for referring to it, and the thought crossed his mind that Lucy's children would be rather a jolly brood to father. He dismissed it, picturing the scorn of his particular friends Sandy and Jock Cranstoun, their cheerful blasphemies and inventive profanities on the subject of women. It was ridiculous to think of them and Lucy in the same breath — so to speak, for he was feeling distinctly muddled — yet there was nothing prissy or missish about Lucy. He could imagine her, if the occasion offered and she thought fit, swearing as comprehensibly as he could himself. Yet nothing more feminine could be imagined than Lucy in her crinoline chair by the fire; the lovely line of her very white arm raising the sewing thread, the young curve of her neck above the demure round lace collar…

He pulled himself out of a dream and told them how far the use of chloroform had progressed since the Queen's accouchement five years before; how in this very year Dr Snow's *On Chloroform and Other Anaesthetics* had been published, though Dr Snow himself had, sadly, died at the age of only forty-five.

On this March day, as Edwin crossed the bridge, his thoughts were still with Lucy. He was faintly annoyed with himself to find it so. He wanted novelty, stimulus, excitement, new faces. He was on his way to a supper party in the rooms of a fellow student, David Ogilvy, high up in one of the tenement buildings of the 'Old Toun': dirty, tumbledown, infinitely attractive. There would be bold rosy-faced Jeannies and Marys and saucy books from Paris and rough wine, and the songs of Burns would be sung in their original versions: 'The Gaberlunzie Man' and 'John Anderson' and 'The Lass That Made the Bed to Me', and before the night was over several of the party would be dead drunk.

It would all be very different from the elegant calm of Eagle Hall and the domestic round of Deansbury.

But life at Deansbury was to change drastically before Edwin came home again. The spring of that year was unusually warm, following a sudden onslaught of snow in March. It was caused by the eclipse, people said. Trees came into leaf and flowers into bloom before they were due, as mild winds and hot sunshine transformed the winter scene, as though by the waving of a wand, into premature summer. Everyone was delighted. It meant a saving on coal and candles, the opportunity to discard heavy clothes for lighter ones;

housewives joyfully turned to flinging bedding out to air, taking up carpets to beat, limewashing walls. As the fine weather went on faces became increasingly cheerful. They said that this year the crowning of the May Queen would be the most festive for years, with roses in bloom for her chaplet and the certainty of sunshine for the revels. May was happier than anyone about this, for she had been chosen as May Queen, suitable both in her name and her birthday. In previous years Joe had insisted that a girl from the estate be chosen, so that no favouritism might be seen to prevail.

'White tulle, I think,' she deliberated. 'Or taffeta. Or perhaps a plain white gauze over a cotton underskirt would be nicest. With a blue sash — or a pink one? Which do you think, Mother?'

'Either would be pretty. But dress simply, whatever you do. Your father would not like you to seem finer than the other girls.'

'I shall wear my hair down, of course — right down. And I must remember to take plenty of pins to keep the crown secure, because one would look such a guy with it slipping sideways. Maggie Lamb's did that last year, and people couldn't help laughing — and of course in the dancing —'

The parlour door opened, and Basil entered. 'If I may interrupt you, Mrs Atkinson —' They had been very formal, these four years, when anyone else was present.

'You're not interrupting. What is it?' She knew him well enough to interpret his grave face.

'Bad news, I'm afraid. There's two cases of smallpox among the hands.'

Dove paled. 'Oh, no! It can't be. Joe has had everyone vaccinated, down to the latest baby. It *can't* have broken out.'

'Well, it has. The doctor did explain to Joe when the first vaccinations were done that the thing wasn't infallible. It seems that there's a margin of error in all cases if the cowpox virus hasn't reached a certain stage. And sometimes the inoculation fails to take on a subject in a poor state of health. I well remember what he said, because I'd been suffering from a low fever just before I had it done, and I feared it might affect the vaccination.'

'All the children here were ill for a week or two … I thought that meant it had taken. Perhaps it had not. Oh, dear heavens, what are we to do? Have you told Joe yet?'

'Not yet, he's in a shareholders' meeting. I will as soon as he comes out.'

May was looking from one to the other of them. 'What does it mean? Is it dangerous?'

'Very, to us all, and everyone in the mill.'

'Does that mean … it couldn't mean there'd be no May Day revels?'

It did mean exactly that. When Joe heard the horrifying news he ordered all gatherings of any kind to be cancelled. Even church and chapel services were not to be attended by anyone from the estate; prayer meetings and school classes were to stop. May wept bitterly at the loss of the glory she had so looked forward to, and she was not the only one to be disappointed and displeased. The men muttered about the deprivation they would suffer in not being able to play billiards in the recreation hall, or bowls on the green; it was taking a working man's pleasures away, they said, and he had few enough with his drinking time watched so carefully.

The Methodist parson spoke sharply to Joe. 'You'd do better to put more trust in God, Mr Atkinson, than in all these fancy ideas.'

'I do trust in Him, Mr Darby. But don't you think He appreciates a bit of help now and then, like the rest of us? We can't expect a miracle every time one infected person breathes on another. The best way's to keep them apart.'

'It strikes me you're out to keep a man and his Maker apart, stopping our meetings.'

'They can pray at home, can't they? Privately, amongst themselves? Just as the children can practise their lessons at home.'

Darby retreated, angry. He resolved to get a bit of outdoor preaching in, whatever Atkinson said. The Church of England rector was more amenable. His congregation came from well-to-do families all round the district; his alms plate would be very little emptier for the absence of the mill workers, and the Atkinsons' pew was paid for yearly. And he very much disliked the thought of smallpox in the rectory.

The women supported Joe, wives and mothers who dreaded the awful disease for their children and themselves. Even if people recovered from it, it left them with scarred ruins for faces.

Dove scolded May, who was still grizzling about the white dress and the crown. 'You might be a little child instead of a great girl of seventeen, not far off eighteen. Marigold doesn't go on so, and she was to have been your attendant. And just remember what your father has said — no going outside the gates or the fences of the coppice.'

'I shall be pale,' May announced dramatically, 'pale and thin — no, I won't be thin, I'll be podgy with taking no exercise. I shall lose my complexion, and Marigold will lose hers.'

'Not half so badly as you'd lose it if you caught smallpox,' Dove told her grimly. 'Do you want a face full of holes like a pepper pot? Well, then, you obey your father's rules. There's a croquet lawn if you need exercise, and a tennis net somewhere in the stables. Why don't you get it out and have some games? Marigold plays quite well. Go along now, do.'

May went along, sulking. She knew quite well that her mother was right, but it was her nature to break rules for fun. The outside world had never seemed so attractive. She even yearned for the Sunday-school class she took, though in normal times she declared that it bored her unspeakably. She took to sitting on the short staircase leading to the attic that was traditionally hers and Marigold's, first a playroom, then a chamber given up to girls' whims, the making of scrap-screens and sand pictures and other fashionable pastimes. Joe, with so much else to worry him, asked wistfully, 'What's become of our merry May?' and Marigold grew even quieter than her usual self, saddened by her twin's moodiness.

'"When the wind blows smoke comes down the chimney," Mother used to say,' Dove observed. 'That's how it is with May.'

'Dear Aunt Mary! She had a proverb for most things.' Joe sighed. 'Well, we must hope the wind will drop soon, when times are better.'

But three more smallpox cases were reported, and a fourth. A child died, then a young woman. Joe paid the funeral expenses, and arranged for a plot of ground to be consecrated and set aside for burials. There was nothing he could do more, unless he ordered the mill to be shut down. He considered this seriously.

'If you do,' Basil said, 'they'll have all the more time on their hands to brood, and you'll find them sneaking off to public houses to drown their sorrows, or getting together for a cock fight or a mill. Your hands are no angels, Joe, even if you're one yourself. Keep them working and trust to luck. If they carry the disease already it will come out, in the mill or at home.'

Every evening Basil himself went the rounds of the mill and the workers' houses. He had had smallpox badly as a child, though it had left only a few marks on his sallow skin. On returning to the Lion House he bathed and changed every garment he had on, washing them himself and drying them in the linen room where there were heated pipes. It was, he thought, like a sort of daily Passover.

May had thought of something to do. A young gardener had recently arrived, Jim Blanchard, to take some of the work off the shoulders of Mr Stone, who was always complaining of his aches and pains. Jim was a comely lad, in the curly-haired and high-coloured style May admired. She thought she had made an instant conquest of him, and followed it up by persuading him to plant a peach tree to climb up the red-brick south wall of the kitchen garden. 'Just for me,' she coaxed, 'just because I dote so on peaches, Jim. My own little tree.'

Jim and the infant peach tree — she would go and visit them. 'You come too, Marigold, for exercise,' she commanded, and Marigold obediently followed her. At first she sat on the ground, enjoying the sun's warmth and making a small bouquet of the tiny-flowered weed called 'shepherd's purse', which had sprung up on the edge of a vegetable patch. She heard May's bright chatter and Jim's slow answers, though what they were talking about eluded her. Tired of doing nothing, she got up and wandered off, singing under her breath.

May was very pleased with herself. She had got an admission out of Jim that she was pretty, and that he would like her for a sweetheart if she were not his master's daughter (her mother would have smacked her hands for that, and her father been deeply grieved). She had also promised him a dance at the

Christmas ball, and a basket of peaches to take home with him if the little tree flourished. Then Mr Stone's hat had appeared among the apple branches in the adjoining orchard, and Jim had murmured, 'I mun get on wi' me work, miss.'

Deprived of further amusement, she turned to Marigold. But Marigold was not there.

May wandered, yawning, into the orchard, expecting her sister to be with Mr Stone, for whom she had a great liking, which was reciprocated — he knew she would not play tricks on him as May did. But she was not there, nor was her pale green dress to be seen among the brighter greens of the lawns and flower beds, or on a rustic bench on the terrace by the side of the house, talking to the friendlier of the peacocks.

The two retriever dogs were there, lying in the sun. May whistled them up. 'Heather! Gorse! come on, good dogs. Find Marigold.' Pleased, they got up, shook themselves and followed her, young Gorse giving sharp excited barks. The three of them traversed the Lion House's two acres of open ground without finding a trace of Marigold, nor was she in the coppice, the sheltered wild land that joined on to the kitchen garden. May had looked there once, but it was worth trying again.

'Drat the girl,' she told the dogs, 'she's gone in, of course. Now I shall get into hot water for losing sight of her.'

Dove was in the morning room with Mrs Skerritt. She looked up in slight irritation; the arrival of May usually meant an argument these days.

'Where's Marigold, Mother?'

'Where? Why, she went out with you, half an hour ago.'

'Well, she isn't with me now. She must have come in. I want to scold her for running off.'

Dove frowned. 'I haven't seen her — have you, Mrs Skerritt?'

'No, madam. But she might be in the kitchen with Cook and Peggy. She's taken a great liking for making cakes lately, and I must say she's a nice light hand for it. That's where she'll be.'

But she was not, nor in her bedroom or the attic, or anywhere in the house. May came down with a very troubled face. 'I can't find her, Mother.'

The storm broke. 'What have you done with her, you naughty girl? How did you come to let her out of your sight? What have you been doing? Of *course* you remember. Did she say nothing?' The questions and recriminations went on and on, until the miserable May was in tears.

'If I knew any more I'd tell you, Mother, but I don't. I've searched everywhere. I'll do it all over again if you like.'

'Indeed you will, and Peggy and Susan can search as well. I don't want an inch of ground left out.'

Mother and daughter and the two maids set off, each in a different direction. This time the unlikely places were tried as well as the likely ones: the large compost heap, the frog pond (though it was not deep enough to offer any threat), even the shed where Edwin had conducted his gruesome experiments, now turned over to Mr Stone's occupation for storing tools and plant pots. There was no sign, anywhere, of green dress or straw bonnet.

They had worked their way round to the main gates of the drive, all four meeting there. Dove saw that the iron hasp that fastened the gates was in place. That at least was a relief — Marigold had a habit of drifting out of rooms without shutting doors behind her. It was unlikely that she would have gone out through the gate and re-fastened it. But there was still no sign of her.

'She had better be found before your father comes home,' Dove said to the downcast May, who nodded. She knew all too well what would happen to her. Her father was the mildest of men until something shocked him into anger, and then his rage could be fearful. Cruelty and injustice had provoked such rages in the past; the loss of his daughter might well set off one of them.

When his key turned in the lock, shortly before six that evening, May looked imploringly at her mother. 'Please will you tell him? I'd rather be upstairs...'

'I'm sure you would. Stay where you are.'

Joe listened to the story in complete silence, stony-faced. Then he said, 'Jim Blanchard. Has he been questioned?'

'He said he never saw her go,' May sobbed. 'He just went on working. He had nothing to do with it, truly.'

'I want to speak to him. Ring the bell. Someone must go to the village and fetch him.' Tom, the lad who worked as odd-man, not being strong enough for work in the mill, was dispatched.

The maid Susan hovered in the doorway. 'If you'd like to go in to supper, madam...' But none of them felt they could eat. They sat in silence, the same horrid thoughts going through their minds: the river, a kidnapper, some villager befriending Marigold who might carry the infection...

Joe got up suddenly. 'I'm going to search for myself. The estate and the river banks. I shall ask at every house. One of you might have thought to do that before.'

'But you forbade us to go near the estate,' Dove said. 'You know you did.'

Joe went out without answering; they heard him ordering his horse to be brought round. May was conscious that she was dreadfully empty and wanted her supper, but there was no question of going out of the room and helping herself to food. It seemed as though she and her mother had been sitting there for ever, watching the evening grow darker.

Then the front door bell clanged. Dove jumped to her feet, there were voices in the hall, and Susan at the door; behind her was a strange young man, with Marigold on his arm.

In the hectic minutes that followed Joe was recalled, Marigold hugged, the young man interrogated, everybody talking at once. Then time righted itself, they were all seated and sensible. The stranger — dark-complexioned, smiling, polite of manner — proved to be an Italian, Enrico Manfredi, a teacher of art and languages in schools and private houses. He lodged, he said, in Glazeheath, the village two miles or so beyond Deansbury.

'I am sketching today in a very pretty lane when I see this young lady walking, with her arm full of flowers, and picking the hedge roses. I would not speak — have spoken — to her, but she stops to look at my sketch. We talk, and I think she has lost herself. She says she wishes to stay with me because no other person has spoken to her and she is a little afraid. Because she is very tired I take her back to my lodging and my landlady make her tea. Then she fall — falls, excuse me — asleep, and it is almost two hours before we can wake her. When she is awake she tells me her name and that her home is here, so I borrow a little cart, dog-cart, from my neighbour, and bring her here. I am sorry for so long delay.'

'We've been out of our minds, but it was not your fault,' Dove said. 'My husband and I owe you a great deal.' She had summed up both Manfredi's and Marigold's mood, which was obviously calm and happy. Nothing terrible had happened to her, and any inquest would wait until the family was alone.

Supper was recalled to the table and Mr Manfredi invited to join them.

What had threatened to be a nightmare evening turned into a delightful occasion, the guest amusing them with stories of his pupils and the problems of an Italian transported to Lancashire. He had been in England five years, he said, but in Glazeheath only a few months. He had come north from London because a scholastic agency had told him that an art master was needed at a boy's boarding school nearby, and that there would probably be opportunities for him to make extra money by giving Italian lessons.

'The people are so kind here — *molto gentile*. At first I am a little frightened of them because they speak...' He floundered.

'Harshly?' Joe suggested. 'We've a reputation for having rough tongues, but we're not so bad when you get to know us.' Manfredi laughed, saying that no such charge could be levelled against his hosts, who were the soul of hospitality. In his honour Joe opened a bottle of wine, which only the adults drank, to May's disappointment. Relief had sent her spirits soaring, and the presence of this agreeable young stranger was quite delightful. She talked even more than usual, flirting outrageously, but he responded only with politeness, giving no sign that her challenge had been taken up.

Dove missed nothing of this. As soon as supper was over she ordered the girls to bed.

'But, Mother —' May began, and Marigold's mouth drooped.

'I want to stay with Mr Manfredi,' she pleaded. 'He said he'd draw my picture.'

'Another time, perhaps. You have both had a trying day and you need plenty of sleep. No nonsense, now — say goodnight.' Reluctantly they did, Marigold bestowing an innocent kiss on

Manfredi's cheek after saluting her mother and father. He accepted it gracefully, without embarrassment.

'How charming they are,' he said when the door had closed behind the girls. 'Two flowers, a rose and a lily. I do not think their names would sound so pretty in Italian — Miss Maggio and Miss Fiorrancio. No, they are better in English, as are not all your names.'

Joe glanced at Dove. She knew what was in his mind, because it was in her own. 'Mr Manfredi,' she said carefully, 'I think we ought to tell you what you may not quite have realised. Our Marigold is not quite like other girls. Though she seems to be a young woman, she has the mind of a child. That is why she wandered away and got lost today, and could not tell you at once where she lived.'

The velvet brown eyes were warm, sympathetic, understanding; a warm tanned hand briefly touched Dove's. 'I did not know this,' he said. 'Thank you to — for telling me. I thought she was perhaps not well or very tired, perhaps. To me, to others, it may be that she does not seem strange, only — *innocente.*'

'Our word for it is *simple*,' Joe said, almost visibly wincing at having to use the word.

'*Semplice*. She is a child of God. Her name means "treasure of Mary", do you know that? — Our Lady's treasure. That is right, for such a sweet young maiden.'

Neither parent said anything to this somewhat original view of their daughter. Dove changed the conversation swiftly, telling Manfredi about the smallpox outbreak. 'You must stay away from Deansbury until the danger is over, but when it is, and we pray that will be soon, my husband and I will be pleased if you will call on us. We may well be able to find you some pupils among our friends.'

He bent his head, smiling. 'I should like that, madam.'

When he had gone, and they were preparing for bed, Dove said, 'I wonder if I should have invited him back.'

'We could hardly have done anything else, love, after he rescued the girl — God knows what might have happened to her without him.'

'I know, but … I feel uneasy, somehow. I'm not sure that I like to hear a man speak of Marigold as if she were a normal young woman. For she isn't, and never will be.'

'He seems intelligent enough to grasp that for himself.'

'And then,' she went on, 'it was so odd, what he said about — well, the Virgin Mary. It made me a little uncomfortable. One isn't used to entertaining Roman Catholics…'

Joe laughed. He would have laughed at anything now that the anxiety of his daughter's loss had been lifted from him. 'You don't object to having a Jew about the place, do you? I can't see any difference.'

Dove turned her head away, feeling her cheeks redden. 'No, of course not. Only…'

'Come to bed,' said Joe.

Edwin wrote to his parents:

I must say I wish I had been with you. Here in Edinburgh there is a great deal of infection of various kinds, including the smallpox, because of the extreme crowding of old tenements and very poor sanitation. It seems odd it shd. break out in Deansbury with so much clean air and Father's modern methods, but these things will have their way. I can but suggest an isolation hospital where nursing can be undertaken by persons guaranteed to be free of the disease and no relatives may visit. The hair of sufferers must be cut short or shaved and the skin bathed, with potassium permanganate solution, the eyes in particular to be frequently swabbed with clear water. Patients must remain in isolation for a clear six weeks. Re-vaccination for all suspects is advisable. Where irritation occurs the hands of sufferers should be gloved to prevent permanent disfigurement.

I have taken up golf, a healthy and v. typically Scottish pastime which...

Joe read his son's letter, recognising with affectionate amusement that the main part of it had been copied from a textbook. But it was welcome enough. That day, while going his rounds of the mill, a loom operator had put her hand to her head before collapsing on the floor. The typical symptoms: vomiting, backache, a pink rash on the forehead. There were four small children at home waiting for her, yet where else could she be sent?

To Basil he said, 'We must have a hospital. At least, some sort of isolation ward.'

'Not at the Lion House, I presume?'

'Good God, no. Aren't there any tenants' cottages available?'

'A double one, wanting repairs, down Greenacre Lane.'

'That will do. Order some bedding, and whatever surgical supplies are needed. Potassium permanganate, he says, and of course there's to be chloride and limewash, cheap cotton gloves, towels and soap, that sort of thing.'

Basil said patiently, 'I can get it all from Manchester, but you'll need nurses, you know. Where do you propose to get them? Miss Nightingale's young ladies have not become familiar figures in the English tapestry, though one reads that she's working to make them so. Drunken old women, or prostitutes out to make a bit extra, seem to be the usual candidates. Do you want them in Deansbury?'

Joe drew a long breath, keeping his temper. Sometimes Basil's mild cynicism irritated him unduly; sometimes he made himself ignore it. 'You know quite well what I mean. Can you find me some honest, sober, clean women to do what the doctor directs? I don't mind what I pay them. Anything to stem this tide of disease. If it spreads further we shall be ruined and the estate will be a failure.' He laughed bitterly. 'I built a public washhouse, put in a water supply, installed boilers in each dwelling, appointed a doctor to do nothing but look after the health of the workers, and this is my reward. Disease. Are we never to conquer nature, Basil, or the devil, or whoever sends these trials to us? *Doth not Death lurk without?* I forget who said that, but it seems true of us, whatever we do.'

He bowed his head on his hands; Basil saw that the grey in his auburn hair had suddenly multiplied.

'If you'd listen, instead of reciting,' Basil said in the flat Lancashire voice which went so oddly with his exotic appearance, 'I was going to suggest something. This new friend of yours, the Italian chap. He's a Roman, isn't he, like all of them? More than likely he knows some nuns. Nobody better for nursing than nuns. Why don't you ask him?'

Joe lifted his head. 'What a good idea. It can do no harm, at any rate. I'll ask him.'

Enrico Manfredi said yes, indeed he did know some nuns. They were a small community calling themselves the Little Sisters of Clare, and they were established on the outskirts of Manchester, in an old house which had been left to them. They had come to England during the French Revolution as refugees. They were not an enclosed order, but worked for charity. Enrico was sure they would welcome a visit from someone in need of help.

And so Joe and Dove travelled to Manchester.

CHAPTER FOUR

The Convent of St Clare was a plain brick building, with no ornament beyond a statue of the saint in a niche and two twisted pillars on either side of the porch. In the solid, studded front door an iron grill was set. In answer to their ring, the sliding panel that blocked it was drawn aside and a woman's face appeared. Joe gave their identification, and the door was opened by a small brown-habited nun who greeted them softly and led them to the office of the Mother Superior.

Dove had expected an atmosphere of dim religious gloom and a mass of holy images. She was all the more surprised to find the interior of the convent not unlike that of Edwin's school — uncarpeted corridors with a clean-scrubbed smell, no attempts at decoration, and a feeling that behind closed doors people were at work.

'Mr and Mrs Joseph Atkinson, Reverend Mother,' the nun announced. The woman who sat at her large desk piled with papers and ledgers raised her wimpled head and smiled in greeting. Another illusion of Dove's collapsed. Abbesses and Mother Superiors in girls' romantic novels tended to be withered crones of Spanish appearance. Mother Marie-Clare was perhaps fifty; it was difficult to tell, for her face was completely unlined, as though she had met all life's troubles with complete serenity. Her blue-grey eyes were calm and steady, her rather large hands beautiful in their shape and whiteness.

'Please sit down,' she said in a voice that was completely English and cultured. 'I believe you need help which we may be able to give you.'

Joe, as taken aback as Dove by the very matter-of-fact atmosphere, explained the situation, though he had a distinct feeling that she knew all about it already, and was taking notes only out of politeness. 'If the epidemic were to spread throughout the mill community it would be quite disastrous. It seems to be spreading, in spite of all precautions. Those who look after the sufferers catch it themselves. I can only think that the answer is to call in professional nurses, and your, er, sisters have a splendid reputation. If you can spare them from, er...'

Laughter played about the Mother Superior's mouth and twinkled behind her eyes, but she answered gravely. 'Their principal work is the care of the sick and poor. Not, as some of your Church seem to imagine, conversion and the worship of idols. I read *Punch,* too,' she added dryly. That journal gave a lot of its space to satirising the supposed influence of Father Newman and the Oxford Movement on the ladies of England. 'Our religious exercises,' she continued, 'are conducted strictly in our own time, not that of our patients.'

Her gentle, almost hypnotic voice began to put them at their ease as she told them how the Order of the Poor Clares had been founded by St Clare — *Santa Chiara* — the friend of St Francis of Assisi, to follow his example of poverty, obedience and chastity; how in later years there had been attempts to make it into a severe closed order, not at all what its foundress intended. 'Now, six hundred years after her death, we think our house is one she would approve. We have no possessions, our life is one of service to those who are far poorer than we ourselves. Solitude and meditation are beautiful things, but

Manchester is not quite the place in which to practise them, do you think?'

Joe said he thought it emphatically was not.

'This is a poor street in a poor district,' she said. 'When we first came here in 1792 people moved near to us because they felt we might help them. The English laws of the time were not in favour of Roman Catholics, so what good we did was done by stealth, and they came in time to understand that we were not witches or fanatics. Now the climate is kinder towards us we go about as we like. That is why we are well known for our nursing.'

Dove asked, 'But do the sisters not catch diseases?'

'Strangely enough, no. Or perhaps it is not strange — frequent contact with infection makes the body immune to it. Our Lord protects us, but by material means.' She smiled. Dove knew that she was very skilfully taking the supernatural element out of her image for their benefit. 'Come and see what we do here.' She led them out, up stone stairs, to another floor, opening one door after another.

'The dispensary.' The two nuns who were working in it bowed their heads almost imperceptibly without raising their eyes. 'Our in-patient hospital.' It was a large, L-shaped room in which the aseptic smell of the corridors was intensified. The plank floor was bare and shining clean, the ten narrow beds immaculately tidy, blanket-covered, each with a plain deal chair beside it containing a mug and water carafe. Dove kept her eyes away from the patients, but had a general impression that most were very ill. Mother Marie-Clare led them out again swiftly. 'Best not to disturb them,' she said.

They were shown the library, the kitchens, and finally the chapel. After so many clinically plain, austere rooms it was a complete surprise. It was small, about the height of the Lion

House ballroom doubled. Round its white-painted walls were the usual Stations of the Cross and some dark oil paintings which Joe, remembering the pictures contained in the City Art Gallery, thought were probably ancient and valuable. But the eastern wall, behind the altar, dazzled the eye. It seemed as though made of ivory: carved ivory niches each holding the figure of a saint, arabesques, angel heads and cherubs, celebrant seraphims with trumpet and harp, all rising to a triumphant peak where stood the Virgin among star-studded clouds, the smiling Infant in her arms, on one side of her St Francis kneeling with his animals and birds about him, on the other a startlingly un-nun-like figure in a flowing robe, long curling hair flying back on some heavenly wind from a beautiful eager face. The whole amazing sculpture — for it was carved in white stone — was lit by hundreds of candles in sconces of different heights, throwing golden light on lovely curves, intricate detail and soaring lines.

Joe and Dove surveyed it in amazement. 'I've never seen anything quite like it,' Joe said.

'There *is* nothing quite like it — in England,' said the nun. 'It was copied from an Italian Romanesque altarpiece by a sculptor who escaped from France at the same time as our order. In gratitude he devoted the rest of his life to making our chapel as perfect as he could. This is his memorial; he is buried under the stones of the aisle. Round here they call this the "Hidden Gem".'

Dove found her eyes held by the candle flames, steady points barely flickering in the still air, faintly incense-perfumed. She was beginning to feel herself hypnotised, as though she could sink down on a pew bench and stay there for hours. Joe's voice recalled her to reality.

'The figure at the top, with the long hair — would that be Mary Magdalene?'

'No, that is St Clare herself, dressed as a bride — as the Blessed Francis ordered her to come to him at the altar, where her hair was shorn and she was dressed for the first time in nun's habit. When her coffin was opened centuries after her death it was said that she was still beautiful, and her hair as golden as ever.' Obviously feeling that the conversation was becoming too spiritual for these two Protestants, the Mother Superior indicated that they should return to her office, where they were introduced to the two nuns who would be coming to Deansbury. They were Sister Marie-Berthe and Sister Marie-Josephe, both very young and very pretty in the calm-faced way of nuns. Dove felt sorry for them, condemned to a life without husband, home or children. She was suddenly anxious to be back at the Lion House, in her own safe surroundings. But Joe, courteous, calm and self-possessed, was making arrangements. There was to be no payment to the nurses themselves, only their food and lodging to be provided; a donation to the convent would take care of the rest. Joe would send a conveyance for them as soon as the hospital building was ready.

The business concluded, the Mother Superior tinkled a small bell on the desk. Within a very few minutes a novice nun appeared bearing a tray on which was a silver chased teapot and china of exquisite delicacy. The tea and the small cakes were of equal quality. Dove stole a glance at Joe, but he seemed quite unsurprised.

In the carriage going home she said, 'What an extraordinary place. I felt quite uncomfortable. Do you think we're doing the right thing, bringing them out to Deansbury?'

Joe patted her hand. 'They won't make it a hotbed of Romanism, love. I've seen a lot of Catholics round and about in Lancashire country places, and I'd say they're what someone called Quakers, a good sort of people. And whatever they are, we need them.'

When they got home it was to hear that four children in one family had developed smallpox. They were the children of the mill-hand who had been the last to succumb.

May was instantly charmed by the two young nuns. Their aura of tranquillity, gentle manners and picturesque costume inspired her with a burning desire to imitate them.

'Did you ever see anything set off the face so well as those wimples? One's complexion would look quite perfect. And the black habit is so pretty against the white, and then that ducky little silver cross ... oh, I should so like to dress like that!'

'So you may, if anyone invites you to a fancy-dress ball,' Dove said. 'You'd find it rather trying for every day, I assure you. Besides, I thought you wanted to wear crinoline when you're eighteen.'

'Oh, I do, of course. But just for now — couldn't I go and stay at the convent and pretend to be one of them? To see what it's like? I'm sure it would be good for my soul, and you're always saying I need to improve. Oh, do say yes!'

Dove sighed with exasperation. 'May, it is not for me to say yes, even if I thought fit. The Mother Superior would certainly not want an untrained Protestant girl on her hands — much less one as giddy as you. This is just a silly fancy of yours — and not the first one, my girl! Besides, how can you think of leaving poor Marigold? Be sensible, if it's at all possible, which I sometimes doubt.'

'Oh, phoo,' May said. She was at the age when nothing her mother told her seemed likely to be right. Secretly she consulted Sister Marie-Josephe; the two nuns were lodged at the Lion House until their hospital quarters were ready. They had been given a handsomely appointed guest room with an elegant lace-draped four-poster and a hardly less elegant half-tester, a quantity of mirrors, a davenport equipped with embossed stationery, and all other luxuries a guest of the Atkinsons might expect. Somewhat to Dove's annoyance, they had come to ask for something else, more simple.

'Perhaps a servant's room. Or two. We have separate cells at the convent.'

'I'm afraid we have no cells here,' replied Dove sharply, 'and the servants' rooms are all occupied. You'll just have to put up with a little luxury, until you can be accommodated at the hospital — which should be spartan enough for anyone.'

'But...' began Sister Marie-Josephe, the elder of the two, not long out of her novitiate and very ardent.

Dove quelled her with a look. 'From your appearance and speech, Sister, I would say you come from a very good home. Pray imagine yourself back there for a short time, and try to tolerate our worldliness. Perhaps you could turn the mirrors to the wall, but pray don't take the bed-curtains down or put the linen on the floor and sleep on the mattresses. The servants would not like that at all. Baths will be brought in to your room after breakfast.'

Marie-Berthe lowered her head; Dove fancied she was distressed, but hardened her heart. The bed-furnishings in the guest room remained undisturbed, wherever its occupants slept If the bathwater, with which maids had toiled upstairs, was used, there was no evidence. Dove seethed quietly, then burst out at Joe.

'Cleanliness is next to godliness, *we* were taught! Do you mean to say they don't wash, and that's supposed to be holy? Good heavens, what rubbish. The less May associates with them the better, and I don't want them here longer than necessary, worthy though they may be. Perhaps you can arrange for their quarters at the hospital to be ventilated by some nice draughts, and import a few rats, if that will make them feel more at home.'

'I expect St Francis extended his charity to rats, love. But I'd prefer not to try the experiment. Do put up with them patiently. They seem nice girls, if one can get over the oddness of it all.'

May thought they looked very odd indeed in the surroundings of the guest room. No possessions laid out on the dressing table, no sign of the beds having been disturbed, no interesting strange perfumes in the air — May always made a point of trying out visiting ladies' perfumes. Marie-Berthe was alone, reading.

'I'm sorry to disturb you,' May said. 'I just wanted to ask you something.'

'Yes?'

'Well, how do you, how does one, get into your order?'

Marie-Berthe looked startled. 'I can only speak for myself. I knew when I was twelve that I had a vocation.'

'What's that?'

'A calling to God's service. A need to serve Him in the monastic life.'

'Oh. And what happened then?'

'When I was sixteen I was presented to Reverend Mother as a candidate. She accepted me as a novice, and I served as one until the time came for me to take my vows.'

'And what do novices do? Sing, I expect, and pray, in that beautiful chapel Father told me about? How I should love to see it! Our church is *so* dull, really quite musty — I don't think the pew-opener ever lays a finger on it, at least Mother says not. Do tell me about the life of a novice.'

Marie-Berthe smiled faintly. 'You want to know about it, day by day? Well, then. We rise at the first bell, when it's still dark, and go to the chapel for prayers. After that we attend to our duties. We scrub floors, clean the hospital, attend to menial work for the nursing sisters, prepare vegetables and meat, dispose of the rubbish... At meals we are read to, and that is a pleasant rest. Then there are more duties, errands, everyday things, preparations for supper. Before the dark we retire, because the bell will wake us for prayers after a very few hours.'

'In the night?'

'Of course. Prayer is our life.'

May was looking thoroughly shocked. 'But that can't be healthy. Besides, it makes one very bad-tempered to be disturbed.'

'*One* gets used to it.'

'I shouldn't. Mother says you don't take baths. That can't be so, surely?'

The nun inclined her head. 'We are forbidden; it would be immodest.'

'Immodest? To be clean?'

'To ... view our own bodies.'

May's mouth was a round of amazement. 'Why ever not?'

The nun flushed. 'You would not understand, Miss May.'

'I should jolly well think not! You mean you don't even wash your hair? Then you must get lice, like some of the children on the estate, but of course Father has them inspected very often. Lice, ugh. How can you?'

She had roused something like temper or defiance. 'It's difficult to get lice when one's hair is shorn, Miss May.'

'You mean like a boy's? I did wonder how you got it all under that headdress.'

With a sudden gesture the nun pulled out pins and whipped the draperies from her head and revealed a head covered with stubble, as ugly as the surface of a field after crops are gathered, and a white scalp under porcupine prickles that had been brown hair. May stared in horror.

The door opened. Sister Marie-Josephe stood in the doorway, taking in the scene.

'Sister,' she said softly.

'I'm sorry, Sister. I will do penance.' The bare, pathetic head was swiftly re-draped.

'Yes.' Nobody told May that it was time she went, but there was no need. She slipped out without a word.

She said nothing of the incident to anyone, even Marigold, who was a sympathetic ear to talk to, even though she failed to take in subtleties. May had been startled out of more than a sentimental infatuation with the nuns' romantic appearance. In the brief interview and the ugly revelation she had grown up a little from her spoilt childhood, and the experience was disturbing. She was ashamed, sorry, angry — she hardly knew with whom: Marie-Berthe, herself, God, her father for bringing the nuns to Deansbury. She was not bad-hearted; she had not meant to pry into other people's ways or criticise them so rudely. She knew, without knowing how she knew, that she had hurt Sister Marie-Berthe, and she had never willingly hurt anybody.

Somewhere in London, far away from Deansbury, the author George Macdonald was writing his allegorical romance *Phantasies*. Its prose was interlinked by lyrics of melancholy sweetness, one of which began *Alas, how easily things go wrong!* It might have been written for the few short minutes in which May had challenged Sister Marie-Berthe.

For the seemingly trivial interview had been a confrontation. The young nun recited thirty Aves as a mild penance for her action; they were not enough to put her at peace with herself. Marie-Josephe saw it, and wisely decided to leave her alone to contemplate, saying that she would walk in the garden before dusk fell. Marie-Berthe watched her there, a figure from past centuries, upright, slender, dignified and confident.

As she was not. In the Protestant girl's eyes she had seen what destroyed all she had believed herself to be; chosen by God, holy, set apart. Brought up a Catholic, she had hardly ever spoken with anyone who was not, other than the poor people in the neighbourhood of the convent. Suddenly a girl of almost her own age had as good as called her a drudge, dirty and ugly. She slipped a finger inside the tight band of her wimple, feeling the sharp stubble on her temples; was aware of the stuffy smell of her body, so different from the sweet smell of this room. She looked slowly round it. It was a beautiful room, far more beautiful than any in the house she had called home, in a small manufacturing town, where she and her sister had been brought up by their grandmother and an aunt, after the death from fever of their parents. It had always been intended that the girls should enter a sisterhood; when Ursula's turn came, everybody was pleased and nobody suggested any alternative. Just as when Bertha — she had been Bertha then — was taken to see Reverend Mother...

What had she said to May? *I knew when I was twelve that I had a vocation.* An appalling doubt came into her mind: perhaps she had not had a vocation. A good child, who went to church without protest, obeyed all the rules, as she had obeyed them in the convent during her novitiate, pleasing Reverend Mother by her obedience; who was to say that she had no vocation? There was nothing she wanted to do in the world, for she possessed no special skill. What could a young woman do, who was not clever enough to teach? Except marry, and she was not attractive enough for that. Her aunt had even told her how fortunate she was not to be cursed with good looks, the snare of the devil.

Slowly she moved to the mirror that stood on the net-draped dressing table. Marie-Josephe had not turned it to the wall as Dove had sarcastically suggested. Strength of will and habit were enough to keep them from such temptation. There were no mirrors at the convent.

Half expecting the devil himself to look over her shoulder, she stared steadily into the glass. The white stuff of her wimple framed a face that was basically oval, though the cheeks still had the roundness of her eighteen years. The eyes were large, of a periwinkle blue, dark-lashed; the nose short and very slightly tilted — surely that was ugly, yet the effect was not unpleasant. Red, full lips, as red as though — dreadful thought — they were *painted.* And the complexion had a town-dweller's paleness, yet was fair and smooth…

She glanced up at a painting on the wall: a woman's head and shoulders, in curls and net ruff *à la* Mary Stuart, a fashion popular some thirty years earlier, though Marie-Berthe knew nothing of that. The woman wore a coy, simpering expression, and for all her curls was not particularly pretty, as May Atkinson was pretty.

As Marie-Berthe herself was pretty, she realised with a shock that sent a wave of heat all over her body.

With a last, lingering look at her reflection, she turned and gazed round the room. When they had first arrived she had taken in very little of its detail, because Marie-Josephe had reminded her to keep her eyes down and disregard their surroundings. There had merely been an overall impression of sinful luxury. Now she took it in, all the wealth of it. The mantelpiece, of veined marble carved with groups of cupids. The walls, covered in heavily embossed wallpaper in a peacock-tail design, were of deep strawberry pink, the colour echoed in the bedspreads of quilted satin and the upholstery of the chairs. The carpet, whose pile was thick and velvet-soft, was patterned with flowers of blue and a darker pink. Dove Atkinson's tastes ran to colourful splendour.

Slowly, with the stealth of a hunted criminal, Marie-Berthe approached the four-poster. She had not been near it before, Marie-Josephe suggesting that they sleep on the floor, in their habits, of course, with only the hoods removed from their heads, and their missals for pillows. It had been no worse than the rock-hard narrow beds at the convent, and the one coarse scratchy blanket.

She climbed cautiously on to the high bed and stretched herself out, lying sideways so that her boots did not touch the coverlet, until she lay quite flat, looking up at the rosy canopy, and beyond it to the white ceiling, covered all over with plaster mouldings of flowerets and leaves. A delicious feeling of languor crept over her, induced by the smoothness of the satin her palms were touching, and the springy softness of the mattress beneath it, under layers of downy blanket and linen sheet. She felt as though she were already experiencing the pleasures of heaven; which she would certainly forego if she continued in the ways of sin. A faint sweet scent came from the bed-coverings, for they had been stored with sachets of lavender and pot-pourri. Her breathing began to slow down; she was on the way to sleep.

Downstairs a door slammed. In one movement she was off the bed, smoothing with shaking fingers the impress of her body on the coverlet. She was trembling all over, horrified at herself and at the thought that Marie-Josephe might have entered and discovered her. She hurried to a window. The tall figure was still pacing a garden path, up and down, up and down, her beads swinging gently from her hand, as though weaving some holy spell.

What will become of me? Marie-Berthe agitatedly asked herself. *I shall never be the same again.*

The worst of the smallpox epidemic was over. In the little hospital seven children and four adults had died, in addition to those who had died in their homes, and several had recovered to be badly marked for life by deep skin-pits. Joe had lost a lot of money with the mill working on half time, but he was profoundly thankful that the loss of life had not been worse.

Gradually things returned to normal. The hospital was no longer in use, but he and Basil agreed that it should be kept as it stood, a spacious clean place available for any further epidemics, or for use in emergencies, accidents in the mill, complicated childbirths, any serious illness among the estate tenants which might need special nursing. They surveyed the bright limewashed walls, the open fireplace, functional high beds and piles of newly laundered linen, and found it all good.

'We're losing the nurses, but that's all,' Joe said. 'It's as decent a hospital as any mill owns in this country.'

'I reckon we could train nurses, as well as yon two moppets.'

Joe looked at Basil under his brows. 'What ailed them, then?'

'Nought, only their clothes frightened the patients, and the little one looked half scared out of her wits when anyone spoke to her. Mrs A was right when she said she'd sooner have had English folk on the job.'

'But they were English, weren't they?'

Basil shrugged. 'Maybe, but they called themselves foreign names. Oh, aye, you can smile at me, with a name like Absalom, but you'd have to go back a good many years to find one of my family that wasn't born in Lancashire. Well, I'm going on my rounds now. We'll lock this place up and put it on the watchman's circuit. There's ragged folk not above breaking in for the sake of a night's lodging or a cotton sheet.'

At the Lion House the early summer days passed pleasantly. A tennis net had been installed on the lower lawn, where Dove and May disported themselves, Dove proud of her agility and the lissom figure which enabled her to dash about in pursuit of the ball almost as spiritedly as her daughter. Joe, amused, watched them; he was too old for such things, he said.

Marigold was happy. Enrico Manfredi was visiting them again — her friend, her special friend — and he was teaching her to draw. He had soon discovered the curious coordination of her hands and brain. She could be taught almost any physical skill, he believed. Perhaps music, one day, but for the moment art was enough. Infinitely patient and gentle, he guided her through perspective, shading, the copying of drawings and the infinitely more rewarding depiction of real objects. She became skilled in drawing a bowl of fruit, a branch of blossom, a wine glass, then, as a sketch, the view of the garden from the window. One day she sat at her easel, working busily, glancing up now and then, but covering it with her arms, laughing, when Enrico tried to inspect it. At last she said, 'You can see now.'

She had drawn a dashing, impressionistic portrait of himself, lifelike even to the points of light in the dark eyes and the faint shadow of beard on the chin. Enrico gazed at it, then at her.

'You are wonderful,' he said. 'A true artist.'

'I can bake cakes, too,' said Marigold guilelessly.

The quaintly sophisticated reply delighted him. For the first time he wondered seriously whether her parents underestimated her. Was she indeed hopelessly imprisoned in a childhood world, or had they not found the right approach to her mind? Slowly, tentatively, he began to sound out her responses. Because he was used to teaching he had a ready ear for speech. When she answered a question in an infantile way he corrected her, made her repeat the correction, and fired the question at her again after an interval. Almost invariably she gave the right answer. She was incapable of deep thought or argument, but he could see possibilities for training even in that. He experimented.

'Marigold, what do you like to do best?'

'To draw.'

'Why?'

'Because of you.'

'Why because of me?'

A pout. 'You know.'

'I do not know. Tell me.'

'You talk to me as if ... I can't tell.'

'You can tell. Try.'

He could see the effort of thinking. 'You talk as Mother does to Father. They talk to *me* as if I were ... Goldie.' Goldie was May's pet canary, a privileged creature allowed to fly about the parlour.

'That is not right,' Enrico said. 'Goldie is only a bird, but you are...?'

'A girl,' she said seriously.

'Yes, Marigold, but not only a girl. Do you know you have — you are almost eighteen years? Soon you will be a woman.' He watched the information sink in.

After a moment she said, 'Like Mother.'

'Yes, like your mother. You are not a child, not a pet.'

She shook her head, again and again. 'Not understand.'

'That is wrong, that is bad English. You must say, "I don't understand you, Enrico." Now say it.'

She looked him in the eyes, a straight direct glance that might have been May's, and said clearly, in an exact copy of his tone, 'I don't understand you, Enrico.'

He clapped his hands in triumph, and she smiled, pleased.

'Very good, very good. Now remember, you are to say that whenever you don't understand me. "I don't understand you, Enrico." Then I will explain to you, make everything clear. Now, we will have a little diversion. You know I am Italian? Not of your country, but of Italy, a long way, over the seas?'

She pondered, brows knitted, then very lightly pointed to his hair with one finger, and after that his mouth.

'You mean,' he said, 'that my hair is black, not your colour or May's or your parents', and that I speak in a different way?'

She nodded, beaming, pleased to have been understood.

'Very, very good. Soon you will be telling me such things in words. Now, because I am of Italy, the words I spoke when I was a child were different from your words. Let us see if you can remember some of them. You see, Marigold, a thing may be called one thing in England, another in Italy. Look, this flower. You call it a rose. We call it *rosa*. Say that.'

'*Rosa!*'

'Good. Now, I say to you in English, you have a beautiful face. In Italian, you have *una bella figura*. Will you say that, now?' She repeated it, again copying his accent perfectly. What a dream of a pupil, after the clumsy attempts he had heard. He tested her on various objects, a glass paperweight in the shape of a frog, a picture, a book, her own shoe, and heard the word come back to him just as he had said it. Then he sensed her tiring, and ended the lesson, beginning again next day, with even more success.

As lesson succeeded lesson she remembered words from the previous one. He thought — he hoped fervently — that he saw something bright in her look which had not been there before, and heard the babyish tone beginning to disappear from her voice. *Dio mio,* he prayed, *let it be so, for I feel that behind this beautiful blank sheet there is a mind struggling to escape.*

May knew of the lessons, though she thought — like everybody else — that they were merely instruction in drawing. She was a little piqued about them. Enrico was the only attractive young man to have visited the Lion House, if one didn't count the local youths who were beginning to respond to the lure of the tennis net. He had taken no notice of her on the evening when he had brought Marigold home, and he was still ignoring her, giving all his attention to her sweet silly sister.

'I think I should take drawing lessons too,' she said to Dove.

'You had some, five years ago, from Miss Prynne, and said you found them very dull. I don't feel like paying extra at school for you to take them up again.'

May kicked a footstool. 'I don't want them at school. Why can't Mr Manfredi teach me?'

'Because he is teaching Marigold.'

'Can't you afford two lots of lessons?'

Joe had overheard the conversation. 'Mr Manfredi teaches Marigold because it gives him satisfaction to improve her mind, and we think it good for her.' Joe knew nothing of the language lessons, nor did Dove.

'Well, I don't think he ought to be in there with her without a chaperone.'

Dove laughed. 'Really, May! Since when have you been so prim and proper? I must say I was a little nervous about Mr Manfredi's visits at first, but your father and I feel now that he is a perfectly nice young man, and the sort of sensible company Marigold needs. Now don't be silly. If you miss your lessons I shall ask Miss Mather to come and coach you in the holidays.'

May gave a hollow groan, and drifted out. They heard her in the hall listlessly playing battledore and shuttlecock with herself. It was not a very amusing pastime, and hardly suited to her years.

She wandered into the ballroom where the grand piano stood, and began to strum idly, then to play snatches of the music scattered about on the lid. Fashionable waltzes: *Georgette, Haunt of the Fairies, Les Clochettes, The Princess Royal.* Her fingers drooped on the keys. If only it had been fine enough to play tennis she could have sent a maid to the vicarage to fetch Georgie and Adelaide and Albert for a few sets. But a fine rain was falling. She closed the piano with a bang and went out.

From the morning room came Enrico's voice, gentle and slow, repeating something over and over again. On an impulse May went in. After all, nobody had forbidden her to interrupt the lessons.

'*...near Woolwich the great ship was met by an American clipper, which looked like a dwarf beside her.* What was the great ship called, Marigold?'

The white brow was furrowed, then cleared. 'Great —
Eastern.'

'Very good. Well remembered. And where did the American
ship come from?'

'Across the sea; in the west.'

Both heads turned as May came into the room. Enrico
greeted her politely, then went on with the lesson. 'Can you
draw me a portrait of the Great Eastern?'

Marigold turned to her easel, where a sheet of drawing paper
was pinned to a backing board, and picked up a pencil. She
made a few tentative marks on the paper, then stopped and
looked at her teacher questioningly. May strolled across and
inspected the scribbled lines.

'My goodness, you haven't got very far, have you? I thought
you were supposed to be quite a dab hand by now. That
doesn't look much like a ship to me.'

Enrico looked displeased. 'Miss Marigold progresses very
well. She must be allowed to take her leisure.'

'Oh, to be sure. Never mind me, go on with the lesson.' She
flopped into a chair, hooked up a stool for her feet, and
disposed herself to be amused. Enrico returned to the account
of the Great Eastern's sailing, but Marigold seemed not to take
in what he said, returning garbled versions of it. He tried her
with single words, to no purpose, then laid aside the book and
set her to copy a print of the ship. But her face was growing
unhappy, her lower lip trembling, and the lines she was
drawing were feeble. Enrico knew that she was losing the
precious concentration he had worked so hard for. At last she
threw down the pencil and burst into tears, burying her face in
her hands. It was unlike her placid nature, and the first time
she had shown anything but pleasure in the lessons,

'Oh dear,' May said, '*now* what have you done to her? She never cries as a rule.'

'I think it is rather what *you* have done, Miss May. It is not good that more persons should attend when I teach her. She is not a...' He floundered for a word ... *commune? Ordinario?* 'She is not like other pupils.'

'I know that. I'm sorry. I'll go, then.' May flounced out, sorry indeed — partly for upsetting her sister, partly that she had put herself in the wrong with a personable young man. She ran upstairs, sobs choking her, and flung herself down on her bed. Dove, hearing the running footsteps, sought her out and heard a gulped version of the story.

'I see. Well, that will teach you to interfere. Now dry your eyes and blow your nose, you look a perfect fright. Have you nothing to do but maunder about the house? No embroidery? Piano practice? Then you could at least tidy up your room — look at it.' Shaking her head, Dove went downstairs.

Without waiting to consult Joe, she sat down to write a letter. It was to her father, suggesting that he and Aunt Margaret might welcome a visit from May; the child was very much at a loose end and in need of a change. Dove felt sure she could make herself useful to them both in many ways, besides being able to renew her acquaintance with her Aunt Belle and Cousin Laurence. As soon as word arrived that such a visit would be acceptable, she would be dispatched by train from Manchester.

A curly flourish in blue ink signed off the letter; Dove sealed it with a satisfied air.

CHAPTER FIVE

Lancaster Castle station was as grey and fortress-like as the castle which towered above it. As soon as May alighted from the train she felt excited by the different air of the place, keener and more northern, with a hint of salt in it from Morecambe Bay and a wind that brought the hills of Lakeland nearer. Her spirits, which had been rising steadily during the journey, soared as she saw her grandfather waiting on the platform.

With a pang she realised that he was an old man. He seemed so much less tall, his shoulders stooped from their height, and his hair under the top hat was white. His nose had taken on a beakiness which made him resemble the late Duke of Wellington. But his smile was as sweet as ever, and from the way he held out his arms to her one would hardly think he depended on his cane at all.

'May, my love! Why, how bonny you're looking. Had a pleasant journey? There's the fly waiting, no sense in getting out the brougham for so short a journey. The lad will bring your luggage. What a heap of it, eh? You must leave some room for buying from our fine shops. Come along, come along. Four years, is it? Well, I can hardly believe it...'

Jogging down the hill from the station they were within the town's compass in minutes. May looked back affectionately at the things she remembered from early childhood. The castle, its cobbled slopes, the ancient leaning cottages, the graveyard between the Priory Church and the railway line, the statue of the White Lady her own mother had found fascinating as a child.

They had left Meeting House Lane behind, the steps where George Fox the Quaker had been pelted with stones; they were in Market Street, passing the old pillared town hall and the market place, and here was Cheapside and Rosemary Lane, that had been a joke many years ago, Mother had said, because an open sewer ran there, giving off a scent that was not of rosemary; and there were the tall grey-gold houses of St Leonard's Gate. They were home.

A very old man and a round cheerful young woman appeared to unload the luggage, nodding and smiling to May. In the hall a lady waited; old, too, though younger than her brother-in-law and very straight-backed. She was tall, thin, handsome in a gaunt way, pepper-and-salt hair beneath an elderly cap with lappets, expensive gold-rimmed pince-nez on her nose.

'Aunt Margaret!' May flew into her arms and received a lavender-scented hug.

'May! You're quite a young woman. No, I'm wrong, there's a look of the babe there yet. Your train must have been prompt. The kettle's boiling and Janet's made some special parkin…'

Her great-aunt was ushering her into the parlour, the one she always remembered from her mother's stories. Mother and Aunt Belle had shared it, and Aunt Belle had been trimming a bonnet there when Uncle George came back from abroad and she didn't know him. Recollections flooded through May's mind, and topping them all was a sense of escape and relief at being away from home, from her mother's sharp eye and her father's abstracted look, and Marigold. Eagerly she answered questions and asked them, looking round at the familiar furniture, the pictures of Great-Grandfather Atkinson in powder and his wife in her high cap with the cameo brooch of the Three Graces on her capacious bosom. In the hall she had passed the grandfather clock on whose face a little sportsman in a red coat forever aimed at a rising pheasant. There on plates in the corner cupboard were the arms of Atkinson, the white bird standing on a knight's helmet, apparently crowing in triumph.

May let out a deep sigh, lying back in her comfortable chair.

'You're tired, child,' said Margaret 'It's the journey. I find the railway very exhausting.'

'Not tired, Aunt. Just glad to be here.'

Margaret was studying her. 'I thought at first you were your mother over again, or perhaps your Aunt Belle. But it's not so. The likeness is only skin-deep. Wouldn't you say so, Ephraim?'

He nodded. 'I would say there was even a look of you, Margaret. And of my Mary...' He watched her with pleasure and concern, remembering how Mary had fussed over her twin daughters, wondering whether Dove managed the life of this one better, now that May was in the difficult years between child and woman. Would he be able to understand his granddaughter, now that he was old, better than he had understood his own daughters? Her life would be so much more thorny than Marigold's, protected by childishness. For that he was thankful. If he had stood out against Dove's marriage with her first cousin, the child might not have been born as she had been. The thought weighed on his conscience.

'And how is Marigold?' he asked.

'Oh, very well. Would you believe it, she's got herself a beau.'

'A ... what did you say, my dear?'

'A beau, Grandfather, an admirer.'

Ephraim's face was shocked. 'I can hardly believe it. Who — what kind of young man ... or a boy, perhaps? She is very pretty of course, but I hardly imagined...'

'Oh, a young man, at least he's much older than us, about twenty-four. He's Italian.' She told the story of Marigold's wanderings and Enrico's rescue of her. But Ephraim seemed to be reading something else into it.

'Are you sure this was a genuine "rescue"? The man could have followed her, or enticed her out in the first place. Your father is well known as the richest mill owner in the district. Not difficult for a scheming person to get an introduction to the family by such a means.'

May stared. 'Goodness, I never thought of that. None of us did, I'm sure.'

'Yet Marigold didn't confirm this man's story?'

'Well, no — but you know her, Grandfather. When she's very tired she doesn't remember much about anything, and she must have walked miles in the heat that day. One wouldn't expect her to say anything, one way or the other.'

Ephraim was brooding. 'And he took her to his lodging? I don't like that.'

'I'm sure it was all quite above-board.' May flushed. 'If … if he had offended her at all she would have been upset, and she was quite calm. She isn't *quite* as silly as that.'

Margaret put in, 'I'm sure May is right, Ephraim. You worry yourself unnecessarily. People like poor Marigold have a special protection from Providence, you know. Besides, if Dove had been concerned she would have written to you.'

'She might not have done. She would not want to trouble me.'

'And she would not want you to trouble yourself, Ephraim. Pray don't think any more of it.'

She shook her head at May, to indicate that the subject should be changed, but Ephraim persisted. What had happened since, how often did Marigold see this man? May answered, truthfully, that he came almost every day to teach Marigold drawing, as she seemed to show a bent for it. How long did he stay? Oh, an hour, perhaps more. May made a wry story out of her own interruption of the lesson a few days before. 'I must say I thought it a very odd way of teaching drawing, getting her to copy a picture of a ship out of a newspaper, and asking her questions about it. He was *very* annoyed at being interrupted.'

'But surely someone else was in the room already?'

'Oh, no, Mother doesn't think it necessary. He's such a serious sort of young man, you see. If you met him you'd understand.'

'I may well do that,' Ephraim said grimly. When May had retired to bed, and the maid had brought in their nightcap of hot milk with a scattering of spice and a drop of whisky, his face was still clouded. Margaret tackled him. She could usually make him see sense when he would listen to nobody else.

'Ephraim, my dear, you are making something out of nothing. Dove is an excellent parent, a little too much on the severe side from what I saw on my last visit — you can surely trust her to protect her own daughter. A mother usually loves her afflicted child best of the family, and Marigold is afflicted in the mind, though it may sound cruel to say so. Now is it not good that she should be taught anything at all by this young man that may improve her poor mind, if only a little? If I were a mother I should be grateful to anyone who would do such a thing. And something else — I doubt whether he is quite as assiduous in his attentions as May's account suggests. There was just the least hint of jealousy there, I thought. You know what young girls are.'

'May is a candid child, and she loves her sister. She would never be jealous.'

Margaret sighed. 'Ephraim, where is your legal mind? *I* am doing the reasoning, not you. You can't see beyond your own suspicions.'

'If you had my experience of the law you would know as I do how unscrupulous men can take advantage of young women. This man is a foreigner, he seems to have no money of his own, if he resorts to teaching for a living. I'm convinced he is after Marigold's fortune.'

'What fortune? What would be the good of a fortune to her? Don't you suppose Joe will make provision for her care after her parents are gone? He may be unworldly but he isn't silly. Now go to bed and forget the whole thing.' But she knew, watching his bowed back as he went slowly upstairs with his candle, that he would go on brooding, until some action came out of it. Nothing she could say would be any use.

The nightcap had failed to soothe her as it usually did. She returned to her study and wrote another three pages of her current novel, a story of passion and intrigue in Henri Quatre's Paris. On her way to bed she looked into May's room. The bedside candle, still alight, showed a calm face, flushed with sleep, a thick fair plait almost hiding one cheek. May looked no more than twelve, perhaps less.

Her great-aunt pinched out the candle flame and quietly went out. She felt certain that whatever Ephraim feared, Dove need not fear for her children.

In a very different bedroom, far away north in Edinburgh, May's brother Edwin was sitting on the edge of a very different bed, his head in his hands. The bed was a typically Scots lie-by-the-wa', a narrow bunk fitted inside the panelling. It looked painfully narrow for one, but it was quite used to holding two, Edwin and the girl who stood over him, her hands pugnaciously on her hips. She was short, pouter-pigeon plump, with a head of flaming red curls and a vividly pretty face, at present contorted with rage.

'I thought ye kent whit tae dae!' she shrieked at him. 'Wha' was it you said — ye'd ne'er let a lassie doon, and I was tae trust ye a' the way? A fine thing for me, findin' masel' wi' bairn after a' yon grand words. Medical student — ye ken nae mair than yon cat aboot medicine.'

'It's not exactly medicine. That is, I thought I did know — what to do, I mean. I must have ... I don't know what happened. You were right — I ought to have left it to you. I'm sorry, Jean.'

'Sorry! A lot o' guid that'll dae us.' Her eyes snapped blue fire at him.

'Well, I *am* sorry. Because I don't know what to do next.' He was almost twenty-one; he felt like a helpless infant.

'Whit aboot David?'

Edwin shook his head. Because his friend David Ogilvy had these rooms in the old house in a close off the Canongate, he had been able to get away from the highly respectable lodging his father had chosen for him and enjoy Edinburgh's night life — too well, as it turned out David merely rented the rooms because his father had rented them for many years, using them on the very rare occasions when the family came to Edinburgh from the Highlands. David himself had no more ready money than Edwin, merely his allowance and enough for laundry and a little private spending. He had obligingly gone out to allow Edwin to meet Jean without having been told why, only that it was important, more important than just another bed-roll. He would have no spare cash to offer, or, Edwin guessed, any advice that would be of substantial help.

Jean stamped her foot. 'Dinna sit there like a gawkie! I played ye fair, didn't I? Ye've no catched the clap. I telt ye I was clean.'

'Yes, yes. Thank you. I mean…'

Her voice softened. 'Could ye no' marry us? I'd mak' ye a guid wife, Eddie.'

'Oh, Jean.' His voice was a groan. 'Don't ask me. You know I can't do that.'

'Whit for no'?'

'Because … must I say it?'

'Because I'm a hoor. Is that it?'

'Well … yes. It sounds terrible — I don't mean to insult you — but I couldn't take you home.'

A silence. Even to her, it had been a cruel thing to say.

At last she asked him, 'Your father's a hard man, is he?'

'No. That is … it would shock him very much. I don't think he'd ever get over it. He didn't even want me to study medicine, you see, but to go into the mill, so this would seem terrible to him.' Impossible to explain to her that his father's simple goodness would be harder to face than the wrath of someone fierce, a father who would knock him down first and harangue him afterwards. He could not face his father with Jean; could not face the prospect of her as a wife, though it diminished him to think that he had used a woman he inwardly despised as he would not have used an equal. It had all been a jolly romp, and it had gone appallingly wrong. Edwin could not even turn to the thought of his mother for comfort; she would be even less understanding.

In the hollow silence the door opened. David Ogilvy peered round it. A natural man about town, two years older than Edwin and many years older in experience, he took in the situation he had already guessed from the swelling of Jean's diaphragm above the artificially tight waist and the stiff spreading flounces of her mauve skirt. Poor bitch, she was in pup and his hapless friend in a dreadful quandary.

'Ah well,' he said, edging himself in, 'have ye sorted things out yet?'

Edwin shook his head. He knew there was no need to explain. Jean began to sniff. Passing her on his way to a chair, David gave her bottom, or what he could reach of it for the flounces, a playful slap. 'Can't expect to rob the magpie's nest and no' get eggs,' he observed. Edwin shuddered.

'I don't know what I expected,' he said, 'but not this, though I suppose I should have done. Davie, what am I to do? I can't marry her, I've told her that.' They were talking as though Jean were not in the room.

'Who said ye should?' He lit his pipe. 'Can ye keep the kid if she has it? Some do it that way. It's easiest, so long as ye don't take on too many by-blows. Think on the late Rabbie and the guid cash his cantie Jeannies and bonnie Marys cost him, puir fellow.'

Edwin had no wish to think of Scotland's national poet. 'I can't keep anyone but myself,' he said, 'and barely that. Father would give me a bit more allowance if I put up a good enough excuse, but I couldn't. I simply could not. Anyway, I expect it would cost…'

'It'd cost a' richt!' Jean exclaimed. 'There'd be a woman needin' payin' for when I was oot at work. I canna work an' tend a bairn, can I?'

'Not all hours of the day and night,' David said gravely. 'We ken you, lassie — a slave to your profession.' His long upper lip curled as he blew out smoke that wreathed into the still air of the room. Outside a raucous fight was going on, shrieks and curses floating up between the steep buildings. A church bell tolled midnight. Edwin knew that he should have been in his rooms an hour ago; Mrs Proutie was very particular about her lodgers keeping decent hours. With the sharpened senses of misery, he was aware of a moth flitting round the lamp, as inevitably doomed to disaster as he was himself; of the shine of the lamplight on Jean's hair, making it glitter like copper through the string snood confining it. He had been fascinated by that hair, and by her earthy charms and salty language. Now he felt ill at the sight of her, and despised himself for it, and wished himself anywhere else, at any other time, so long as it was before all this had happened. He knew he should feel sorry for Jean, yet though she was crying softly and mopping her eyes with her sleeve cuff he sensed that she was not as unhappy as himself.

'Well, then,' David said, 'there's the needle.'

Jean looked up alertly. 'I'm no' gaun' through that.'

Edwin had not reacted instantly to what David had said. Now he realised. A constant procession of the victims of backstreet abortionists came into the hospital wards, to die there in nine out of ten cases from massive haemorrhage, infection, or a combination of both. He could not face the thought of being the cause of such a death, and shook his head violently.

David shrugged. 'I'm out of suggestions, then.'

With an effort Edwin roused himself to deal with the situation somehow. 'You'd better go, Jean. Don't fret yourself too much, we'll think of something. I'll see you tomorrow. Go along, there's a good lass.'

'"Don't fret yoursel'!"' she mocked. 'Some hopes o' that.' Then, realising that her best plan was to keep him soft towards her, she came towards him with a coaxing smile. 'Gie's a kiss. Ye were aye kind tae me, Eddie.'

He made himself kiss her cheek, then almost pushed her towards the door. When she was gone he said, 'Davie, man, what am I to do? I'm desperate.'

'Have a drink. Or several.' He was pouring two large measures of whisky, one of which he handed to Edwin. After downing almost half of it the worst of the tension began to recede.

'Well,' he said, 'a fine mess I'm in. What am I to do, I ask you again? It's like some awful nightmare.'

David laughed. 'A body would think *you* were having the bairn. I tell you, it's happened before and it'll happen again. I hardly know a man it hasn't happened to, and that's the truth, so don't think yourself any special case.'

'To you?'

'Aye.'

'And how did you deal with it?'

'Money. That's aye the answer. You'll need some jemmy o'goblins, wherever you can get 'em from. Don't look at me, old son, I'm as skint as a St Giles's mouse. Won't your dad cough up if you tell a good story?'

'No. I can't ask him. I've told her that.'

'Well, your grandad, then? I've heard you say he's a sporting old boy.'

'Not as sporting as all that — and the twins are his favourites, anyway.'

'Any rich uncles?'

A glow was beginning to pervade Edwin, who had now finished his first glass and was well into the second. Not a rosy glow, perhaps, but one that cast a warmer light on his problem.

'There's my Uncle Jesse...'

David hooted with laughter. 'What kin' o' an uncle is that? Sure you don't mean your Aunt Jessie?'

'No, I don't, you great fool — Jesse as in the Bible, if you've ever read it — *the stem of Jesse* and all that. He's a Member of Parliament and lives in high style. I could tell him — I think. He's always struck me as a broad-minded sort. But I hardly ever see him — he's either at Westminster or in his constituency, down south somewhere. I daren't risk a letter to him getting opened … oh, Lord!' He buried his face in his emptying glass.

'Does he not take a vacation when Parliament rises, or whatever they call it?'

Edwin thought. 'I expect so — yes, he does, of course. Last time I stayed with them it was the holidays, and he was there. I could —' he slapped his knee triumphantly — 'that's it, I could ask if I might visit them on my way home at the end of term. It's only a fortnight. Nothing can … happen before then, can it, Davie?'

'The process takes nine months, laddie, or have your studies no' revealed that to you? Aye, well, that's settled. Let's turn to brighter things. I'm bidden to a wee bit fling at the Cranstouns' lodging tomorrow — will you no' come too? Jock's got a new madge-howlet, some lass from Aberdour, fresh in town — maybe she'll have a sister…'

Edwin shuddered. 'No, thank you.'

The Bradshaw family reclined in comfortable cane chairs on the lawn behind Eagle Hall, under the wide-spreading branches of the Spanish chestnut. They had just partaken of a sumptuous five o'clock tea: delicate cucumber sandwiches, strawberries with cream from the farm across the lane, tiny biscuits and sponge fingers. Edwin had eaten more than his uncle, aunt, and cousin — possibly more than all of them put together. Lucy regarded him with curiosity.

'Do they starve you in Edinburgh?'

'Heavens, no. They're very strong on food in Scotland. Particularly porridge, and oat cakes, and finnan haddie with bread and butter, and good meat — oh, we eat very well on the whole. But the, er, quality of English food is so much better, tastier.' He could have added that even his twenty-year-old appetite had failed him since his confrontation with Jean, and had only come back when he was safely over the border and ensconced with his favourite relations. Now the whole thing seemed unreal, or at least less real by a dimension. Warm and replete with tea and food, he surveyed his Aunt Eleanor, elegantly thin as ever, chatting vivaciously to two equally elegant lady friends, his Uncle Jesse, plump, smiling, half asleep under the tree's shade. Tonight he would talk to him, some time after dinner, away from female ears — especially Lucy's. She looked as though she would know without telling what people were saying to each other, whole rooms away; not that she was prying, it was a kind of wise look she had.

He knew so much more about women than he had done last time they met. Everything, indeed, he told himself, almost taking pleasure in his latest grim experience. It should be easy to solve Lucy's riddle, to find the answer that lay behind the calm broad brow and the eyes like clear lakes. How would she be if...

The scene that came into his mind was vivid enough, audible and tactile, a girl sprawled on a bed, himself above her, the sounds and sensations. And none of it related in the least to Lucy. Whatever it would be like with her, it would not be like that. He saw her smile at some lazy remark of her father's, and thought how unlike the smile was to May's ebullient giggle or Marigold's sweet blankness. It made her look for a moment very like Uncle Jesse, though they were so different in their general appearance: Jesse over-plump to flabbiness, Lucy so compact and firm, straight-backed as a governess. Edwin admired the strong creamy column of her neck above the prim round lace collar, and the neat graceful movements of her rather large hands. It occurred to him to wonder if she had ever thought of becoming one of Miss Nightingale's nurses. How different the hospital wards would be with such clean and capable angels to superintend them...

He lay back in his chair, watching the play of sunlight in the boughs above him, aware of the heavy hum of bees round the flowers in a classic urn, feeling comfortably replete after the substantial tea, yet pleasantly conscious that supper would follow in due course. After that he would find a way of getting his uncle alone and making his daring request. Perhaps it would not be too difficult, after all.

In another place, miles away across the beautiful Trough of Bowland, another, very different young man was also dreaming of Lucy Bradshaw. Laurence Dilworth gazed out of the window of his small office on the first floor of the building in Moor Lane, Lancaster, where his grandfather's legal business was conducted. Nowadays the active partner in the business was James Booth, son of Ephraim's one-time associate, dead ten years since. James was a born lawyer, happy with all aspects of his work, and tactful enough to let Ephraim think he was doing far more than in fact he was. The old man's memory was not what it had been. James was expert in showing him the documents in a case, seeking his advice and diligently recording it, then acting as he himself thought fit, confident that his senior would have forgotten what he had said by the time the matter was raised again. Seventy-eight; it was a great age.

James had not been entirely happy when Ephraim insisted on bringing his grandson into the firm as a very junior assistant. Laurence had left school with no particular academic qualifications and no real bent for any trade or profession. His mother made it quite clear that he was not going to live on what money his father sent home for her own keep and the running of the house. Laurence must earn his own living; the less she saw of him the better, was the implication. Ephraim was sorry for the boy. Had Laurence shown any strong inclination for the law he would have sent him to university. But that would clearly have been a waste of money for such a dreamy, unworldly youth. Fortunately Laurence wrote a beautiful clear hand and had a certain turn for arithmetic, and Latin had been his best subject at school. He would do quite well for a clerk's duties.

It annoyed James Booth that he had not been given the opportunity to appoint a clerk of his own choice. There were plenty of young men, he felt sure, who would have filled the chair and shown a great deal more enthusiasm and animation than Laurence did. A head full of dreams and nonsense was no qualification for legal work. If James had only had a son himself he was sure the lad would have turned out ideally for inheriting the business. Laurence was very much aware of his master's disapproval, worried by the necessity of not making the slightest error in copying or accounting, lest he should be dismissed, sent to waste his time in the unhappy home where his mother made it clear he was not wanted. She liked to entertain her friends, usually male, without a great hobbledehoy there to remind her of her age, a thing she worked hard to forget.

Laurence had no friends. He was too shy to cultivate them, not very fond of the society of other youths; schooldays had

been in the main a torment to him. Girls had little appeal —
those he had met so far, at least. With one exception: his
cousin-by-courtesy Lucy.

His pen idle, he looked out at the passing traffic, the busy
corner where five roads met. A few yards away was his
grandfather's house in St Leonard's Gate, and the theatre,
which he had hardly visited in his life. He had very few
pleasures or recreations, because he had not yet found anything
that fulfilled him or made him happy.

Only his great-aunt Margaret understood anything of his
make-up. Her eyes might be short-sighted but were
extraordinarily perceptive. When the Bradshaw family had
visited Lancaster the previous year she had not missed
Laurence's silent adoration of Lucy, a sensible girl of whom
she had thoroughly approved. Laurence was encouraged to
haunt her library and borrow her books. She smiled when her
copy of Wordsworth's poems was kept for months, and said in
the end, 'Don't bother to return it, child.'

Laurence was grateful. He knew the 'Lucy' poems by heart.
He read his idol's name over and over in them, sometimes
appropriately, sometimes not.

And vital feelings of delight
Shall rear her form to stately height,
Her virgin bosom swell;
Such thoughts to Lucy I will give
While she and I together live
Here in this happy dell.

It troubled him to read the elegiac verses on Lucy: *But she is*
in her grave, and oh, the difference to me. Great-Aunt Margaret had
explained that the real-life Lucy was the poet's sister, Dorothy,

and that for some strange reason he had killed her off prematurely in his verse. Ephraim had known the Wordsworths long ago, and had visited them in later years, often, until Dorothy and William had died within three years of each other. Laurence was relieved to know that the prototype of Wordsworth's Lucy had not died young. He felt that if premature death took his own adored girl he would have nothing left to live for. She was the calm maternal figure his own mother had never been: Lucy, the strong, the beautiful, the wise.

His love for her had begun, he thought, when he was only fifteen, and had seen her descending the staircase of Eagle Hall. He visualised her so, still, though he knew her now for a human creature who ate, talked of quite ordinary things, danced the fashionable dances, and acted as her adoptive mother's social secretary; yet she was still his angel.

How rich that forehead's calm expanse!
How bright that heaven-directed glance!
So looked Cecilia when she drew
An angel from his station;
So looked — not ceasing to pursue
Her tuneful adoration!

He began to draw her on the sheet of paper in front of him, which was in fact meant for the copy of an important letter. It was such a strongly characterised face, yet so difficult to draw. He managed a rough sketch of the brows, the broad cheekbones and smooth wings of hair, but gave up at the mouth, his pencil training away into Wordsworthian echoes.
'Well? Is the Haythorp letter ready yet?' James Booth's voice broke sharply in on his reverie. Laurence started, blushing, his

arm going protectively over the paper. But Booth had seen it already.

'What's all this? *Myself shall to my darling be...* What do you think we pay you for, young man? Mooning and idling? I protect you often enough from your grandfather, God knows — or rather I protect him from finding out what a useless wastrel you are. If that letter isn't ready in twenty minutes he shall hear about this, believe me. And no blots, mind.' He swept out.

Miserably Laurence put aside the spoiled paper, and began another sheet.

Dear Sir. Further to our client's instructions...
Dear Sir.
Dearest Lucy...

CHAPTER SIX

Sister Marie-Berthe was working her way through an enormous pile of dirty dinner plates. She had washed some thirty, and as many again remained from the convent's midday meal, shared by the sisters and the hospital patients. Every plate had to be scraped before washing, so that any scraps of food on it (not that the sisters left many) might go into a bucket which would be taken out to the pig. The pig lived in a sty at the back of the convent; it was considered a great privilege to be given the job of looking after her and her young, when they arrived, and after the few fowls who pecked about in the yard. There were tears when any of the creatures had to be slaughtered; what would St Francis have to say to that? But it was necessary. Weeping, the tender-hearted sisters forced themselves to do it. Marie-Berthe dreaded the day when it would be her turn.

One after another the greasy plates went into the increasingly cold grey water in the stone sink, were taken out and piled into drying racks. If only the water would stay hot, or the towels could be of good thick quality, really drying, instead of thin scrawny panels of ancient huckaback. She wrung her hands together, red, wrinkled and sore from the water and the soap the sisters made themselves from fat scraps. When the washing-up was done there would be that to see to, and the setting of mousetraps (another un-Franciscan necessity) and the lining-up of cups for the next meal. The kitchen smelt of old food, and wet stone, and the rags with which the plates were washed, that had not been recently boiled to sweeten them.

Marie-Berthe's back ached. She suffered every month from a crippling pain in it which could last up to four days. Her feet were tired from standing and her ankles swollen. She would have liked to sit down, but no chairs were provided. She was feeling sick, in spite of having had a frugal meal that went nowhere towards sustaining a growing girl.

And the worst of it was that no light in her illuminated the drudgery and the aches. The kitchen chores should have been as joyful to her as the lighting of the altar candles. Reverend Mother, whose reading was most comprehensive, was fond of quoting to her novices the words of George Herbert:

Who sweeps a room as for Thy laws
Makes that and th'action fine.

It was difficult to remember what His laws were, in her tiredness, and that depressed her spirits more than the cold greasy water or her raw hands. Something had happened to her, something she found hard to remember in detail, though glimpses of it occasionally flashed across her memory. It had happened in the guest bedroom at the Lion House, when she had seen herself in the mirror and wondered who she truly was: Sister Marie-Berthe or Bertha Moorhouse, supposed to be dead and buried from the moment her hair had been cut and the Lord's wedding ring put on her finger? She looked down at it, almost swallowed up in the swollen reddened skin; it seemed meaningless.

She was not eighteen yet, and she had never thought for herself, never wondered what her best way should be in the world. Her mind was not clear enough to reason out that she might be better employed in washing up for a family of her own, wearing her mortal husband's ring. The poor and sick were her family, the convent sisters were her family. Mortal husbands, as she knew well from those in the dwellings around, were much given to heavy drinking and beating their wives and children. She shuddered at the thought of life with one of them; indeed, it was impossible to imagine.

And yet her heart was very heavy, and felt as though it, too, ached and was sore. It was quite true that the heart was the centre of emotions. Just under the top ribs on the left side of her chest was a sensation as though a lead weight were suspended in a black cavity.

Only one strong idea sustained her to the end of the weary tasks. As soon as they were finished, the cups ranged on the board and the cloths hung on a rail to dry, she made her way to the office of Sister Marie-Blanche, directrix of domestic works.

'I have finished in the kitchens, Sister. May I have permission to go to the chapel for an hour?'

The sister glanced at the clock. 'What is your next task?'

'Laying the tables, at five o'clock.'

'You may have an hour. Wait — are you unwell?'

It was not permissible to admit to such a thing, unless one was actually dying. 'Quite well, Sister.'

A nod. She was dismissed.

She sat alone in the chapel. Not too close to the altarpiece, but some rows back, humbly shrinking in a corner. She should have been kneeling, but her body ached so much that she felt she would have fallen to the floor without the support of the pew back. The candle flames danced before her eyes, doubling and trebling themselves in a dazzling dance. She tried to fix her gaze on the holy group at the top; they seemed indistinct, the features coming and going. Marie-Berthe wondered if she were indeed ill, and rather hoped so. That would be better than an illness in the soul.

She looked in turn at each little saint in his or her niche. Unlike the great figures they seemed motionless: dolls, puppets. She tried to keep her eyes fixed on her special saint, St Margaret of Antioch, on whose name day she had been received into the order. There she was, the little shepherdess saint, with her crook and a lamb at her side. *Holy Margaret, help me, show me the light again. I should have taken your name that day, not kept my own. I promise to take it now.*

But there was no sign, only a carved ivory profile turned away from the suppliant. She was alone in the chapel; quite alone. The beads of her rosary were cold lifeless wood between her fingers, no longer living prayers.

Marie-Berthe spent a week in hell before asking for an audience with the Mother Superior. A small, drooping figure, she stood before the desk, her hands clasped. Mother Marie-Clare took in the girl's loss of weight, grey face and heavily pouched eyes. Even her steadfast heart sank a little. So many things could be wrong. She hoped it was not a grave sickness or the result of one of the terrible things which could happen to a young nun who went about in the world.

'Sit down, my child,' she said. When the heavy head was shaken she repeated the order, and this time it was obeyed.

'Tell me what ails you. I can see there is something. Whatever it is, I shall not be angry.'

Marie-Berthe's voice was hardly more than a whisper. 'I've lost my faith, Reverend Mother.'

So that was all; how many times she had heard it before. She smiled.

'We have all committed that sin at some time in our lives. The only cure is prayer, and more prayer.'

'I have prayed, Reverend Mother, all day and all night. I haven't let myself sleep this week. I spent last night in the chapel, on the floor before the altar, and still it was no better. I'm not God's child any more.'

'Nothing can make you anything else.' But the Mother Superior's face was grave. 'Tell me about it, anything that will help me to understand.'

Out came the rambling, confused story; how she and Sister Marie-Josephe had gone to the house at Deansbury and at first had resisted its luxuries, and how she had talked to one of the young ladies, and then yielded to the allurements of the beautiful bedroom and felt the pull of the world so strongly that her former state of mind seemed to have disappeared like a dream, and ever since she had fought with the devil to get her soul back, because it must be he who had done this thing to her, and the weight of sin was too much to bear...

The words were not coherent but the sad sense was there. Mother Marie-Clare let her talk on, nodding gravely now and then, touching the silver crucifix at her waist for help and reassurance. The more she heard the more sure she became that she had before her a very bad case. She knew all about the girl's background: the dull enclosed home, the lack of normal family life, the grandmother's religiosity. Bertha Moorhouse had had little choice in the way she should go, and so had come to the convent. Her conduct during her novitiate had been so obedient and humble that nobody had seriously questioned her vocation. There had been no great evidence of spirituality, but that was not essential; a down-to-earth young woman who might in other circumstances have made a successful housekeeper and mother might be of exactly the right temperament for a working nun.

Mother Marie-Clare reproached herself that she had not gone more carefully into Bertha's qualifications. It had all seemed so simple, no sudden conversion or vision-seeing (always suspect, particularly in young girls), no violent conflict of will: just a very ordinary Catholic girl dedicating herself to a life of service. Yet perhaps it had all been a mistake.

She set about questioning Marie-Berthe, no easy thing. What had Miss Atkinson said that had shocked and distressed her so much? What was there about the room in which the experience happened to provoke such a change of heart? She re-phrased the questions, watched carefully for reactions to her words, and learned very little. From answering her in a tearful, childish wail, Marie-Berthe dissolved into monotonous sobbing and incoherence. Mother Marie-Clare diagnosed the onset of hysteria.

'You are excused your duties until you are better in health. Go to the infirmary now, and tell the sister in charge you are to stay there, in bed, on an invalid diet. Go along. I shall pray for you.'

Not content with prayer, she sat by Marie-Berthe's bed some part of every day, in the room set aside for nuns too ill to work. The girl's apathy and obvious wretchedness distressed her. She talked gently, on soothing topics, without getting a word in response; she read from the books most popular with the sisters, ordered special little delicacies for Marie-Berthe's meals, watched them eaten with no sign of enjoyment. After two days she said, 'I can see my presence is no help to you, Sister. I shall leave you alone to think in quietness. Remember that God alone can afflict us with trials, but that He very often expects us to find the cure for ourselves.'

The cure. Marie-Berthe lay for hours, staring at the low ceiling, or round the room with its five narrow beds, all empty except for hers. The only ornament was a large crucifix hanging between the two windows, that were draped in cotton net. There was nothing to occupy the eye or fix the attention, and nobody came near her. She was, indeed, being allowed to think in quietness, and as the hours passed a slow build-up of resolution was taking place in her mind. When, distantly, she heard that evensong had begun, she slipped out of bed.

Her folded habit and a set of clean coarse under-garments were neatly disposed on a chair beside her, and her boots beneath it. She took off the shift that served as a nightdress and began to put on her clothes, fumbling at the fastenings with nervous fingers. At last all the little buttons of her habit were fastened. But she discarded the bib of starched linen that should cover her breast, and the wimple; they would give her away for what she was. Yet she must hide her dreadful hair.

Among her petticoats was one of black cotton, threadbare with wear. She took a firm hold of it at the placket, and ripped it down the seam. Now it was a manageable size, and she wound it round her head and shoulders, so that it looked like a shawl; or so she hoped, having no mirror to tell her what sort of strange appearance she presented.

She felt neither apprehension nor fear as she left the room, closing the door behind her quietly, though there was no chance of anyone hearing. Their voices came to her, clear and sweet, in the evensong chant from the chapel. The main door of the convent would not be locked yet, but to make doubly sure of escape she went out by the door that led from the kitchens to the yard.

The pig raised its head above the sty door, thinking she had come to feed it. 'Goodbye,' she said, 'goodbye, poor thing.'

The workman standing before Joe's desk looked his employer firmly in the eye. 'I've come up to see you meself, Mr Atkinson, to put things straight, like.'

'Yes,' said Joe wearily; he had heard the same statement several times in the last ten minutes.

'It's not right, Mr Absalom dockin' me pay because I were late a couple o' times. I told him, I'd a headache on me like t' Day o' Judgment, I could no more work nor fly. So I laid in a bit, till I were better, then I went in as usual, only a bit after time.'

'Two hours, I'm told.'

'Not near as much — he can't have told t'time proper. You tell him how it was, Mr Atkinson. I need all t'brass I can get, wi' t'wife sick an' all.' He was a small man, with a dogged look to him; like many small men, he seemed to fill the room with some inflation of his personality. Or perhaps it was the sheer repetitiousness of his speech. Joe hated argument.

'All right, Donnell. I'll speak to Mr Absalom. And I'll arrange for you to see the doctor.'

'Oh, there's no call for that, Mr Atkinson. It's nobbut now and again it comes on me, lights flashin' afore me eyes an' me head fit to split...'

'It sounds quite serious enough to me. Now, I'm very busy.' He dipped his pen in the inkwell and prepared to write — anything, to get rid of the man. 'And by the way — there was really no need for you to come up to the house. I shall be in my office at the mill this afternoon.'

'Well, like I said, I come to put things straight, Mr Atkinson...'

It was all of five minutes before he left, talking still. Joe's own head seemed to ache by now. Sighing, he began to go through the pile of letters before him. A tap at the door interrupted him; he called, 'Come in!' with unusual irritation in his voice.

'Yes, Peggy, what is it? I'm extremely busy.'

'I'm sorry, sir,' said the housemaid. 'But there's a young person waiting to see you.'

'A young person? What sort of young person? I'm not expecting anyone.'

Peggy looked acutely embarrassed. 'A young woman, sir.'

'Can't Mrs Atkinson interview her, whatever it is she wants?'

'Please, she asked for you, sir.'

Joe placed a paperweight on top of the pile of letters. He was beginning to feel hounded. 'Very well, show her in — and Peggy, tell her I can only spare five minutes.'

Outside the door there was a muttered colloquy before the visitor appeared. Joe stared at the extraordinary figure, then put on his spectacles to inspect it more closely. The Franciscan habit he recognised, and there was a familiar look about the pale, weary, none-too-clean face, swathed in a rough black cloth, but he could hardly believe that this was one of the nursing nuns who had left almost three weeks before.

'Sister...' He struggled to remember the name. She bowed her head.

'What in heaven's name...? Sit down.' He pulled out a chair. She sank down on it, her back very straight, but he could see that she was tired out. She said nothing, only looked at him with begging eyes, while he floundered for words.

'I don't understand. What are you doing here, Sister, and what's happened? Are you ill, or in some trouble? Did you not reach the convent safely?'

'Yes. Thank you. But I've left.'

He saw the dust on her draggled skirts, the streaks of dirt on her face. 'How did you get here?' he asked.

'I walked.'

'But why, in heaven's name? The coach is not very expensive.'

'We have no money,' she said flatly. 'It's not allowed.'

Completely baffled, he stretched out his hand to touch the bell that would summon Peggy, anybody, to take care of this mysterious female. As he did so, she slipped sideways from her chair and collapsed on the floor in a dead faint. Joe banged on the bell and shouted at the same time.

Some time later, trying to concentrate on his correspondence with his mind still on the visitor, he looked up as his wife entered.

'Well?'

Dove sat down. 'I don't know what to make of it, Joe — any of it. Coming here, after *walking*, in that extraordinary costume — I don't remember exactly what they wore but I'm sure half of it's missing — worn out and half starved, obviously ... oh, dear, what are we to do with the girl?'

He shook his head. 'I wish I knew. Has she said anything?'

'No. She came round when they carried her upstairs, and we got her to take some soup — then she fell asleep — at least I think it's sleep, not another swoon. When Peggy and Susan started to undress her she fought them, but they took no notice and got her down to a sort of rough shift. I haven't the faintest idea what to do with her when she wakes.'

'Send her back?'

'In that state of weakness? No, we shall have to wait for her to explain — if she can. Do you suppose she might be mad?'

'How should I know, my dear? But I shall be quite mad myself unless I am left to get on with my correspondence.'

Dove smiled, patted his shoulder and left him.

Much later that day, before dinner, she went up to the maid's bedroom to look at their visitor, who was awake, looking languidly about her. Her colour was high now. Dove felt her brow, which was hot.

She sat down by the bedside, hoping she looked calm and cheerful, and quite in command of the situation. 'Now, my child,' she said, unconsciously echoing the Mother Superior's form of address, 'tell me about all this. Has someone been cruel to you?'

The cropped head was shaken.

'But you ran away.'

'Yes. Had — to go.'

'And why did you come here?'

'Nowhere else, in the world,' Marie-Berthe whispered. Dove was puzzled, until it occurred to her that 'the world' might mean everywhere not enclosed by the convent walls.

'I see. But why did you ask for my husband, not me?'

'He was kind.'

'Oh, dear. Meaning that I was not.' *Well,* she thought, *I suppose I wasn't, very. I did speak rather sharply to them about not taking baths and refusing to sleep in the beds.* 'I'm sorry if I was unkind,' she said aloud, 'I suppose I didn't understand your ways. I am really quite nice when you get to know me.' There was no smile, only a faint relaxing of the troubled face. *What blue eyes the child has,* Dove thought, *and what a curious cast of features — I suppose one might call it elfin. Quite attractive, but for that shocking hair.*

'Madam,' Marie-Berthe said in the silence, 'may I ask — something?'

'Of course. Anything that will make you feel better.'

'The room.'

'What room? This one? Are you not comfortable in it?'

A feeble head-shake. 'Could I be in … the other? Where we were?'

Dove thought rapidly. The pink guest room. How very odd, when those two seemed to despise it so much. Perhaps this was a sick fancy.

'Certainly,' she said briskly. 'It will be no trouble to prepare it for you.' *And I only hope she won't be taking the smallpox or something nearly as bad into it,* she thought, watching the heavy lids drop over the blue eyes.

When they carried Marie-Berthe into the guest room she looked about it, smiled, and fell into a sleep that lasted until the morning. Dove's instinct had begun to tell her something of the truth. She ordered breakfast for the girl to be sent up on a silver tray with a lace cloth on it, the china delicate, rosebud-sprinkled, the toast wafer thin and the tea the best Orange Pekoe. A small brown egg was cooked perfectly, and by its side, in a little crystal vase, sat a pink rose. *The touch of luxury,* said Dove to herself. *One may be starved of more than food.*

She went up to inspect the results of her experiment. A perfectly recognisable human girl was sitting up in bed, propped by embroidered pillows, her face washed and one of May's nightcaps framing it in lacy frills.

'Well,' said Dove, 'you look a very great deal better. We were afraid you might be ill, but I see you've taken your breakfast very well.' Only the egg shell and the rose remained; egg, toast, marmalade and scrolls of butter had disappeared.

'Thank you, madam,' Marie-Berthe said. 'It was...' She faltered. She had been taught in the convent that one must not speak of food as lovely, beautiful; it was simply the means of sustaining physical life, not worthy of emotional descriptions. 'I liked it,' she said lamely.

'So I gather. And you like this room, since you asked yesterday to be brought to it. It *is* pretty, isn't it? I chose the furnishings myself. Now, if you really feel better, will you try to tell me something about how you came to be here? Not tiring yourself, just telling me whatever comes into your head.'

But Marie-Berthe was quite unable to give a satisfactory explanation. She murmured something about a change, a shock, a talk she had had with Miss May, and life at the convent seeming different, so that she was not happy there and none of it mattered ... then she crossed herself and muttered a prayer. Dove saw that trying to talk it out was distressing her.

'Yes, I see,' she said. 'Never mind. Do you know, I have no idea what your name is. We were all in such a state when you and your — friend were here that I hardly noticed.'

'Bertha.'

'Oh. I thought it was something longer than that.'

Bertha Moorhouse shook her head. Marie-Berthe was gone forever, lost on the road from Manchester to Deansbury, and she was never coming back.

Joe and Dove went to see Mother Marie-Clare that day. She thanked them warmly for putting her mind at rest about the whereabouts of her strayed lamb.

'I fear I allowed myself to think of the river. Not the clean Mersey, but the Irk or the Irwell, where so many poor people end their troubles — or believe they are ending them... The child was very confused in her mind — anything might have happened to her. What has she said?'

Dove repeated as much as she recalled of the rambling words, and waited for an outburst of anger against the runaway, even against herself for not returning her immediately to the convent. But the Mother Superior's face was as inscrutable as ever, calm and mild as a statue's. She nodded slowly.

'I think I understand. I have seen it before, but not in such violent form. Marie-Berthe had no vocation. She was not meant for the religious life, even in an order as free as ours. Unfortunately that was not discovered early enough. I blame myself very much; I should have known, before she took her vows.'

'Vows,' Joe repeated, with thoughts of the apprentice's oath. 'They are very binding, of course. Can they be cancelled, or whatever you call it?'

'A vow once made is made for ever. Nobody in heaven or earth can cancel it. But it cannot hold an unwilling spirit. Marie-Berthe may ask to be released from her vows, since she had only served two years since her novitiate. But give her time — let her experience the worldly life she thinks she wants — then, if she feels she needs to remain in the world, I will make arrangements for her release. If not, we shall welcome her back joyfully. Can you keep her without trouble?'

'Easily,' Dove said. 'We have plenty of room.'

They thanked Mother Marie-Clare, who showed them out courteously, apparently unruffled at the loss of one of her flock. In the carriage Joe mopped his brow. 'I'm glad that's over. I thought they walled them up alive. What a very sensible woman that is. I'm not sure that Bertha's made the right choice, you know.'

'I shall see to it that she has,' Dove said firmly. 'They're excellent people, especially Mother Marie-Clare, but I don't at all like the idea of young girls living like that — it's quite unnatural, no husband and no children. Imagine our May ... and by the way, what do you suppose May *said* to the girl in the first place, to start all this?'

'I'd hate to guess at it, love. It might have been anything. You know her, she speaks before she thinks. Whatever it was, it's put the cat among the pigeons.'

'Or the pigeon in the Dove's nest,' said that lady. 'Poor little grey thing, we shall try to brighten up her feathers for her.'

It soon became very clear that Bertha had no intention of leaving the outside world again. Up and about after the two days in bed insisted on by Dove, she took a lively interest in everything that went on at the Lion House. With difficulty she was restrained from helping the servants: 'People who occupy a guest room are guests, and Cook would much rather be left to herself.' So Bertha strayed into Marigold's lessons, and, strangely enough, was not resented there as May had been.

Imbued with the habit of quiet obedience, she listened intently to everything Enrico said, watched his drawings and Marigold's and tried to copy them herself. 'She is a natural scholar,' Enrico said. 'I could teach her anything.' But it was the practical that interested Bertha most. She sewed beautifully, was intensely tidy, and loved to do anything that would beautify the house. In the convent a much-envied job had been the arrangement of the altar flowers. At the Lion House it was something she could do almost every day, collecting armfuls from the gardens and setting them out with an artist's eye for shape and colour. Marigold followed her about, finding in Bertha's quiet simplicity something she could understand, copying her. Dove was pleased at first, then, unreasonably, a little worried.

'Don't you think she is a little too much like Marigold? Oh, not in the same way, but in her childishness?' she asked Joe. 'She's very sensible, but not altogether … I don't know. And then — I'm afraid she may have some sort of return to her past. She never mentions her church, or priests, or anything like that. We have no Roman Catholic churches nearer than Manchester, of course. But should she not be taken there, to settle her conscience?'

'We don't know that she has a conscience, love. She may just be like a child let out of a school that was hard for her. If you like, I'll write to the Mother Superior and ask her advice.'

Sister Marie-Clare's advice was, *Let her be. If she needs us and the Mass she will come back. She has the habit of private prayer, which may be enough.*

'There's another thing,' Basil put in, 'she feels she ought to be working for her living. She asked me the other day if there was nothing to be done in the mill — "tidying up", as she put it. You'll not keep a girl like that happy, letting her live as a lady.'

'Well, is there anything?' Dove asked.

Basil shook his head. 'It's all taken care of. I tell you something, though — you were too soft with yon Donnell, and so I told you at the time. Megrims, indeed! Last time he was late I took a good sniff of his breath, and there was spirits on it. He's been taking something to deaden the smell, dry tea leaves or mint, so I missed it before, but it was there, all right. Drink's what's the matter with his head, and his wife's too, if I'm any judge. He's only first generation cotton, think about that. His father was an Irish navvy working on the railroad. I'd not trust him an inch near a pint pot nor a spirit measure.'

'Well, what am I to do, then?' Joe asked. 'Follow the man about? Get a certificate from Doctor Ainslie?'

'You might have done that last time. He never went to the surgery.'

'Basil's right,' Dove said. 'I don't care for the man. His wife came round to the kitchens last week, begging, though she said it was because her neighbour was sick and she needed scraps.

Cook sent her away, but told me afterwards. Why don't you send for him and straighten it all out? Then, if he's what Basil says, get rid of him.' But she knew as she spoke that Joe would do nothing of the kind. Benevolent rule was his watchword. A workman would have to commit a major crime before he was sacked, and if he was Joe would contrive to be somewhere else at the time. She loved him and understood him, but Basil was right, he was soft. Basil was always right.

She caught his eye; they exchanged a long, highly communicative glance. Her expression said, *See to it yourself*, and Basil's, *Never fear, I will.*

The next morning's post brought three letters. Dove pounced on them.

'Thank goodness, the children write.' Three sheets of her father's beautiful embossed writing paper followed each other to the tablecloth. 'May seems to be having a splendid time. I thought life at St Leonard's Gate would quieten her down, but it seems the other way round. Two evenings at the theatre … a picnic on the rocks at Heysham, and a boat trip … a dance at Ellen's house. Ellen! Remember her, Joe, one of my bridesmaids? Letty Chirnside was the other. And now Ellen's the mother of five boys. No wonder May had a good time. It seems she took Laurence as a partner, and he — listen — *It was very hard to get him to dance at all, I'm afraid he is quite a muff. I believe he must be in love, but not with any of the young ladies here, it seems. I have tried to tease it out of him but he won't tell me…* Well! Poor Laurence, at that one's mercy!'

'May is a puss,' said her father. 'Who are the other letters from?'

'This one from Eleanor.' Dove read two pages of elegant spidery writing on gold-coloured paper headed with little coloured decorations of cupids and flowers, then looked up.

'Lucy is taking up charity work. She says she has not enough to do and needs to enlarge her sphere of activity. Eleanor hopes it will not turn her into a complete frump. I'm sure she need not worry. What sort of charities, I wonder?' Dove was gazing through the window of the morning room; in the garden a sturdy young figure was determinedly following Mr Stone, a sacking apron round her waist and a spade in her hand. Bertha, determined to be useful, whether anybody wanted her or not. A thought struck her.

'My dear. Lucy and her charities. Would she — do you think Bertha might help? We should have to ask Eleanor, of course. I doubt whether Bertha would mix well with fashionable house parties. But do you think…?'

Joe smiled at her. 'I think it might be a very good notion of yours. At least try it. Does Eleanor mention Edwin?'

'Oh yes. They are so enjoying his company. _Quite the young man now_, Eleanor says. He's riding a lot — Jesse hopes he can stay for the shooting — a ball at Sir Something's, can't read it, in Clitheroe … well, that's nice. How very lucky we are to have such sociable children. I sometimes feel, when I get a letter like this, that we need hardly worry about them any more.'

CHAPTER SEVEN

The story Edwin had told his uncle Jesse on the night of his arrival at Eagle Hall might have worried his mother a little if she could have overheard it. The appetite Edwin had discovered at tea time on the lawn did not endure through the evening meal, tasty as it was. A delicate shrimp soup, made with shrimps fresh from Morecambe Bay, was followed by galantine of chicken — a suitably light dish for the hot weather — a fillet of beef with small new potatoes and asparagus, and an iced pudding.

Edwin's throat grew dryer and dryer as he ploughed through the dishes. He felt himself in honour bound to tell his uncle about Jean that evening. To postpone it would be to remain under that roof under false pretences. Smiling stiffly, he listened to Jesse deploring the fact that the Liberals were in power again after a year out of office.

'The Queen's delighted, of course, even though Gladstone is Chancellor of the Exchequer — he's no favourite of hers, or mine, for that matter. I must say for old Pam, though, he works like a dog, never misses a sitting when the younger men are staying away in droves. Palmerston, I'm talking about, Edwin. Fine old boy: pity he left us and turned Whig.'

'He must be a great age,' Eleanor said. 'I remember him as quite a buck in the Regent's time.'

'Still is. Always neat as a new pin, trousers cut in the old style, even his hair brushed forward in curls as the bucks used to wear it.' Jesse smoothed his own thinning fair locks. 'Wish I'd thought of it first — very becoming.'

'And that reminds me,' said Eleanor, 'what a shocking thing in the paper this morning — Vauxhall is closed! After those years of pleasure, the dear gardens are no more. Do you remember it, my dear, the time you took me there when we first went to London? The lights, the beautiful statues, the singing and music, and those dark romantic walks ... I thought it was paradise, after dull old Lancaster. You young people will never see anything like it.'

'No.' Lucy's eyes were seeing the vanished scene; Edwin almost fancied he could see it, mirrored in those clear depths. 'We shall never see anything like that again, Mama. Vauxhall was closed because London ... because all our cities are growing bigger and dirtier, and the small pretty things don't fit into them any more. You and I are going to have to face evils our parents never knew, Edwin.'

'Yes, I suppose so.' He was uncomfortably conscious of the particular slice of evil he had on his mind. It would have been pleasant to linger over the meal, and particularly to talk to Lucy, but he was glad when the dessert came and went and the ladies went into the drawing room for tea. To his relief he was not expected to accompany them.

'If you'd care for a glass of port,' Jesse said, 'I don't suppose you're too young to savour a good one?' They adjourned to the library, which was just what it purported to be, a room filled with books which were well used, its most prominent piece of furniture a huge desk covered with documents, more books, files of newspaper cuttings, every sign of a man who took his duties seriously. After a couple of glasses of port and an excellent cigar he would return to the work he enjoyed, though it pleased him to have the company of an intelligent young nephew for half an hour. The boy seemed uneasy and *distrait,* though he had accepted eagerly the invitation to join his uncle.

Jesse hoped he was not intending to ask for Lucy's hand in marriage. A number of young men had already done that and been politely rejected, to Jesse's relief. He had thought none of them good enough for his jewel.

Edwin gulped the port without reverence for its age and bouquet. Then he sat up very straight on the edge of his comfortable chair and told his story.

He was too involved in it to notice Jesse's ruddy cheeks pale. By the time the tale was told the man who was normally so benign and relaxed looked as stricken as though his nephew had brought bad news. Even Edwin, tense and inwardly trembling, saw the change and feared that it meant anger. Jesse did not speak immediately, but picked up an ivory paper knife from the table at his side, and followed its intricate carvings with nervous fingers. Then he said, 'This girl. Do you love her?'

'Oh — no, indeed, Uncle. That's why I...'

Jesse cut in. 'Are you quite sure she's a whore? Quite sure she is not just a feather-headed young woman who's been indiscreet?'

Edwin would have smiled in other circumstances. 'Indiscreet' was a somewhat mild word for Jean's behaviour.

'No,' he said. 'She's on the town, there's no question about that. A quean, they call it up there. You'd know, if you saw her. I mean, it was obvious. Otherwise...' he floundered.

'Otherwise she wouldn't have been fair game.'

'Well ... there's no need to go on, Uncle. I know how wrongly I've acted.' He was surprised at the shocked sorrow on Jesse's face. It was not a pretty story, but surely a very usual one to a man of the world, a virtual Londoner. Everyone knew what London was like. He was defending himself mentally, though he knew he should be admitting, pleading. This was nearly as bad as his father's hearing of his confession would have been.

'How old is she?' Jesse asked.

'Oh — I don't know. About eighteen, I should think. They always look older, because they — well, they paint, and all that.'

'Younger than Lucy. Two years younger.' As young as that other young girl, more than twenty years before. The ghost of dead-and-gone Sally Winterslow was between them, though only the older man could see it. Young, and poor, and alone in the world. But for early death she might have become what this Jean was now, and all thanks to him for starting her on the downward road. He would always owe reparation to her for that lonely workhouse death, and for the priceless gift of Lucy.

Edwin watched him, puzzled. He had not expected his uncle to take it like this; he wondered what the outcome would be.

'You will want to support the child.' It was a statement, not a question.

'I — of course. If you could — when I begin to earn I would pay you back, every penny. I hate to ask. If you don't feel you can help,' he said in a rush, 'please forget all this, and I'll find another way, Uncle.'

Jesse was at his desk, writing. After a moment he handed a cheque over to Edwin. 'That will take care of the girl until her delivery, and buy whatever the child needs. You must see that she has a decent place to live in, and enough to eat.' That seemed very important to Jesse. Sally had not had enough to eat during her last wanderings. 'And, of course, you must keep her out of bad company.'

Edwin thought bleakly that he would have his hands full, doing all that and following his studies at the same time. But the cheque was for a hundred pounds, a fortune. He began to stammer his thanks, but found himself hastily dismissed.

That evening Jesse did not rejoin his womenfolk. He sat alone in his library, the lamp unlit until darkness fell, and his pen untouched on the desk.

The ordeal of that evening over, Edwin began to enjoy himself. He rode well, and Lucy better. Together they galloped in the rich countryside, along quiet lanes and between gold harvest-fields, down to the slopes of Pendle to look for the witch image that appeared on the mountain in certain lights and certain weathers; up to the top of the hill on fine days to see the distant prospect of York Minster, far away to the east; into busy Clitheroe to take dinner at the Brownlow Arms. Edwin was proud to be seen with a young lady who sat her horse superbly, and wore her clothes so well that people noticed only her looks, not muslins or taffetas. She might have dressed like a boy and would have looked equally handsome. Everybody seemed to know her, and she them, from workers in the fields under Pendle to the eminent Parker family at Browsholme Hall. Edwin noticed that she smiled more away from home, a wide sunny smile that transformed her face. Sometimes she could look quite plain — sometimes as grave, almost as stern, as the caryatid he had thought she resembled — though now he had almost forgotten that comparison; but when she smiled she was beautiful.

As they walked their horses by the banks of the Hodder, one still day of calm skies, he asked her suddenly, 'Are you content, living at home?'

She gave it a moment's thought, then said levelly, 'If you mean do I wish to live at home always, the answer is no. That is, unless I can be of more use than I am now, answering Mama's invitations and helping to entertain Papa's friends.'

'But you'll marry...' Why was it just a shade painful to say that? 'Then your life will be your own, surely.'

She raised an eyebrow. 'To send out my own invitations and entertain my husband's friends?'

'Well, then. What *use* do you want to be?'

She moved to her horse's side, where he stood cropping the juicy grass by the river's edge, and stroked the white streak that ran down his chestnut nose. 'Of use to him.'

'Sir Walter? He looks very well to me. What on earth can you do for him? Really, Lucy, you're a most mysterious girl.'

She pushed her hat back so that her snooded hair was free of it, and pulled off her riding gauntlets one by one. She was gazing at the slow-moving river, seeing things, he knew, that he could not see.

'Sir Walter is perfectly well,' she said. 'I mean to help others like him, but less fortunate. And not only horses ... things happen to creatures, in the country and in towns, that I don't like at all. I intend to improve matters for them.'

'But why? I mean, what's wrong with them, and what sort of creatures do you mean?'

She raised her eyes to his. 'Why did you decide to study medicine?'

'Because it interested me, I suppose.'

'Not because you felt that people needed your special knowledge and help?'

If Edwin had answered quite truthfully, it would have been to say that this had not really entered his head. The craft of surgery called him, anatomy fascinated him, but he had given no particular thought to the patients who would come into his care. Since he had walked the wards they had become real to him — people, not merely cases — though like all fledgeling surgeons he had had to put up barriers so that emotional involvement should not unsteady his hands or cloud his brain.

'I feel that now,' he said. 'But ... animals?'

Suddenly his mind went back to a dinner conversation they had had in his second term, when Lucy had asked him very forthrightly whether he approved of animal experiments. Something told him that he would lose her esteem for ever if he were to come out with some facetious or callous remark. At this moment he felt a very long way from her, and curiously desolate.

'Yes, I see,' he said quickly. 'Animals. There must be a lot of ways in which their conditions could be improved. It's very commendable of you to think of it, Lucy. Most girls would be far too, er, frivolous.'

'I am not most girls,' Lucy said. 'Shall we ride? We could be at Slaidburn by tea time.'

'Dear me,' Eleanor said, laying aside Dove's long letter. 'What will our family think of next, I wonder? I merely drop a line to Dove telling her of Lucy's intention of passing her time in good works — though I shouldn't think the charity organisations would count things like fighting cocks and hares — oh dear, are we to have no more hare pie? How I do run on; I meant to tell you, my dear, that Dove says she is sending us a runaway nun.'

Jesse put down his newspaper and began to laugh as only his butterfly wife could make him laugh. 'I think you must need your spectacles changing,' he said. 'Dove's writing is rather on the dashing side. I'm sure she means something quite different. Nun, indeed!'

'If you don't believe me, read it for yourself.' He took the letter and read it.

'Well! I must say, you were right. I should never have believed it. Do you know anything about this, Edwin?'

Edwin, his mouth full of toast, shook his head, then said, 'Not a word, Uncle. Mother wrote to me when she was in a taking about the smallpox, telling me not to come home, but nothing about nuns. What's it all about?'

'Read it.' He read it, whistled incredulously, then passed it to Lucy. 'Rum sort of place, this, to send a nun.' He looked round the elegant morning room. 'Not quite what she'll be used to.'

'Your mother says the girl seems starved for luxury — though I should have thought there was plenty of that at the Lion House. It's a novel idea, I must say…'

'You needn't have her to stay if you'd rather not, my dear,' Jesse said.

'Oh, but I'd like it. It sounds quite a romantic story, and I've never actually met a nun … have I? Besides, she should be perfectly at home in this part of the world. Half the country people are Roman Catholics. Do you suppose she'll wear that strange garb? They remind me so much of crows!'

'And what does Lucy think about it?' Jesse's eyes were on his daughter's faintly smiling face.

'I entirely approve, Father,' she said, picking up the letter again, and reading. Dove had written, *We found the nursing sisters at the Convent of St Clare; they are a Franciscan Order…*

Bertha was overcome with nervousness when Dove told her of the impending visit. To go so far, further than she had ever travelled before, to strangers, just when she had become accustomed to life among the Atkinsons; uncertain of herself as she was, she shrank away from it. Dove hardened herself against the pleading eyes.

'It's for your own good, Bertha. If you are to lead an ordinary life you must go among people and find out what the world is like. Mr and Mrs Bradshaw are our relatives, kind and sensible people, and I'm sure you'll find a friend in Lucy.'

'You would rather I went,' Bertha muttered.

'No. You know we are happy to have you here. I am only afraid that if you stay too long it will be like the convent all over again for you. Now I won't hear any more, and I don't want any tears. Everything is arranged, you are to go next week.' *Before May returns,* Dove thought, *to stir up any more trouble.*

She turned with relief to her household accounts. Mrs Skerritt's arithmetical mistakes were a relief from the manipulation of people. It was so much easier to be a man than a woman. Joe involved himself deeply in his model estate, the classrooms and Sunday school and the new bathhouse he had installed, but he saw no further into his operatives as individuals than their outward appearance. She thought back to the days of their youth. Perhaps he had never learned to understand people. He had been indifferent for so long to her infatuation for him, then blinded by his own infatuation for Rosie to the girl's utter unsuitability to be his wife. His head was high above the clouds, while she was left with the personal problems of those about her. He was, and had always been, a dreamer; sometimes, lying by his side in the night while he slept, she thought that she was no longer included in his dreams.

He was as kindly, as affectionate as ever. Whatever she said, he would listen to; whatever she wished would be done. She would never for an instant suspect him of unfaithfulness. Yet a gap was widening between them, Joe growing away from her. She had borne his children, put his house in order, graced his table, welcomed his friends; her vigilance had kept troubles away from him, her perception had often saved him from making expensive mistakes. They were as much equal partners as husband and wife could be. Yet something was missing, something that had once been between them.

She had tried to tell him that she was not entirely happy with the relationship between Marigold and Enrico. 'Do you think it altogether wise to continue with the lessons?'

'Why not? They do no harm, surely?'

'I don't know... He's explained to me how he is teaching her, and that she responds to it. But I find that she remembers very little of the lessons when he has gone, and she seems more disturbed than she used to be. Perhaps we're unwise to let him force her mind.'

'I think you're seeing goblins where there are none, love. Enrico is obviously devoted to her. How can his teaching do anything but good?'

'That's another thing,' Dove said sharply. 'She follows him round like a puppy. I don't want any mistaken ideas on his part about a romance — or any delusions on hers, I know I told May it was nonsense to insist on her having a chaperone for the lessons, but I'm not sure now. There can be no normal life for Marigold; she has a child's mind in a woman's body. And if you're going to tell me he knows that, he also knows that you're a rich man and would be bound to give her a handsome dowry if he persuaded her to marry him.'

'How could he?' Joe's tone was impatient. 'She would never understand a formal proposal. And I should never give my permission — have no fear about that.'

'There are other ways ... such as elopement, forcible abduction...'

'Can you see young Manfredi forcibly abducting anyone, even Marigold? It would be like a gazelle setting out to rob coaches.'

'Very well, don't take any notice of me.' Dove went out hurriedly before she could let angry words escape and upset them both. She wished very much that she could talk to Aunt Margaret, for so long her guide and counsellor. Impossible to pack Marigold off to her, as Bertha was to be packed off to Eleanor. Ephraim adored Marigold, of course, had asked if she might be entrusted to him, but it was impossible — two old people in charge of a girl who needed constant vigilance, a girl who could dance like a fairy and draw prettily, but might at any moment dash out into a busy street under the hooves of horses or set the house on fire playing with paper dolls and matches. And Eleanor would be quite unsuitable as a guardian.

Dove sighed heavily. There was nothing for it but to let the lessons continue for the moment. If anything happened to alarm her seriously she would put an abrupt end to them, whether Joe liked it or not.

It would have consoled Dove a little to know that her father's thoughts had travelled along the same lines as her own. From the moment when May had light-heartedly mentioned Enrico and the lessons, Ephraim had brooded on the danger they presented to his beloved grandchild. It was clear to him, after some weeks of May's company, that she was not a mischief-maker, and had plenty of sense under her frivolous manner. If she had seen the Italian as a possible beau rather than a mere tutor, then there was some ground for Ephraim's fears.

Waking at dawn, as the old often do, he would lie awake for hours, uneasy visions forming in his mind. It became obsessively important to him to save Marigold from a nightmare marriage. He shuddered to think of lust exercised on her unprepared body — of neglect, the wastage of her fortune, for, once in possession of it, this adventurer would regard her as disposable. Perhaps she would be committed to an asylum. He remembered visits to the local one on Lancaster Moor: the eerie gibberings and mirthless laughter, mad posturings and blank, blank eyes. A person merely of weak mind could be driven hopelessly insane or into a vegetable state of stupidity by being there, with no conversation, no normal life going on around them. The horrors endured by lunatics in Ephraim's youth had gone: whips, darkness, starvation and jeers. But what remained was bad enough.

Sometimes, in fevered dreams, he saw her bear a child and murder it, like Margaret in the German legend. Or he would recall a news item of years before: a lunatic breaking out and assaulting his keeper with a razor. That would mean close confinement; he saw Marigold in a dark, damp cell. His mind went back beyond the present humane conditions at the asylum to which Royal Albert himself had lent his name: back to old King George III and the dreadful stories of the treatment meted out to him in his dark days. Ephraim, the calm and reasonable, had become a troubled, irrational old man.

Margaret worried. He refused to tell her what was on his mind, fearing that she might try to talk him out of it. Nobody should do that.

One day she entered his study; a message had come which must be dealt with. His desk was unusually clear, and he was sitting at it, writing, a pile of virgin paper before him, the inkwell full. He hardly looked up at her entry.

'Mr Booth has sent this note, Ephraim. He would like a reply quickly — the boy is waiting.'

Her brother-in-law looked up with a frown of irritation. 'Why the devil … oh, give it to me.' He read, scribbled an answer on the back of the paper, and returned it to her. 'Tell the boy I'm busy.' Thrown off his thinking by the interruption, he read his work back from the beginning of the document, murmuring the words under his breath.

This is the last Will and Testament of me Ephraim Atkinson of St Leonard's Gate, Lancaster Gentleman made published and declared this eleventh day of August in the year of Our Lord Christ one thousand eight hundred and fifty nine. I order and direct all my just debts, funeral and testamentary charges and expenses, to be in the first place paid off and discharged, and with the payment thereof I give and bequeath unto my dear sister-in-law Margaret Bateman…

The clauses ran on through page after page: clear, emphatic, unpunctuated. Bequests to his daughters, Mary Anne Dilworth and Maria Doveton Atkinson, separate legacies to remain in trust for Edwin and Maybelle Atkinson and Laurence Dilworth until they should attain the age of twenty-one years, with various provisos for the disposal of the monies if they should die under age.

Then followed the section which was the purpose of his re-drafting of his will.

I give devise and bequeath unto my dear granddaughter Marigold Atkinson the sum of £5925 to remain in trust for her care and maintenance during her lifetime, the sum to be made up from Stock in Three per Cent Consolidated Annuities together with…

An impressive list followed, then the edict. The substantial yearly dividends, interest and produce of the legacy were to be administered by James Booth, attorney-at-law, and John Dilworth, George's brother, who had become a highly respected accountant, and were not to be paid into Marigold's hand or to any person or persons that she might from time to time, by any writing or writings under her hand, order or require the same to be paid to. In effect, even her signature or that of anyone she nominated as her agent would not secure a penny of the money. *My said daughter Maria Doveton Atkinson and my son-in-law Joseph Atkinson to be Joint Trustees during their lifetime.*

More followed.

It is my express Wish that any marriage contracted by the said Marigold Atkinson should be entered upon only with the signed and sealed approval of all four Trustees and a minister of the Established Church, with the full understanding that no monies due to her shall be payable to any person with whom she may contract marriage.

So much for penniless Roman Catholic foreign adventurers, Ephraim thought with satisfaction as he inscribed the final words, *in the twenty-second year of the Reign of Our Sovereign Lord King George III by the Grace of God...*

Something about what he had just written niggled at his mind. He read it again slowly. Good heavens, he had wandered back in time and named the wrong monarch. Shaking his head he crossed out King George, initialled the error, and substituted the name of Queen Victoria. Then he sat back, satisfied.

That night he slept peacefully through the dawn hours, and woke refreshed.

Margaret read the will slowly, twice. 'It seems to me an excessive precaution. And don't you think Joe will have taken steps himself, if the situation is as bad as you think?'

'No, I don't. Joe always did believe the best of everybody.'

'Well, I hope you won't be offending anyone.' In fact, Margaret was embarrassed by the emotional tone of the document. She hoped Ephraim was not verging on the senile, for there were suggestions of that about it. He was reading it again, with satisfaction, mouthing the words.

'I shall deliver it myself, of course,' he said.

'You'll do nothing of the kind! Go all that way, merely to hand over a document which speaks for itself? What's wrong with the post? You're not a young man any longer, my dear, to go dashing about on trains in this hot weather.'

'I could escort May back.'

'May has no wish to go back yet. She enjoys herself greatly with Laurence and the other young people Belle seems to have found for her. It does Belle a great deal of good to have to conduct herself as an aunt, for once. She has never been a good mother to poor Laurence, you know; she spends far too much time dancing and playing cards. I wish George would leave the merchant service and come home for good. That young woman needs a firm hand. Young woman, indeed! She must be … yes, nearly forty-five. All the more reason for May to remain and provide some youthful competition.'

Which was exactly what May was doing. Belle could not pretend even to herself that she did not enjoy having a lively young girl to giggle with, take shopping, and educate in the latest fashions. But there was another less pleasing side to May's society — her young freshness showed up Belle's age, so carefully camouflaged and successfully concealed. Against the pink and white and gold of her niece, Belle's cherished complexion showed pale and lustreless, her hair — rinsed with camomile and lemon juice — the uninteresting colour of string. Her figure was impeccable: tiny tight-laced waist, handsomely swelling bosom, her ankles and feet were well worth a roving glance, her hands white and elegant. But May's looks were the looks of youth, and Belle was hurt by them. In company she referred to May as 'this child', or 'my little niece', anything to make her seem infantile, a habit which May resented, being at the age when she tried hard to look older than she was.

But it was a small price to pay for moving in the most frivolous society Lancaster had to offer, and for being away from her mother's sharp critical eye, Marigold's helplessness, the boring company of the Deansbury folk, Georgie and Adelaide and Albert fighting amongst themselves and their mother going on about the eminent persons the vicar was preparing for confirmation, Jim Blanchard avoiding her eye and moving to another patch of garden when she went out in search of a mild flirtation, all because of the bother over Marigold's disappearance that day... It was much more fun at Lancaster. Great-Aunt Margaret had given her a bracelet of moonstones, the most beautiful thing she'd ever owned ('I should have had that,' Aunt Belle had said in a snap of temper) and Grandfather Ephraim spoiled her dreadfully, though not as dreadfully as he would have spoiled Marigold, because he liked helpless females. She hoped Marigold was not missing her, but Signor Manfredi seemed to be taking care of her, judging by the letters from home.

They were bathing in Morecambe Bay, from machines anchored on the gold sands. Bathing-women were coaxing or manhandling some inexperienced customers, but not herself or Aunt Belle or Laurence, all experienced swimmers. Swathed in all-enveloping bathing dresses, the two women frolicked in the water like seals, while Laurence swam efficiently at a discreet distance. He should have been on the men's beach, by rights, bathing in the nude like the other males. But Ephraim had intruded on the routine of the office and given him the afternoon off, to James Booth's disgust. So he was here, splashing about quite pleasurably, for the sun was warm and the water clear, though as usual he felt half-grown and clumsy and incapable of being comfortable in the society of ladies.

He swam to the shore for a rest, among little barnacle-studded rocks. May came towards him, her hair streaming out wetly behind her, a modern-day mermaid. As she settled luxuriously at full length beside him he was blushingly aware that his maleness was as unmistakably emphasised by the clinging cotton costume as was May's femininity, her alert erectile breasts. She saw his embarrassment, and made her teasing most of it.

'Laurence? Look, such a pretty shell.'

'Yes.'

'You're not really looking at it.'

'Yes, I am.'

She wrung out her hair, then spread it on the crook of her arm, her head back, relaxed and laughing. 'What a funny boy you are. I know plenty that would — well, take advantage, flirt. Why don't you?'

'You're my cousin,' he said roughly.

Her face softened. 'And cousins shouldn't marry. Mother told me all about that. I don't mean to be serious, Laurence. Only *you're* so serious, I just want to amuse you. Don't you ever think about girls?'

He had been staring out to sea, over the fishing grounds towards the Furness hills across Cartmel Wharf. He turned his head towards her, unsmiling. 'Yes. But it's nothing to do with you.'

May shrugged one shoulder, almost baring it, turning her face up to the sun in defiance of everything Aunt Belle and her mother had told her. 'I think you're spoony,' she said, her eyes closed. 'Spoony and moony. That's why you won't dance and don't listen when one talks to you. Who is it? Anyone I know? Oh, all right then. But I do think you might be civil to one. Aren't I pretty? I'm old enough to be married, you know.'

Her eyes glinted at him under long, damp lashes. For an instant he felt a surge of desire, and moved towards her, then lay back, inert. She was too like his mother in her ways, and he wanted none of her. With a snort of annoyance she plunged back into the water and swam away.

A movement on the beach caught Laurence's attention. His mother, draped in a very becoming pink bathing wrap, with her hair loose on her shoulders, was talking animatedly with two men in summer attire, one in a suit of sporting check, the other more soberly dressed but wearing a Scotch bonnet. There was laughter, some gesturing, then she disappeared into her bathing machine, leaving the men to wait. Laurence guessed that he would be taking his cousin for tea, ices, and a long, long interval before his mother reclaimed them; or, more probably, told them to get back to Lancaster by themselves.

Lucy, he said over and over in his mind. *Lucy, Lucy, if you were here.*

CHAPTER EIGHT

The arrival at Deansbury of a copy of Ephraim's will caused consternation.

'You see, I was right,' Dove said. 'Father has summed up the situation from whatever May has said to him, and he sees it just as I do. Mr Manfredi will have to go. Surely you agree with me now?'

'I'm not at all sure that I do.' Joe was scanning the will, frowning. 'This seems to me a lot of nonsense involving people who have nothing to do with us. I don't want Jack Dilworth mixed up in our affairs, and I don't like the implication that my daughter is an idiot, or that I'm not capable of making provision for her. Your father is failing, if you ask me.'

'He's your uncle as well as my father, and his brain is as good as ever. I think this is a very clever will. He realises how important it is that Marigold should be provided for all her lifetime, and after all, who knows what may happen to our fortunes? The mill could be burnt down or the bank could fail or our stocks and shares collapse.'

'There would still be enough, you know that.' They were almost quarrelling.

'That's not the point. The point is that after this we *must* dismiss Mr Manfredi. Whatever May has said, she must have noticed something that has alarmed Father. It would be an insult to him to ignore his wishes.'

'It would be an insult to Manfredi to send him away because of the unreasoning prejudice of someone who has never set eyes on him.' Joe tired of the argument, as he usually did of any conflict. 'However, have it your own way, and I only hope we shall not be sorry for this.'

Normally Dove would have consulted Basil about such a problem. But her feelings were ruffled and she had deep respect for her father's judgment. She decided not to chance his swaying her opinion, and in any case he was away in Liverpool; she wanted to act the following afternoon, when Enrico was due to give Marigold her next lesson.

From the morning room came a peal of laughter that might have been May's. But it was Marigold's, and she almost never laughed. Dove paused outside the door, then went in. Pupil and teacher were looking at a drawing Enrico had copied from *Punch,* a simple joke which he had carefully explained to Marigold and which had amused her. It was the first time he had been able to arouse her childish sense of humour, and he felt triumphant. Both bright faces turned as the door opened.

'Would you kindly look in on me before you leave, Mr Manfredi?' Dove requested, her tone giving nothing away. He was pleasantly expectant: in his present euphoric state he thought that she might have decided to raise his modest salary, and that would be very welcome, much as he enjoyed the lessons for their own sake. Teaching was a poorly paid business if the teacher lived in private lodgings, not at a boarding school with all found, but he did not wish to do that, knowing something of the conditions teachers were expected to put up with uncomplainingly.

Dove's first words disillusioned him. 'Sit down, Mr Manfredi. I might as well tell you this at once. My husband and I have decided to discontinue Marigold's lessons.'

He felt as though the breath had been knocked out of him. 'But — why, madam? I do not satisfy?'

'Not that exactly. But we feel that they are not doing her any real good. She sometimes appears disturbed in her mind —'

'It is because she thinks more!' he interrupted eagerly. 'I have awakened something that slept in her.'

'I am afraid you might awaken the wrong thing,' Dove said, with meaning. If he had been making sly advances that would touch him. But his face was blank, uncomprehending, shocked. 'You see,' she said more kindly, 'a mind like our poor girl's could so easily be — well, overworked, strained, so that she became much more difficult. And, if I may speak frankly, it is not entirely wise that she should be thrown together with a young man like yourself. She might take a fancy to you, which would be, of course, a dreadful thing to happen. She must never marry, even if — if the person were suitable.'

To her horror, Enrico's eyes filled with tears. 'I did not mean … I have never … I love her…'

'Exactly.'

'No, no!' He broke into a flood of Italian which she did not comprehend. She caught the words *amore del spirito* and *innocente*, but she was too embarrassed and anxious for the interview to end to ask him to explain in English. In any case, it would be pointless, as he had confirmed her suspicions. Not looking at him, she turned to her desk and counted out money. 'I'm sorry, I've nothing more to say. Here is your salary for a month ahead, instead of notice. I hope you will soon find another pupil. And thank you for your kindness and patience with Marigold.'

He was at the door, his hand on the knob, tears running down his face unchecked, and a look in his eyes Dove had never seen in any others. Was it reproach, bitterness? She was afraid he would break out again, but he only said, choking, '*Addio*, madam.' Then he was gone. She listened in case he went back to the morning room, but the front door closed behind him.

So that was done. She should have felt relieved. Instead, she was filled with a mixture of shame and regret, and a strange heavy fear that she had not only done the wrong thing, but something dangerous, menacing Marigold's happiness.

There had been a time, many years ago, when Dove's mother had turned away Belle's lover, Will Raven, because he was a married man and twice Belle's age. Belle had been heartbroken; and then Will's mad wife had died, leaving him free, but things had gone wrong and Belle had married George Dilworth on the rebound. They had never been suited to each other after the first fires had died down.

Dove had cried for Belle's broken life then, and for Will's. Her mother had done the wrong thing and altered lives. Had she herself done just that? She wondered if she was turning into a copy of her mother, inflexibly hard-hearted toward any who might seem to threaten her family. Time was when she had been the gentle one of the sisters, Dove by name and nature. It seemed to her that she had been pleasanter altogether, then. Perhaps living with Joe, having to be strong to make up for his weakness, had changed her.

She was tempted to run out and call after Enrico, telling him to come back. But he would be far out of sight by now. And she was not sure that she had been wrong; only afraid she might have been, because of the weight on her heart that only came when something very bad had happened to her.

Marigold was calling her in the hall.

'In here, Baby.' Why had she called her by that old name? Joe and she had agreed to drop it, long ago.

'Mother, where's Enrico?'

Dove hesitated. 'He's gone, dear.'

'He didn't say 'bye to me.'

'No. He was in a hurry. He … Enrico won't be coming back, darling.'

Shock was on Marigold's face, her mouth turning down at the corners. She was beginning to tremble. 'But I want him. I want 'Rico.'

'I'm afraid he … try not to upset yourself, dear. It's best that he should not come back. I can't explain why…'

'*You* made him go — you did it!' Marigold stamped her foot violently and went into a fit of temper such as she had not suffered since her childhood. Scarlet-faced, she screamed, cried and babbled unintelligibly, while Dove made vain efforts to calm her with words and touches. At last she threw herself down on the floor and lay there, writhing and uttering loud mechanical sobs and animal sounds.

Dove flew to the bell-rope. Mrs Skerritt entered before a maid had time to answer. 'What's all this awful noise? Oh, madam! Whatever is the matter?'

'Miss Marigold's very upset. Please help me — we must get her upstairs.' Together they tried to raise her, but distraction had given her abnormal strength to resist them. The maid, Peggy, appeared, and stood horrified in the doorway. Dove motioned her to stay where she was. Eventually the dreadful sounds quietened and the tense heaving body grew still, until it lay unmoving on the carpet. They lifted her, heavy in unconsciousness for all her slender build, and somehow carried her upstairs and into her bed. She seemed to be in a troubled sleep, her eyelids twitching and her lips forming words silently. Dove sat by her until normal sleep seemed to have set in, then tiptoed downstairs.

She had hoped Joe would be there, someone to whom she could confess the recent happenings. But he was not yet home, and it was Basil who disturbed her as she sat brooding in the room where the scene had taken place. A vase had been knocked over during Marigold's convulsions: Dove had retrieved the flowers scattered on the carpet and put them back in it, not noticing that all the water was spilt. Now there was nothing to put right, nothing to do but think.

Basil put his head round the door. 'Joe not here? I looked in at the mill but they said he'd left ... what in heck's the matter with you?'

'Oh, Basil.' Before he had time to sit down she began to pour out the story of Enrico's dismissal and its results. He listened impassively, leaning on the mantelpiece.

When she had finished he said, 'You didn't think to consult me, then?'

'You weren't here. I wanted to get it over quickly... Do you think I did wrong? She was so ... oh, it was dreadful to see her. I should have asked you first, I know that now, you're always so sensible.'

'Thanks. All compliments gratefully received. I've had my uses up to now. If you *had* asked me I'd have said leave things as they were. The lad was doing no harm, and quite a bit of good from what I gathered. As to your father's will, he's an old man, and old men get strange notions. You were here, on the spot, it was for you to sit tight and wait till something concrete happened. I'm surprised Joe let you. No, that's untrue, I'm not. I suppose you nagged at him and he got up and went out.'

Dove nodded miserably. 'I wish he'd fought me. He did argue, but not enough.'

'That's Joe all over. Do you know where I was this morning? Down on the estate, at Donnell's. He was the chap that came here ranting because I'd docked his pay for repeated bad time-keeping. Joe listened to him, not me. I thought I'd catch him out for a liar, and I did, not long before he was due at the mill. His wife answered the door, half naked and reeking of spirits. If you'd struck a match near her she'd have burst into flames. I saw Donnell over her shoulder, snoring on the bed, too sound to wake even when I shouted in his ear. There were bottles on the floor, and he knows well enough what the rule is. But do you think I'll be able to persuade Joe to sack him? I'd as soon expect a mouse to bark.'

'Perhaps he will, this time, if he's angry enough. And he *will* be angry when he hears about Marigold. Oh, Basil, what shall I do?'

'How can I tell you? I'm not the girl's father.' *And I wish I were,* he thought. He looked down at the beautiful face upturned to him, so much older than when he first knew it, marked by little lines of care and discontent; the round throat beginning to sag; the faint tracks from nose to mouth-corners; the figure half-hidden by the ridiculous crinoline, not so lissom as it had been. Yet she was still his love and his idol, the only dream he permitted himself in his hard lonely life; the virtuous woman whose price was above rubies, fairest among women, rose of Sharon, lily of the valleys… If he had had the luck to wed her he would have given her the strength she needed, so that her softness would not have had to harden in the constant fight to protect Joe. He would have given her an undivided passion, the unquestioning faithfulness of a good Jewish husband, he for whom industrial ideals were not allowed to become rivals to a woman.

And Marigold would have been born a normal child.

'Don't look so down,' he said. 'Cheer up, the war's not lost yet and worse things happen at sea. I'll go after the lad. I can be in Glazeheath in no time, my horse has had no exercise today.'

'Thank you,' she whispered, and put out her hands to him. Bending, he took them, and kissed her full on the mouth. It was their first kiss since that day long ago, and it left both of them shaken.

He was unlucky in his quest for Enrico. The landlady at the cottage in Glazeheath said that her lodger had come home earlier than usual in a terrible taking, hardly talking sense, and had said he was going away for a time. After paying her he had left the house with only a small bag, not even his sketching things. She was very bothered about him, and not only for the loss of the rent.

Marigold laughed no more after Enrico's banishment, and showed no interest in drawing. One day Dove found her tearing a picture she had drawn into small neat pieces, and feeding them into the fire. She became very quiet, almost sullen, so abstracted that people spoke to her repeatedly without getting an answer.

The house was much changed, Bertha thought, yet she was bitterly unhappy to be leaving it for a strange place. Her face streaked and swollen with tears, she sat glumly in the railway carriage, staring sightlessly through the grimed window at the passengers and porters milling about on Manchester's Exchange station. Dove was there, seeing her off conscientiously, glad of the chance to get away from home and do some shopping. As the train began to move she waved and smiled, but Bertha was too dejected to raise more than a grimace before applying her handkerchief, now reduced to a soaking ball, to her eyes again.

Yet even misery was not proof against the interest of the changing landscapes of the journey; the station left behind, the industrial ugliness of the city giving way to areas of scattered building, a glimpse of hills away to the east, her first sight of the 'backbone of England', the Pennines; other towns, Bolton, Blackburn, and wide fields with cottages and farms, stately houses nesting among trees; and suddenly the train was crossing a wide river, and hills were rearing their heads, smiling in the sun that had come out.

'Clitheroe next stop, love,' said the stout lady sharing her compartment. Dove had whispered to her to look after the solitary girl and tell her where to get out, for she was very inexperienced in travelling. A shock of excitement went through Bertha. She fumbled with her gloves and her ticket, staggered as she took her portmanteau down from the luggage rack. She was horribly nervous, apprehensive of the horrors she might encounter among strangers, yet the habit of moral thought inculcated at the convent made her remind herself that all this tribulation was good for the soul.

Clitheroe. The noticeboards said so in bold letters; there could be no doubt that this was where she ought to leave the train, though she did so with an awful fear that she would find herself alone in a wilderness.

The station was reassuringly small after the vastness of Manchester, and the people on it seemed in less of a hurry. Some were carrying fowls in small crates, there was a woman with a huge dog which leaped with delight at seeing its master descend. A boy was leading a loudly protesting goat towards the guard's van. And the air was strangely sweet, even allowing for the steam; different from the air of Deansbury, which Bertha had thought so fine.

As she stood uncertainly, looking about her, a voice behind said, 'Hello!'

She turned to see a portly gentleman dressed in what even she recognised as very expensive country clothes. His jacket was of heather-coloured tweed, his breeches of finest twill, his high boots shining. He raised his hat in a sweeping courtly gesture, his ruddy face breaking into a warm smile.

'It must be Miss Moorhouse, surely?'

'I ... yes, sir.'

'I thought so, an unescorted young lady. Come along, come along. The trap's just outside. Thought I'd fetch you myself, rather than send a groom. Well, well. Had a comfortable journey?' Jesse did not miss the tear-stained cheeks and swollen eyelids, but he was a supremely tactful man, and he knew the value of light chatter when dealing with such a very nervous young person. She seemed a plain little thing, but then she was pale, travel-soiled and thoroughly frightened of him. He had been curious to know what an ex-nun would look like: on the whole she was what he expected.

As she sat perched beside him he pointed his whip at various sights to be seen: Clitheroe castle, a much admired church, the handsome house of a local landowner. She barely turned her head (and what a hideous hat she wore, like an inverted mushroom swathed in brown net, the usual pleasing wealth of hair showing not at all).

Bertha was, in fact, too alarmed to take her eyes off the road in front. Jesse enjoyed driving; they went along at a spanking pace behind the fresh young horse, sometimes turning corners so sharply that Bertha gasped and clung to the arm of her seat. She was quite unused to travelling in this way. Dove had taken her for drives in their sedate brougham round the local flat countryside, but this was something far more perilous. Ahead there were mountains. Would this Jehu dash up them?

Even if her murmured replies could have been heard above the noise of the wheels and the passing traffic, she was able to think of nothing to say to him, for after they had set off she had realised that this was the Member of Parliament Mrs

Atkinson had said was the head of the household. A governor of the country, a man high in council; she had never even seen such a personage before, much less conversed with one. He was subtly much grander than Mr Atkinson, that private gentleman with more than a touch of Lancashire in his speech. This deity spoke with a London accent and had a manner that was rather loud and assured, though he meant to be kind. Men were a strange land to Bertha. Brought up with no father or brother, accustomed in her convent days to meet only the low-born, apart from priests, and at Deansbury in charge of the desperately sick, she had not known what a gentleman was like until she had encountered Joe Atkinson, and found him not at all alarming. Mr Bradshaw was something else altogether.

Another worry occupied poor Bertha's mind. The train had carried no washing facilities (that was the nearest phrase she dared think of) and she had had a cup of tea before leaving Manchester. What with nervousness, fear, and discomfort her plight became increasingly desperate. She shuddered away from the thought of what it would be like to be received by strangers in such a state. What would she say, how could she bring herself to express her need?

Jesse was a far more intuitive man than his bluff outside suggested. The strain that showed on the child's face became unmistakable. As they approached a small village some three miles from their destination he thought of the Fleece Inn, a comfortable little tavern where he had often paused. It came in sight; Jesse drew rein and stopped.

'We'll take a breather here, my dear.'

She stared at him, uncomprehending. Surely this was not the end of their journey.

'Just a pause — a cup of tea and a slice, anything you feel like.'

Bertha knew only too well what she felt like. Her relief was unbounded when, once inside the little flagged passage of the inn, he went before her and murmured to the landlady who appeared, smiling, from a back room. Bertha hardly knew what the woman said as she conducted her upstairs.

And after that everything was quite different. They sat in front of a cheerful fire, Bertha realising for the first time how chilled she had grown on the drive. Her companion took a mug of ale and she was served with tea, hot, strong, with a very curious taste to it quite unknown to her. She had sometimes administered brandy to sick persons, but had never touched it herself. It did her a lot of good. When they resumed their journey she was almost, if not quite, looking forward to reaching Eagle Hall.

The house was silhouetted against a sky glowing with the orange and pink of sunset. Swallows twittered round the ancient chimneys and swooped over the gardens. Bertha had never seen such a house before, except in pictures, the drawings which decorated magazines at Christmas time. *The stately homes of England, how beautiful they stand...* The Lion House had been something beyond her experience, wonderful in its elegance and comfort, but this was as different again, a dream place.

She stood looking up at it, the sunset light on her face. A groom had appeared as soon as the trap had entered the drive, and was leading the horse away to the stables.

'Come along,' said Jesse, 'you'll get cold standing here.' But she barely heard him speak, for the old house had reached out and touched her with its finger.

Eleanor swam gracefully out of the drawing room, crinoline rustling, a tiny flowery cap perched on the smooth hair which might have been either blonde or white.

'My dear Bertha! Goodness, what a cold face. Meg, take Miss Moorhouse's wraps. There, that's better.' She chattered away, not giving away by a flicker of expression her astonishment at the sight revealed by the removal of the mushroom hat: a seemingly naked head covered by a small, tightly gathered net cap. 'My dear,' she said to Jesse, 'I expect you'll be sharp-set for your supper, and it shall be served soon, but first I must take Bertha to meet Lucy and Edwin — then, if she likes, she can take supper quietly by herself after that fatiguing journey. I really think after all you should have sent the carriage for her — up the stairs, Bertha, and to your left, we're all stairs in this house…' Skipping in front, she pushed open a heavy, carved door, with an iron ring for a handle. The room it revealed was long, low-ceilinged and panelled. At a small table in front of the richly ornamented stone fireplace sat a young man and woman, playing chess. Both looked up. Edwin leaped to his feet politely, and Lucy half-turned, giving Bertha the benefit of her broad sweet smile. There were welcomes and enquiries, an invitation to sit down by the fire, enough talk to cover the fact that Bertha herself had little to say.

She took in the pair, the tall young man with the thick mane of hair and a fleeting look of Joe Atkinson, though his features were stronger and his manner laughingly bold; the graceful sturdily built girl, who also had a resemblance to her father, Jesse. Bertha had not been told the adoption story. They in turn surveyed her, without seeming to, under cover of Eleanor's light talk. The cinnamon-brown foulard dress she wore had been made for Marigold, who never liked it. Bertha's clever fingers had re-made it entirely to fit herself, taking in the fullness of the skirt so that it only just covered her modest hoops. The feeling of being in a cage, however fashionable, was strange and not altogether comfortable to her, but the dress as it was after altering suited her well. Her face, which she had washed at the wayside inn, glowed from the ride and the heat of the fire. It was forthright Lucy who voiced what all three had been thinking.

'What a charming little cap. I suppose your hair was shorn — before?'

'Lucy, dear,' protested Eleanor. But though Bertha blushed she answered readily.

'Yes. I'm afraid it looks sadly ugly. Perhaps you had better see it, and then you will know the worst.' She unfastened the cap-strings and took it off.

'But it's charming!' Lucy exclaimed. 'Or it very soon will be. How can you call it ugly?'

The small head was covered with tiny close curls clustering round the ears and touching the brow with their soft rings. The effect, on top of the slender childlike neck rising from the prim collar, was curiously piquant.

'Really very pretty — like a little lamb,' Eleanor said. 'Why do you wear that cap at all? You'll set a fashion, just see if you don't. Talking of lambs, I remember — good gracious, how long ago? — Lady Caroline Lamb wearing her hair just like that, and disguising herself as a page to get into Byron's lodgings. The town was very shocked, but someone painted a most striking portrait of her, and I declare, Bertha, she had just the same pretty pointed ears and *retroussé* nose as you have. What a coincidence. Poor Caro, I believe she went quite demented, and that unfortunate son of hers, too…'

Throughout his aunt's reminiscences Edwin was staring at Bertha. He could very well see her as a page *en travestie,* with that turn of the head and the pert nose above the full lips. Nun, indeed! He had seen faces not unlike that looking out of coaches and down from horseback in Edinburgh, and had on occasion been the recipient of a meaning glance or even the faintest of winks from them. What, he wondered, had his mother been thinking of to let this demure charmer loose, when she had a marriageable daughter of her own? Of course, the newcomer's light was dim besides Lucy's, and he would not waste any thought on her, but she was damnably fetching for all that.

Suddenly he caught himself at his favourite pastime of weighing up female allure, and his heart dropped like a coal from the grate to grow dull and heavy, for he remembered that when he returned to Edinburgh it would not be to flirt with charmers but to face the prospect of unwilling fatherhood, and Jean, and whatever horrors that entailed. He sighed deeply, and withdrew his gaze from the young woman by the fire. But not before she had seen it, and read — inexperienced as she was — something of what it meant. Bertha had received her first look of admiration from a man's eyes, and found it strangely warming.

The door opened, slowly squeaking on its old hinges, and a very large cat entered. It was tortoiseshell in colour, a mixture of black, brown, ginger and white which was hardly beautiful; but its measured, rolling gait and the proud carriage of its tail made its entrance impressive.

'Ivan,' Lucy said, 'where have you been since breakfast, you very remiss cat?'

'His name is really Ivanhoe, Bertha,' Eleanor explained. 'I only tell you so because Ivan sounds altogether too Russian a name, with the Crimea still in our minds. Lucy calls all her animals after the characters of Sir Walter Scott. She has a hen called Merrilees which we shall never be allowed to kill, and a...' Her thoughts wandered. 'My sister Margaret and I used to be *so* fond of Sir Walter's poetry, but girls nowadays seem to think nothing of it, so I was pleased when Lucy began to call her menagerie by these romantic names...'

The cat Ivanhoe advanced towards them, paused, stretched, and became intent on tearing up the carpet, slowly, deliberately, with loud ripping sounds. Then, ignoring Lucy's extended hand, he walked up to Bertha, sniffed casually at her skirts, and jumped on her lap, where, after turning round once, he composed himself to sleep.

'Well!' Lucy exclaimed. 'In all his life Ivan has never gone straight to a stranger — and he never sits on anyone but me. What fascination do you exercise, tell me?'

Bertha laughed, the first time they had heard her do so. 'None, I assure you. But the pigs at the convent were very fond of me, I remember. I thought it was because I would offer to feed them when the other sisters were not inclined to.'

Lucy shook her head. 'Oh no. It was because when you fed them you did it with love.'

A maid appeared at the door. 'Supper, madam.'

Bertha would never know what they ate, or how she got up to the room at the top of a twisting stairs where she was to sleep. There was only a hazy impression of comfort: a fire burning, the voices of autumn winds round the house, the tossing of trees. Even at the Lion House there had been village sounds; here there was only peace.

At breakfast Bertha said to Eleanor, 'It was kind of the old lady to look into my room last night. I was almost asleep, but she was so quiet that I was not disturbed at all.'

Eleanor's hand, stretched out towards the tea urn, was instantly withdrawn. Lucy began, 'But there isn't...' A look from Eleanor silenced her. Jesse was hidden behind his *Times,* not listening to the conversation, but Edwin glanced up from his plate with interest.

'Yes, she is very quiet,' Eleanor answered in a curious tone.

'I suppose she has been here a very long time, as she wears such old-fashioned clothes.'

'She has been here a *very* long time. May I give you more tea? Yours has gone cold.'

Bertha did not recognise the hint that the subject should be changed. Social gambits were outside her experience. 'Was she Lucy's nurse, perhaps?' she asked, unaware of her hostess's air of shock and the puzzled faces of Lucy and Edwin.

Eleanor took a deep breath. 'In a sense, yes. That is, she took care of her as a baby.'

'But I don't remember any old lady,' Lucy said.

'Where do you keep her during the day, Aunt?' Edwin asked facetiously. 'In the cupboard under the stairs?'

'Neither of you knows quite everything that goes on in this house,' Eleanor said, shortly for her. 'There are old people — round about — who visit us sometimes. Is there anything new and interesting in the paper, my dear?'

'Oh, a great deal about the Italian wars, of course. More stuff about raising volunteers. And a vessel has returned with some news of Franklin's expedition — it seems they've found some evidence that he had to abandon ship off King William's Island, in the ice, eleven years ago ... no, let's see, he himself had died by then. Poor fellows, what an ordeal they suffered. And yet in my opinion they'd have been better employed righting wrongs at home than gallivanting about in the Arctic. When I think of the things there are to be done ... I tell you, Nell, I shall be happy to get back to the seats of the mighty.'

'Which will be very soon now, dear. That reminds me, your court breeches lack two buttons. And stockings, remind me to check the stockings. Now if we have all finished breakfast, shall we go about our various tasks? Lucy, your cat is on the sideboard again after the haddock remains, will you remove him, please. Then you must take Bertha to see the rest of your menagerie, and perhaps Edwin would like to go with you.'

Edwin replied with alacrity that he would.

Left alone in the breakfast room, Eleanor leaned her head on her hands. As years had passed she had thought less and less about the apparition she had seen — or thought she had seen, or dreamed, on that night when she had been crazed with jealousy, ready to turn the infant Lucy, Jesse's bastard daughter, out of the house. It had seemed to be a vision of old Madam Bradshaw, Jesse's grandmother, who had made it possible for Jesse and herself to live together in the first place. And it had warned her that if she rejected the baby it would die, and her empty arms would be empty for ever. Whatever the apparition had been, something she had really seen or a wild figment of her imagination, it had brought her a complete change of heart. Instead of sending the child to the poorhouse and breaking with Jesse she had accepted it as her own, the daughter she had always longed for.

And by the time the longing for physical motherhood had died away Lucy had become her own dear daughter, hers and Jesse's, as though the poor servant-girl, Lucy's real mother, had never been. Lucy had been christened Lucetta, after the ghost. Another Lucetta Bradshaw, Old Madam's great-granddaughter.

Eleanor had not told many people about her experience. Telling ghost stories round a Christmas fire was one thing, and announcing that one had a personal experience of a ghost was quite a different matter. She had no wish to be thought mad.

Jesse would have stared and patted her consolingly, saying that it was a freak caused by her woman's change of life, and Lucy — somehow it was not the sort of thing one told Lucy. Dove, her favourite niece, had been told, and had certainly relayed the story to Joe, and Margaret, Eleanor's beloved sister, knew. That was enough. She hoped the subject would not arise again now that breakfast was over. The look she had exchanged with Lucy satisfied her that Lucy was quite aware that here was something not to be mentioned further. Bertha would soon forget about it.

But what did it mean? The first time Old Madam had appeared had been a solemn warning to her, Eleanor. But for it, her life and Jesse's and Lucy's would have been very different: a broken home, a child reared on the parish to domestic slavery. What did the glimmering form of Lucetta, in its cobwebby Georgian finery, portend now? Nothing bad, surely, for it had looked kindly on Bertha...

Eleanor resolved to put the thing out of her mind. She rang for the breakfast table to be cleared.

CHAPTER NINE

Storm clouds scudded across the sky above Edinburgh, veiling the summit of Arthur's Seat and turning the castle to a grim bulk hovering over the city like a roosting black eagle. Heavy drops of rain began to patter down; soon they were lashing against the windows of the lecture room, causing Dr Morison to raise his voice.

'If you will turn to your diagrams, gentlemen, you may observe that an imaginary line may be drawn from the supraorbital notch between the bicuspid teeth to the jaw which will cut the exit of the fifth nerve — I refer to the second division of that nerve, of course — from the infraorbital foramen...'

Edwin sat slumped at his desk, one arm across the diagram he should have been studying. His spirits were as low as the temperature in the room. He had got back from Downham deliberately late on the evening before, having paused at Lancaster for a meal at St Leonard's Gate with his great-uncle and great-aunt. May had been very agreeable to him, thus proving how separation may improve the relations between a brother and sister. Otherwise it had been fairly dull, much chat about the household at Eagle Hall, curiosity about the arrival of Miss Moorhouse and her religious background, general family gossip. Ephraim was growing rather deaf and Margaret absentminded, though her brain was as sharp as ever, the mutton was cold and there was no wine. But Edwin had longed to stay there, to sleep in the familiar 'nursery attic' and not to have to return to Edinburgh.

When he reached his lodging, in trepidation, he found no message there. Mrs Proutie said, sniffing, that a Mr Ogilvy had called some days before, and she had told him when the term would resume. So he might expect some word this evening. It was a relief not to have found Jean sitting brazenly on Mrs Proutie's stairs — for she would never have been allowed inside — but he would certainly have to confront her before long. He had sent her, through Davie, news of his uncle's generosity and an advance payment. That should keep her satisfied; perhaps she would stay away from him for the moment. And perhaps not.

He was recalled to the present by the realisation that heads were turned in his direction, amused stares directed at him. Dr Morison was speaking.

'Do we gather that Mr Atkinson is not held captive by the anatomy of the human face? Can it be that his thoughts frolic in other pastures — toy, perhaps, with Poupart's ligament or Scarpa's triangle, or descend even lower, to Nelaton's line?' He playfully tapped the swinging leg bones of the skeleton suspended beside him on the platform. 'If so, may we hear those thoughts?' A laugh ran round the lines of students. It was always a welcome break when old Morison let rip with his famous sarcasm.

'I'm sorry, sir,' Edwin said. 'I was attending.'

'Ah. An amazing feature of the human face, gentlemen, is its ability to conceal the disposition of its wearer. Mr Atkinson was attending; I should never have guessed it. Shall we proceed?'

They proceeded. By the time the class finished it was dark outside, heavy persistent rain falling. Edwin stumbled across slippery cobblestones down the hill in the direction of his lodging, other huddled figures dispersing with hurried goodnights. He was tempted to slip into one of the taverns whose lighted windows were the most cheerful things in sight, and take a glass or two of punch. But it would only delay the inevitable meeting. It was not that he was afraid of Jean, or of facing up to the situation as a man should — a man turned twenty-one, if only just. But it had all become distasteful to him, the daft student pranks that had led to his getting into this scrape, and getting Jean into it. The weeks at Eagle Hall had seemed idyllic, compared with what he had come back to in this dour city, as different as his aunt's pot-pourri and rose-petal fragrances from the sour miasma of anatomical specimens preserved in spirits. And the thought of Jean was equally distasteful after the companionship of Lucy in all her beauty and good sense. As he toiled up Mrs Proutie's dismal unlighted stairs, stumbling over holes in the oilcloth, he wished he could go back to the day he first came to Edinburgh. Why the devil hadn't he stuck to his books, worked towards passing the stiff examinations, kept himself pure for marriage as he had been taught, and left the young whores alone?

There was no answer, he knew.

Holding his breath, he turned the key Mrs Proutie graciously allowed him for the door that shut off her three rooms from the staircase. But there was nobody in the sitting room that also served him as a bedroom. He called, 'Mrs P! Any messages?'

She appeared: lean, drab, with the looks of an old woman though she was hardly older than Edwin's mother, wiping her hands slowly on a grimy apron. The doings of her lodgers did not interest her, so long as they behaved themselves and paid regularly. 'Nah. Naebody called,' she said.

'Thank you,' Edwin said aloud, and to himself *Damn, damn, damn, damn.* He would have to go out again, on such a miserable, bone-chilling evening, to seek out news. The thought lent a dusty taste to his supper.

Yet again he was climbing stairs, up to Davie Ogilvy's apartment. Halfway up a chatter of voices told him that Davie had company. Perhaps she was there, and the meeting would be less trying with others in the room.

But there were no women present, only four lads beside Davie, three known to Edwin. There was a punchbowl in the hearth, a pleasant odour of rum, lemons and spices coming from it.

'Young Eddie! Come in and sit ye doon. Whit a black de'il of a night. Man, you're steaming like a railway engine. Get yon coat off before ye go down with pleurisy. Andy, mix a glass.'

It was pleasant enough to sit down among them, feeling the warmth steal through his body from the fire and the punch, and talking of the holidays, the Scots boys' grouse-shooting and fishing, Andrew McNab's adventurous sail from the Moray Firth as far as the Orkneys and back along the coast of Sutherland, past Cape Wrath into Hebridean waters. Andrew was nut brown and tough as a whip. Edwin felt faintly ashamed of his own unmanly holiday, lolling about being waited on and sleeping late in the mornings. It would be good to embark on such a sail, to explore the wild Highlands and islands, to have not a care in the world, as one should not at twenty-one. But Andrew was free, and he was not.

He finished a second glass of punch to get up his courage, then drew Davie aside. It was easy to speak privately against the laughter of the others.

'What news of Jean? I thought she might be at my place, or here. Did you give her my letter, and the money?'

Davie looked uncomfortable. 'Aye, I did. Naturally.'

'And what did she say? Was she pleased?'

'Pleased enough. But then...'

'Then what?'

'Weel ... to my thinking she made up her mind to eat her cake and have it, if ye follow me.'

'No, I don't at all. Come out with it, man, what did she do?'

'Went to someone — an auld wife, maybe. It went wrong, as it aye does. She got this far, to ask me for help, but I couldna do a thing by that time. So I got her to the hospital, and — eh, weel ... ye ken what it's like.'

Edwin nodded. 'Did she ... come through it?'

'No. No. They mostly don't. Septicaemia and fever combined. She was further on than she said, and there was very bad haemorrhaging. She could never have lasted.'

Edwin sat down heavily. He knew that Davie was trying to spare him the mental picture of the results of a botched abortion, a dirty needle applied by dirty hands to a shrinking patient. He shut his eyes, feeling the vision would never leave him, however hard he tried to shut it out. Jean had been such a sporting little thing — exciting, good company, right up to that last scene in Davie's room. And to end like that, in a mess of blood and pain and delirium.

Tears were choking him; Davie put a hand on his shoulder, standing between him and the others so that they should not see.

'She was ... a jolly pretty girl,' he got out. 'I can't bear to think...'

'Aye. Aye. It wasna your fault.'

'It was! It was! If I hadn't...'

'Someone else would have. Dinna blame yourself, laddie. If it was anyone's fault it was Jean's, puir wee bitch, thinking she could cheat you by keeping the money you sent her every month, and no' telling till it was plain there was going to be no bairn. Maybe she'd even have moved away and let you send as long as you were daft enough to do it. Try and see it that way and you'll no' feel so bad.'

Edwin forced back the tears. 'Spare me your bedside manner, Davie. I'll take more punch, if you please, and for God's sake don't tell *them*.'

He got very drunk that night, so drunk that Davie made him up an improvised bed on the floor. Next day he was more ill than he had ever been in all his healthy life, obliged to cut lectures, and subjected to the full wrath of Mrs Proutie's tongue. It took him two days to return to normality, during which time balance was restored and he had got over the worst of his shock and guilt. He thought of the tragedy of Jean more calmly, in the light of what Davie had said, and began to accept that in time she would probably have come to an unhappy end without his assistance.

But the manner of it troubled him, all the more for its commonness in the filthy wynds of Edinburgh. When he finally forced himself to write to Jesse, telling him what had happened and pouring out his contrition (little knowing what effect his letter would have on the man who had once felt such guilty pain in a similar situation), he added:

It seems to me that the whole miserable business of abortion should be dealt with at a high level. At its worst it is double murder, at its best a nasty remedy for something which should have been avoided in the first place (and I well know your views on this, Uncle). Do you not think it should come under the law? And can you not with your influence take some steps about it? I suppose it would still go on whatever was ordained, but at least it could be made more difficult. I can do nothing about it myself; I wish I could.

He began to work very hard, and was rewarded by excellent results in the next examination. And as he studied he found the tenor of his thoughts changing. His ambition to become a surgeon was waning. Because of Jean, his mind dwelt a great deal on gynaecology. He began to read obstetrics in his leisure time, becoming more and more interested and involved. Here, he felt was something he could do, to help not only Jean and her kind but all women.

And when he had qualified, as he was determined to do, and could put up a brass plate with his name and an impressive string of letters on it, he would go to Downham and ask his uncle for permission to speak to Lucy.

Lucy opened the door of the outbuilding called the Little Barn and ushered Bertha inside. The atmosphere was an overpowering aroma of horse, pig, fowl, other unidentifiable odours, blended with the scent of hay and a general essence of farmyard. Bertha stepped back and took a breath of fresh air before venturing inside. Light from high windows illuminated a number of pens which held a variety of animals — a pony, squealing piglets, a thin mangy dog, some hens, a goose, two goats, a family of kittens. Every day the numbers changed as Lucy rode about the countryside collecting invalids. Bertha had been nervous at first of these expeditions, afraid that a farmer might produce a gun and order the girls off the estate, or a cottager subject them to violent language.

But nothing like that had happened. There was something about Lucy which drew respect and even friendliness from those whose sick animals she commandeered. They were used to her now, driving up in her trap with the loosebox in tow, ready for the receipt of anything, large or small. Sometimes she addressed them forthrightly about the condition of an animal, and they took the reproof meekly. After all, it was easier to let a weak or sickly beast go to be tended by her than to keep it oneself. They would have looked on anyone but Lucy as being a bit daft, not quite ninepence to the shilling, but her natural authority made such thoughts impossible. If she wanted to tend creatures that were neither use nor ornament, and had the money to keep them, then good luck to her. Just once, since Bertha had been accompanying her, a gang of boys had sworn at her when she had demanded to know the contents of a sack they carried, which writhed and squealed.

'Very well,' Lucy said. She dismounted and pulled the sack away from the boy who was holding it before he could resist. It was tied at the neck, but she knew its contents without looking. Some housewives would give a penny or two for superfluous kittens to be taken away, rather than go to the trouble of drowning them personally. Lucy put the sack in the trailer and remounted. A stone struck her horse on the shoulder, making it jump. She waited until it was calm.

'All right, Ned Barnes,' she said, 'I know you — and you, Dick Patterson. Just one more stone and I'll have you up before a magistrate. Do you understand?'

Sullenly they began to move off, then one turned and shouted a filthy word at her. Bertha had never heard it, but blushed at the very tone. Lucy took not the faintest notice.

'Aren't you ever afraid?' Bertha asked.

'Why should I be? I'm as strong as they are — and much stronger-minded. They want to destroy things. I want to save things. That's the difference.'

'But — why do you do it?'

Lucy raised an eyebrow. 'Did you love the patients you nursed when you were a nun — the poor people round

Manchester, and Uncle Joe's smallpox patients? Really love them, and feel passionately about them?'

'I ... no. Except as we are all bidden to love our neighbour. And we Sisters were obedient to the rule of the Blessed Francis.'

'Exactly, the Blessed Francis. Now, as I understand it — and I'm very ignorant about your Church — he imposed poverty, chastity and obedience on you, which don't seem to me either very important or very interesting. What does interest me about him is that he championed animals, the whole beast kingdom, calling them our brothers and sisters. So because of him a few people, I don't say many, have been kind to them, thoughtful of what they might be suffering. Well, never mind him, though I'm sure he was an excellent person. *I* feel that animals are indeed our brothers and sisters, and that we are no better than them — and I wonder why you look so shocked, Bertha.'

'The soul...' Bertha began.

'Yes? Has anyone proved that animals haven't a soul? I would admire the Christian religion a good deal more if it said that they had. I've been brought up to revere Christ, and of course I do, but I would *like* Him a great deal better if He had said rather more about looking after the furred and feathered things. There's something about God knowing whenever a sparrow falls, of course. But round here they set a halfpenny a head on sparrows, and shoot them and take them to the farmers' wives, who make pies of them. Has God said anything about that? If so, I haven't noticed it.'

'But ... we should think first of our neighbour — of mankind.'

Lucy pulled a long stalk of grass and chewed it slowly. 'Why? People can look after themselves. They've tongues, haven't they? They'll get their wrongs righted one way or another, in time. Children are another story, of course, but there are those who fight for their cause, without me joining in. I'm not a particularly motherly person, I fear. My passion is for the small ones.' They had stopped, far away from the stone-throwing boys. Lucy untied the sack in the trailer and extracted a tiny ginger kitten, mewing pitifully. She held it against her breast, murmuring to it. To Bertha's surprise its cries lessened, until it was quiet, nestling in Lucy's hands, moving its head and paws as though suckling its mother.

Bertha watched and marvelled. At last she said, 'I think you must be a kind of saint, though I know very little about them, really. I begin to think I know very little about anything. What is it you want to do, Lucy? You see, I can only think of two kinds of women — us, that is nuns — and wives and mothers, like Mrs Atkinson and Mrs Bradshaw.'

Lucy gently removed the kitten, which was now asleep, to her lap. 'There are others who wish to follow a profession. I don't know any — I've only read of them. But I intend to become a veterinary surgeon. That,' she explained, seeing Bertha's puzzled face, 'is an animal doctor. With a surgery, like any other doctor, and a practice.' She went on to explain that the Royal College of Veterinary Surgeons had been founded in London some fourteen years earlier. 'I know perfectly well that I should not be admitted to their ranks. I'm a woman, and therefore wouldn't be tolerated. So I shall study what they study by myself, and Edwin will lend me books of elementary medicine which I shall work from. I have nothing at the moment but my own instincts and what I know of country remedies. And one day I shall present myself to them in London, and they'll be utterly horrified and shocked and tell me to go away and produce babies. But I shan't. I shall make them accept me, if I have to fight until I'm an old woman. You'll see.'

Bertha shook her head slowly. 'I don't understand. You're so beautiful, and ... a lady. Does Mr Bradshaw approve all this?'

'He wants what I want.'

'Well ... you *are* very like him.'

Lucy regarded her curiously. 'Am I? Well, perhaps I am.' She put out a hand impulsively. 'Don't fret about it, little Bertha. Just remember your Blessed Francis. I wonder what he did to tame Brother Wolf? No, I don't. I know. Or I think I know.'

Bertha furtively crossed herself. 'Edwin admires you greatly. Could you not marry him and share in his work? Then you would perhaps feel you were fulfilling your mission in life.'

'My dear Bertha, you haven't understood one word I've been saying. Shall we move on?'

A wild October wind howled round the Lion House, flinging fallen leaves against its windows with a ghostly rattling. Dove, by the fire, heard Joe's arrival home, the door shut and chained after him, a servant helping him off with his greatcoat and boots. As he came into the room she rose, went to him and kissed him. His face was chilled and damp. He sat down wearily, shutting his eyes. Marigold, on the hearthrug dressing a paper doll, looked up without greeting her father, then went on with her play.

'A bad day?' Dove asked.

'A long one.'

'Anything particular?'

Joe sighed. 'A frame's gone wrong. Mending or replacing it's going to come expensive. Bibby came over to look at it, but I doubt if he knows what he's at. And there's some bad feeling over Donnell going.'

'You got rid of him, did you?' Dove was surprised.

'I'd no choice. Apart from Basil's find, the doctor said the man was pickled in drink — he'd had the cunning to hide it, that was all. And it seems to me some of his mates were in on it, to judge by the black brows this morning. Handing it out, perhaps. Lord knows where he got the money for it. Some fiddling business on the side. There's a smell of corruption in that shed — I hope we're not going to have a strike on our hands.' Joe struck the arm of his chair with a fist. 'I won't have debauchery in my mill, whatever the cost.'

Dove patted his hand, but he moved it impatiently away. His eyes were on the kneeling figure of Marigold.

'Doesn't that child ever speak these days?'

'Yes, of course. She's absorbed just now, that's all.'

'Absorbed. In playing baby-house. That's a fine thing for a young woman of — what is it? eighteen, nineteen? You'd better send for May. She's been away long enough. Time she came back and brightened up her sister — and all of us. This house is like a morgue.'

Dove watched him anxiously. It was unlike him to be bad-tempered, but of late she had noticed signs of a change in him, a hardening of the habitual sweetness of his expression, new lines on his face. She thought it dated from his anger at the dismissal of Enrico, but it might have begun before that. At a venture, she said, 'Would you like me to get another tutor for Marigold?'

'Where? What use would an ordinary teacher be to her? You had the perfect one, and you threw him away.'

Marigold looked up. ''Rico's gone,' she said sadly. 'Gone and left Marigold.'

'I'm sorry, I'm sorry!' Dove exclaimed. 'But don't say any more before her. Talk about something else. There was a letter from Edwin today; he sounds very busy and interested. He says —'

'All right, don't tell me. I prefer to read things for myself without having the meat taken out of them first. Is supper ever going to be ready?'

Dove's eyes filled with tears. It was deeply hurtful that Joe should speak so to her. He had not kissed her when he came home for some time now, and she had to try to ignore it because she knew that he had much on his mind, but tonight she felt it, an aching smart. After Mrs Skerritt had summoned them to the meal she lingered behind, swallowing the tears. Trying to seem cheerful she said, 'Come along, Marigold. Supper. And smile at Father, won't you, dear? He feels rather sad tonight.' It was impossible to tell from Marigold's blank face whether she had understood. For an awful moment Dove felt she hated the daughter who had come between her and her husband; then hated herself for the thought.

She felt a desperate need to talk to Basil. Since the moment when their lips had met, and the door of a new world had seemed to open for her, she had avoided him as much as possible. Such things meant danger, for both of them; for all of them, perhaps. But now she needed him, not for the love he could give her but for his strength of mind and his good sense. The difficulty was finding the right time and place. She could hardly call on him at the mill, and he seldom came to the Lion House during the day. It would be impossible to speak to him when he took supper with them, as he did once or twice a week; after the meal he and Joe always retired to talk mill matters.

The solution seemed to be a letter, asking him to make time to call on her. It might seem strange to Joe, if he accidentally found out, but she would risk that. She wrote it carefully, keeping it short and impersonal.

The boy Sim Lund, who had taken the letter to the mill, was away so long that Dove grew increasingly impatient. What could have happened to him? Had Joe received the letter by mistake, and questioned Basil about it? In his present incalculable mood anything was possible. Or had the boy met with an accident?

The morning dragged past. Dinner, as the servants firmly called luncheon, was on the table before Sim made his appearance. He was sent in to her at once, as she had asked.

'Well?' There was a letter in his hand, which she feared was her own.

''E weren't theer, Mrs Atkinson. A man said to tek it round to wheer he lives, 'cos he'd been took sick.'

'Oh. And what then?'

'I were sent up to see 'im, and 'e read letter and give me this one back.'

She took it, relieved. 'Thank you, Sim.'

The letter said that Basil had caught a chill and thought it best to stay away from work for a day or two, but he was sure it was not infectious. If the matter were as urgent as it sounded he would be pleased if she would call on him.

Basil lodged at the end of the high street of Deansbury, in a house owned by a solicitor, who practised on the ground floor and lived elsewhere. The house was old, plain, pleasant in red brick and a graceful portico. Dove had been there once or twice with Joe, and knew her way through the hall off which the solicitor's offices opened, and up the stairs to the landing. A door once opening into a double drawing room, in the house's grand days, was now Basil's front door. She knocked, wondering whether a servant would open it.

But it was Basil who appeared, wearing a neat, even elegant dressing gown of damson red trimmed with black braid, a woollen muffler round his neck. As he gestured her in, she said lightly, 'Well, how smart you look! Quite a fashion plate. I expected to find an invalid.'

'Oh, there's not much wrong. I'm a bit chesty, that's all, and I don't want to make it worse in the damp of the mill. Come in. There's a good fire, and tea if you want it.' The front half of the double room was arranged as a sitting room; quite an elegant one, for a bachelor, with chairs upholstered in rich blues and reds, and a stripe of gold in the wallpaper. Over the mantelpiece hung an oil portrait of a beautiful dark young woman in the dress of the 1830s, wearing a carcanet of gold and jewels round her neck, and long sparkling earrings.

'My mother,' Basil said, seeing her looking at it. 'Handsome, wasn't she? Still is.'

'Very. And your room is handsome, too.'

'Not too flashy, you think?' He motioned her to a chair on the other side of the fireplace from his own, and she was glad of the distance, feeling a dangerous intimacy in their proximity here, on Basil's home ground. She looked round for signs of any other occupancy.

Basil understood. 'No, I don't have a domestic. No room, just this, and the bedroom through there, and another small room. Old Mrs Lomas comes in twice a day and looks to things. For the rest, I do for myself. I'm quite handy about the house.'

'So it would seem.' She dared not settle back to enjoy the charm of the room, and of his company, though she had felt a lightening of the spirit on her entry into it, after the gloom that hung round the Lion House. She plunged straight in to the reason for her visit.

'Basil, I must talk to you. I'm very troubled about Joe.' She described the change in him, the irritability and dark moods. 'I don't know how long it's been going on, but it seems to have been worse since I sent Mr Manfredi away. Do you think that could be it?'

'Might be. Partly, that is. I've seen this change in him, mind you — have to be blind not to. But there's other things, Dove, A bad spirit in the mill, for one. Joe spoils those hands, if you ask me. He's given them all they could want: the best housing in Lancashire, education and medical care, a helping hand whenever they want one. And do they appreciate it? The women do, yes, but the men — the more they get the more they want, and the rules he lays on 'em they resent. No drink, above a few pints at weekend. No cards, or cock-mains, or wenching. They're too well taken care of.'

'He got rid of Donnell.'

'Yes, because I made him. But I was wrong, I ought to have done it myself. From me it would have come naturally, because they think I'm a hard man. But Joe — it's a curious thing, and I've often noticed it, that when somebody easy-going turns angry, people say, "Well! what a serpent! Fancy that, deceiving us all this time, and such a nasty temper behind it. We'll never trust him again." I ought to have sacked Donnell, then there'd have been no ill feeling.'

Dove sighed. 'I thought it was good that he should take a stand occasionally, but it seems it wasn't.'

'No. There's another thing. Have you thought he might be ill?'

She was startled. 'Ill? No. Why?'

'Because he's changed the way a man might if he thought he'd got something bad gnawing away at him. Has he any symptoms? Eats well, sleeps well, does he?'

'I suppose so ... I haven't noticed any difference. He was never a great eater, and he hardly touches wine. As for sleeping...' Basil's eyes were asking a question she could only answer with a blush. 'I think so, yes. I sleep well myself, so I haven't noticed.'

Basil nodded. His question had been answered. 'It may not be that, then. What is he — fifty?'

'Yes ... Edwin was twenty-one this year, you know, and not at home to celebrate. Joe was sad about that; it might have helped to put him in low spirits. And then Enrico ... I've been thinking, we didn't try hard enough to find him. Marigold has grown so much worse since he went, with disappointment, I think. Couldn't we have him traced, somehow? He might have come back to Glazeheath by now, or be teaching at one of the schools round about. If we could only find him! I think he might agree to teach Marigold again, if I explained, and apologised.'

'You'd have to do more than that. You must have hurt the lad's feelings for him to run off like that. I doubt he'd come under your roof again. Do you know what I think? I think he's gone back to Italy to Garibaldi's war. Did you know he'd strong feelings about Garibaldi and liberation? He talked to me about it — the crossing of the Ticino and the freeing of Italian land from the Austrians, as far as the Tyrol. It's the sort of thing a young Italian with imagination would think of as a refuge, when he'd taken a bad toss in a foreign country. There's a lot of feeling for Garibaldi here — he'd have heard him talked of as a hero. If you want to find Manfredi, look for him in the Alps.'

'How can I? Even if you're right. Besides, I have a feeling he's not far away. Watching us, perhaps.' She shivered.

'Rubbish. You've thought about him too much, that's what it is. He's gone — let him go, and stop brooding. Why don't you get May back? That might cheer Joe up.'

'Yes, he said I should, for Marigold's sake. Father will want her to stay for always if he gets too used to her. She would be company for me, too, and heaven knows I need it.'

She leaned her head back wearily in the chair, closing her eyes. The little pork-pie hat she wore was ugly, in Basil's opinion, and so was the way she wore her pretty silver-gilt hair, in a sort of onion bag, and her wide skirts and loose Zouave jacket completely hid the lines of her figure. He crossed over to sit on the chair arm. She made no objection when he unpinned the hat and took it off. He found the ribbon that tied the snood on top of her head, loosened it, and freed her hair so that it fell over her shoulders. She opened her eyes, smiled faintly, and said, 'Don't,' as he picked up the tresses, one by one, and stroked them, and her brow.

'You mean "do", I think.'

'Yes … no! I don't know what I mean. Except that we mustn't.'

'If I hadn't the on-comings of a cold, my dear, and wasn't afraid to give it to you, I'd treat you as I want to, and as you want me to. I know what's right and what's wrong for us, and so do you, if you'd only admit it.'

'Joe,' she said.

'Joe. Is he a husband to you any more?'

After a pause, she said, 'No. Not as he used to be.'

'Your hair's like corn in moonlight… Isn't that a poetic fancy for a chap like me? You think I'm disloyal to Joe, don't you. Well, I'm loyal to him to the last stand, where it's appropriate. I've backed him up and defended him and seen he wasn't cheated for years now, and I'll go on doing it, just as you'll go on being a loyal wife to him — downstairs, because he doesn't want you anywhere else.' He kissed her hand, warm in his, and the slender childish wrist, then suddenly put it from him and stood up.

'Put your hair up and go, Mrs Atkinson. I've said what you came to hear. I'll make enquiries about Manfredi, but I don't hold out much hope of finding him. You write to your father and get May back. That's all I've got to tell you.' He turned aside, coughing. 'Go on. I should never have let you come here.'

'Don't speak so roughly to me.' Her voice was trembling. 'I get enough of that from Joe — I thought you'd be kind.'

'*Kind?* If you knew what I'd like to be...' He was at the sideboard, mixing lemon juice and spirits in a bowl, his back to her. She pinned on her hat and put on the gloves which had fallen to the floor. At the door her 'Goodbye' was hardly audible, and he did not answer.

CHAPTER TEN

When May came home she was much changed. Far from growing restless in the company of the two old people, she had taken on from them a sobriety and an air of good sense that startled Dove, remembering the madcap May of barely three months ago. It was very true, she reflected, that grandparents often have a better understanding with children than their parents. Who would have imagined that May would actually enjoy reading aloud to her grandfather from the ponderous novels written by Great-Aunt Margaret, or the poems of the late William Wordsworth?

'But you detested your literature lessons with Miss Wynne,' she said, 'and I'm sure I never saw you open a poetry book for your own pleasure. Whatever has happened to your tastes?'

'Well, I suppose I never read things properly. When Grandfather told me about knowing Wordsworth, and how close he was to nature, poems like *The Excursion* seemed to fit into place, instead of being long boring things I couldn't be bothered to understand. We even went for a long drive, a whole day out, last month, as far as Lake Windermere, so that he could show me Wordsworth's country, and the lane in Kendal where Father was born.'

I spent my honeymoon in Kendal, Dove thought, with a pang of bitterness. *The little inn was heaven to me. There was a pink geranium on the windowsill and a patchwork quilt on the bed.*

'And then,' May went on, 'he has so many amusing stories about his practice, and the trials at the castle. And Aunt Margaret is most amusing too. Did you know she was once an actress — and then turned to writing and met all sorts of famous people like Count d'Orsay? And she had a play performed at Drury Lane Theatre, imagine that!'

'Yes, I did know. She once took me to London and quite dazzled me with her acquaintances. I'm glad you appreciated her company. But you saw something of Aunt Belle, surely, besides all this time spent in improving your mind?'

Dove's tone was dry, but May replied earnestly. 'Yes, of course. We had some pleasant shopping expeditions together, and a few balls at the Assembly Rooms. I like Aunt Belle, Mother, but … she would be so much better looking if she would only leave her looks alone, as you do, and not dye and paint. It makes her look much older than you, though of course one can't tell her so.'

'I'm sure one can't. What a pity. Many people thought her much handsomer than me when we were young.'

'Well, she isn't now. And besides — she is so inconsiderate to Laurence. Poor boy, he seems to have no friends, because he only meets her sort of people, who are not his. And she speaks to him as if he were some kind of dog. I felt truly embarrassed sometimes, and tried to make it up to him, but I don't think anyone could. He's such a sensitive boy, and so serious-minded, not in the least like Edwin. I tried flirting with him, I confess.'

'Did you, Puss?'

'Yes. But it seemed to disturb him in some way, so I stopped. I think the trouble is that he's in love and she doesn't care for him. I caught him writing poetry one day, and he hid it, and blushed dreadfully. And he doesn't like Aunt's gentlemen friends, I know, because he let it out. It would be so much better if Uncle George would come home and take care of both of them. Aunt needs a husband, in my opinion.'

My goodness, you have *grown up,* thought Dove. May's revelations threw an unpleasant light on Belle's household, and confirmed Dove's uneasy feeling that her sister's life was moving in a downward direction. Perhaps it might be wise to invite her to stay, and talk to her. But Belle and Joe had never cared overmuch for each other; her presence at Lion House might make things worse.

May turned the bracelet on her arm round and round, so that the lamplight drew rainbow colours from the round milky stones linked with gold. 'Isn't it pretty, and wasn't it kind of Aunt Margaret to give it to me? It's the nicest thing I've ever had.'

'Yes. I remember it. But I wish it had not been moonstones.'

'Why not? They're beautiful.'

'Oh, no real reason. Just that they're supposed to be unlucky, like opals.'

'Aunt Margaret's owned them for years, and they haven't brought *her* bad luck.'

'No... They would hardly have the impertinence. But she is such a strong lady.' Dove did not go on; it was in her mind that her own household was far from strong, a citadel besieged.

To her disappointment, May's return had very little effect on Marigold's condition. May was as protective as ever, but the likeness between the two had subtly diminished with May's added maturity. Marigold seemed to regard her now as a grown-up person, not the playfellow she had once been, and was as dull and unresponsive in her company as she was with her parents. The courtesy and gentleness of the two old people in Lancaster had rubbed off on May, lending her infinite patience; at least she took Marigold off Dove's hands for much of the time.

Basil's chill had turned to a fairly sharp bout of bronchitis. For three weeks he lay ill, unable to make any progress with enquiries about Enrico Manfredi. Dove visited him sometimes, with delicacies his daily servant might not think of buying him; but always accompanied by a maid. She would risk no more indiscretions. Joe's irritability seemed on the increase, coping alone at the mill as he was. He blamed Basil for his absence, as though catching a chill were a deliberate indulgence. Evening after evening he came back late, making it impossible for Mrs Skerritt to organise supper perfectly, and then blamed her, the cook, and Dove.

'Mutton cutlets. I'm sick of mutton cutlets. Are we never to have anything else? Don't we eat chicken any more, or beef, or fish?'

'Yes, dear. But roast dishes get so overdone if they're kept hot, and you know you don't like boiled fowl…'

'No, I don't. Pap.'

At last Dove stopped apologising. The meal was put on the table, he complained, ate part of it and left the rest. And she said nothing. They had almost ceased to converse. Only May kept up a stream of gently cheerful small talk to which Dove replied mechanically, eyeing the man across the table as though he were a stranger, not her beloved husband. May was quite aware of her role as keeper of the peace.

'I think Father must be ill, Mother,' she said when they were alone.

'That's what Basil thinks. I don't know … he seems to have no symptoms, and he won't see the doctor. I suggested it, and he snapped my head off. It's so terribly unlike him … oh, May.'

Her daughter's arms went round her, warm and comforting. 'Dearest Mother, don't cry. We can't possibly understand what worries men have in their business. He probably doesn't want to bring his troubles home from the mill, so he keeps them to himself, and it makes him irritable. Would you like me to talk to him — just hinting that he's being rather a bear? I'm sure he doesn't realise it.'

Dove shook her head. 'He'll only think I've been complaining.'

But May did have a quiet word with her father, and he listened to her. Dove could see him biting back sharp words, trying to be equable, and the obvious effort he made hurt her almost more than his unleashed impatience. At last the moment came that she had been unconsciously dreading.

She went to their bedroom as usual, thankful to be going to bed, and found that his belongings were missing. Brushes and combs, stud boxes, razors and pomade had all gone, and the leather jewel box where he placed watch chain, fobs and cravat pin at night. Cold with apprehension, she went to the bed and lifted the counterpane. Only one pillow was there, on the bolster, and her nightdress, neatly folded. His tartan dressing gown was no longer hanging behind the door.

She ran out into the landing. He had come upstairs, and was standing outside the door of one of the unused bedrooms. Not the pink room where Bertha had slept, but a more austerely furnished one that was given to any bachelor male visitors. He glanced at her uneasily, not meeting her eyes.

'What's this about, Joe?' she managed to say. 'What have I done?'

'You? Nothing. But I'm sleeping wretchedly these nights. I've tried to keep still, not to waken you, but it won't do, I must have a room to myself so that I can get up if I want to, and read, or have a drink. I asked Peggy to move my things.'

'I see.' She was cold all over, as cold as though she stood there naked in the November chill. 'I hope you sleep better for it.' She turned and went back into the bedroom, slamming the door. It was some time before she heard the door of his newly adopted room close.

She stood in the middle of the room, her hands clenched at her sides, fighting to control herself. But no effort could stop her face convulsing or the rush of tears that overwhelmed her. She threw herself down on the bed and abandoned herself to noisy grief, uncaring whether she was heard or not. Let them come in and find her; she would let them know of the hideous humiliation that had been put upon her, the ultimate rejection.

It seemed that she cried for hours, until her eyes were slits between swollen flesh and her nose raw. Breathing clearly was impossible, she could only snuffle. At last, exhausted, she got to her feet and looked round. The bedroom fire was almost out, the candles guttering. She lit two more, and took clean handkerchiefs out of a drawer.

Then, moving like a sleepwalker, she went quietly downstairs, candlestick in hand, to do a thing she had never done before. In a corner cupboard in the dining room Joe kept bottles of brandy, a decanter and glasses, for such guests as liked a liqueur after dinner. Dove chose a bottle and returned upstairs with it, closing doors softly behind her. It would not do to alarm the household with sounds that might mean burglars.

Back in the bedroom she undressed, put on a nightgown and wrapper, and made up the fire. She drew up a comfortable chair and occasional table and settled down for the night to drink herself to sleep.

Some coherent thoughts flitted across her stupefied brain. Had she done something quite unknowingly which had alienated Joe? Nothing suggested itself. The dismissal of

Enrico was surely not enough to have antagonised him to such an extent. He had worries at the mill, it was true. But in the past, until only a few weeks ago, he would have shared them with her; they had always shared things, since they were boy and girl.

Again, bad temper might be a sign of guilt, though it was hard to think of Joe and guilt together. Long ago there had been Rosie, the flaunting handsome factory girl who had allured the idealistic young Joe into a mistaken marriage. Was there another Rosie now? Dove tried to summon up the faces of the women operatives she knew. On Christmas Day she and Joe called at every house on the estate with greetings and gifts. Had an open door ever shown her a girl black-haired, red-cheeked, with a bold laughing charm? That had been Rosie's type, and men, Dove seemed to remember reading, always pursued the same image.

Rosie had been fond of drink. Dove poured herself another glass, hating the taste of the stuff, glad of the burning pain it brought. A moment came when she realised she could take no more. She reeled towards the bed and crawled into it; the first time she had occupied it alone since her last miscarriage, seventeen years ago. At once she fell into black insensibility.

In the morning she was not at breakfast. Joe had left the house long before she came down. Mrs Skerritt regarded her with alarm.

'Aren't you well, madam? You look very poorly to me.'

'No, I'm not at all well, Mrs Skerritt. I was ill all night — I must have eaten something that disagreed with me. Please don't concern yourself, it will pass. Tell Miss May I'll spend the day in my parlour, quietly. I have a very bad headache.'

She was glad when the housekeeper had gone. The smell of brandy seemed to be still about her — the woman must have noticed it. And by now Peggy would have told the rest of the staff that the master had removed himself to another bedroom. There would be whispers, speculations. She felt unable to face them, and turned the key in the door.

But May came knocking. 'Mother? Mrs Skerritt says you're ill. Please let me in. I promise not to bother you.'

Wearily Dove turned the key. May took in her mother's appearance at one glance, and went to her swiftly.

'What is it, dear? Are you in pain? Can I fetch you anything?'

But pride would not allow Dove to tell her daughter the shameful thing that had happened to her.

'It's really nothing. I had a very bad night, and my head still aches. No, there's nothing I want, truly. Thank you, dear. Just let me be quiet.'

'It's Father, isn't it?' May said flatly. 'He hardly spoke at breakfast. I thought then there was something very wrong. Won't you tell me? Perhaps I can talk to him again. He listened last time.'

'No, thank you.'

May's smooth brow was creased with worry. 'I've never seen you like this, Mother.'

Dove smiled tightly. 'Not surprisingly, dear. I've never been like this before. Now go, there's a good girl.'

As the afternoon wore on she began to feel better. Her head cleared; the nasty physical effects of the drink disappeared after a bowl of strong savoury broth and some of Cook's good brown bread. By six o'clock she was herself again; or not herself, but someone very cold, collected, determined. Joe would not be home for at least an hour yet. She went upstairs and rang for a bath to be filled. Warm from it, she dressed herself in the best lingerie she had — a satin-bound corset, a chemise of finest India cotton, petticoats of silk and satin trimmed with lace. On her dressing table was a flask of Eastern perfume sent by her brother-in-law, George. She had hardly touched it, finding it too rich and musky for daily wear; now she sloshed it lavishly on to her skin. Then she put on her best day dress, a soft flowing gown of rose-pink challis trimmed with creamy lace, and over it a hooded cloak of thick wool, one she had worn in her youth and liked too much to part with. Then she rang for her new maid, Alice, a girl from the village whom she was training. Alice stared to see her mistress dressed, without assistance, and ready for outdoors.

'Will you tell Mrs Skerritt I shall not be at home for supper?' Dove said. 'I am going on an errand.'

'Yes, ma'am. What time shall I say you'll be back?'

'No particular time. Perhaps she will leave the front door unchained for me.'

'Yes, ma'am.' Alice was mystified. Dove knew that the rest of the household would be mystified, too, and felt a savage satisfaction at the thought. Even Joe might be slightly disturbed.

She met nobody on her way out. The night was crisply cold, the moon appearing from cloudy wraps, then veiling itself, the November stars large and bright. Dove walked swiftly along the lane towards the village. The river glinted through bare trees, its banks deserted now of the fishermen and boys who lined it in summer. Lights still shone in the mill windows, but as she watched they began to go out, one by one. A horse and cart passed her, the carter shouting a goodnight; a dog ran out from a cottage garden, barking. The high street, when she reached it, was deserted but for the village shop which doubled as a post office and sold everything from sweets and patent medicines to haberdashery. It stayed open long after the rest had closed, to oblige the mill workers. Dove hurried past on the other side of the street.

A light showed on the first floor of the solicitor's house. She pulled the downstairs bell, hearing it jangle in the quiet. After a minute or two footsteps sounded on the stairs, a bolt was drawn back and the door unlocked from the inside.

Basil stared at her, transfixed. 'What in the name of ... what are you doing here?'

'Aren't you going to ask me in?'

'Of course.'

She followed him upstairs to the living room. A lamp was lit, and two candles, but it was cold enough for her to keep her cloak tightly wrapped about her.

'I'd only just got in,' Basil said. 'The fire's not properly alight yet.' He knelt and added more sticks and small coals to it, until it began to blaze. Dove seated herself on the small, uncomfortable sofa. At last he stood up, and looked down at her.

'Well? Is something the matter? You shouldn't be out alone at this time of night.'

'Last time I was here you seemed glad enough to see me.'

'That was one thing,' he said impatiently, 'and this is another. Don't tell me you've gone to the trouble of calling for the pleasure of my company.'

'Something like that.' She unfastened her cloak and let it fall away from her, revealing the rose dress and the twinkle of jewels at her ears. Basil stared.

'You're very fine. Are you expected at a party? Come on, Dove, what's all the mystery? There's something wrong at home, isn't there? Why didn't you send someone? I'd have come up straight away.'

'That would hardly have done,' she said composedly, spreading out her skirts. 'I needed to see you alone. Won't you sit down? You make me uncomfortable standing over me like that. And it's not easy, saying what I have to say. Joe has turned me away, Basil.'

'*What?*'

'Oh, not from the house. From his bed. I went up last night and ... I should have expected it from his behaviour recently. He's hardly been able to tolerate me for weeks. I don't know how I've offended him. I told you about his moods, but now there's only one mood, towards me. Oh, what's the use of going on about it all? Basil, I came here to tell you that I'm yours, if you still want me.'

Basil sat down suddenly. For a moment he made no answer, his face grave and troubled. Then he said, 'I can't believe it. Either that Joe should do this to you, or that you should take such a revenge on him. It's not like either of you. You've got it wrong somewhere.'

'No. I told you. He doesn't want me. No matter what we used to be, we've both changed — or rather he's changed me. I mean every word I've said.'

To her disappointment, Basil did not seem overjoyed. He looked tired and harassed, and older than before his illness.

'I don't know what to say. I didn't expect anything like this.' He clasped and unclasped his hands restlessly. 'Dove, I ... you'll have to forgive me if I can't play courtier to you. The fact is I'm tired and I'm hungry. It's been a long day. I can't take — all this — in.'

Quietly she said, 'I can see that. I'm sorry, I should have thought of it. I'll get you some supper. Where do you keep things?' Ignoring his protests, she went out to the mesh-fronted cupboard on the landing which was his food store.

'What's this — a pie? It doesn't look very fresh. Haven't you anything else? Meat — that should have been wrapped. Never mind, I can pare off the outside.'

Basil put his feet up on a footstool, and lazily watched her as she moved about calmly among foodstuffs and crockery, a beautiful vision very unlike old Mrs Lomas. He was very tired, and slightly shocked. More than ten minutes had passed when she came back to find him asleep, his head turned against the chair cushion, long dark lashes lying calm on his cheeks. Gently she touched his shoulder.

'Wake up. I've heated some soup and made the meat look as presentable as it ever will.'

'You shouldn't have troubled. But it's welcome. Thank you.'

She sat watching him as he ate, saying nothing; then, without asking, boiled the kettle and made coffee, drinking some herself. The colour came back to his face as he relaxed.

'That's better. I didn't expect to have service like this tonight. *Some have entertained angels unawares.* Is that your testament or ours? Yours, I think.'

'St Paul. To someone or other.'

The fire had blazed up, burning for frost, and the room was snugly warm. Their eyes met and held, until Basil said, 'Come over here.' She went to him, perching on his lap, her arms round his neck, her exotic scent heavy on the air.

'You took my hair down last time,' she whispered. 'Do it again.'

There was a silver net confining the mass of it. Loosening it, he said, '*Apples of gold in pictures of silver.* There's some more Scripture for you. How does this thing come off?'

She unpinned the brooch at her throat, and began to unfasten the tiny buttons that ran from neck to waist, raising his hand to help hers, and smiling up at him.

'Oh, Dove,' he said thickly. 'Dove, you're too much for me.'

'I mean to be.' Her fingers found the last of the buttons. 'Apples of silver,' she said. His hands were on her breasts, caressing them urgently, as he said her name over and over again. She slipped from his arms, and standing before the fire undid one garment after another, letting them slide to the floor until they lay there, a pool of silks and laces, herself a white lovely nymph in the rosy light, small breasted and long-legged. Then she kicked them to the end of the hearthrug. 'They'll make a nice pillow. Basil, come to me.'

'Oh, my love. So pretty — so pretty!'

When he came to her she forgot Joe, and her hurt pride and her revenge. A soaring delight took her and carried her back into lost youth, into passion such as she had never known. All the years when she and Basil had denied each other were gone in a moment, burnt in bright searing fire that was acute pain followed by acute pleasure, and then utter peace.

They talked in murmurs, his head on her shoulder, her hair spread all about them. 'I didn't mean it to be like this,' she whispered. 'I came here for the wrong reason. I love you.'

'Hush. You women talk too much. But you can say one thing again.'

'What?'

'"I love you."'

She repeated it, kissing his shut eyes, then his mouth.

'I didn't mean it to be like this, either, come to that,' he said. 'I told you I wanted you. But I didn't know how much. *O thou fairest among women, thy love is better than wine.* I wish I'd seen you first, before he did. I wish I'd seen you my bride, under the canopy, with flowers and music and people wishing us good luck and long life. Not this.'

'I was twenty-four when I married. You'd have been a little boy.'

'Not so little. There's only seven years between us. It makes no difference. Oh, God!' He rolled over, staring at the dancing shadows on the ceiling. 'What's the use of talking?'

'None. Let's make the most of what we have. You and me.'

He turned her face towards him, searching her eyes. 'Are you happy, my Dove?'

'Happy. Oh, so happy!'

It was late night before she left him, refusing to let him escort her. As she turned into the lane leading to the Lion House she saw torches bobbing in the fields and gardens, and distantly on the river bank. Her household was out searching for its lost mistress.

CHAPTER ELEVEN

'How dreadfully quiet it is now May has gone,' Belle said petulantly. 'At least it was some sort of diversion for me, even though she was staying at Father's. *You're* very poor company, I must say, Laurence.'

'I'm sorry, Mama. I don't quite know what you want me to talk about.'

'Well, you never say anything about your work. You must hear some amusing things, surely? Aren't there any local scandals? Any bits of gossip? I should have thought a lawyer's office was just the place for interesting snippets.'

'If there are any, they don't come my way. All I get are things like conveyancing and leasing. You'd find them very dull. Mr Booth doesn't handle clients' personal affairs, and Grandfather only takes part as a consultant now.'

'How boring. It was so different when I was young — younger. Murder defences and all sorts of strange cases — Father would never talk about them to us, of course, but we used to pick up the details somehow. And of course there was Joe's famous divorce — now that was *really* scandalous. Oh, dear!' She yawned and stretched, frowning at the rain that trickled down the windows. 'No whist party this afternoon. How tiresome of Louie Brierley to catch the flu! I'd have held it here if I'd known in time, but of course it's too late... What shall we do for Christmas? I'm sure it will be very dull here; a woman without a man is never asked to Christmas parties unless she's a poor relation sent for to keep the children in order. We could go to Deansbury, of course, but Dove quite

189

clearly doesn't want us. Joe's having business worries, and there seems to be something else — more from what she doesn't say than what she does. Has May said anything in her letters?'

'Only that Marigold is no better and that her father seems very low in his spirits.'

'Joe always was a dull fellow. I don't know how Dove's put up with him all these years. Who's this Mr Absalom she mentions?'

Laurence thought. 'There was a gentleman, when Uncle Joe showed us round the mill — a manager, I think. I don't remember his name.'

'Really? Dove remembers it very well, since she mentions it so often. How odd. I wonder…'

A nightmare vision flashed through Laurence's mind in which his mother made mischief and set the inhabitants of the Lion House at loggerheads with each other. 'Mama,' he said hastily, 'could we not go to Downham? Aunt Eleanor likes to entertain.' He began to blush. 'And … Lucy has a companion now. You'd enjoy some young company.'

Belle shrugged. 'Lucy is so earnest. All those animals! I suppose she has them warming themselves round the fire every evening. And then there's this girl, a runaway nun, Eleanor said. *That* doesn't sound very entertaining. But I suppose you'd find it so, dear boy?'

At her sly look Laurence's painful blush returned. Belle had sometimes gone so far as to taunt him with his infatuation for Lucy, and he had suffered the taunts in silence rather than drag the name of his idol in the mud. He made no answer. To his rescue came the tap of their young servant at the door, and her voice.

'The post, if you please.'

Belle surveyed languidly two or three letters, tossing them aside, then, excitedly, flourished another.

'Your father! Quick, the paper knife. Where is he writing from? Oh, I can't make out these names.' She needed spectacles but refused to order them. Laurence watched her eagerly reading the one sheet of his father's bold handwriting. Then she looked up, shimmering with excitement.

'He's coming home! He's on his way. So we shan't need to go anywhere for Christmas — we'll have our own. Oh, how wonderful!' She flew at Laurence, who embraced her with pity and affection.

He remembered so many homecomings, so many arguments and fights, his father raging, his mother in tears. This could hardly be very different. And he would not see Lucy at Christmas after all.

George came home on a winter evening when snow lay thick on the quays. Belle had been waiting all day, running to the door when Laurence came home from his work, stamping with temper because he was not his father. She had dressed in her best almond-green silk which set off her fair skin and rather over-gilded hair. But for once, Laurence noticed, there was no rouge on her cheeks, and she looked all the better for it. She would be forty-six soon, but nobody would have guessed it tonight.

Laurence had gone into St John's Church in his dinner hour and prayed that his father's homecoming would be a happy one for her, for all three of them. It was almost Christmas: prayers should stand a fair chance of being heard. He had thought of poor Great-Uncle John, who had died in that very pulpit, in mid-sermon. Perhaps his spirit still lingered in his church.

At last they heard wheels crunch in the snow, and cheerful shouts. Belle went pale, then scarlet. She was at the door before George's knock came, and in his arms before he was fairly inside the house. Laurence hovered, watching his big handsome father embrace his mother. The snow lay lightly on George Dilworth's bared head, where grey mingled with the tarnished golden curls. George raised a laughing nut-brown face.

'Laurence, my lad! How are you? Come and give me a hug. Lord, you're peaky-faced. Don't they feed you? I've got a crate of fruits aboard, coming ashore tomorrow, such a treat you never saw. And there's a box of tricks for *you*, my beauty.' He aimed a playful slap at his wife's rear, recoiling in mock agony. 'What's all this wire they cage you ladies up in now? Can't a fellow smack his own wife's bottom?'

'George, you're perfectly awful, as usual. Come in, let me look at you. Oh, what cold hands! Laurence, pour your father some Madeira. Let me take your coat. Gracious, it's soaking — how long were you out in the snow? What kind of voyage did you have?' Belle chattered and ran about in her happy excitement, poking the fire, plumping up cushions behind George's broad back, more alive than Laurence had seen her since his father's last homecoming. Perhaps this time things would be different.

Drawing the curtains closer, Belle peered out. 'George, the cab's still there — didn't you pay him off? Laurence, go and—'

His father interrupted. 'Just a moment, Laurence. I told the man to wait because there's something to come in.'

Belle clapped her hands. 'My box!'

'Your box, of course, my love. But something else. I'll go and fetch it. Shan't be long.'

Laurence shivered, not knowing why. What could a chest of presents do, except give pleasure to his mother?

There was talk outside, then the driver's word to his horse, and the fading rumble of wheels. Belle was waiting, fluttering with excitement, as the door opened to admit George, a large cedarwood box in his arms. He put it on the table, saying, 'Wait,' with an odd look, and went into the hall again.

When he re-entered a girl was on his arm.

She was neither tall nor short, but of a perfect height, with an hourglass figure shown off to perfection by her unfashionably tight dress of cerise silk, daringly low at the bosom, hugging her small waist, breaking into a froth of frills at the hips. Above it she wore a loose coat of peacock blue, patterned all over in raised silks, and on her head was a round hat wreathed with mock fruits and flowers, purple, gold, pink and sharp green, shapes and colours that never grew in an English garden.

And the laughing face framed in glossy ringlets was black. Or so it looked to Laurence, in the uncertain lamplight, against the startling vividness of the hat and the clothes. When she advanced he saw that it was, in fact, brown. He had seen plenty of brown-skinned men about Lancaster, sailors and ship-workers from the quays, but never yet a female one.

The silence in the sitting room was almost tangible. Belle had gone white to the lips, the absence of her usual rouge making her appear almost corpse-like. George was looking at her intently, willing her to be civilised and good-natured to the newcomer. Laurence was frozen with apprehension.

It was George who spoke. 'Belle, I want you to welcome Magnolia. Her father was a good friend of mine in the Service, dead a year ago. She has nobody now in Haiti, so I brought her home, for the winter at least. Will you give her a berth?'

'How do you do?' Magnolia ventured at last. Her voice was warm, fruity, rich sensuous music. She put out a hand in a canary-yellow glove; Belle did not take it. George saw that he must handle the situation.

'My wife's struck all of a heap, Magnolia; we don't see many strangers. Let me take your things, my dear, and come close to the fire. Laurence — this is my son Laurence, Magnolia — Laurence will make you comfortable. That's better. It's a terrible night, turning to a blizzard, I shouldn't wonder. I thought the old tub would get blown back to sea as we limped up the river. Luckily we made port. Now what about some refreshments? We're pretty sharp-set, I can tell you.'

Without taking her eyes off the girl, Belle said, 'There's something ready.'

'Oh, that's good,' said George, falsely hearty. He drew her sharply aside and whispered, 'Be civil, can't you? She's a stranger, it's Christmas.' Belle made no reply but left the room, her rapid footsteps audible on the stairs to the kitchen-basement. Laurence, uncomfortably stationed opposite Magnolia, tried to think of something to say, but failed. Without her hat and in the full light he could see that she was astonishingly beautiful. Her skin colour was creamy-brown or dark gold, as the light caught it, with a rose-flush on the wide cheekbones, her eyes enormous pools of black. She smiled widely at Laurence.

'Your mama's afraid of me. You aren't, are you?'

'Of course not. No. I ... I didn't expect anyone, that's all. I'm very glad to see you.' It was not true, for he had been looking forward to a quiet reunion between his parents. Nervously he poured Madeira for her and his father, and sipped some himself, hoping it would give him Dutch courage.

When Belle returned they were nursing their wine glasses, apprehensive of her mood. She was unsmiling and tight-lipped, but immediately broke into the social chatter expected of a hostess. Where had Miss — what was the name? Ah, Brown — come from? Haiti. That was an island, was it not?

'Of course it is,' George said, 'between Cuba and Porto Rico. Magnolia was born in Santo Domingo — near Barahona on the south coast, palm trees, melons, oranges and limes, grapefruit and mangos growing wild, there for the picking. Beautiful blue sea, nothing between you and Venezuela but the Caribbean. Isn't that so, my dear?'

'Yes, P — sir.'

What had she been going to say, Laurence wondered?

'Glorious climate, too. Just the odd hurricane, and the rainy season, of course, but none of this stuff. Snow and ice, horrible. Don't know why we left it, eh, Magnolia?'

'I don't know either,' Belle snapped. 'You were obviously more suited there than here. I'm afraid we've nothing of that kind to offer you. There's some food downstairs if you'd care for it.' She was addressing nobody, her eyes directed above their heads.

'Downstairs? Don't we eat here when we've company?' George nodded towards the double doors that shut off the room used as an additional parlour and a dining room.

'It's not convenient tonight. Perhaps you'd follow me.'

Oh, dear God, prayed Laurence, *don't let her fight him in front of me and the girl. Don't let me have to listen to all that again. I know what she thinks, and I don't know what to think myself, but she mustn't say anything.*

The meal was indifferent. Possibly it would have been so in any case, for Belle was uninterested in presenting food attractively, but to the wretched Laurence it seemed as though his mother had breathed a bad spell on it while on her visit downstairs. The Windsor soup was tasteless, the steaks of cod wet and pale, the boiled fowl stringy, the stewed ox tail insufficiently cooked. George, ever hungry, ate his without comment, but Magnolia obviously had difficulty in disposing of even half her portions. Belle, watching maliciously, asked her whether she were used to such food.

'We have good fish — we eat a lot of it. And game, wild duck, partridge and guinea fowl. Chicken we eat, yes, but usually with a sauce.'

'Oh, your mama keeps a good table, then? Plenty of servants, I expect?'

Magnolia looked down at the tablecloth. 'My mama's been dead for many years.'

'Oh. I'm sorry.' (*Then sound so,* thought Laurence.) 'And have you any other family?'

'A half-brother.' She shot a glance at George.

'I see. And your father was ... European. And you knew him well, George?'

'Very well.' Unhappily George demolished the far-from-tempting sponge pudding that wilted on his plate. Laurence saw that Magnolia's eager smile had faded, and that her look was melancholy. Now and then she shivered uncontrollably. In the poky little room off the kitchen where they were eating, a meagre fire gave off hardly any heat; there was a damp feeling in the air, as though the falling snow were piling up round the basement to bury them. The girl's dress was only of summer weight, not at all adequate for an English winter. The pretty colour that had lightened her dusky cheeks when she first arrived had faded; Laurence thought she looked almost grey. He was deeply sorry for her, remembering old tales of slaves in the last century who had died young of nothing but the

English climate. Suddenly, against his own nature, he spoke up for her, stammering slightly as he did sometimes when moved.

'Miss B-Brown must be feeling very cold, Mama. Shall I heat some b-bricks for her b-bed?'

Belle raised her eyebrows. 'Well, how gallant of you, Laurence! He's not generally so thoughtful, I can tell you, Miss Brown. Do as you think best, Laurence — the attic room will have to do, I'm afraid, as I had no warning.'

The attic bedroom was the coldest in the house in winter, as it was the hottest in summer, right under the slates. It was also the barest, being furnished with a servant's requirements in mind, though Emily, the cook-general, preferred to sleep on a mattress in the kitchen. Laurence pulled together the thin curtains, put hot bricks wrapped in flannel at the foot and in the middle of the bed, then remembered a warming pan hanging on the landing and filled it with coals from the sitting-room fire. He raked the dank coarse sheets of the bed with it until a faint warmth was detectable.

Still not satisfied, he went down the ladder-staircase yet again to his own room, returning with a blanket from his bed and a heavy greatcoat. Magnolia appeared before he could arrange them, his father behind her. Laurence held them out to her.

'For the b-bed. Goodnight.' He fled, embarrassed at having been found even so innocently in a lady's bedroom, but not before he had seen the gleam of tears in the great eyes. Behind him, he could hear the murmur of talk between the girl and his father.

In his own chilly, denuded bed, he resigned himself to overhearing the scene downstairs, predictable, yet none the less distressing to him.

'What a homecoming! Sitting here waiting for you — parted for almost a year, living like a nun or a widow — and what do I get when you *do* come back to me but a dressed-up trollop!'

'She's no trollop…'

'Oh, no, I suppose not, pure as snow — or soot, more like. And you might have thought of a better tale to tell me. Friend's daughter, indeed. A very close friend, for you to make sheep's eyes at the girl all through supper, and put a voice on you never use to me! And what did this *friend* think about your extreme partiality for her? I suppose he left her as a legacy to you when he died — if he *is* dead, for I don't believe that part of it either, or that the man ever existed. It's easy to see with half an eye —'

'Belle…'

'…easy to see what she is. Not that I know much about these people. Perhaps she's a slave, if they still have them in that place, wherever it is? How you must sympathise with the man in Virginia, John Brown — another Brown, how curious!' Belle gave an artificial laugh. 'He's trying to make the slaves there rebel, I read — doubtless he'll keep a few for himself, a man would…'

'There are no slaves in Haiti.'

'Of course there's a long tradition in Lancaster of keeping them. Are you going to renew it? Dress her in a boy's suit with a silver turban and make her follow you about the streets with a fan? I can just see it. And all the time, I, your wife, am expected to house the creature! The wicked, downright impudence of it, to bring your whore home to me —'

There was the sound of a ringing slap, a cry from Belle, and George's voice, loud and desperate.

'Damn you! Magnolia is not my whore. She's my daughter.'

Because George was too benign a man to keep anger alight, he spent hours in trying to explain, console, negotiate peace with the sobbing, half-hysterical Belle.

'I've told you, it was long before I met you. After I came back from sea, that is, when I was still engaged to Dove. When I married you, Magnolia was almost two years old, and Julius her half-brother —'

'By a different woman!'

'Well, yes, by a different woman — we did put in at different ports, and sailors are as much flesh and blood as other men — Julius was a year older. I loved them both, and I was fond of their mothers, but it was you I married.'

'Thank you for nothing at all.'

'So it's been nothing, all these years of housing and clothing and feeding? I didn't do that for the others, I may tell you, though I made them an allowance for the children, and they both married men of their own colour and did very well, I believe. When Magnolia's mother died her husband wrote to tell me, and after a long time the letter caught up with me. I went to see her, and found the girl had had a bad time of it with his second wife. I scooped her up and brought her home. I thought you might have tried to give her a welcome, Belle.'

A furiously shaken head and more tears answered him.

'I might have known,' he said sadly. 'I might have guessed you'd still be jealous of every female who crossed your path. You always were and you always will be. A good thing for Dove she married and got out of your way — you'd have clawed her eyes out, too, wouldn't you? Well, my daughter's here. What do you mean to do about it?'

'Turn her out. Send her back where she came from.'

'Can't be done. That door's shut. The stepmother's another off your pattern. Come, Belle, you'll be none the worse for giving her house room. Nobody's to know what the relationship is — she'll just be what I told you at first, the daughter of a shipmate. She speaks well, she's had a good education, she'd fit in with your friends. Why should there be any scandal, if you keep a still tongue in your head?'

'I'd tell them all, just to shame you — and her.'

'Where's the shame to her, poor child? But I believe you would.' George re-lit a Havana cigar which had already gone out twice. Its taste was bitter, like the flavour of the pointless conversation, if conversation it could be called when one side of it was unreasoning invective.

He was angry with himself for not being enough of a man to tell her the truth at first, for having precipitated this, for being so foolishly optimistic as to think Belle's nature would have changed in his absence. She would never change, and he was landed with an impossible situation. There was nobody he knew in Lancaster with whom he could lodge Magnolia. Indeed, he knew very few people, being absent so much, and those few tended to be Belle's circle. To put up the girl at an inn, with full board, would cost more than he could afford, and would never do in any case, even at a respectable place like the King's Arms, young, beautiful and vulnerable as Magnolia was. That would be the certain way to scandal.

He thought of the dreadful evening, the shivering girl sent up to a servant's attic, poor downtrodden Laurence trying in his humble way to comfort her, Belle carrying on like a Poulton fishwife. Suddenly rage swept over him. He threw the cigar into the fire and shouted at Belle.

'All right, enough of this. Get up to bed. Go on! I'll show you who's master in this house.' Heedless of her protests, he pushed her through the door and propelled her upstairs in front of him. Frightened, she grew quieter, until he slammed and locked the bedroom door.

She crawled under the bedclothes, where she lay, too frightened to stir, almost afraid to breathe. George lay down beside her, as far off as possible, looking out at the cold, impassive moon. If only, all those years ago, he had not been rash enough to marry the first pretty face he saw on coming home from sea, he felt he would have made an excellent husband to someone, for nature, he knew, had intended him to be quite a jolly fellow.

Magnolia had known spite before. Her stepmother had been an expert at slights and rebuffs, even sly blows and pinches when her husband, who was fond of Magnolia, was not there to see. Stepmother, indeed — she had not even been that, being only the second wife of the man who had married Magnolia's mother. So it had been easy to be aloof and uncaring about her behaviour. One day her real papa would come and take her away, and in the meantime she was contented enough, first at her convent school and then with the friends whose homes were happier than her own.

But she had expected England to be so different. Everyone on the ship had been charming to her, even though she was supposed to be only a *protégée* of the master's, not his relative, and George himself had told her so many tales of his boyhood in Lancaster, and the snug little house near the quays, and his son who would be pleased to have some cheerful young company. He had not said much about his wife, and Magnolia was too innocent to interpret this as a warning sign.

The woman who hated her on sight had been as much of a shock as the bitter English weather. Magnolia, lying under Laurence's blanket and greatcoat, felt as though she would never be warm again; just as she felt she would never trust anyone again. Her kindly cheerful father had brought her into a small, freezing hell out of which she could see no way, unless someone outside it took pity on her. She remembered the boys who had wanted to marry her, allured by her beauty, her white blood, and the comfortable fortune of her adoptive father. They had not all been coloured. One had been a Spaniard; what a fool she had been not to take him, just because of the promise that one day she would go to England. Now he, and the others, were at the other side of the world, and she could never go back.

She thought idly of the voodoo magic that was practised in Haiti. The nuns frowned on any mention of it, but all their pupils knew about ritual sacrifices, black cockerels and goats, spells and wild dances and hypnotic chants. A person could be killed by such means; Magnolia imagined the slaying of her father's wife. It made a pleasant picture.

Ephraim took off his spectacles and passed his hand wearily across his brow. It was time he retired from legal work. It imposed too much strain on him, and in this case depressed his spirits.

'Are you quite sure, George,' he asked, 'that you want to put your name to this document? It seems a very drastic step to take.'

'It's the only one left to me,' said his son-in-law. 'Belle and I can't live together happily, even during my time ashore. We're like cat and dog. Always have been, I think, under the lovey-dovey stuff. I came home in good enough fettle, and she's made my life hell ever since. Best to make a clean break.'

Ephraim sighed. 'It was very unwise of you to bring your daughter home. You might have known how Belle would take it. And it was hardly fair on the girl herself. Laurence tells me he thinks her very unhappy, though she puts on a bold front.'

'Oh, yes. No weeping and wailing there. It's "Papa" to me and "Brother" to Laurence and "Madam" to Belle. I can't say I blame her. Belle knows she'll get as good as she gives if she raises a hand to that one. She's mad jealous, of course, of the attention Magnolia gets — it's like a royal procession every time she walks down the street — and by Jove, how she can walk! She's got the carriage of a queen. You ought to see her, sir — won't you change your mind?'

'No, George. It would not be fitting for me to receive a young person whose presence is an affront to my daughter. Now read this indenture over and see whether I have interpreted your wishes correctly.'

George took the folded double sheet of paper with its ominous title page: *Re Master & Mrs Dilworth. Deed of Separation.* He read, slowly and carefully, the charter of his freedom.

…between George Thomas Dilworth of the one part and Mary Ann Dilworth the Wife of the said George Thomas Dilworth of the other part. Whereas unhappy differences have arisen between the said George Thomas Dilworth and the said Mary Ann Dilworth and whereas there has been one Child of that Marriage and no more namely Laurence Ephraim Dilworth who is now of the age of twenty-one years. Now this Indenture witnesseth that it is hereby mutually agreed and declared by the parties hereto…

Ephraim was watching him narrowly. 'Do you follow it?'
'As far as a layman can, sir.' He read on.

1. The said George Thomas Dilworth and Mary Ann Dilworth shall henceforth live separate and apart from each other and as if they were unmarried and neither party shall take any proceedings against the other for the restitution of conjugal rights and neither of them shall in any way molest or interfere with the other.

2. The said George Thomas Dilworth shall during the joint lives of himself and the said Mary Ann Dilworth and so long as the said Mary Ann Dilworth lives a chaste life and observes and performs the Stipulations herein contained and on her part to be observed and performed pay to the said Mary Ann Dilworth the annual sum of one hundred pounds from the first day of January One thousand eight hundred and sixty.

George looked up. 'Good. You've put in the clause I wanted.'

'Against my will,' Ephraim said, frowning. 'It was very distasteful to me to draw up a document suggesting that my daughter was likely to lead an unchaste life. However…'

'You don't hear rumours, sir, and if you did you wouldn't listen to them. I do hear them, from various quarters, and if young Laurence weren't loyal to his mother I could confirm them from his lips. Well, I tell you now, I'm not having Belle dragging my name in the dust any longer. I'll support her, just as this paper says, but I'm damned if I'm going to finance adultery.'

'Of which you are quite guiltless yourself, of course.' Ephraim's tone was dry.

'No. I won't pretend to that. It's impossible, in a life like mine. I should never have married at all, I see that now, but it's too late. At least I keep it away from my own door.'

'Hardly, since you brought the product of it to your home.'

'I know, I know. I've admitted I was wrong. Let's not fight about it. What does the rest of this say? *Monthly instalments … she shall at all times keep indemnified the said George Thomas Dilworth from and against all debts and liabilities* ... yes, that's pretty important. Right, sir. Where do I sign?'

'Where your name is pencilled in.'

Summoned by Ephraim's bell, his head clerk appeared and witnessed the deed. A point occurred to George.

'You're sure Belle shouldn't sign it too? I don't want to find the whole thing's not watertight.'

'I think you may trust me for that.'

When George had left the room Ephraim heard him talking to Laurence in the outer office. Stiff with sitting, he levered himself out of his chair and went to the window. People wearing what were obviously their best clothes were coming away from St John's Church, from which wedding chimes were ringing out. He thought back mournfully to the day he had given away twin brides, his two lovely daughters, in that church, and what happiness that day had seemed to promise. Now the life of one of those brides was in ruins, a shattered marriage and a loveless home, and the shadow of her misery darkening the young life of her son. And the other bride ... he had been so certain that Dove would be happy, and for years it had seemed that she would. Then came the birth of Marigold to sadden them all; and now some threat which could not be put into words, but showed itself in all Dove's letters. She was much disturbed, her father could tell, knowing her simple, self-betraying style of writing so well. Something was badly wrong at the Lion House. May had said nothing in her dutiful letters to himself and Margaret, only that her father had worries. Ephraim toyed with the idea of going to Deansbury, rather than endure any more suspense. But he was old and frail now; the journey daunted him too much.

So was there nothing he could do, but fret impotently? He thought of one thing, and acted upon it. At the sound of his bell, pressed twice, Laurence entered.

'Yes, sir?' Formality was observed between grandfather and grandson in the confines of the office, but Ephraim was about to waive it.

'Laurence. Christmas is ten days away. Have you any plans?'

'Plans, sir? No.' Laurence went fiery red. 'Mama did say something about going to Downham. But I don't think ... I don't think...'

'You don't think she will do so now.'

'No, sir. My s-sister — Magnolia, that is — is moving to an hotel with Papa. Mama has not mentioned anything, but I shouldn't think she will go away.'

'Then will you take a letter to her from me, Laurence? I'll tell you what it will say. I shall ask her, from myself and Aunt Margaret, to come to us for the Christmas and New Year season. I think you'll find she will accept the invitation — if I use all my powers of persuasion. I shall not ask you to come with her, because I think it would be best if you were to be out of each other's company at the moment.' Ephraim paused delicately. 'How would you like me to write to Mrs Jesse at Downham, and ask her, as a favour to all of us, to have you as a Christmas guest?'

Laurence's face brightened. 'Oh, Grandfather! I should like it so much! B-but for two days ... it would hardly be w-worth...'

'Not worth the journey? Well, then, suppose I extend your holiday by a week, so that you need not return to work until the day after New Year? I'm sure Mr Booth could dispense with your services for that time.'

'That would be … wonderful. Grandfather — I do thank you, so much.' Laurence was transformed with joyful expectation.

'Good. Don't build on it, mind, in case Mrs Jesse has a house party. But I think we may allow ourselves to hope.'

CHAPTER TWELVE

Christmas at Eagle Hall meant fun and feasting, and services in the old church by the little green, looking down to the bridge and the stream. It felt quite different from St John's, with its haunting associations and the distracting rattle of passing traffic, even on a Sunday. There was nothing to trouble Laurence in Downham's church; only peace, and food for his spirit. It was bliss to be with Lucy, and a pleasant surprise to find Bertha not the strange creature he had expected, but a calm and sweet young woman with whom be felt instant affinity. Bliss, too, that his cousin Edwin was not there, to rival him in Lucy's favours.

Edwin's holiday was less happy. The change in the atmosphere of his home struck him like a chill. They were pleased to see him, proud of his medical progress, ready to listen to his news and stories. But there was tension in the air, which his experience of patients made him quick to recognise. There was a sort of bright coldness about his mother: she seemed to look at and speak to his father very little. His father's warmth of manner was quite gone, replaced by irritability and silence. Edwin noticed that he spent little time at table, or in family chat, and had not the patience he once had towards Marigold. In her, too, there was a deterioration which Edwin did not like.

To May he said, 'What's the matter with everyone? Except you — *you're* all right, much improved, in fact.'

'Thank you, you're too kind. Eddie, I simply can't tell you what's wrong. It's been going on for months now. I've dropped hints to Mother, but she won't talk to me about it, and Father's impossible. It seems as though he can't help being disagreeable, and it's so terribly unlike him. As to Marigold, that tutor upset her — it would have been better if he'd never come here. But, Eddie —' she lowered her tone — 'there *is* one thing. I can say it to you because you're a doctor, or going to be, though I wouldn't mention it to anyone else.'

'Well?'

'Mother and Father don't share a bedroom any more. I can't help knowing — the servants talk, and I've been in Mother's room — there's no sign of Father's things. What can have happened?'

'Oh, Lord. How should I know? After twenty years, I suppose ... look here, May, I'm not one of the Three Wise Men just because I'm a medico. I don't like the sound of it, though. And it's not the sort of thing one can ask. *Botheration.* I thought this vacation was going to be spiffing, but it's turning out like Black Monday.'

'What's that?'

'Start of exam week. Come on, I'll teach you some college songs.'

'But we're not to play the drawing-room piano. That's only for practice and musical parties — not that we ever have any. I know, there's the one in the old schoolroom.'

Edwin could not read a note of music, but had a flair for playing by ear and an instant memory for words. With a flourish of chords to impress May, he launched into song.

I yince was a light-headed laddie,
A dreaming and daundering loon,
Just 'scaped from the rod o' my daddie,
And the skirts o' my minnie's broun goun.

But now I cut loftier capers,
And the beer that I drink isna' sma',
When I see my ain name in the papers,
Capped and doctored an' a'.
Capped and doctored an' a',
Doctored and capped an' a',
Right sure 'tis a beautiful thing
To be capped and doctored an' a'!'

She clapped. 'What a splendid Scots accent you've acquired. Do they really sound like that?'

'More or less,' Edwin replied modestly. 'I say, though, I shouldn't be singing that, not yet. It's flying in the face of Providence, with another two years to go. I know, let's have a bit of Latin. Bet you can't join in this one:'

'Concinamus, O sodales!
Eja! quid silemus?
Nobile canticum, dulce melos,
Domum, Dulce Domum, resonemus.'

'Bet you I can, if I miss out the words!' May interrupted. 'Carry on, and I'll la-la them.' She added her soprano to his strong baritone.

'Domum, domum, dulce Domum,
Dulce, dulce, dulce Domum,
Domum, Domum resonemus.'

The joyful young voices floated down to Dove, where she sat at her dressing table. She was no Latin scholar, but the old student song remained in her memory from some time in her youth, when her father would sing to them all to his own accompaniment at the old tall piano. *Sweet, sweet home, let us sing of it ...*

She grimaced at her reflection. What a home Edwin had returned to; she was glad he could sing and sound so carefree. She would try to cast off her own dark mood while he was on holiday, and make something of a Christmas for him and May.

Christmas. What a hollow sound it had. Basil would not be in Deansbury for the festival which meant nothing to him. When the mill closed he would go to his family home on the other side of Manchester. So there was no point in dressing the Christmas tree in special glory for his benefit, or making up the kissing bush she and Belle had always made in the old days, before the tree came in with Prince Albert: two hoops of wire intertwined with holly and mistletoe and yew, and hung with gilded oranges tied with bright ribbons. If Basil were with them at Christmas he would have to kiss her under it. That way, at least, she would get a kiss.

Since that wonderful night at his lodging he had not touched her, except by accident, and then had hastily moved away. Time and again she tried to get him alone, and each time he avoided her, until at last she contrived that they should be the last to leave the dining room. She clung to his arm, holding him back.

'Basil, I must speak to you. What is it? Why are you avoiding me?'

'You know that very well. My position here is impossible — or it will be if we let ourselves slip again.'

'Slip? It was you who wanted it. You went on about it for years — and now you make it sound as though it were all my doing! How can you be so unfair?'

'Aye. I suppose I am being. A man can want a thing without thinking what getting it will be like. It's no use, Dove. Even if Joe's no good to you I can't cuckold him in his own house — or in mine, for that matter. Be a sensible girl, now.'

She laughed, a high mirthless laugh. 'Girl? I'm forty-six. Am I to have no more love? Am I just a thing, then? Shall I go into cap and shawl? What sort of life are you condemning me to? Basil, please…'

He shook his head and pulled his arm away from her grasp, then hurried after the others. She knew she had lost him, unless she could establish some new hold. She was left with her longing, and her guilt on Joe's account, and the great hurt to her pride, and her bitter disappointment.

Their Christmas was tolerable, though joyless. They went to Deansbury Old Church, to hear the usual sermon and be greeted by the vicarage children and other Deansbury neighbours. Then there were the presents to be distributed; to the women servants ribbons, lace collars, new caps, to the men, neckcloths and leather purses. Of the family, Edwin had a pipe, a handsome manly thing he prized on sight, though he had never truly taken to smoking. May had a new dress, made secretly at her mother's orders, to her measurements, and Marigold a set of small dolls dressed like a family, parents and children, of German manufacture. Nobody pretended now that she would enjoy anything more advanced. The roast goose, now fashionable, came and went on the table, and the mince pies and pudding.

Edwin watched his father carefully. He had begun to work out his own theory of what was wrong in his family. The food half touched, the wine almost untasted, the frequent helpings of water from the carafe. Over the leisured meal he covertly studied his father's waxen colour, the wastage of his once-comely face, the nervous twitches and the moody fixed stare. When the meal was finished and the clock struck four, Dove and May retired. Marigold had long since been taken off to bed by Susan, the maid who attended on her with motherly devotion. Edwin chose his moment.

'Shall we take a glass of port, Father?'

'Port? You take one, if you like. I don't care for it.'

'Oh? You used to, I remember. Haven't you some rather decent bottles stowed away in the cellar? Cockburn's, Martinez's, that sort of thing? Pity to waste it, especially after a jolly good meal like that. You should try my landlady's cooking — whew! What about sending Warburton down for a couple of bottles? I'll do justice to them if you don't.'

With a shadow of his old smile Joe rang the bell. The bottles, when they appeared, looked in prime dusty condition. Warburton, the young man who was rather more than a footman if not yet quite a butler, pulled a cork and produced two fine glasses. Edwin drained one.

'Merry Christmas, Father. Though you don't look particularly merry. Aren't you sleeping?'

Joe threw him a suspicious glance. 'Moderately well. Why?'

'Thought you didn't look up to snuff, that's all. We get used to the signs, in our line. I'd say … let me take a look at your ankles.' With a sudden movement he stooped and drew forward his father's foot, ignoring resistance. The once-slender ankle was puffy, folds of flesh above the house slipper, matching the heavy bags under the eyes. Just what Edwin had expected.

'Having a bit of pain, are you?' he asked, as casually as though enquiring the time of day. He was aware of a change in his father's expression: fear, on the surface, naked.

'A little. Nothing to speak of. The weather, I suppose.'

'What weather? This hasn't just started, has it? You find exercise painful — tenderness on both sides of the spine? Been a little feverish at times, have you? Not quite yourself?'

Joe's voice was low. 'I've heard myself raving. A lot of nonsense. Nobody else has heard — yet, so far as I know. I seem to grow ... hot, and then I'm not myself. How did you know?'

'Why, it's nothing unusual — just an occasional high temperature. You might have one later today, or you might not. Have some more port, Father, it won't hurt you, and we're getting on so nicely. What about other things, then? You've been seeing blood, perhaps? Having acute discomfort, er, where you'd least want it?'

Joe was staring at him. 'How do you know? I've told nobody. How do you know these things?'

'Because I hope to be a doctor in a couple of years, Father, and even though I'm specialising in female complaints I have to know about the rest of it, too. In my opinion you've been keeping things to yourself you ought to have come out with, and so caused a lot of bother to the family. Now, won't you tell me all about it? A doctor's got to have the eye of a detective policeman, but it helps him to have a bit of evidence as well. Now, then.'

Joe swallowed a glass of port. That, or his son's honest approach, loosened his tongue, and he talked. Edwin listened, not quite as cocky and cheerful as he appeared, to a recital of misery and fear.

'I can't describe to you what the pain's been like. I never knew what agony was, before. I could barely keep still in company, or control my face. I tried to keep away from people; it was very difficult — I must have seemed sharp in my manner. I thought it would show, and somebody would make me see a doctor.'

'Why in heaven's name didn't you? Doctor Ainslie's there, he's on call if one of your workers has a finger-ache — what about you, the master, then?'

'I should have called him, I know. I was afraid. I'm afraid now, Eddie, though it's better since I've told you. Can anything be done?'

Edwin smiled reassuringly, not meeting his father's appealing eyes. 'I don't know. It's not my subject, but I'll go into Manchester and talk to people as soon as the holiday's over. Only two days — this being Sunday. Don't worry yourself. Shall I make you something up? What have you been taking?'

'Morphia. It was the only thing that did any good...'

'All right, I know. I'm a dab hand at mixing things — lead me to it.' Gently he put his arm round his father's bowed shoulders and led him from the room. Their roles were reversed; now his father was the hurt child, he the comforting adult. Suddenly his chosen profession weighed heavily upon him.

Later he sought his mother out. She was in her parlour with May, reading.

'Excuse me, ladies,' Edwin said. 'Pussy, would you like to go and busy yourself with household tasks, or put your hair in curlers, or whatever you girls do? I want a word with Mother, just on our own.' He lowered an eyelid in a long slow wink. May nodded. She had a high degree of respect for Edwin.

He perched himself on the arm of Dove's chair, looming benevolently above her. 'I've been talking to Father. I thought somebody should.'

She started. 'Oh! What about?'

'Did you think I hadn't noticed? I'm not so green as I'm cabbage-looking, you know. All this moping and silence — well, it's not like this house, is it? — not what the poor old lions are used to. I heard 'em growling before I'd properly rung the doorbell. No, but seriously, Mother, listen. Father's ill. He's been ill for months, getting worse and afraid to tell you. If he seems to have been avoiding you — all of you — it was because he thought you'd notice his symptoms. He's in very great pain; enough pain to need morphia. That, and ... other things, made him think he was in a very bad way. And the condition makes people extremely irritable, as you may have noticed. Even slightly rambling in their wits at times.'

Dove had gone paper-white. 'Dear Lord. What is it?'

'Renal calculus.' Edwin tried not to make it sound too alarming. 'Kidney stone. A rather hard case, it sounds to me, with complications. It's a thing that — excuse me, Mother — can take away a man's virility, for the time, anyway, and change his whole nature. I'm sorry; it's not nice. But I had to tell you. It may explain quite a few things.'

'It explains everything. If you only knew ... I've behaved so badly to him ... wickedly!'

'You couldn't be wicked if you tried, Mother. I expect you've been just a bit cool sometimes, that's all.'

'It's more than that — much more!' she said wildly. 'I've ... oh, Eddie, I can't tell you. You wouldn't believe me — nobody would!'

'Then don't try to tell me. It won't do any good — confessions never do, whatever the Romans think about it. What we must do now is to get Father well, if it's possible. I'm afraid it will mean an operation, you know.'

Her hand flew to her mouth. 'Oh, no! We've never ... none of us have ever needed...'

'No, and aren't we lucky that we haven't, considering that chloroform's only been in use for operations this past ten years or so. Pity we weren't quicker to follow America's lead.' He forebore to tell her that major surgery under an anaesthetic was still a dangerously chancy thing, since the chloroform must be inhaled for as long as the operation lasted, and the patient well might die on the table. 'I know a fellow at the infirmary,' he said brightly, 'very well thought of for this kind of thing. I'll ask him to come out and see Father, then we shall know more where we stand.'

Dove nodded. Edwin thought she seemed to have aged years during their conversation. 'I must go to him,' she said. 'What can I say? What can I possibly say that will make it up to him?'

'Just be your ordinary cheerful self. Behave as though there was never any coolness. Tell him I've told you all about it and that things will be better from now onwards. Go *now*.'

'Yes, I will. Thank you, Eddie. You've been wonderful. I don't know where we should have been without you, my dearest boy.'

She went to Joe with a bright face and a cheerful manner, making the lightest she could of Edwin's news and chiding Joe gently for not having been frank with her. 'Now it's all over, darling, and you know nobody will mind if you're a bit cross when you're in pain. I'm sorry I didn't know before.'

Sleepy with the morphia, he smiled at her, murmuring, 'Doesn't matter. All my fault.'

She sat by his side, holding his hand, until he slept. She was indeed sorry she had not known before; how sorry, she would never tell him. The remorse would be hers to bear alone. Only Basil might guess something of it.

A letter rustled in her pocket; it was from Belle, giving a hysterical account of the separation and George's shocking behaviour. With her sorrow for Belle was mingled the thought that she must treasure all the more the husband who had been always faithful, and had never consciously given her a hurt.

Edwin's friend, James Mellyn, came out to Deansbury as quickly as transport could bring him. After an examination which left Joe exhausted with pain he took Edwin aside.

'I don't like the look of him at all. We shall have to operate, and soon. Otherwise ... there seems to be an infection, and you know what that means. I wouldn't give much for his chances.'

'Oh, God. Can you do it yourself?'

'I'd prefer to give it to Sefton. He's had more experience. But I'd like to assist if he'll let me. There are some very interesting features ... I'm sorry, I know it's your father and I mustn't indulge in professional enthusiasm. But you know how it is.'

Eddie smiled wryly. 'I know how it is.'

In the first week in January, Joe was taken to Manchester Infirmary. Dove and Edwin went in the carriage with him, trying to keep him entertained with light talk, though the sweat stood out on his brow with pain and there was a fever on him, so that he answered them sometimes with nonsense. When they reached the infirmary in the centre of Manchester, Edwin summoned a hospital porter to help him carry his father in quickly, out of the cold air. Dove began to follow them, but he gently sent her back to the carriage.

'I'll see him into bed. You go home.'

Looking back anxiously, she obeyed him. Now there was nothing to do but wait.

Basil had taken over the affairs of the mill and the estate. He was wily enough to ask Dove to help him with the accounts; she was good at book-keeping and it would help to take her mind off Joe. Another benefit was that it would bring them together as a working partnership in which all shadows of the past might be forgotten. Or almost forgotten. He knew that now he would never have to repulse her again, while Joe lived.

Mr Sefton postponed the operation for a few days in order to examine his patient at leisure and take tests. Every day Edwin travelled to Manchester, coming back in the evening to report his father's condition. It was impossible for Dove to tell how much of the truth he was telling her. He had stood by the beds of so many desperately ill patients that he was adept at concealing any emotion he might feel beneath an exterior of cheerful calm.

On the third day after Joe had been taken away, Edwin came home with definite news.

'It will be tomorrow, they think. The fever has gone down, and Father seems stronger. That's good, isn't it? The suspense will soon be over.'

'Yes. The best news. No — the best news would be a successful operation.'

Edwin patted her hand. 'We must wait and hope, Mother. What about a few hands of whist tonight, if Mrs Skerritt will make a fourth? Or would you two like to have a shot beating me at billiards? Come now — May?'

'Oh, no, Eddie. I find it so boring walking round and round that huge table, and I can never stretch across it without bursting a seam or losing a button. And whist is so dull.'

'Mother's very good at it,' Edwin said pointedly, in a tone that conveyed, 'so that's what we'll play, to take her mind off things.'

'Yes, of course, Eddie,' she said meekly. 'Goodness! how the wind howls. Was it rough driving home?'

219

'Dreadful. Extraordinary weather — bright sunshine when I left Manchester and almost a blizzard by the time I got back. More like April than January.'

'I know,' said May. 'We were actually in the garden this afternoon, until about an hour ago, looking for snowdrops, but there aren't any yet. Do you know a blackbird nested in your old shed last year, the one where you used to do those awful experiments. I hope so much they'll come back in spring. Ugh! I hate this weather. I hope Father's warm enough in that great barn of a place.'

'Warmer than we are,' Edwin said. 'He's in a nice small room, with one other patient, an army officer. There's a good fire in the grate and plenty of blankets — every comfort, in fact. I should be proud of that little ward if I were in charge of it.'

Dove shivered. 'Draw the curtains, May — why are they still open? And ring, please — I expect Eddie would like some tea.'

Only a few seconds after May had pulled the bell-rope Susan appeared.

'Madam…'

'Goodness, that was quick. Can we have tea, please, Susan?'

'Yes, madam, but — I came to see if Miss Marigold was here.'

'No, she isn't. Have you tried her room? She must be dressing.'

'She's not there, madam, and she never dresses without me to help her. To tell you the truth, I was getting a bit alarmed, then I thought she must be here all the time.'

A faint cold fear began to steal through Dove, and to communicate itself to May, remembering vividly the last time Marigold had disappeared. But this could not possibly be like that. 'She was perfectly all right in the garden,' she said sharply.

'She may have gone to sleep somewhere in the house. What a nuisance. Well, put all the lights on, and take candles into the bedrooms. What a naughty girl, just as we were comfortable.'

The search party set out independently, the three of them, two maids, and Warburton, with candles and matches, calling Marigold's name in every corner of the house. May, unthinkingly, began to hum a tune, and was pounced on by her mother.

'There's nothing to sing about, May.'

'Was I? I didn't know. I'm sorry, I won't do it again. Marigold! Do come out, there's a dear.'

But Dove had recognised the tune. 'The Mistletoe Bough' was a popular ballad; she remembered Belle's account of the party given at Eagle Hall after their wedding, and how it had been part of the uproarious charades. And she remembered the words that had set off May's humming:

They sought her that night, they sought her next day,
They sought her in vain till a year passed away...

The old story ended in a fast-locked chest, and a skeleton bride. Dove shuddered and pushed it out of her mind.

Seven o'clock came, eight, nine. They had had no supper. They were cold, weary, dusty from hunting in attics and cellars. When, the whole house explored, they met in the hall, nobody had any further suggestions.

'We must search the garden,' Dove said.

Edwin protested. 'Mother! It's pouring, and pitch dark. The wind would blow candles out if we took them.'

'Then you must take storm lanterns — there are some in the stables. Just you and Warburton. Put on heavy coats and boots, you'll find plenty out there.'

The two boys came back wet, muddy and with no news. 'We've looked everywhere, Mother, and not a trace. The sheds, the greenhouses ... there's nothing else we can do, truly there isn't. Look, this is useless. Wherever she is, she's not going to turn up till morning. Let's all have something to eat and go to bed. She'll be all right, you see if she isn't. She's fallen asleep somewhere, you know what she is for doing that.'

To May he said, under his breath, 'Just for once I could spank Marigold for this. I know she did it before, but this is too much, with Mother so worried.'

'Marigold's worried too. We had to tell her Father was ill and had gone away, but she's kept looking for him. That's it, I'm sure. She's in some place we've never thought of searching. Wait till morning and she'll come out, you'll see.'

But when morning came to the uneasy house, no Marigold appeared. Dove was openly frightened by now. She sent a message to Basil that would catch him before he went to the mill, and he appeared as breakfast was being served. Hurriedly she told him what had happened.

'Get everyone you can to start searching — anyone who isn't at work. Search the mill — she might just have gone there to look for Joe. And — oh dear, what else can we do?'

'The police. I'll get them to send someone out from Manchester, if there's no sign of her when we've gone over the mill. And there's the —' He had been going to say 'river', but thought better of it. 'The village,' he substituted. 'If she's gone wandering she might be curled up in somebody's outhouse. Don't worry, I'll see they look everywhere.'

'Don't worry! All very well ... Oh, Basil, I'm sorry. Thank you.'

The clock was striking eight when he left. Dove started violently. Another day was beginning: the day of Joe's operation.

May was dressing, heavy-eyed and yawning from the tiring evening and late night. She put on a dark green stuff frock, sensible enough to wear if another search was necessary, then thought it looked depressingly drab, and opened her jewel box. The bracelet of moonstones shone blandly up at her.

'You!' she said to it. 'Mother was right. We've had nothing but bad luck since Aunt gave you to me. Hateful thing!'

She slammed the box shut and went down to breakfast unadorned.

CHAPTER THIRTEEN

Edwin had no choice but to go to Manchester, anxious though he was not to leave his mother and May in their suspense. But if he stayed he would only be one more searcher. Reluctantly he rode off through the steady cold rain, relieved at least to see his mother composed and apparently calm.

During the watches of the night she had found a kind of strength. The evil times which had come upon her family were not to be met with tears and weakness. She had been strong when Joe was weak, all their married life and before; it was no moment to break now. There was something which came to one's aid when disaster threatened. Perhaps it was God, perhaps some hidden weapon in the human spirit's armoury, In any case, she thanked God that May, her good May, was at her side, and Edwin at home. But for Edwin his father might be beyond the help of surgeons by now.

All that day no news came from the searchers. Dove and May watched the rain turn to sleet, then snow. May said, early in the day, 'There's no point in sitting here staring out of the window, we need to keep busy. What is there to do that we've kept putting off? Now's the time to do it.'

Dove thought. 'Grandmother's counterpane.' Laid carefully in lavender in a press was a bedspread more than a hundred years old, worked in silks by the hands of Dove's grandmother, Ann Atkinson. It had begun to fray long since, and had been taken out of use in case it should fall apart altogether. Dove had always meant to set aside some leisure time in repairing it herself, not liking to trust it to the fingers of servants. Now they unfolded it carefully and spread it out.

'It's perfectly beautiful,' May said, as the elaborate design of birds, flowers, fruit, leaves and scrollwork was revealed. 'Look, there are the initials, *A* and *J* entwined.'

'Ann and John. My grandparents. She died before I was born, but I did know Grandfather John, I believe, though I don't remember him. Your father remembers him well — it was a blow to him when the old gentleman died.' As they sorted out embroidery silks and wools, matched colours and cut with infinite care and tiny scissors such patches as had gone threadbare, Dove talked gently on about her childhood, Joe's coming to them, the old Lancaster days before Queen Victoria came to the throne, the excursions they had taken; and May listened and asked questions. She had heard most of the stories before, but they were ever-fresh, and never so welcome as now. She felt closer to her mother than ever before. For the first time it was just the two of them together.

By dusk the counterpane was half repaired. In the early evening Basil returned, grim-faced.

'Nothing. I've not been out myself all the time, I'd work to do. But plenty of others have, and nobody's seen her. It's snowing hard now, so they've had to give up. They'll start again in the morning, with any luck. There's three policeman on the job, from Manchester, but they're not taking it all that seriously, seems to me. Runaway girls are ten a penny to them, from what they say, and I reckon they don't believe what they've been told about her affliction. Hard-headed lot. Any news from Manchester?'

'Not yet.' But almost as Dove spoke a messenger arrived with a letter from Edwin.

'Father came through the operation reasonably well and seems to be a little stronger, though not conscious yet. Still not out of danger, so I shall stay overnight. I hope so very greatly there is news of Marigold.'

'She's hiding, if you ask me,' May said. 'She knows very well when she's been naughty. She'll come back when she thinks she's forgiven.'

Basil did not seem to hear her. 'They're covering the road to Manchester tomorrow. Just in case she's gone looking for her father.'

Dove smiled at him, as though nothing more serious than a silver spoon had gone missing. 'They'll find her,' she said, 'you'll see.'

She was going over the household accounts the next morning with Mrs Skerritt when the knocker sounded, a loud and purposeful *rat-tat*, followed by an energetic pulling of the bell.

'Somebody wants to get in, no mistake!' said the housekeeper. 'Why don't they break the door in while they're about it, I wonder?' Dove closed her eyes, feeling as though her breath had stopped, as Peggy entered, wide-eyed.

'There's a man to see you, madam. Important, he says.'

The man was waiting in the hall; a burly, moustachioed man, in a heavy caped coat. He was standing on the doormat, glancing apologetically from his large muddied boots to the carpet. Dove said something, perhaps inviting him into the morning room, for they were in it, he still standing, looking straight in front of him, not at her.

They had found Marigold. The earliest searchers had found her, for most of the snow had melted overnight, making it possible for them to go back over the tracks and look more thoroughly. She was lying in a ditch in a narrow lane, about two miles south of Deansbury, with fallen branches hiding her. She would have remained hidden if one of the seekers had not noticed a glimpse of blue among the sodden browns of the wood and leaves. It was her jacket, the one she had been wearing in the garden.

Dove tried to form a question, but it would not come out.

'I'm deeply sorry, ma'am,' the policeman said. Questions would have helped the job he had to do. 'She was quite dead. For two days, we think. It's to be treated as a case of murder. I really am sorry. Shall I ask them for some water for you?'

'No. Thank you.' Dove heard her own voice coming back to her from an infinite distance. Then May was in the room, and Mrs Skerritt, their horrified voices rising and falling, the policeman's low rumbling tones going on and on. Somebody must have put her on the sofa, for she was lying there with a glass of brandy being held to her lips. It was not real, of course, any of it, just a vivid morning nightmare, and she would soon wake up.

But the nightmare did not end, only fused itself with reality. Dr Ainslie appeared, summoned by Mrs Skerritt, and gave Dove a sedative. Almost at once, before she could be taken upstairs, she fell into a heavy sleep.

'Severe shock,' the doctor said. 'Cover her up and leave her here to be quiet, and we'll go to another room. May, you ought to take a draught too.'

May, whose eyes were like dark holes in her white face, refused. 'I must be about to look after Mother. Give it to Susan, Doctor. She really needs it.'

Susan had collapsed when the news was broken to her, and the other maids were in little better case. The doctor himself was badly shaken. He had brought May and Marigold into the world, had been the one to break the news of Marigold's mental deficiency to her parents, and had treated all three of them for their childish ailments. In all his years of practice in his pleasant riverside villa no murder case had ever occurred, apart from an occasional killing by a young servant of an illegitimate child. He signalled to the policeman that they should talk alone, and said to May, 'If you'd leave us for a little, my dear? Go and sit by your mother. She'll probably not sleep for long, and it would be best for her not to be alone when she wakes.' May went out silently.

'Well, Doctor,' said Inspector Burgess, 'this is a nasty business. You'll be handling the medical side at the inquest, I take it.'

'I will. What happened? You're sure it was murder?'

'Quite sure, sir, more's the pity. The body had been deliberately covered — might have lain there for months, given a long hard winter, and that lane's about as lonely a thoroughfare as there is round here. Lovers' Lane, they call it. Not many lovers using it now. And there was no question of accidental death — the back of the skull was smashed in. Not only that, but — I'm afraid this will shock you, sir — the unfortunate young lady had been ravished.'

'My God. Are you sure?'

'No need for a medical man to tell that,' Burgess said grimly.

The doctor went to the window and stood there, his back to Burgess, struggling to control himself. 'May God punish the villain that did it. I'm not a vindictive man, Inspector, but if I had him here... That child — for she was no more, in her nature — that pretty, harmless, affectionate child.' He swung round. 'How am I going to tell them? It will kill her mother. Her father's near death himself; better if he didn't recover, with this to face. The brother's a medical student — he could be told the facts, but the others...'

'I think we can put it aside for the moment, Doctor. The body's been taken to the mortuary, so they won't see it until it's been tidied up, so to speak. If I might make a suggestion? The worst details of the business could be kept from the ladies of the family, as they'd not be coming to the inquest. What we must know from everyone concerned is who might have done it — anyone who might have a motive, or might have got at the victim easily. Motive and opportunity, the usual pointers to the murder. Perhaps you can think of someone yourself?'

Ainslie shook his head. 'I've not seen all that much of the family for some months. It appears that Mr Atkinson should have consulted me long ago about his symptoms, but he didn't; and nobody else has needed medical attention, except for one of the maids with an inflamed hand. The girls were always very healthy. No, I can't tell you who might have been likely to do this awful thing.'

'Well, thank you, Doctor. I shall have to report back to the Manchester station, but I'll be back tomorrow or possibly tonight, and enquiries will be put in hand round the district. Perhaps you might talk to Mr Edwin when he gets back?'

'I'd stay until he does, but I've my rounds to do. Someone should be with these poor women. I'll get my wife to come round, she's a very passable nurse.'

It was May who told Edwin, when he burst in full of the news that his father had spent a comfortable day with no sign of returning fever. They sat up into the night, the two of them, by the fire in Dove's parlour. She had been in bed all day, sometimes asleep, sometimes half-dozing in a laudanum haze, answering mechanically when spoken to. Now Mrs Skerritt was with her; the only member of the staff to remain sufficiently calm.

'It's God's will, Miss May,' she had said. 'Harsh it may seem, but He knows best. She's out of whatever pain she suffered and at rest, and who can say but what she's been spared worse than this, if she'd lived?'

'Edwin, I think I knew,' May said suddenly.

'What?'

'That she was dead. I said I thought she was hiding, but I don't believe I really did. I used to know where she was and what she was doing, nearly always. It's something twins have. And I didn't feel her — sense her being anywhere.'

'No. I can believe that. I was too busy thinking about Father. May, he mustn't be told, for a long time yet. He's very weak — any bad news might give him a relapse. I'll say nothing when I visit him.'

'The police want to talk to you. You'll have to see them tomorrow.'

'Then you must go. That's it — you'll be better out of the house and I can look after Mother and see them as well. Come along, bed. It's almost two o'clock.'

He slept instantly, and May, worn out, hardly knew that she was upstairs and that Mrs Skerritt was gently undressing her. In another room, all Marigold's clothes had been tidied away.

All Inspector Burgess's experienced persuasion was needed to convince Edwin that the case was not only one of murder.

'But who would do such a thing? To Marigold, of all people. She was like a child, she had no admirers, nobody who would have thought of her in that way.'

'Very young children have been victims of rape before now, Mr Atkinson.'

'Yes. Of course. But in this case ... no, I can't think of anyone who would be known to the family.'

It was May who, without knowing the true facts, gave them the name of Enrico Manfredi, and the story of his dismissal. 'But I can't think he would ever have struck her, he was so quiet and gentlemanly, and so fond of her. I thought it was a mistake to let him try to teach her; but he *was* fond of her, and she of him.'

'Fond of her.' Burgess stroked his chin. 'Fond enough to hang about the neighbourhood and lure her away to the very lane where he found her the first time she was lost — or said he did?'

'He would never do such a thing! Why should he?'

The inspector was silent, seeming to make notes. 'It was the same lane, that seems clear. Would she have gone there of her own accord, hoping to meet him?'

'No, of course not. She forgets — forgot things very easily, and it was months ago that she wandered off there. Even then she was half in a dream, as usual. She did mention him often, yes. Well, ask for him. But as for going there, on a cold winter afternoon, no. She'd been quite happy, looking for snowdrops with us. I'm sure the thought of him never entered her head that day. Somebody must have enticed her away. Besides, Mother says a friend of ours thinks he went off to the Italian wars.'

'I see. Thank you, Miss May.'

When Dove came out of her deep shock, within two days, she was quietly resigned to Marigold's death. Under the continuous effects of the sedative her mind had worked out without conscious effort that she must not grieve too much over the ending of a flawed young life, only the manner of it, and of this she knew nothing but that Marigold had died of a blow on the head. Yet she would never quite recover from the tragedy. A subtle change had come over her looks, taking away the freshness they had kept so long. In her mourning wear she could have been fifty or more. She cared nothing for it, only that Joe should be spared the news that would set him back, even when he came home in a fortnight or so. They would lie to protect him, they would set up a conspiracy so that he might never find out the whole of the truth, said Dove, unaware that such a conspiracy had been set up to protect her.

But it was to her that Warburton, unable to find Edwin, ushered in Inspector Burgess. He brought the news that Enrico Manfredi had been found in his old lodging in Glazeheath, and was being held at the local police station which also did duty as a prison. The magistrate would be pleased if a member of the Atkinson family would be present during his questioning.

Dove shrank into her chair. 'I would rather not. I can't believe he would have injured ... and I'd rather not see him. Please.'

'No, no, madam,' Burgess assured her hastily. 'We thought Mr Edwin might oblige.'

May had come in and was listening. 'But he never met Enrico. *I* did, and I could tell you whether he was speaking the truth. I'd like to talk to him, anyway — he knew my sister so well. When do you want me to go?'

Burgess quailed. Awkwardly he explained that it would be impossible to question the man thoroughly in a lady's presence. There were details ... facts might come out that... He floundered. May rescued him.

'Why should not you and Edwin talk to him first, and I'll see him after? Then you can get over your details and facts, and someone can stay with me if you think he's likely to be dangerous.'

Anything less like a dangerous criminal than Enrico could not have been imagined, when Edwin was admitted to the cell in the small lock-up. Slight of build to start with, he seemed to have shrunk inside his clothes with fear and cold. Shabby and unwashed, he looked the very opposite of the flashy charmer Edwin had imagined. He had had many hours of imprisonment and rough questioning from men who shouted at him as though he were an idiot because his speech was foreign. Under the pressure his memory for English words had begun to fail. The Italian phrases he used in desperation only baffled and annoyed his captors, Burgess and a constable. They were quite certain he was guilty, so took no pains to understand him; all they wanted was an intelligible confession which could be taken down in writing and used to transfer him to Manchester's Strangeways gaol.

'Seems to me he's wanting in the head,' Burgess confided to Edwin in Enrico's hearing. 'We can't get a straight answer out of him.'

'Perhaps he doesn't understand the questions.' Edwin had taken in the situation swiftly. 'I think you'd better let me have a talk with him, while you take notes.' He drew up a rickety chair, the only one in the cell, and faced the prisoner, perched nervously on the edge of his pallet bed. His arrival had done nothing to reassure Enrico — another large stranger, who would bellow incomprehensibly at him like the others. Only one ray of hope came to him — could this young man be a lawyer, come to help him?

'*Avvocato?*' he ventured.

Edwin knew no Italian, but his Latin was sound and his studies had kept him in practice. 'No,' he said, and his light gentlemanly voice was a relief to Enrico after the heavily accented voices of the police. 'No, not an advocate. My name is Atkinson. I'm the brother of Miss May and Miss Marigold.'

The Italian's face lit up. 'Mr Atkinson. Will you tell me ... I don't comprehend these men ... they say things about Miss Marigold, that she is dead, that it is my ... I don't know, I forget words.'

'Your fault. That you have killed her. Did you, by the way?'

Enrico shuddered. '*Dio mio.* Then she *is* dead. But that *I* killed her? How could it be?' He crossed himself.

Edwin, summoning his best bedside manner, carefully chose simple words and spoke slowly. He explained that it was thought Enrico might have a grudge against the Atkinsons for dismissing him, and might have returned to the neighbourhood with revenge in mind and lured his one-time pupil away. It was also thought (and he chose his words with particular care) that the tutor might have had an unsatisfied passion for Miss Marigold, and killed her when she resisted his advances, since she had been found to be ... he tried *ravished*, saw that it made no impression, and ventured on *violata*, which he hoped might be recognisable to an Italian ear.

He was understood. Enrico's expression changed from bafflement to utter horror.

'*Madonna!* Not possible! A child, a young maiden, one of God's innocents. What beast would offend Him so? A savage, an animal...' He buried his head in his hands and began to sob. Edwin looked on, embarrassed yet reassured that whatever beast and savage had assaulted and murdered his sister, this was not he. With a glance towards the vigilant constable, who was looking disgusted, he touched the weeping man on the shoulder.

'All right, old chap. I can see this has been a shock. Do you think you can tell me — quietly — where you have been, since you left our house, and why you returned?'

Haltingly the story came out, the constable laboriously taking down Edwin's rapid clarifications of anything obscure in it. At first, shaken and saddened by his dismissal, Enrico had decided to go back to Italy and fight for Garibaldi. It was not disappointed love for his pupil, he explained, since he had felt for her only as a brother might, a great affection. But he had not had enough money for his passage, and had had to stay in London, in poor lodgings among other Italians in Soho. Since he had left his sketching materials in Glazeheath he had no means of earning a living, until a kind fellow lodger had loaned him some paints and told him of a landlord who wanted a new sign painting for his inn. Enrico's bold and original design had pleased him, and the commission had led to others, until the onset of winter weather had made the life of a wandering artist impossible, and, drawn by the memory of happiness, he had come back to Glazeheath to find his old room free and the landlady welcoming.

Yes, she had told him someone had called to ask him to go back to the Lion House, but so much time had passed that he felt he would no longer be wanted, and feared to be rejected again.

'And you swear to me you have never seen any of the family, or been near the house?'

'No. No. I would not have been so bold.' He had found work, he said, teaching the five daughters of a farmer; it brought him enough money for his rent and food, and they were kindly people.

Edwin was not his grandfather's descendant for nothing. If Inspector Burgess wanted the law satisfied, it should be satisfied with that useful thing, an alibi. Or so he hoped.

'Did you go to the farm recently — within the past few days?'

Enrico looked surprised. 'I have stayed there since before the *capo d'anno*. The New Year. The lady invited me to join them for the festival. Then the snows came and she would not let me leave until yesterday. And when I arrive at my lodging, the policeman waits for me.'

Edwin drew a sigh of relief. 'That settles it, then. Did you get it all down, constable?'

'Not all, sir. Be glad if you'd go over it with me.'

'Of course. I'll do that while my sister talks to Mr Manfredi.'

'Sister?' A gleam of superstitious fear crossed Enrico's face, as though the murdered girl might be expected to appear.

'May,' Edwin said. 'She very much wanted to come and see you. And, Mr Manfredi — say nothing to her about the … the … *violata* business. Not suitable for her to hear, you understand.'

'I understand,' Enrico said gravely.

When May came in he stood and made her a courtly bow. She gave him her hand, which he kissed, to the increased disgust of the constable. Edwin took her aside and told her briefly what had been said. 'So he couldn't have been guilty, you see.'

'I knew that. That's why I came, to tell him it would be all right.'

'O wise young judge. Then do it — he's had a bad time, poor chap.'

He left them alone, motioning the constable to do the same, and in the corridor listened to the murmur of their voices,

May's soothing, Enrico's emotional. He hoped that nothing May should not hear was being said. When she came out she looked sad but composed. 'I think,' she said, 'it's worse for him than for us, in a sort of way. You see, he worshipped Marigold as a kind of saint, so far as I understand him, and to be accused of killing her was like — well, being accused of insulting the Virgin Mary. And then he's so sure that if he had been allowed to go on teaching her he'd have done her good, made her brighter. He doesn't think he's anything left to live for, now.'

Her eyes were filling with tears. Edwin took her arm and hurried her away.

In Burgess's office he wrote out his statement of what the prisoner had said to him, and gave the address of the farm where Enrico had been staying at the time of the murder. The inspector was surprised and disappointed. A very promising case, which would have helped his promotion, looked like slipping through his hands.

On their way home in the trap May, who had been quiet, said, 'There's something I haven't been told, isn't there?'

'About what?'

'Marigold's death. Was it just a blow on the head?'

Edwin hesitated for a second, clicking his tongue to the horse, which was going quite fast enough and very sensibly took no notice. 'That was what killed her, yes. Nothing else.'

May glanced at him. 'You can't deceive me, Eddie. Remember how I always knew when you were telling a lie, you were so bad at it? There was something worse, wasn't there, and I can guess what it is.' She shuddered. 'Mother thought of that the first time she was missing. It was true this time, wasn't it? Oh, poor Marigold.'

'I doubt if she knew much about it,' Edwin said grimly. 'From what Burgess says there was a violent blow on the skull from behind that killed her almost instantly. Anything else was … after. I shall know more when the inquest's held. Nobody else from home is to attend it — not you, certainly. Thank God Father's still in the infirmary. I'll have to break it to him before I go back to Edinburgh. I wouldn't leave that job to you or Mother.'

May leaned sideways and kissed his cheek. 'Thank you, Eddie.'

The coroner's verdict was murder by a person or persons unknown. They brought Marigold home afterwards in her coffin, dressed in a white gown she had liked; May had sent it to the mortuary. The damaged head was hidden on a lacy pillow, the marble-white face a statue's. May filled the cold crossed hands with snowdrops from the garden, the snowdrops she had been searching for on the day she died.

After the quiet funeral they came home, the three of them and Basil. A red sun was setting on the horizon, a robin singing on a bush by the door. In the house, Basil asked Edwin to come into Joe's office.

'I want a word with you, away from the women's ears. I've got a pretty fair idea who the murderer is. I wish I'd known before they put that teacher through the mill for it. If I hadn't had to go to Bolton that day I'd have stopped all that.'

Edwin stared. 'How can you know? They only arrested Manfredi because they thought he had a motive. Who else had?'

'Someone with a grudge against your father and a habit of going crazy with drink. He got sacked last year, and I let Joe do it personally. He's been back since, drinking with the hands, stirring up trouble. Your dad never guessed who it was, but I did, and I got on his track. I've just found out where he's living. I'll get Burgess on to him in the morning. Don't say anything to your mother about this — I won't have her bothered any more, she's taken enough.'

Within twenty-four hours his prediction was fulfilled. The police discovered William Donnell in a working men's hostel in Manchester, sober for once after a bout of drinking. At Basil's suggestion, they let him have more drink after he had been arrested. His sullen refusal to talk led to a burst of maudlin confession. His wife had run away from him with another man, he was crazed for a woman. So he had walked back to Deansbury and seen Marigold alone in the coppice that adjoined the gardens, and had asked her to come for a walk, promising to find her the flowers for which she was searching. When she had failed to understand what he wanted of her, and tried to run away, he had picked up a stone and brought it down on her head.

So it was Donnell whose arrest brought praise for Inspector Burgess, Donnell who went to Strangeways gaol and was subsequently hanged there. Marigold was avenged. Her wistful presence would dwell in the Lion House for months, for a year and more, while her family wore mourning for her, and would gradually fade from the place, almost from their minds.

Edwin packed his bags to return to Edinburgh as eagerly as though he were going on holiday. Away from the shadows and sorrows of home, back to his friends and his studies. His boyhood was over, and May's girlhood. When they met with their cousins again they would be men and women, and their lives quite changed.

CHAPTER FOURTEEN

Two years brought changes to Eagle Hall. Its master was no longer Jesse Bradshaw, MP, but Sir Jesse, proud possessor of a knighthood graciously bestowed by Her Majesty during a period of pique against Lord Palmerston, her prime minister. Jesse was not, like her dear lost Lord Melbourne, a Whig, but the sharp-eyed monarch was well aware of a certain resemblance he bore to that lord, a warm cheerfulness and a gift for extending it to all sorts and conditions of people, and a quality at once fatherly, courtly and protective which her woman's instinct found out during his holding of a minor office in Derby's very brief ministry of 1858. He had been charming to her angel, the Prince Consort, and had discussed a favourite project of the Prince's as though it were the one dearest to his heart.

So when her Angel died in February 1861, taking a great part of her life with him, she awarded this not particularly eminent northern politician her accolade, as it were a memorial brooch to wear for Albert. True, his wife had been involved in scandal and so could not be received at court, but she took no part in London society and so no difficulty arose. The royal sword touched Jesse's shoulder, the plump royal hand was extended, and Jesse rose up a knight.

Eleanor was delighted. She was not precisely a snob, but there was no doubt that a title did something for one. White-haired and elegant, Lady Bradshaw swam about in Clitheroe society, such as it was, enjoying the compliments and congratulations and edifying the young with tales of life at the court of the Prince Regent, some apocryphal but all entertaining.

Only one thing flawed her pleasure: Lucy was not by her side. Now twenty-three, Lucy had asserted her independence and gone off to lead her own life; something unheard-of for an unmarried young female to do, but then, the gossips said, Miss Bradshaw was and always had been most shockingly spoilt. So odd and eccentric, too, devoting herself to the care of animals, as though they had sensibilities, when everyone knew that the proper recipients of charity were the poor, and heathens and lepers, and it would have been a great deal more becoming in Miss Bradshaw to be seen distributing alms or taking part in a ladies' sewing circle.

Sublimely oblivious to criticism, Lucy went her own way. From her father she extracted the money to buy a neat four-square house in the village of Halton, by the River Lune, just north of Lancaster. Its attraction for Lucy was the large stable yard at the back, with outbuildings enough for all the creatures she took in. She was wise enough not to deal with horses and cattle, since there were men whose living it was to doctor them. Her patients were smaller and more manageable, creatures too unprofitable to warrant money being spent on them — and Lucy made no charge for her services, only invited contributions in aid of the patients' food.

To her natural gift for handling beasts and birds she had added a considerable knowledge of veterinary matters. From Edwin she had borrowed works on anatomy — human, of course, but translatable into animal terms — and others from which she learnt simple surgery and basic medicine. She made mistakes, sometimes fatal, and wept over them, the only times anyone saw Lucy in tears. But for the most part she could cure anything that was not beyond curing when it was brought to her. Of the four large rooms on the ground floor of her house she had turned one into a surgery, carpetless with whitewashed walls and a large well-scrubbed kitchen table. Antiseptics were still unknown, but Lucy believed firmly in cleanliness, and everything that touched her patients was as spotless as her own large beautiful hands. Sometimes the patients objected to being cleaned up, but none escaped it.

Eleanor was horrified by Lucy's domestic arrangements. 'But that room *smells,* my dear! One can smell it all over the house.'

'Nobody's yet invented a scentless animal, Mama.'

'Of course not, but still … could you not use one of the stables?'

'Surrounded by flies in summer and icicles in winter? Thank you, no.'

Eleanor surveyed the front parlour disparagingly. 'You could have made this a good deal more elegant. A few good pictures from home, and one or two nice pieces instead of this plain stuff. And there's some porcelain you could have for the mantelpiece, instead of those two common china dogs.'

'The people who come here, Mama, are mostly cottagers. They're used to plain furniture and china dogs. If this house were full of elegant costly things they'd be frightened off and not come again. Besides,' she added, 'I like plain things myself. I know I was brought up with beautiful ones, but there's something in me that enjoys rocking chairs and kitchen dressers.'

Eleanor said nothing. She wondered if Lucy's liking for the unpretentious could have come from the serving-girl who was her real mother, Sally Winterslow of Wendslake in Buckinghamshire, who had shared Jesse's bed for a night. They had often talked of Sally, she and Jesse, when her first angry jealousy had died out and her frustrated motherhood had been fulfilled by the bringing up of Sally's baby. Sally had been gentle and defenceless; Lucy's purposeful attitude to life was all Jesse's. Like him, she knew exactly where she was going. But that was not to say one should not try to guide her.

'I do think you should have a companion, my dear. It looks very strange, a young lady living alone as you do, and men coming to the house.'

'Men? I don't run a bordello, Mama.'

'Don't be naughty. You know what I mean — men with animals, birds — oh, anything you like. It isn't right that you should receive them alone.'

'As a matter of fact very few men come here. Too lazy. They send their wives or their children. And if any men did behave badly, I fancy I could deal with them.' She looked complacently at her brown forearms, spangled with freckles, revealed to the elbow by her rolled-up sleeves. 'If not, I'd only need to let Brushy out. He snaps at everyone but me.' Brushy was the fox she had taken in as an orphaned cub, who had developed an obsessive love for Lucy, following her about like a spaniel and sleeping on her lap when opportunity offered. 'Besides, Mama, I'm not alone. Joan is a perfectly capable chaperone.'

'Joan Butterworth? But she's a maid, a servant. She worked in our kitchens until you decided to bring her with you.'

'I don't care if she worked down a coal mine. She's honest and sensible, and twice my age, and we get on together extremely well. What would I do with some fussy lady companion, shrieking and reaching for the sal volatile every time a mouse looked out of the wainscot? Joan likes animals and they like her. She can hold one down while I'm working on it, and that's more use to me than airs and graces.'

Eleanor tried her last bid for Lucy's respectability. 'I'd be quite willing for Bertha to live with you. That would make everything look…'

'Mama, Mama! Do see things as they are, I beg you. Bertha would hate this sort of life. She's nervous with animals, St Francis or no St Francis — and she adores Eagle Hall and flower-arranging and paying social calls and languishing in the arms of young men at hunt balls. Anything less like a nun I never saw — she's much more like you than I am, I'm sure. No, don't wish Bertha on me, if you please, though I like her well enough.'

Eleanor sighed, not without relief. It had not been entirely true that she would have been willing to let Bertha go. The girl who had come to Eagle Hall as a timid waif had become almost a part of it, certainly a part of the Bradshaw family. She was, indeed, just the daughter Eleanor had expected Lucy to be: gentle, feminine, domesticated, delighting in beautiful furniture and decorations. Sometimes Eleanor would find her lovingly stroking the linen-fold panelling of the oldest rooms in the house or sitting in a deep window seat, touching the smooth surface of the deep rose silk curtains Eleanor had sent for to France, her eyes dreaming. And she was so much a girl of the period, the once-cropped hair now grown into shining ringlets, the piquantly pretty face and neat figure greatly admired by the eligible males of the district, and some less eligible. She was something of an intriguing mystery, too. At her own request Eleanor had not revealed her origins, describing her only as a *protégée* of her niece's. Could she be an Atkinson, people wondered? Not that she was in the least like the family. Another rumour was that she was a by-blow of Jesse's; something which, ironically, had never been said about Lucy, who was.

Her marriage chances were much on Eleanor's mind. She dressed well, on Eleanor's generous allowance, but was always scrupulously honest in admitting to those who fished for information — usually mothers with sons to marry off — that she was an orphan dependent on the Bradshaw's charity. So there was no father to bestow a handsome dowry on her, no landed property to accompany the giving of her hand. Such a pity; merely an ornament at parties, much in demand for the supper dance. If only she had been the Bradshaw daughter, and not that strong-minded tomboy Lucy — who, it was whispered, had been seen wearing *men's clothes*.

It was not quite the case, but near enough. For her work about the stables and the half-acre field where she grazed her two horses, Sir Walter and Peveril, Lucy wore tailor-made riding breeches and high boots, a rough cord jacket and what may have been a blouse but looked remarkably like a shirt. The neighbours averted their eyes, or else stared rudely. Edwin, when he visited her, was all admiration. She was at the height of her beauty now, her complexion rich from sun and air, for she refused to hide it under a hat as other women did, her brown hair, shot with touches of gold, flying loose about her shoulders. Edwin thought she looked like a nymph, or one of the ladies admired by the poet laureate, a daughter of the gods — divinely tall, and most divinely fair — or the Princess Ida who sat between two tame leopards...

...such eyes were in her head.
And so much grace and power, breathing down
From over her arched brows...

He was not sure that he was exactly in love with her, in a spoony sort of way, only that she fascinated him, and had done for years, that he was entirely comfortable and at home in her company, and that he would willingly spend the rest of his life seeing a great deal of her. He visited Lancaster during every vacation on his way back to Scotland, having paid a dutiful, if not very enjoyable, visit to his home. Marigold's death had aged and saddened his parents and thrown a dark shadow over the Lion House. His father would never be the same man as before his illness; grey, bowed, very silent and given to melancholy, he would sit for hours without speaking. Unable to run the mill and the estate as he had done, he had taken Basil into partnership; the firm was now Atkinson and Absalom. Behind Dove's eyes there was always trouble lurking, a fear that some terrible thing might strike at another of her family. And May looked after them both, her natural frivolity quenched, for her father was too tetchy these days to appreciate jokes and her mother needed a soft voice and quiet ways about her. Edwin hoped May was not going to turn into an old maid, but it began to look like that. He tackled her about it.

'You'll be old before your time if you don't get out more and have some fun. You watch out.'

She shrugged. 'How can I? Mother pretends she wants me to, but I can tell she doesn't mean it. It's impossible to ask people here, and I feel so guilty if I leave the house for more than an hour. Heigh-ho! How gay it used to be, when we were young. Do you remember the night Mr Dickens came to dinner, and I was so rude and pert to him? We never see anyone interesting now. But it can't be helped. You can just think yourself lucky, Eddie. A man can get away — a girl can't.'

'What would you do, though, if someone asked you to marry him?'

'Do? Well, I suppose I should have to refuse. Unless — yes, unless I were to fall wildly, madly, excitingly in love. I know I could, with the right man. Then I think I'd do anything. It would have to be someone frightfully rich, so that we could afford a really good companion for Mother and perhaps a nurse for Father — I'm sure he needs one. Yes, that's what I need — a prince on a snow-white charger.'

'I hope you mean all that,' Edwin said seriously. 'Do you know what you said just now? *When we were young.* You're young now, but you don't feel it, and small wonder. Women don't improve with keeping — look at Mother and Aunt Belle. The sooner your prince rides up, with or without the snow-white charger, the better.'

'Oh, fudge. I was only romancing. I'm perfectly well as I am. I might as well settle down to being a dutiful spinster daughter in any case, if we're going to be poor people, as it seems we are.'

The American Civil War had been raging for over a year, and the Federal Navy had at last succeeded in blocking the seven main southern ports from which raw cotton was exported. In the cotton districts of England the result was disastrous. Mills began to close as supplies diminished. No cotton, no work, no work, no pay, no pay, no food. Desperate, the mill workers began to sell off anything that would buy bread for their children: the family Bible, a treasured watch, furniture, even the baby's bedding and shoes. For the shadow of the workhouse hung over them, a place of shame and dread. Pavements rang with the desultory sound of clogs, not hurrying to work but idling at street corners, lingering wistfully around bakehouses and the pubs where men could no longer afford even a weekly pint of ale. Charitable people wrote

touching ballads to be sold for the Operatives Relief Fund, and
street singers invented their own.

'We can't get our cotton from the old Kentucky shore:
Oh short time, short time, come again no more!'

By the summer of 1862 Atkinson and Absalom's mill was
closed. Joe sold some of his shares to provide what he could
for his workers, besides remitting their rent. At least they
should have a roof over their heads, and as much food and
clothing as he could afford to buy. The Lion House kept a
poor table, every scrap that could possibly be spared going to
the estate. Even so, the workers suffered. Some of them
walked to Manchester to sing in the streets, shamefaced and
pitiable, for what few coppers their music could earn them.
They sang hymns and sacred songs known to everybody. Some
had kept concertinas or cornets out of the pawn shop, and
played instead of singing. Joe had never thought to see the
dwellers on his proud estate reduced to such humiliation.

Some cotton was coming in from India, but it was hardly
worth the handling. 'Surat' was a vastly inferior cotton which
cost twice as much as the American variety: dirty, dry, hard to
handle and sometimes full of pebbles. The spinners hated it.
Basil had tried two consignments of it, to keep the mill
working, then refused to buy any more. 'Throwing good
money after bad, that's all it is.' He added to Joe, 'We're in for
a long war, here as well as in America. I don't give a lot for
Lancashire's chances of coming out of it the same as she went
in.'

The summer passed gloomily at Deansbury. Edwin had
visited the family at the beginning of the vacation, then gone
with friends on a fishing holiday in the Highlands. Then, as the

time for him to return to Edinburgh drew near, a letter came which brought new cheerfulness with it. The postmark was Lancaster; the letter had been written from St Leonard's Gate.

'My dear Parents and May,

Rejoice, the deed is done! I'm passed, quailified, ready to be capped, a Bachelor of Medicine! Edwin Atkinson, MB. How does that sound? Pretty good, to me. Mind you, I swotted hard enough for it, so I suppose I deserved to pass, but it comes as a very agreeable shock, and the long grind was worth it all. Now all I've got to do is to rise by rapid degrees to professional eminence...

In Lancaster, too, there was quiet rejoicing. Ephraim sent down to the cellars for two bottles of specially fine old wine, 'laid down before you were born, my lad.' The silver plate bearing the family crest was polished up for use at dinner, Margaret wore her best cap and a silk gown, and at the table, after they had raised their glasses, Ephraim presented his grandson with fifty guineas.

'A reward for diligence and application. Do what you please with it, but if I were you I'd save it, and put a little to it from time to time. That way it will grow.'

Edwin blushed with pleasure. 'I *do* thank you, Grandfather. It's jolly kind and generous of you. Yes, I will save it, only ... I might buy just a little something to keep as a souvenir.'

The souvenir was not for himself. He had sufficient sense not to buy it without making certain enquiries, though he window-shopped eagerly at every jeweller's in Lancaster, gaining himself some sharp looks from proprietors who happened to be looking out. Then he rode to Halton.

The day was bright and cold. He walked round the side of the house in case Lucy were in the stable yard or the paddock, but there was no sign of her. He found her indoors, in the parlour adjoining her treatment room. She was sitting by the fire in a rocking chair, covered from neck to foot in a coarse sacking apron, and on her lap, wrapped in a blanket, was what looked at first sight like a baby but proved to be a very young pig.

She glanced up, smiling. 'Edwin, how nice, I didn't know you were in the town.'

'I'd have come earlier today, but to tell the truth Grandfather did me rather well last night with the rosy — the flowing cups, you know — and I woke up slightly boozed this morning, so I took some exercise to get my head clear before presenting myself.'

'Very civil of you to think of my feelings. Would some tea complete the cure, and some of Joan's scones?'

'I should just say it would, if it's no trouble.'

'None. Joan!'

The buxom Joan Butterworth loomed up in the doorway, bringing a scent of cake-baking with her, and glowing from her work. 'Eh, Mr Edwin, I'm glad to see thee. We thought we'd seen last o' thee till Christmas.'

Edwin kissed her on both cheeks, to her evident pleasure.

'Well, I never. What's that for?' she asked.

He had been meaning to keep his news until he was alone with Lucy, but the temptation was too much.

'Because, Joan — because, Lucy — it's not Mr Edwin any more, but Doctor Edwin. There!'

Joan flew at him and caught him in an enveloping embrace. 'Nay, that's grand! A real doctor, after all this time... Us'll have to mind our manners now, I can see. Wilt tha look at my chilblains for nowt?'

Lucy put out a hand, with a warm smile, and took his. He held it until she gently withdrew hers. 'I'm so glad, Eddie. Well done, indeed. I always knew you would, of course.'

'So did I — I think. It's the most tremendous relief, though.'

'Tell me all about it while Joan gets the tea.'

Only too ready to oblige, he took her through his pre-examination nerves, the papers, easy or alarming, the fearful *viva* with an examiner who delighted in pipping one with impossible questions; then the long wait for a result, and finally the result itself, his feelings on receiving it. To all this outpouring of youthful egotism she listened with maternal patience and only the faintest hint of amusement. Pouring tea, which was served in kitchen china of a thickness to make Eleanor wince, she said, 'I'm glad we have a doctor in the family now. Papa's politics are all very well, but who knows what good they're doing? And law is so stick-in-the-mud. Poor Laurence seems quite stupefyingly bored with it. Now *you* are going to devote your life to something which will benefit from the advance of science in this wonderful age. I shouldn't be surprised if another twenty years saw medicine quite revolutionised.'

'I say, what a platform speaker you'd make!' Edwin exclaimed admiringly. 'Quite the New Woman, aren't you.'

'What, with a red nose and steel-rimmed spectacles?'

'No, indeed, far from it. With a beautiful straight nose and eyes like … well, I don't quite know, but quite spiffing, anyway.' He gulped down a scone, determined to come to the point. 'Lucy. I want to ask you… you must know what. Will you marry me?'

'*What?*'

'You heard me the first time. I've given it a great deal of thought recently, when I was up in the Highlands with those chaps, on my own fishing a lot of the time, among the mountain silences and boundless lochs. And I decided that you and I would make perfect mates. I've always admired you like anything, and made no secret of it. I say, can't you put that pig down while we're having a serious conversation?'

'No, I can't. It needs warmth and reassurance. When it was brought in this morning I thought it had pneumonia, but now —'

'I don't care what it has. Lucy, listen to me. We could have such a splendid life together, both with medical interests —'

'And what would we live on?' Lucy interrupted.

'Why, my fees, of course.'

'Now? When you're not even capped?'

'I am — bar the ceremony.'

'That doesn't matter. You're going to have to struggle for a long time, Edwin. If you have ideas of putting up your plate in some fashionable district and immediately attracting a stream of titled patients, forget about it. Without a great deal of money — and I'm sure your father hasn't a lot to throw about at the moment, from what May writes — the best you can hope for is a partnership in a modest sort of practice, or an assistant's place on the staff of a hospital. *That* won't keep two people.'

Edwin looked sulky. 'You seem to know a lot about it.'

'Only because,' Lucy's cheeks were faintly pinker than before, 'I've thought sometimes about your prospects. You're a very optimistic young man, you know, because nothing has ever gone really wrong for you. There *is* hardship, even in a doctor's life, at first, unless he's particularly lucky. If you and I were to marry now, we should both be very uncomfortable. And you need more time to be free — to gain experience.'

'I've plenty of experience. I haven't lived on my own in Edinburgh for nearly five years without seeing a bit of life.'

'And love? Oh, there's no need to be embarrassed. Everybody knows what medical students are like.'

'I wouldn't call it love,' Edwin protested. 'Adventure, perhaps. Gaining experience.'

'I hope the young ladies were gaining it as well,' Lucy said drily. 'I rather doubt whether you thought about that. Speaking of which, what about my point of view? I want to go on doing what I'm doing now, for some time at least, without complicating my life with a husband. I know you think my work with these creatures is some sort of amiable eccentricity, and the local people look on me as something between a white witch and a loose woman. "A young lass living on her own, eh dear, it's not seemly." Well, I really don't mind what you or they think, or whether I'm making any great contribution to the world.'

She stroked the pig, which grunted, or snored; Edwin was not quite sure which. He was tempted to snatch the thing from her lap and try some ardent persuasion of a different kind, but at that moment a scratching began at the door, and Lucy gently deposited the pig on a chair and got up to let in the young fox. It jumped up at her to be caressed, its strong feral scent and the very sharp teeth it displayed in a dog-like grin, causing Edwin to move his chair back in some apprehension.

'You see,' Lucy said, quite aware of what his thoughts had been a moment since. 'I'm very well protected. Brush makes a splendid Cerberus, don't you, pet? Now, dear Edwin, I think you'd better go. Don't be angry with me; I promise you I'm right about this. I do thank you for all the help you've given me, the books and the advice.'

'Does that mean I'm not to see you again?' Edwin was dismayed, and showed it. Lucy patted his arm consolingly.

'Of course not, you silly person. Come and see me whenever you like — though you won't have much time once you start looking for somewhere to practise. I wish you all possible good luck.'

To his surprise and pleasure she embraced him lightly and put a warm kiss on his cheek. She was not much shorter than himself. He thought of other girls who had kissed him, and had smelt of perfume and flowers. Lucy gave off an aroma of fur, feathers, strong soap, and something that could only be pig. It was curious that he felt not in the least repelled.

At the door, on a strong impulse, he said, 'Will you do one thing for me? Something that will make me very happy?'

She hesitated. 'What?'

'Will you come to the ceremony — to see me *capped and doctor'd an' a*? It's a long way, I know, and I don't suppose you can spare the time. It's just … that I should like to see you there.'

'Of course I will,' she said simply.

She kept her word, and was the only member of the family to be present when the name of Edwin Atkinson was sonorously proclaimed as having gained the degree of Bachelor of Medicine. Proud of his cap and gown, fully aware of the classically handsome figure he cut, he was almost as proud of Lucy, spectacularly beautiful in lupin blue, the wild-rose freshness of her face standing out amongst the pale ladies round her, serenely conscious of masculine admiration. There was a graduates' party in the evening, a noisy drunken celebration at which Edwin was unusually quiet, and drank much less than usual. His comrades accused him of being smitten; he denied it, but not too emphatically.

Some six weeks after the ceremony, Lucy received a letter telling her that Edwin had been appointed Assistant Physician Accoucheur to a Preston hospital. 'You wait,' he said, 'one of these days it will be Consulting Obstetric Surgeon, and there won't be room on my brass plate for the string of letters.'

One person who was not enthralled by Edwin's success was his cousin Laurence. He was well aware of Edwin's frequent visits to Lucy, and now she had travelled all the way to Edinburgh to be with him. Night after night Laurence wrestled with his conscience, trying to exorcise the obsessive jealousy that wracked him. He knew he should be glad for Edwin, happy that Lucy had chosen to witness his triumph. But he was not. It seemed that Edwin was high in her favour. Why should he not win her, handsome, talented, light-hearted as he was?

Laurence knew himself to be painfully shy, without wit or charm; not a young doctor with prospects but a lawyer's clerk kept in his job more by his grandfather's charity than anything else — he was often made to feel Booth's contempt for him, and the other clerks' impatience with his slow work.

Yet Lucy meant so much to him. She was the one beautiful thing in his life, his dream, his ideal. Hopefully he travelled out to Halton every Sunday, to take tea, and gaze at her, and make what conversation he could. Lucy had normally no time for social calls and small talk, but she put on a fair display of entertainment for Laurence, sorry for his loneliness. If ever there was a fish out of water it was he, a man with a child's problems, at twenty-three still torn between his father and his mother. He had not enough money to take bachelor lodgings, and still shared Belle's house, painfully, shamedly aware of the men she entertained in direct defiance of George's deed of separation; only now it was done furtively instead of openly. Laurence lived upstairs, in the room he had converted from a spare bedroom to a parlour, holding his books and enough furniture to make him reasonably comfortable. He ate by himself in the bare little apartment off the kitchen, leaving the dining room to his mother and her guests.

His father was living in Lancaster now, since a recurrent feverish illness had kept him from sea. He had taken lodgings in Common Garden Street, rooms above a shop which he shared with his daughter. Magnolia's very existence had alienated the Dilworths from George. To come home with a daughter born out of wedlock, and black! Belle had made sure that her own wrongs were known far and wide, so the *protégée* story had never even been aired. It suited George very well to live with Magnolia, whose tastes fitted in very nicely with his own, but neither of them cared for the idea of being joined by Laurence. In the company of his pleasure-loving father and half-sister, Laurence's feelings of inadequacy were even stronger than in his own home. With them he had nothing to say that seemed to matter. He knew that his presence cast a damper on them, amiable as they both were to him. Magnolia had never forgotten the night he gave her his own blanket; she remembered such things, just as she remembered slights. Poor Laurence ... but how deadly boring he was.

Lucy no longer called him poor Laurence. Even her patience was wearing thin with him, his aura of unhappiness and the adoring melancholy gaze which never left her. His looks had not improved with manhood. The fair hair had turned to a nondescript mouse colour, and the large hare-like eyes looked out through small, ageing spectacles. Wishing very much that he would not stare at her so, she went on with her usual tasks instead of sitting with her hands folded in her lap, as befitted a lady receiving a social call. Watching her rolling up newly washed bandages into neat rolls, and pinning them firmly,

Laurence asked her, 'Would you like me to read to you while you are doing that, Lucy? It might relieve some of the tedium of the task.'

'I don't find it tedious, thank you. And I don't particularly like being read to.'

'I have just read a very thoughtful novel, *Adam Bede*. I think you would find it excellent, and I don't in the least mind reading it again.'

'I do happen to have read it myself. I'm not a complete vegetable, you know. I did have rather a good education. Oh dear, what a pompous thing to say, and how ungrateful of me. Laurence,' beginning on the hem of a small blanket for an animal invalid, 'why don't you write yourself, instead of reading all the time? You used to compose poetry, I remember.'

Laurence flushed, also remembering his pallid and pining imitations of Wordsworth, addressed to Lucy. He had ceased to write them, since she had received them with brisk matter-of-factness and sometimes criticism, instead of meltingly, as he had hoped. 'No,' he said. 'I do so much copying work that my hand is too tired by evening to wander over the paper.'

Lucy suppressed a laugh. 'How sad. Excuse me, something's whining.' She went into the surgery, where Laurence heard her talking as if to a person. Returning, she said, 'Just a splint getting uncomfortable. That spaniel has the sensibilities of an aristocrat — give me mongrels every time for bearing things cheerfully. The better the breed, the worse the patient.'

Laurence was struggling for expression, twisting his hands together. 'My dear Lucy — I hope you will not think me impertinent, but I do wonder whether you are right to spend your time and your great talents on these animals. After all, they are only beasts of the field, not human souls in need of rescue from all kinds of perils. Would it not be better to turn to more womanly duties, the care of the poor or even the nursing of the sick, if you feel you have the gift? There are little children...'

Lucy's expression stopped him. When she was angry, and it was seldom, she could look very like her father making a vehement speech from the back benches of the Opposition, a tide of hot colour flooding her face and her eyes dangerously bright.

'Cousin, I've had to listen to remarks like that from other people — too many times, but I'm damned, yes, damned, if I'll take them from you! If it comes to beasts, may I refer you to the columns of the newspapers for beastly behaviour on the part of things walking about on two legs? Are animals treacherous, or immoral? Do they steal for gain, or murder for revenge? Do they waste their time and other people's in a lot of empty talk? If it comes to simple virtue I'll back animals every time, yes, and birds and fish and anything you care to name. Do you suppose there are any animals behind that bitter struggle in America which is condemning our mill workers to famine? — unless you count wretched horses innocently dragged into the bloody business. And another thing — I'm sorry to find you among the ranks who assume that because I devote myself to animals I must be some sort of cold-hearted fiend to my fellow humans. You might be interested to know that a gang of children from the mill families come here every day and do work for me, mucking out or feeding or going errands, for money. It's not much, but it helps to keep them alive. I do it partly because I feel as responsible for them as all of us with enough to eat must feel, and partly because it's good for my father's reputation as a humanitarian.'

She stopped for breath, and saw Laurence's stricken look. Her wrath dissolved into smiles.

'My dear boy, I'm sorry. I didn't mean to speech-make at you like that. What a virago you must think me.' To her horror, tears were starting in his eyes. 'It was just that I'm tired of hearing these things and I can't bear that anyone close to me should misjudge me…' He was on the floor, at her feet, his head buried in her lap, his shoulders heaving with sobs. 'Don't, please. Oh, don't. I've said I apologise, but only because it's you. I don't take a word back, mind. Come, now, get up.'

He lifted a tear-stained face. 'Am I … close to you? Lucy, do you love me at all? I love you so much, so very, very much … always have…'

'Yes, I know.' She stroked his hair. 'You've made that very plain. Of course I'm very fond of you.' She murmured consolations, as though he were a hurt dog. Gradually the tears subsided, and he scrambled to his feet and returned to his chair. 'That's better,' she said. 'Can you bear another lecture, do you think?'

He nodded.

'Well, then, dear Laurence, please forget all about loving me except as a cousin. No, don't protest. I'm not at all the right sort of woman for you, if you'll only think about it. You've had a very unhappy time with your mother, and you need a wife who is absolutely her opposite. That is not to say anything against Aunt Belle, and I won't say any more about her. But what you need is somebody motherly — which I'm not — and utterly feminine — which I'm not — and altogether sweet and gentle and full of good works. There are plenty of them about if you'll only go out and meet people.'

'They wouldn't want me,' he muttered.

'Yes, they would. Oh, why are you your own worst enemy? Do you know, if I were you I shouldn't read *Adam Bede* again, I should read Samuel Smiles's *Self-Help*. I expect you could get it from the circulating library. It shows, by many examples, how to improve one's lot in life and make oneself altogether a better person. Will you promise me to read it?'

'Yes, Lucy.' He fished in his pocket for paper and pencil, and meticulously wrote the title down. Lucy was watching him, hoping he would not break out again, wishing fervently that he would go, studying the bent head, stooped shoulders and anxious pale face, and wondering why some other image was in her mind. A ray of late sunshine filtering through the window faded behind a cloud, then shone out again, illuminating him and throwing a far brighter light into Lucy's mind.

'Laurence!' she cried, startling him. 'I've just had a flash of inspiration, and I *know* it's the right one. Laurence, you must take holy orders!'

Uncomprehending, he stared, as she talked excitedly on. 'Don't you see, you would make a perfect clergyman — studious, pious, devoted to your fellow men and all that, shunning worldliness ... oh, I can just see you in the pulpit. Did you do Greek at school?'

'Yes, but...'

'There you are, then. You'll need a bit of Hebrew but I expect you'll soon master that. You must start training at once, and if your grandfather complains about you leaving the office tell him I'll talk to him about it. As to the money, I'm sure that will come from somewhere, it always does. Now go away and think about it.'

'I shall pray. Yes, I shall pray.'

'You do that. Go along now, and you'll be in nice time for evensong at Halton church — it's only just over the way, and there's a most interesting Roman altar and a Danish cross...'

She shut the door on him and leaned against it, puffing with relief. Joan looked in. 'I heard a lot o' that. Sorted him out then, have you?'

'I don't know, but I hope so. Oh, dear, I wouldn't go through that again. Poor boy, I pity him, but he does wear one out so. I hope he's praying now, like anything, and getting the right answers.'

'Praying never did any harm, Miss Lucy,' Joan said severely.

'Oh, I know, and I'm not mocking, because I swear I had a kind of vision. He was sitting there, with the sunlight just catching his head, and then it came to me — the portrait of his great-uncle John at St Leonard's Gate, the one who was vicar of St John's and died in his pulpit. Laurence is the very image of him. How could I not have seen it before? And I thought of course, that's what he must do.'

'And what you think's allus right, I don't doubt,' observed Joan drily. 'Well, time'll tell. And now you've got your cousin's troubles washed and ironed, what about tackling his dad and that Magnolia? Strikes me it's her as needs praying for.'

CHAPTER FIFTEEN

Magnolia felt in no particular need of prayer as she sat before her dressing-table mirror and contemplated herself. There was no shortage of light from the extravagance of candles in the room — two flanking the mirror, two branches on the mantelpiece, besides a lamp on the table. Papa was always warning her that one day she would set herself on fire, but she laughed at him.

She was very pleased with what she saw. Her ball dress for the Assembly Rooms that night was cut immodestly low, exposing her shoulders and threatening to slip off them altogether. But all ladies dressed, or undressed, as daringly as that for evening, and not all could boast of shoulders like Magnolia's: golden-brown, gleaming with health, with a tempting swell of bosom below and a full round throat above, setting off the necklet of twined gold and pearls George had given her for her birthday.

Her face was in a dark glow of excitement, the firefly reflections of candle flames dancing in her huge eyes. Tonight her hair was brushed back as rigidly as its texture would allow, and massed on her neck in curls like a great bunch of black grapes. She leaned forward, anxious that it did not look too like native hair. No, the elegant small wreath of artificial mistletoe with pearls for berries camouflaged that, and the heavy application of Papa's pomade had put a good shine on it. It was the best that could be managed for one who had not European hair and longed for it.

She had wanted a dress of bright yellow, but George, who would have given her anything, discouraged her. It would be too gaudy, he said, for her colouring; she must not look cheap. So, protesting, she compromised with a golden apricot tarlatan, agreeing in the end that it suited her very well. The tight bodice gave way to a wide spread of skirts, looped here and there with more artificial green leaves. There were gold bracelets on her arms, long earrings of gilt filigree swung from her ears, and her fan was of ivory, cream silk and feathers.

'Yes, dear girl,' she said to her reflection, 'you'll do.'

It was very necessary to keep her pride fed in this town where she was the only female of her colour, unless one counted a few sailors' women round the docks. At first she had minded very much the stares, loud comments, and turned heads as she passed; had shrunk at the jeers of children and youths. She had been facetiously asked whether she was on her way to Gillow's to be made into a mahogany what-not, and whether she had run away from the war in the 'Mericas because Abe Lincoln was losing. It had been instinctive to answer back, with the sort of words she would have used to louts in Haiti. But when she went home to George, weeping, her gown stained by thrown dirt, he told her to ignore such insults in future. 'You're as much of a lady as their mothers — a dam' sight more of one, in fact. And you belong in Lancaster because that's where the Dilworths belong. Hold your head up and look like the princess you are.' After that she had no trouble, and as she learned to dress less showily, the stares and comments grew less.

Except from young men. They had never seen so exotically desirable a creature before. Drawn like toys on a string they followed her, whistling admiringly at the proud turn of her head, her innocently sensual swaying walk. If only, instead of these puppies, she could have attracted the notice of respectable young gentlemen who would treat her honourably. George tried hard. But his own relations had turned their backs on him and his daughter. His sister Sophy had two daughters of her own, both spinsters, who still went into society in the hope of catching a husband; Sophy, therefore, would not raise a finger to help a rival to them, even if she had been able to countenance Magnolia's existence. His sister Amy, already a grandmother, had left the district, and his elder brother Jack had only sons. Any well-placed mamas he did happen to know were careful to issue only invitations which could not possibly lead to Magnolia's encountering their dear boys.

So Magnolia went walking and shopping unescorted, except by her maid, Eliza, a plain quiet girl who was grateful for her mistress's good nature and kindness and enjoyed looking after her pretty things. Eliza remembered her grandparents talking about the slaves who had once been shipped to Lancaster to wait upon the slavers' wives and daughters, and had more often than not died of misery, ill-treatment or sheer cold. It seemed to Eliza a great shame that her mistress should not make a really fine match, for the sake of all those dead girls — to show them that the luck had turned for their descendants. She did not put it exactly in that way in her mind, but such were her notions, for she was deeply romantic and a great reader of the newspapers, with their pathetic pictures of chained slaves pleading to cruel Simon Legrees of masters, 'Am I not a man and a brother?' It was sad that Miss Magnolia had no young gentleman.

But tonight would be different. George had bought tickets for a ball at the Assembly Rooms. Nobody could stop his daughter meeting young men *there*. There was a ticket for Eliza, too; not that she presumed to dress up and dance, but she would enjoy seeing the company; and there was another ticket for a lady living in Middle Street with whom George had a discreet 'arrangement'.

Magnolia stood up and twirled round the room, glancing back over her shoulder at herself in the mirror as she sang:

'Camptown ladies sing this song, doodah, doodah,
Camptown race-track five mile long, Oh, doodah day.'

She stopped herself. It was a very popular American song, but suggested a sort of society very different from the one she was going into tonight.

A knock at the door. 'Master says time to go, miss,' came Eliza's voice.

The Georgian Assembly Rooms bore traces of former grandeur: moulded ceilings, marble fireplaces carved with cupids and goats, pillars with chipped capitals and dirty cream paint which had once been white and gold. But the people who were dancing, chattering, sitting out or drinking were more intent on pleasure than on criticising their old-fashioned surroundings. The ball was a charity function, in aid of the Cotton Workers' Relief Fund, a worthy cause. Among the whirling figures of the dancers, the men in black, the ladies in as many colours as a public flower garden, George could see an apricot dress that appeared and disappeared, in the arms of a tall partner.

'She's enjoying herself,' he said to his companion, Mrs Cathie Ashcroft, the attractive youngish widow who was his only female consolation these days.

'Seems so.' Mrs Ashcroft shot a knowing look at his beaming face. 'You care a deal about that, don't you?'

'I do. She's not had a lot out of life so far — and precious little out of Lancaster. I sometimes wish I'd not brought her home, you know.'

'Oh, go on! What would she have done out in that heathen place?'

'Married, maybe. I don't know. She was too good for a lot of the fellows I met out there. I thought she'd have a better chance here, but I didn't reckon on all the stiff-backed folk that look down their noses at her. Belle's done a lot of harm, talking round the town about me and my bad ways, and Maggie's mother being a trollop ... sometimes I wish I could go back and take my girl with me, and be damned to the whole pack of 'em'.

'Not me, George?'

He squeezed her arm. 'Not you. Well, at least I've the money to keep her since Jack went.' His elder brother had died some months before and the family sail-making business was now being run on George's behalf, much to his pocket's benefit. His half-pay pension would have been nothing like enough to pay for Magnolia's dresses and jewels, not to mention Belle's allowance and Mrs Ashcroft's modest rent.

'Who's that she's dancing with? I don't like to wear glasses with my best cap.'

George peered. 'Billy Sherston. Well, well. There's one that can afford to put something in the charity box, twice over, and have plenty left after that.' Sherston was that somewhat unusual thing, a gentleman farmer whose lands were tilled by hirelings. A wealthy man already, he chose to run the farm for pleasure as much as for profit. He provided employment for a large number of people, could afford the best equipment, had as good an eye for a beast as any man in north Lancashire, and made a habit of walking round the whole compass of his acres with gun and dog at least once in the week. It kept his tall figure trim, unlike those of many of his contemporaries.

Magnolia thought his figure beautiful, and his long high-nosed face impressively aristocratic. He waltzed as well as she did, with a long-legged grace and perfect command. In his arms she felt like a feather borne along by a powerful wind.

The waltz came to an end; it was the fifth dance they had had together. 'Tired?' he asked, smiling down. 'Shall we take a pause?'

Magnolia was panting slightly. 'Just a little out of breath. I've never danced so much, all at once.' And with one partner, she might have added. He led her to one of the chairs lining the sides of the room, where chaperones watched their charges and unclaimed ladies sat smiling hopefully. Just as he was about to hand her to a seat, he paused.

'Would you rather take a turn on the balcony? I find the atmosphere in here quite suffocating. Perhaps I can find your wrap for you?'

'Oh, pray don't trouble. My maid will get it.' She signalled in pantomime to the watching Eliza, who appeared with the fur-lined cloak, becomingly hooded. Sherston helped her gallantly into it, and led her through the crowd to one of the long French windows at the back of the room. He parted the curtains and opened the window, ushering her out.

A full moon cast its brilliant light down on the colonnaded balcony, made mysterious shapes of the roofs of the houses and cottages clustering behind King Street, and lit with magic the great castle beyond them. Magnolia gasped with pleasure.

'How beautiful! I never saw the moon so bright in England before.'

He was watching her face, amused. 'Is it bright where you come from?'

'Oh yes! Sometimes gold like a big melon. And the stars are brighter, too, and much bigger than these.'

Like your eyes, he almost said, then changed his mind. 'You don't feel the cold, I see, Miss Dilworth. That surprises me, for such an exotic lady as yourself.' Seeing that she did not recognise the word, he added, 'I should have thought a beautiful bird from the tropics would die in our climate.'

She shrugged, a more exaggerated shrug than an Englishwoman's.

'I am used to it now. At first I thought I *should* die. But my father sees to it that we have good fires, and so keeps me alive. I am very expensive to keep, you see.' She smiled up at him, teeth flashing white in the dark flower that was her face, framed in soft fur, and he thought her breathtakingly attractive. He knew that he attracted her; she was too naive to play the coquette with him as an English girl would. Expensive to keep, indeed: what a daring remark, made by anyone else! More and more amused, he made polite conversation, not touching her, but close, quiet-voiced, intimate, getting her trust and goodwill.

George had seen them go out. When they had not come back by the end of the next two dances he wondered whether he should follow them, for propriety's sake. Cathie Ashcroft dissuaded him.

'Mr Sherston is a gentleman. So far as I know, that is. Since he seems so taken with her, why not let them alone, George? She'll come to no harm out there.'

The couple reappeared. Magnolia was radiant, clinging to Sherston's arm. Just before returning her to her father he asked her, 'May I call on you?'

She knew nothing of the etiquette of morning calls and their possible significance, but answered, beaming, 'Please, I should be very happy.' She would have liked him to kiss her hand, as a

Spaniard would have done, but he made her a stiff little bow before turning away.

George was disturbed by her obvious state of rapture. She was too truthful to deceive him, he knew, and when she said that they had only talked about the weather and life in the West Indies he believed her. And yet — five dances, and a disappearance from the public scene. Could the fellow be serious? George did not move in farming circles, particularly such elevated ones as Sherston's. He decided to make enquiries.

For a week Magnolia waited for the expected call. She had not mentioned it to anybody, for she had a superstitious feeling that if she talked about it, it might not happen. There was a new light in her eyes, a dreaming smile on her lips. Little Eliza saw, and hoped that the tall gentleman with the proud face had brought happiness into her mistress's empty life.

Day after day went by, until Magnolia's expectation began to turn into anxiety. He would not come; it had only been a whim.

Then, on the seventh morning, Eliza bustled in to say that there was a gentleman to see Miss Dilworth — the gentleman of the Assembly Rooms. But she had no need to say it, for Magnolia had known as soon as the knocker sounded. She leaped up and ran to the glass, glad that she was wearing her best day dress; she had put it on each morning, to be ready.

Then he was in the room, looking even more handsome than he had done that night.

'Miss Dilworth. Good of you to receive me.' He took the chair she indicated, seating himself with composed grace, his hat, cane and gloves on the floor beside him, as etiquette dictated. To leave them in the hall would have implied an improperly long stay. Magnolia fetched a decanter of wine and another of Madeira, clumsy in her excitement, almost breaking a glass. She knew her hands were shaking, and feared that he would notice when she raised her own glass to her lips, but he was talking lightly of this and that, putting her at her ease, giving her leads so that she would talk herself. When she heard that his farm was at Creston, south of Quernmore, she said delightedly, 'Oh, then you are not far from my relatives at Downham.' He smiled inwardly as she floundered through an attempted explanation of the link between her father and Sir Jesse Bradshaw of Eagle Hall, who had married Papa's wife's aunt.

She hurried on to chatter about the splendours of Eagle Hall, described to her by Laurence: the furniture, the gardens, the size and grandeur of it all, the fabled beauty of Lucy and her curious hobby of tending sick animals.

'It sounds remarkably fine,' said Sherston. 'I had heard of Sir Jesse, yes, but we're not acquainted. A farmer's life is too busy for a great deal of socialising. I must seek him out, as a relative of the beautiful Miss Dilworth.'

Magnolia's blush grew deeper. 'Oh, I don't think they would know much about me. I've never visited them, nor Papa. Things are very —' to her horror she forgot the English word for the awkward situation, and came out with, '*desmañado,* since Papa parted with his wife.'

Sherston hastened to cover her embarrassment by changing the subject to the ball of the previous week, the excellence of her dancing, the pleasure of spending a civilised evening in Lancaster, a town not noted for its sophistication. He often visited the south, where life was much gayer. Perhaps she would see London one day, and discover all she had been missing.

Almost without a pause, he went on, 'Will you do me the honour of dining with me one evening?'

Completely taken aback, she stammered, 'At — at your farm, sir?'

'At Creston. I can offer only modest hospitality in a bachelor household, but my cook is not at all bad. My sister will be pleased to have your company — we see very few people.'

Her breath taken away by surprise and delight, she said, 'Thank you. I — should have to ask Papa. And...' There was some objection she should make, but nothing came into her mind.

He said swiftly, 'The proprieties would be observed, of course. Was that your maid who let me in? Then let her accompany you. I shall, of course, send a carriage for you.'

She could only smile; it seemed as though she would never stop smiling again, since life had suddenly become so sunny. When he left a date had been agreed, four evenings hence. She ran to the window and watched him emerge into the busy street, and stride towards a magnificent chestnut horse, its reins held by a boy, mount it gracefully, and ride away as if no other horses or vehicles existed in Common Garden Street.

It took Laurence a good deal of courage, and time to muster it, before he faced his grandfather with the news that he intended to give up his work in the office and train for the Church. He made the confession at the house in St Leonard's Gate, where Ephraim spent his time now except for an hour or two a week. Having finally got it out, he sat staring at the carpet of Ephraim's study, not seeing it, waiting for wrath to break over his head.

But Ephraim only said mildly, after a long pause, 'I think you've chosen well, lad. Your heart was never in the law, was it. I could not in all conscience have left the practice to you.'

'No, sir. I was never much good.'

'Don't say that. You're a good boy, very good. It was not your fault that they ... that Dove...'

'Who, sir? Aunt Dove?'

The old man shook his head impatiently. 'I forget names so. Not Dove, Belle. Not your fault that those two couldn't agree. I've always said that half the matrimonial troubles of this world come from absentee husbands. Yet Eleanor seems quite happy, even though whatshisname is away in London. Well, well. They've not done rightly by you, have they? An Atkinson never needed spectacles at your age. And you're too thin. Doesn't your mother tell you so?'

'No, sir.'

'Dear me. My Mary would have seen it at once. If I lost as much as a pound of weight she would start feeding me like a fighting cock. Time you took a wife, lad.'

Laurence looked away. 'I can't afford one, Grandfather. And — my heart is engaged, but — I'm not favoured. I've given up all hope.'

'And decided to turn to holy orders, eh? Good thing you can't become a monk and spoil your chances for good. Well, well. And where are you going to learn your trade? I suppose some sort of apprenticeship is needed.'

Laurence explained that he would have to enrol at a theological college outside Manchester, the largest and best establishment of its kind. It would mean living in for some four years. Pressed to name the fees, he did so, adding hastily that his father was prepared to pay them, though not altogether happy about the business.

Ephraim leaned forward to poke the fire, drawing bright flames up from a smouldering cave of coals. 'No,' he said, 'no. I will pay the fees.'

'But Grandfather! I didn't come for … I mean, I don't expect you to do anything for me.'

'I shall pay them. What have I to spend my money on now?' The faded old eyes in the lined, fallen face were sad. 'No wife, a sister-in-law almost my age. Belle, your mother, has made her own bed; she can lie on it, for me. Only Dove left.'

'I think Aunt Dove and Uncle Joe are suffering very much from the cotton troubles, sir, and would be very glad of help.'

'Yes, yes, I know. I'm here if they need me, aren't I? And then there's the little girl. May. Yes, May. She was pretty, I remember. She came here, you know — when was it? — to stay with us. But it's very strange, I can't recall her face, only Marigold's. My poor little Marigold. You know she died?'

'Yes, sir.'

'Yes. Went wandering off on a snowy day and got lost. They found her in the snow, like a dead bird…' He stared into the fire, seeing the face of the one who had been his darling. Nothing had been said to him about the way Marigold had met her death. It had not been reported in the local papers, and they had hoped he would escape seeing an account of it elsewhere. Margaret had been told, just in case the truth should reach him; she would know how to console him best.

His mind came back from the past. 'I made a will, Laurence, apportioning a certain sum to Marigold in her own right, not to be operative in favour of any person who should trap her into marriage. Well, it's void now; cancelled. I shall devote as much of that sum as is necessary to your training. Don't thank me, lad, it gives me pleasure to do anything that will help you young ones. Edwin, now … I've no fears for that young

273

cockerel, there's gold dust on his wings. Did you hear that he — what was it he did? Got some even better place than we thought, or passed some high examination? I forget. Never mind. I'll pay your fees, I say. In any case they're very modest.'

Laurence might have told him that the accommodation was equally modest, a spartan carpetless cell to each young gentleman of the college, and the food not encouraging to the development of worldly tastes. But it was of no consequence to him. He was happy, for the first time in years, happy to be going away from his troubled home and divided parents, and to be doing something Lucy wanted for him. In a glow of goodwill to all, he said to Ephraim in parting, 'Sir, would you receive my sister? She's very much alone and would take it very kindly, and she hasn't done any wrong...'

The old man frowned. 'Don't be silly, boy. You have no sister. Mind's wandering, as mine does sometimes — you're far too young for that.' They shook hands, and Ephraim, looking affectionately into Laurence's eyes, said, 'Goodbye, John.'

The days dragged like years for Magnolia until the Friday evening when she was to dine with Billy Sherston. George did his best to dampen her excitement. He had not met Sherston, apart from a few words at the Assembly Rooms. His enquiries had produced nothing beyond the information that the man was unmarried, that there was no scandal about him in Lancaster, that he rode into the town very little, usually on market days, and that his wealth was rumoured to be immense. George could not believe that such a man could be seriously, matrimonially interested in a girl of no pedigree with a half-pay officer for a father. He said as much, as gently as he could, to Magnolia, yet knew as he said it that she was completely ignorant of the customs of English society and took in very little of his warning. It seemed from her account of the two conversations she had had with Sherston that nothing in the least improper had been said or done; the man might be genuinely attracted. George had met a great many white men who fancied dark-skinned women far more strongly than their own kind. Sherston could be one of them, and Magnolia's white blood an added charm for him.

He tried to look on the best side of it, since he could not disappoint the girl by forbidding her to go. 'But I wish the fellow had spoken to me first,' he said.

'How could he, Papa? You were out.'

'There's such a thing as a civil note asking permission. This Mr Sherston of yours seems uncommonly high-handed to me.'

Magnolia smiled tenderly. 'A king among men, Papa. A true gentleman.'

'Hmm. I hope so. I wish young Eliza were a more suitable chaperone for you. Dam' shame you've no mother to take you about, Maggie. Wish I could come with you myself, but it ain't done, fathers escorting daughters.'

'I wish too that you could come.' He stroked her hair back from her face, knowing that she meant it, that she had no guile in her.

When the neat carriage drawn by a spanking pair of brown horses drew up at the door, she was ready and waiting, as she had been for almost two hours. She wore her best dress, the apricot tarlatan she had worn at the ball, and a necklace and earrings of intricate West Indian work, the fur-lined cloak enveloping her. George kissed her cheek. 'Look after your mistress,' he told Eliza. He felt a strong impulse to get out his own horse and follow the carriage to Creston.

Magnolia and her host faced each other across the long highly polished table in the dark, severe dining room of Creston Hall. For he lived not at the farm, as she had thought, but in this dignified Queen Anne house from which the cluster of farm buildings could be seen in the midst of crop- and grazing-lands, dark shapes with lighted windows here and there, like the pictures in which children make pinpricks and hold them up to the candle. The sister he had mentioned was not present — called away on a visit, he said, apologising.

The meal had been simple and light, chosen for a lady's tastes, served by a manservant who scarcely spoke, seeming to know his place and his duties without direction. After the dessert was placed on the table he vanished silently, leaving them alone. There was no sound of life in the house, yet somewhere below stairs Eliza was being entertained in the kitchen, Sherston had said.

'How did you get such fruit in winter, sir?' Magnolia asked Sherston. Through a haze rising from golden aromatic wine she could still taste mangoes and peaches, plump green figs and dark grapes.

He smiled. 'I have sources for such things. I like to please my guests. Did I please my guest of tonight?'

She glowed at him. 'Oh, yes, sir!'

'Don't call me sir. My name is William. Friends call me Billy. Take your choice.'

'Billy, then.' Magnolia giggled. 'Papa calls me Maggie, and I like that. Not so pretty a name as my real one, but it sounds so much more English. That is what I would like, to be quite English.'

'Venus has no nation and no colour.' She looked up, puzzled. 'I mean that beauty may be English or Haitian, where's the difference? Shall we move to the fireside?'

Magnolia got up, staggered, and clutched her chair, to find him at her side, his arms round her. He led her to where a log fire burned quiet and steady in an open hearth; a chaise-longue of the old style was beside it. He laid her on it, and knelt by her side, looking intently into her face. She felt curiously weightless, as though floating on air, carried away by the glory of the evening and the strength of the wine. Billy was saying something to her which she could not quite take in, but certain words filtered through to her consciousness, words that she knew were shocking, but she had neither the will nor the energy to chide him. He kissed her lingeringly, and she let him, she who had never known any kiss warmer than a father's; then he was half-carrying, half-leading her, along a corridor and up stairs lit by an overhead lamp. Somewhere below them faint sounds of argument were going on, but her ears, ringing with the effect of the wine, failed to recognise Eliza's voice.

Then they were in a room with a great four-poster bed hung with dark red and gold, candlelight flickering in dark austere presses and chairs and oil paintings, the pale faces of their sitters springing into life and fading again. Because her legs felt so weak and her head so giddy she subsided on to the bed, feeling her slippers being removed, the hooks of her dress unfastened, the dress lowered to the floor, the tapes of her petticoats untied. Something still sober in her knew she should protest, but she was unable, and the experience was delicious, sending her into a half-sleepy haze of excitement.

He left the candles burning.

When Magnolia had not returned by midnight George's anxiety became intense. He sat by the window, leaning forward at every hoof-fall and rumble of wheels. Until three o'clock next morning he sat there, stupid with weariness, going over and over in his mind the things that might have prevented her return: she had been taken ill, there had been an accident on the road, a wheel off, a horse gone lame. He found a map of the district, carefully measured the distance to Creston, worked out the carriage road, thought of the possibility of going there. At last he went to bed, where he lay sleepless at first, dozing fitfully towards morning. It was the longest and darkest night of his life.

About the time when he came out of an uneasy dream to see, thankfully, that his watch said eight o'clock, Magnolia woke in the wide bed, alone. Her head felt heavy, her mouth furry, but now she remembered vividly everything that had happened the night before. Her body was sore, aching; there were bite marks on her shoulders, breasts and throat. She touched dried blood, and the tender area of a large bruise. Her lower lip was bitten, tender to the touch. Billy had been an ungentle lover.

He was standing by a dressing chest with a mirror over it, shaving. He wore an elegant waisted dressing gown, and something about the set of his head suggested high good humour. Magnolia was not angry. She had been tricked into submission, violated without her consent, hurt more than ever before. But it was the lordly way of such men as Billy to take women like this. Now she was his indisputably, and glad of it. In her own country it could never have happened so, but customs were different in England. Ashamed, and shy, yet glad, she spoke his name softly. He turned.

'Ah, awake, m'dear? Come on, then, up with you.'

'But...' She looked round helplessly. She was naked, her clothes out of sight.

Sherston laughed. 'Don't be modest. I've seen all there is to see of you. Here, then.' He took a towel from its rail and threw it to her. 'Drape yourself in that and get dressed. They'll bring you up some coffee, I dare say, then someone will drive you back.'

She shook her head, bewildered. 'But, Billy. Are you not going to kiss me?'

'Why the devil should I? We had plenty of that last night, if you remember. *I* certainly do.' He wiped the lather from his face, threw off the dressing gown, and assumed a checked waistcoat, carefully selecting from a jewel box the right chain and fob to go with it.

She was trembling, not with cold. 'But I am your bride now — sir,' she said.

Sherston spun round, staring his hard grey stare, laughing.

'My good girl, what *are* you talking about? Bride? Why, I do believe you mean it. Good God, what a little savage you are! So that's marriage, where you come from, is it. Well, it ain't here, let's be thankful.' He came closer. 'Just look at you. Pretty sight for a bridal morning, eh?'

She managed, her throat swollen with tears, to say, 'Why? Why? You were so kind, before…'

'Why? What a damned silly question. Don't you know anything, Miss Maggie? I was kind, as you put it, because a certain degree of civility's expected before a conquest. How would you expect me to behave, in order to get you into bed — kick you from Lancaster to here? A little party first, the serious business afterwards. I was very curious about you, you know. I've had more women than the days of the year, I'd say at a venture, but never a black one yet. My apologies — brown. They said there were interesting differences, and I'd agree. But one thing did surprise me, I must say. Why didn't you mention you were a virgin? I thought your father lived off you, hired you out so to speak. Perhaps you've always gone so far and no further, is that it? Well, it don't signify. Get dressed now. I must be off.'

He was gone. Magnolia was ice cold, her teeth chattering, tears pouring down her cheeks. Somehow she found her clothes and put them on, her hands shaking too much to fasten the buttons and tapes properly. She placed her cloak about her and heard the faint jingling from a pocket. In it were three gold sovereigns.

'I haven't seen her,' Lucy told George. 'I only wish I had.'

He heaved a great sigh of disappointment. 'I thought she might have come here. She always liked you, and you were the only one of the family to admit that she existed and visit her. Apart from Laurence, of course. Well, he's at college — she can't have gone there.'

'I think she was a little afraid of me,' Lucy said, 'poor girl. How long is it that she's been missing?'

'Two weeks and three days. I've been out there four times. Each time he was away, or they said he was. I could hardly smash my way in to see for myself.'

'But the servant was gracious enough to admit that she'd been there?'

'"A young person dined here." They were pretty sure she'd left, they said. You don't suppose he could be keeping her prisoner, Lucy? God, I don't know what I fear most — that, or that she's dead. Eliza knows nothing. They got her stupid with drink. I've told the police she's missing, and where she went that night, but the man they sent got no further than I did. What the devil can I do next?'

Lucy surveyed compassionately the tired, haggard face and the droop of the broad shoulders, once jauntily held. She was about to remark, in her direct way, that the family appeared to specialise in missing girls, then thought better of it. A reminder of Marigold's fate would hardly cheer Magnolia's father.

'I wish I'd never brought her home,' George said. 'I thought I was giving her chances she wouldn't have had out there, but I was doing just the opposite. Must have been out of my senses. A damned, miserable, snobbish crew, all of 'em, even Belle's father. And then to be taken in by that villain's foxy scheming...'

'Cousin George,' Lucy said, 'I've been thinking. I believe I might be able to go where you can't, and perhaps find out things that wouldn't be said to you. It's plain to me that Mr Sherston's servants have been told to say nothing to a man enquiring about his guest. But they haven't been warned about a female. It's worth a try.'

When she rode over to Creston on Peveril, her handsome grey, she was the picture of ladylike elegance, in a perfectly cut riding habit, a hard hat with a becoming veil, and her hair neatly put up. She was not known in that area, Sherston having a reputation for disliking strangers on his property, but it was as well to look respectable. She avoided the Hall, and went to the main farmhouse. A stout woman was feeding hens; Lucy reined in and addressed her pleasantly, starting with a comment on the fine weather for February and proceeding to remark on the isolation of Creston. The woman responded, glad to have a word with a civil stranger; it was fortunate that she was not the dour kind. Hands on hips, she chatted volubly. Aye, it was a sight too quiet for anybody as liked a bit of life, out at Creston. To Lucy's gratification she proved quite a gossip, and obviously not over devoted to the master. Sly, well-placed questions drew information: there *were* guests sometimes up at t'Hall, and in her opinion some funny things went on. It was not long before Lucy got out of her the story of the foreign girl

— "black as night, Egyptian or summat" — who had dined with Mr S. one night and not been seen afterwards, though he had ordered a groom to drive her back to town in the Victoria next morning. A maid had told another servant, who had told one of the girls at the farm, that the foreigner had been as drunk as a fiddler's bitch when the footman served the dessert.

Lucy let her ramble on to other matters, putting in an occasional encouraging word, before consulting her watch and riding away with a friendly wave of her whip. She had learned enough to assure her that Magnolia was not being concealed at the Hall. With servants like that, it would have been no secret by now.

Something else had emerged from the conversation with the obliging hen-wife. Sherston was not away from home, but in the past fortnight he had been absent two or three times, visiting Sir Jesse Bradshaw at Downham.

Lucy rode thoughtfully home, her methodical mind hatching plans.

CHAPTER SIXTEEN

The woman at Creston Hall Farm would not have recognised the figure riding over Skerton Bridge in the twilight, then turning his horse left along the river opposite the Custom House. He was an ordinary enough young countryman wearing breeches, high boots and a rough cord jacket with a woollen muffler round his neck and a round workman's cap pulled well down over his brow. He rode with assured ease a grey horse which was becoming tired of this stopping-and-starting journey. Already they had visited eight public houses and one seaman's hostel, the horse's rider having taken no drinks anywhere. The people in crowded, shabby riverside Skerton were not used to being asked questions by well-spoken persons; they had given some short and occasionally obscene answers. But the rider was patient and determined, and following a strong scent.

At the ninth public house he dismounted again, tied up the horse and strolled into the bar, smoky, reeking of ale and the rum the men of the shipyard loved. This time, for a change, there was a woman behind the counter, a red-cheeked Amazon built to resist both insults and cajolery. Her small dark eyes flashed about like searchlights, ready to spot troublemakers, drunks and those who tried to get their drink money put on the slate. Suspiciously she watched the approach of the stranger, the easy walk, the fresh, comely, beardless face, the frank smile with which she was greeted.

'Evening, missis. Half of your best, if you please.' It was the first drink of the quest, and went down well. Business was slackish; the landlady was soon drawn into a conversation about ships that had recently put into the port and the number of different nationalities who must visit the Ashton Arms. Aye, there were all sorts, she agreed, some worse nor others.

The rider drew a thoughtful pattern on the counter with the base of his beer mug. 'You've not by any chance come across a young lady friend of mine — dark-complexioned, well spoken, nice manners?'

The landlady's brows drew together in a frown. 'I don't answer questions about other folks' business.'

'What business?'

'Never thee mind.'

Lucy leaned one elbow on the counter and fixed the woman with a look of sweet soulfulness and trust. 'You've a kind face, missis. I knew that soon as I walked in.' She lowered her tone. 'Now this young woman, she's a sort of relative of mine. One of those marriages, *you* know — right enough overseas, not so well received here. She wasn't made welcome, and she's run away. Now, I figured she might make a bid to get back to her own folk, board a ship West Indies bound.'

An unresponsive gaze met hers. 'Well, then?'

'Well, then. She's wanted back home, here in Lancaster. Things have changed, it's a long story, but there's many a tear been shed since she went missing. I swear to you, on the Bible, if you've seen her and can tell me where to find her you'll be doing her the best turn anyone ever did.'

The landlady turned to serve a customer, her face giving nothing away. Lucy sipped beer, staring nonchalantly round the bar at a gloomy-looking parrot in a corner, a beam hung with trophies brought home by seamen, but alert for the moment when the woman's attention should switch back to her. The moment came.

'I don't know why I should trust thee,' said the landlady in very untrusting tones. 'But tha seems a decent kind of lad, and too young to do a lot of harm.' Lucy forebore to say that she was twenty-four, not the stripling youth she appeared. 'Can you promise me she'll not be hurt?'

'I told you, I'll swear on the Bible if you'll fetch me one.'

'Nay, I'll not bother.' A long stare. 'She come to me the most part of a fortnight ago, wanting work. Didn't say what sort o' work — didn't know, I reckoned. Well, I'd nowt for her here — my daughters do all I want — and I told her straight, them as works in sailors' pubs gets what they're asking for, going into such places. Not but what mine's a respectable house, you ask t'constable. She said she'd tried this and that place, but they didn't want her, only some as put to her … what weren't right. Bedroom work.'

Lucy nodded gravely.

'I were sorry for t'lass. Maybe it were soft of me, but she seemed honest enough, and frit out of her mind. She said she'd no money for her passage to some foreign place. She'd had some bits of jewellery as had been stolen, and pawned summat, a cloak, I think she said. She looked no better nor a draggle-tailed cat.'

'Please, can you tell me where to find her? I know you helped her. God bless you for it.' Lucy threw all her powers of persuasion into her voice and her look. It was fortunate for the strength of her disguise that the voice was contralto, and her features strong enough to pass for a boy's.

The woman half-turned away, then turned back. 'Powderhouse Lane. Just after you turn off the Torrisholme Road. It's nobbut a little alehouse, no name, just a sign up. My sister keeps it, Mrs Greenall. Say Ellen sent you. And I hope I'm not bringing more ill luck on yon poor lass.' Abruptly she moved round the counter and began to berate a customer whose voice was raised in argument.

Mrs Greenall's alehouse was not easy to find in the dark, among a confusion of narrow lanes, open country, and tiny hamlets. Lucy found it at last, an insignificant small building only identifiable by the publican's sign above the door, almost illegible without a lantern.

The inside proved to be as far from festive as the exterior. The bar room was little more than a farm kitchen with hardly any furniture in it. In front of a low fire, on facing upright settles, two old men were silently playing a game with counters. A grizzled mongrel dog lay in a corner. Behind the rough table which served as a bar-counter an elderly woman whom Lucy presumed to be the landlady was washing glasses and mugs in a tin bowl. She looked up, surprised. Evidently her establishment saw few customers.

'Mrs Greenall?'

'Aye.'

'Your sister Ellen told me to come to you.'

A deeply suspicious glance raked Lucy from head to foot. 'What for?'

'I think you have a relative of mine staying with you.' Hastily she repeated the story she had told to the woman at Skerton, feeling as she talked that it was not going down well. The old men took not the slightest notice of the conversation, for which Lucy was thankful. When she finished a dubious silence fell, before the landlady said, 'How do I know you're not one o' them she's run from?'

'So she *is* here?'

'I niver said that. I'll tell thee straight, I don't like t'look o' thee, young man. Art some kind o' player? They say there's some funny folk come to yon wicked playhouse in t'town. This is a God-fearing home, this is. We don't want none o' your sort here, so be off with you.' She advanced threateningly round the table, a big-boned, flat-chested figure who might have alarmed a weakling, but not Lucy.

She smiled winningly; not that smiles were likely to soften Mrs Greenall's heart.

'I'm not a player, I'm a — well, an animal doctor. Come now, your sister believed what I told her, and she's not one to be taken in easily, is she? Please let me see my cousin. If she's afraid of me, I promise to go away at once.'

After another long, critical stare, the women went into a room at the back of the bar. Lucy heard her say, 'Maggie. Someone to see thee. Don't do owt you don't want to.' Emerging, she beckoned Lucy to follow her.

The small parlour was as crammed with furniture as the bar was bare. At a table, sewing by the light of an oil lamp, sat Magnolia: thinner, lacking her old lustre, dressed in a shabby dark gown.

At Lucy's appearance she dropped her work and jumped up with a shriek. Mrs Greenall interposed herself between them, glaring. 'You see? She's scart out o' her wits.'

'She needn't be. Maggie, it's me.' Lucy snatched off her cap. Her sunny hair fell about her shoulders, transforming her. With a cry, Magnolia rushed to her and clung round her neck, sobbing incoherently.

Lucy murmured, 'If you please, Mrs Greenall, could we have a little time alone? Just a few minutes.'

'Well, I don't know … I niver saw owt like it. First a lad, then a lass. It's not decent.'

She went out, muttering. Lucy led Magnolia back to her chair, drew another up beside her, and talked reassurance to her.

'I'm so glad I found you. I'm sorry to have startled you, dressed like this, but I could hardly go round the publics as Miss Bradshaw, could I? I guessed you'd make for the quays. You were thinking of taking ship, wasn't that it? Yes, of course. Now there's nothing to be afraid of. Tell me all about it, Maggie, and take your time. Mrs Greenall won't bother us — I think she trusts me with you now.'

'I can't go back, Lucy,' Magnolia said, her head turned away. 'Not after — what happened. That's why I … I can't go back, even with you.'

'Suppose you tell me what happened, before we talk about that?'

'Don't look at me, then.' Hesitantly, hardly able to get out the words, Magnolia told her story; the details she could not bring herself to say were perfectly clear to Lucy, who seethed inwardly with an anger she would not reveal. She nodded calmly, as though the tale were quite ordinary.

'So you didn't wait to be driven back to Lancaster.'

'I couldn't. I knew Eliza was somewhere, and I ought to have waited, but I couldn't. I walked, on and on, I don't know where. I got quite lost. Even when I came to the edge of the town I didn't know where I was. Then I saw the bridge and remembered. Oh, Lucy, people stared at me so!' She laughed half-hysterically. 'I had my best gown on and my cloak with the fur lining, and my slippers were all in pieces…' Remembered distress shook her. 'I didn't know what to do, then I found a pawn shop. He let me have some money for the dress and the cloak, and I bought another, a dress, I mean — this one, and a shawl. He charged me a lot for them, nearly as much as he gave me for the other ones. And I took my necklace and earrings off and put them down while I was changing, and when I came to look for them they were gone. Somebody took them, perhaps it was the man. I don't know.'

More composed now, she went on with the story. She had gone to St George's Quay to enquire for a ship bound for the West Indies, but there were none sailing, would be none for a month or more. So she started to look for work. Lucy could guess from the thin narrative how much was being left out: insults, attacks, hunger and humiliation. At last she had come to the Ashton Arms and found the landlady honest and well-meaning towards her. 'But she said Skerton was no place for me to be, and she brought me here to her sister's. Almost nobody comes here, just a few travellers, and people from the cottages. Usually I stay in here and help with the house, and do the sewing. I learnt to sew nicely at the convent.'

'I'm sure you did. Well, we must be very grateful to Mrs Greenall and Ellen whatever-her-name-is. Thank God you fell into their hands. But now it's time to come home, Maggie.'

The dark eyes widened with fright. 'I can't! Never. Nobody must see me, not Father nor Eliza, nor anyone.'

'Why, pray?'

'I'm disgraced.'

Lucy gave what she hoped was a convincing laugh. 'Stuff and nonsense. If anyone's disgraced it's that wretch at Creston Hall. My dear girl, nobody knows anything of what happened there except you and I — for I imagine you didn't give the two ladies any details. So far as the world is concerned, you had a rather indiscreet meal with a bachelor who had no business to invite you, took too much to drink and wandered off without waiting to be escorted home. We could say you had a fall and lost your memory; it's been known to happen. Your father is breaking his heart to know where you are and see you again.'

Tears started to Magnolia's eyes. 'Is he? Does he not hate me, really?'

'He loves you very much,' Lucy said gently. 'Whatever happened, he loves you. I should try not to tell him everything, if I were you, but even if you do it will make no difference. Won't you let me take you back?'

After a silence, Magnolia asked, 'When?'

'Tomorrow. I must rest my horse tonight. Mrs Greenall will probably find me a bed, or I can sit in a chair all night — I don't mind. Then tomorrow we'll hire a trap and take you home. Don't cry any more; it's all over.'

Lying in the parlour on the pallet bed a still bewildered Mrs Greenall had rigged up for her, Lucy stared at the dying fire. She had played God, no less. Perhaps it had been wrong, but she thought not. A discreet question had reassured her that Magnolia would suffer no dreadful consequences from Sherston's brutality. Left to wander, she would have come to disaster and real disgrace, Lucy was sure of that. One must not be tempted to play God too often: it was a heady exercise. Animals were one thing, when it came to the manipulation of lives, human beings quite another.

But there was one thing she intended to give God a hand with: the paying-back of Billy Sherston.

Lucy's carefully written reassurance to Laurence that his half-sister was safe made Laurence much happier. He had been deeply disturbed by his father's half-coherent letter about her disappearance, and had hurried to the Lion House to share his trouble with May. She had urged him to keep it from her parents, because of the alarming parallel with Marigold. Now it was all over, and Magnolia found safely. Lucy omitted any more details, only remarking that the poor girl had suffered some kind of lapse of memory.

'*So all is well again,*' Laurence read out. '*Cousin George is taking her back to Haiti, where he feels her health will be better, and his own as well. Lancaster's climate is notorious. What must it be for a person born and bred in sunshine? He will be writing to you himself and I know he means to tell you that when you feel you can take a rest from your studies he will arrange a passage out for you to join them.*'

'What a happy thought,' May said. 'I'm sure you can't wait to sail. Don't I just wish someone would invite *me* to the West Indies. I tell you, Laurence, I begin to feel three times my age. Four, perhaps. Can you see any grey hairs? I'm sure I pulled one out the other day. What with the awful situation on the estate, the people more than half starved and living like rats, Father worried out of his mind for them and Mother worried for him, it's like living in a morgue.' She cupped her chin in her hands, gazing out at the cheerless landscape, late snow lying on the gardens, trees still bare.

'There must be plenty of work to do among Uncle's employees,' Laurence suggested. 'Bible classes…'

May gave a mirthless hoot of laughter. 'What do they want with Bible classes, when they've no food, and hardly a stick of furniture left? I've seen a woman cry inconsolably to see the cradle taken away to be sold. I hope you're not one of those who believe the poor only need to be good to be happy. What rubbish! I'm sorry. Of course it's your job to believe that of everybody. But I'm not like you, I'm a frivolous, feather-headed creature that would rather be dancing her feet off than sitting here like … like a piece of pie going slowly cold on a plate. Oh, Laurence, do *smile*. I shall go mad, I know I shall. Do let's talk about something amusing. Have you got over Lucy?'

Her cousin flushed. 'What?'

'You know what I mean. Have you got over being spoony about her, now you've found something you really want to do with your life?'

He did not answer at once, taking the question seriously, as he took everything. His talk with Lucy, when she had so forcefully recommended him to go into the Church, had subtly changed his attitude to her. He still thought her the most wonderful of girls, but what she had said about her unsuitability for him had impressed him deeply. He still had no idea why deprived animals mattered more to her than human souls. If they argued until the Day of Judgment he would never understand it. She made him feel inadequate and weak, whereas among his fellow students he felt himself a person of at least some intellect, whose opinions and aspirations were respected. Lucy had also used language more suitable to a smoking room than a lady's parlour; to make a clergyman's wife, she would have to revise her manners very radically, and something told him she would never do that. Whatever her charms, and they were dazzling, he would never quite approve of her again. He turned to May.

'I shall always be fond of Cousin Lucy,' he said.

May grinned. 'Good. That tells me everything. I hope you'll find a dear little deaconess, or whatever they call them, one day.'

May's life these days was so dull that she was sorry when Laurence left to return to college. Nobody could call him entertaining, poor boy, but at least he was a different face. Basil, coming from her father's study, heard desultory tinkling from the drawing-room piano. On impulse, he went in. May was sitting in the half-light strumming snatches of tunes, with no music on the stand.

'Don't you want a lamp lit?' he asked.

'No, I don't. I want a hundred thousand fireworks let off, with millions of stars and Catherine wheels and things that run along the ground banging. I want a rocket display and a grand transparency showing the Queen dancing a Highland fling with Mr Disraeli.' She crashed her hands down on the keys with a discordant thump.

'Well, well,' said Basil. 'That's not much to ask, if you can wait till Guy Fawkes Day. Though I reckon nobody else fancies fireworks round here, at the moment.'

'I know. I'm selfish. I'm horrid. Oh, go away, you're making me more miserable than I was before you came in.' She began to play a lugubrious air, singing in a tone to match, *'I'm leaving thee in sorrow, Annie...'*

'Hold your noise,' Basil said. 'If you're as low-spirited as you sound, I'll take you for an outing.'

'A — what? When? Where?'

'Only if your mother doesn't want you, mind. Don't jump out of your skin at me, it's not a fancy ball, just a visit I'm paying. I didn't reckon to take anybody with me,' Basil was thinking aloud, 'but it seems to me you're going daft for want of company, and they'll be glad to have you.'

'*Who* will? Oh, do tell me, don't tease!'

'My people. It's my mother's birthday tomorrow, she's eighty-five, and they'll all be there. We go in a lot for ceremonies. It was your mentioning fireworks that put me in mind of it. We'll go early, in the afternoon; I might as well, for all there is to do here,' he added gloomily.

Dove made no objection to May's 'outing'. Basil was like an uncle to the girl. If he thought it would do her good, then it would. Her mother was aware, without admitting it, of May's repression in the quiet house. Joe's gloom and silences affected everybody, even the servants, but most of all the daughter he had once loved to play and laugh with. May could not be denied what might lighten her way, if only for an evening and a night.

Wistfully she watched them get into the brougham, May in her best white dress, her colour brilliant, chattering and laughing with excitement. Nobody should know how Dove longed to be going herself, robbed of Basil's company as she now was and must be.

To the end of her long life, May would never forget her first entry into the Absalom home. The house, on the north side of Manchester, was more like a mansion, standing massive, modern, mock-Gothic in its own large grounds. A liveried servant answered the door. In the large, ornate hall, marble-tiled and hung with bright, contemporary tapestries, May remembered what Basil had told her on the journey: that his first English ancestor had come over from Portugal during the Napoleonic wars, driven out by the Peninsular War, and with his savings had built up a general merchant's business, dealing, among other things, in textiles, as another Jewish exile, Nathan Rothschild, was also doing. But when Nathan moved to London, Aaron Absalom remained in Manchester and became involved in cotton manufacture, first as a middleman, then as the owner of a small mill bought with his substantial profits. From such modest beginnings had come the Absalom riches, added to by each generation. Basil had not boasted about them; his home was all the more of a surprise.

The large high-ceilinged drawing room seemed to May to be completely full, without an inch to spare, of people and objects. More people than she had ever seen in a private room milled about among furniture: gilt chairs in the Louis XV style, fragile little tables covered with knick-knacks and photographs in silver frames of modern Sociables, a massive mahogany chiffonier doubling the scene in its mirrors, over the fireplace a huge overmantel rearing its burden of curlicues and laden shelves to the ceiling.

Basil led her through the throng to where, in a throne-like chair, the queen of the occasion sat, robed rather than dressed in a flowing, spreading gown of purple, with a good deal of lace about it and a lace mantilla on her head. May thought that given the Sceptre and Orb she would have made a splendid model for a statue of the Queen.

Basil kissed his mother's cheek, greeted her in Yiddish, and propelled May forward. 'Mama, may I present Miss May Atkinson?'

His mother smiled, holding out a plump hand almost invisible for rings. May shook it, feeling that a reverent kiss would be more appropriate. Basil was explaining that May was his partner's daughter, and trusting that his mother would not mind his having invited her for the happy occasion.

Esther Absalom smiled graciously. 'Delighted,' she said in a heavy foreign accent. For her age she was amazingly handsome, her dark eyes as bright as jet and her face discreetly touched with rouge and powder. Her hair was improbably black and shining, arranged in plaited masses under the mantilla. May found out later that it was a wig; Esther had been brought up as a strictly orthodox member of the Sephardim sect, and like other such Jewish wives had cut off her hair on marriage. She had obviously been a striking beauty in her youth.

Basil led May into the throng of his relations, presenting her to one after another. 'Moses ... Benjamin ... Hannah ... Rachel ... Serena ... Mayer...' Incapable of taking them individually, she smiled and nodded. Everybody said 'Mazel tov,' to her, and she began to say it back, to Basil's amusement.

It was difficult to hear anything else they said for the uproar of chatter. She had expected to feel like a fish out of water among these people so different from her own, but to her surprise a curious feeling of belonging came over her before she had been in the room many minutes. Perhaps it was that her nature, made for happiness and starved of it, responded to their warmth, the sense of family identity and closeness they exuded, their obvious and reassuring prosperity, so different from the pale faces and lean ragged bodies of her father's workers. She felt herself beaming, returning hearty handshakes, and was aware of the attention her blonde looks attracted.

Soon there was a summons to the dining room, where a vast meal was spread.

'I hope you won't find the food unpleasant,' Basil said. 'It's not altogether what you're used to, but of course it has to be kosher.'

'Of course,' she replied, knowing nothing about it.

He laughed. '*Kosher* means *proper, suitable, right* — something like that. Right for us, that is, prepared as our laws insist.'

'I never knew you were, well, *really* Jewish. I mean, you don't seem so at home.'

'Ah, a good many people present tonight would say I wasn't. I'm a back-slider, a bad Jew who doesn't go to *shul* — the synagogue — as often as he ought, and rides horses on the Shabbat. That's Saturday, not your Sunday Sabbath. I do look in at the Reformed Synagogue when I can, I'll say that for me. Mama thinks I'm practically a lost soul, but, between you and me, a good many of our friends and relatives here tonight are pretty lax as well. It's difficult in a business life, when one has to eat with Gentiles and keep their hours. Have some of the stuffed fish they're bringing. It's one of our great dishes, and it's very good.'

May enjoyed the fish, and the fowl, and the lavish helpings of perfectly cooked vegetables. There were light wines to drink, in which Basil joined her, but she noticed that tea and coffee were more generally popular, and that those who drank wine seemed not to be affected by it. At the head of the table Mrs Absalom presided expansively, her eldest son at her right hand, eating very heartily and talking a great deal. She seemed not to be in the least deaf.

The faces round the table seemed to be mainly of two kinds, plumply cheerful or aquiline and slightly melancholic. Basil was of the latter group, now May came to compare him with others of his race. But beside them, and his mother in particular, he seemed almost colourless and very English. There were obvious Gentiles present: business associates, perhaps, or neighbours.

May's neighbour on the other side from Basil was one of the jolly variety, Asher Cohen, who was 'in cotton' and had a lot to say about the present situation and the prospects of an end to it. She was so busy making what she hoped was intelligent conversation with him that she hardly spoke to anyone else. At the end of the long meal people began to rise and drift away, but Mrs Absalom remained at the head, holding court. Suddenly she fixed May with her glittering gaze, and beckoned.

'I am very pleased to see you, Miss Atkinson,' she said. 'My son tells me much of you and your house.' May understood *house* to mean *family*. 'Your father is as a brother to him, he has said. But you know nothing of us? You have not attended a *bris* before?' At May's baffled look, she explained, 'A *bris* is a family feast; a wedding, a birthday, a circumcision, a *bar-mitzvah*, when a boy attains manhood. So, how do you like our celebration?'

'I like it very much, Mrs Absalom, I don't think I ever enjoyed myself so. I…' She began, flounderingly, to try to express what she felt, the elation and sense of security.

Mrs Absalom nodded. 'We are a family, all of us. Judaism is one great family. It is very important to us.'

'Yes, I know. My family used to be a happy one, until my sister…' Half-horrified, she found herself telling the old lady about Marigold, wondering how she dared, yet filled with an urge to confide. At the end of the story her listener nodded slowly, with understanding.

'Basil told me something of this. I am sorry for you. You should have had more sisters, more brothers. When Basil was born to me I was past a woman's age for bearing, but I was glad, as Sarah rejoiced when she was with child of Isaac. You will have many children, because you know this need.'

'Will I?' A cold shiver ran down May's spine. Was she hearing a prophecy?

'Maybelle.' Again the imperious beckoning. How did Basil's mother know her full name? Nervously she approached, was folded in silky, perfumed arms, received a ceremonial kiss on each cheek. Then, with a gracious nod, she was dismissed.

Basil appeared. 'May, have you met my nephew, David?'

May looked up, and it was as though her body flamed with white sweet fire and her heart became a soaring lark. He was tall and slender, with the look of a prince from the Arabian Nights; as black as coal, as white as snow, as red as blood, said a memory from an old nursery tale. Yet the white skin was tinged as though with a scatter of gold dust, and the dark eyes were meltingly beautiful, soft, like a deer's eyes, the soul shining through them. He put out his hand and took hers, holding it a long time, and in that moment May fell in love, just as she had once told Edwin she might: wildly, madly, excitingly.

She was terrified that he would leave them and be lost to her, but he stayed with them, looking often at May, saying little, yet his deep gentle voice seemed to her like the heavenly music of a great symphony. Soon Basil slipped away, leaving them together in the corridor outside the dining room.

'Shall we go and see the fireworks?' David said, and, smiling, offered her his arm to the French windows where people were already gathering. On the lawns outside servants were letting off dazzling explosions of light, rivulets and cascades of fire, bursting stars of emerald and diamond and pink, white fountains, golden wheels, rockets that soared high above them and turned to airy torches.

'Great-Aunt Esther should have been born at Hanuka,' David said.

'Hanuka? What's that?'

'The Feast of Lights. It comes in midwinter, about the time of Christmas. Every household puts an eight-branched candlestick, the *menorah,* in a window, so that passers-by can see them, and remember a time in our history when one day's supply of oil burned for eight days, so that help might come to the Temple.'

His arm was close and warm against her. There was a calm about them, a oneness, though surging excitement was in her heart. All the rest of that evening he stayed with her, while others watched them, and speculated, and smiled.

The guests were going, but she was to stay the night. She said goodnight to David, wistful to see him go, yet knowing he would come back to her soon. Basil appeared at her side.

'Well,' he said, 'you wanted fireworks, and you got them.'

'Yes, I did. Thank you.' She kissed him; she would have liked to kiss the whole world.

Basil watched her go up the stairs, light-footed, light-hearted, the bright image of her mother in youth.

When May announced her intention of marrying David Absalom a family storm broke. Joe was furious at the thought of his surviving daughter leaving home, and for a virtual foreigner, Dove distressed. May faced them with apparent calm.

'You haven't thought of Basil as a virtual foreigner all these years, Father. When did you ever think of him as a Jew — and if you had, what difference would it have made?'

'That's nothing to do with it. We only see him away from his own kind. You don't know what you'd be taking on — all that mummery, and those un-Christian customs, and plenty of bad feeling. You'd be the black sheep in that fold, I'm telling you straight.' He was trembling with anger, the old nagging pain starting up in him.

'Not at all. They're very kind people, and I think they like me.'

'They would now. Not when they know about this ridiculous notion of yours.'

'It's not ridiculous, and it's not just mine, it's David's as well. We knew as soon as we met that we were meant for each other, whatever anyone else said. You don't think he'd let me run my head into the lion's mouth? The Lion of Judah, ha, ha,' May added with a hysterical giggle.

'There's nothing to laugh about, May,' said her mother sharply. 'We've not met this young man, but he sounds thoroughly unsuitable. Your father and I don't like the idea at all. For one thing, dear, it's most unwise of you to commit yourself to a person you hardly know.'

'I've known him a whole month.'

'Don't quibble. You'll be sorry one day, if you act on impulse. I know you've been very much alone, and met few men, so I can understand a little. But girls can be very foolish, May.'

'All right. You think David's unsuitable, and you don't approve of him, and you don't think I can possibly be really in love with him, but you haven't met him. Very well, then, you *shall* meet him. You'll see.'

They saw, though reluctantly. Dove was forced to admit to herself that David was possibly the handsomest and best-mannered person who had ever crossed their threshold. He was quiet, far from the Flash Ikey image with which Joe had taunted May, yet when he spoke it was with great good sense. He managed to convey, without saying much, integrity and intelligence; his attitude to May convinced Dove that he loved her as deeply as she him, though without the flying of romantic banners. When he had gone she tried to weaken May's case by this very lack.

'But he *is* romantic!' May broke out. 'He doesn't just look like Romeo, he *is* Romeo, and he makes me feel like Juliet. *Her* family didn't think much of their marriage, either, and look what happened. Don't worry, we shan't stab or poison ourselves, we shall be very, very reasonable. If Juliet had been reasonable with her family they'd have come round, and there wouldn't have been a tragedy.'

Dove sighed. The ground seemed to be slipping away beneath her feet. One objection, that David might not be able to support May, had been demolished before it was raised; he was a merchant banker, following in the footsteps of his father.

301

Yet Dove could not bring herself to approve the match, or try to persuade Joe to do so, even though he was making himself ill again over it. The thought of losing May was unbearable. There was something else. David was Basil's nephew, son of his brother. In his features she could see a glimpse of the younger Basil, and she was bitterly jealous of May.

The ripples spread wide, as far as Lancaster. Ephraim was at first incredulous, then furious. The idea was preposterous, unthinkable. His granddaughter to marry a Jew! He would never countenance such a thing.

Margaret reasoned with him. 'My dear, I know it seems odd to you. But remember, in our young days the Jews were outcasts in this country. They had almost no rights — to hold office under the Crown, to enter Parliament, or go to university...'

Ephraim smiled grimly. 'Indeed. I remember Lord Coke stating that the Jews were devils' subjects and there could be no peace between them and Christians — and that view was upheld in court. I could even give you the date of the hearing.'

'Pray don't. I am trying to say that those days are over — people are not so ignorant now. They are as free as us, and just as good. You read the papers, dear. Do you despise men like Sir Moses Montefiore, or Sir David Salomons, who was Lord Mayor of London? I don't think you should. If you object to their religion, remember that we are all equal in God's eyes; and perhaps their God and ours are the same. Sometimes I think they are.'

'Don't talk heathen rubbish, Margaret. My grandchild's life is at stake. I shall go and settle the whole thing myself.'

'Oh no! You're not well enough — it will upset you too much!'

He pulled himself away from her affectionate grasp. 'I shall go, and there's an end of it.'

And go he did. Dove was appalled to find herself with an angry, ailing father on her hands as well as Joe. Their days and nights seemed to be one long wrangle, two dogs using May as a bone — with Dove herself a bitch joining in, she reflected bitterly. But her mind was made up. The marriage was quite out of the question.

For a time May kept up her valiant defiance of them. After all, it mattered not at all whether she had their approval or not. She was twenty-one, she would simply leave home and marry David. Her father could keep her dowry; the Absaloms had no need of it.

The only difficulty in her path was David himself. When she wrote him a long, passionate letter declaring her readiness to marry him whenever he chose, she received a cool, balanced reply.

I understand your feelings, dearest May. Of course you are free to marry without your parents' consent. But I would have the greatest scruples about it. To defy them would be to rob us of their goodwill, and, believe me, we would be unhappy without it. In our Faith a wedding is a time of great rejoicing with no place in it for resentment, a family festival; and both families must be as one. Forgive me for adding to your worries. I have my own, you know, for our rabbi refuses to marry us in view of our different faiths. My darling, try your best to persuade them.

This reasonable letter was the last straw to May. She rushed to Basil, who had been carefully keeping out of the way of the strife, feeling responsible for it having come into being at all.

'You see, even David's against me now! I suppose he wishes he'd never proposed. As for this rabbi, how *can* he refuse to marry us? A vicar doesn't refuse to marry people if the banns are put up. Silly old man, whoever he is!'

'Don't be childish, May. David belongs to the Reform Synagogue, but even their rabbis dislike mixed marriages — won't perform them, more often than not. I've known a couple travel all over Europe looking for a rabbi broadminded enough to tie the knot between a Jew and a Gentile.'

'Very well, that settles it — I'll become a Jewess, and they can like it or not, I don't care.'

Basil clutched his head. 'O God of Jacob! I wish I'd never introduced you two. Listen, there's only one thing for it, you must talk to Mama before you take any such decision. It's a very grave thing, do you realise that? No, I thought not. Well, my mind's made up. Go and get ready, and I'll take you to Manchester.'

'But ... they won't let me.'

'You keep saying they can't stop you, don't you? Brace up, then. I'll go and tell them, that'll settle it.'

A somewhat awed May was led into Esther Absalom's bedroom. She reclined, propped up on lacy pillows, in a large, ornate brass bed inlaid at head and foot with mother-of-pearl, and she wore a peignoir of dark gold silk and a cap of snowy lace. Her fine eyes were kind as she held out a hand to May; it carried just as many rings as on her birthday night.

'So, the fair young Maybelle is in trouble. Sit down. Tell me.'

May found herself pouring out everything; her love for David, her affection for her family and resentment that they should not want her to be happy, her determination to do anything that would enable her and David to be married, even to giving up her religion.

'So Basil has told me. How much does your religion matter to you, my child?'

May was taken aback. 'I ... never gave it any thought.'

'No?'

She blushed. 'Well. I go to church, of course.'

'Why?'

'Because — because we all do.'

Smiling her sybil's smile, Esther extracted from May that piety had never meant a great deal to her. Some girls *were* pious, she supposed — they did things like getting up to go to early service, and taking Bible classes, which was of course very worthy, but not really interesting to May. The hymns were nice, and Christmas, but...

Esther listened to the innocent confession of a girl in love with love and life, a nice, good girl, but one who would qualify neither as a Catholic nun nor an Anglican spinster. She was infinitely relieved, a great weight lifted from her mind. When she had heard enough, she said, 'You have told me that you do not truly practise your religion. Shall I tell you what it would mean to practise ours?'

Slowly and clearly, feeling for the right words, she talked of Judaism: of the mysteries of the Shabbat and its restrictions, of the Holy Days and the great Feasts of the year, of the laws that have come from ancient times which help exiled Jews to survive as a community. 'We are one great family. It is this belief that makes us what we are; and the mother is the head of the family. It is the mother who prepares the food that begins the ritual of the Shabbat, who lights the candles for Hanuka, who cleanses her house for Passover, who bears the children that will make her marriage fruitful and joyful...'

As May listened, her face grew more and more thoughtful. Esther stopped. 'You are afraid. I am telling you more than you wish to hear.'

'No. No. Only it's so much more — serious — than I thought. Mrs Absalom, I've been very silly. I didn't know what I was saying when I told Basil I would join David's faith. I didn't understand.'

'You understand now?'

'Not altogether. You told me so much, but there must be so much more.'

There was a silence in the room. A perfume like incense hung on the air. May, her mind in turmoil, saw without seeing the garden trees dressed in the tender green of early spring, the passing traffic of the suburban road. She felt pulled in two between the claims of convention, habit, fear of great change, and the curious feeling of belonging that had come over her in this room, as it had done on the night of the birthday party. Esther watched her, anxious, though nothing in her look showed it. At last May said, 'Please can I think about it?'

'But of course. And I would ask you one thing: come to our synagogue. David shall take you. Then you will see things clearer.'

'It's not true, of course,' Dove said; 'You're saying this to try and force our hand, you wicked girl. Joe, tell her.'

'Come on, love,'Joe gave her a shadow of his old smile. 'Mother and I know you and your ways. You always were a bit of a rebel, but you mean no harm. Only it's doing us some harm, May, having to fight you like this. Now just come and sit down by me, like you used to do, and tell us it's all nonsense.'

May stayed defensively where she had placed herself, where the lamplight fell full on her face, showing them her resolution.

'Not nonsense, Father. I intend to become a Jewess; next week I shall begin instruction with David's rabbi.'

CHAPTER SEVENTEEN

'Well, I never. Our May arisen a mother in Israel.'

'Don't laugh, Basil. I was never more serious in my life. And it's solved everything.'

'True.' May's dramatic resolution had been the end of her family's resistance. They were completely uncomprehending, but it was clear that she was deeply in earnest, and not only in her desire to marry David. Something had come into her life that they had never been able to offer her, and Dove knew they would be wrong to oppose it The best argument on May's side had been David himself. He came to them as though no bad feelings had ever been and no strife existed. As he sat by their fireside, beautiful as an angel, wise and gentle and unselfconsciously at home, he seemed already like their son, May at his side, mild and loving as they had never seen her, even at her best. Her rebellion had disappeared since her talk with Esther Absalom. Now it was not a matter of winning or losing, but of acceptance: hers, of David's belief and way of life, theirs, of what she must become for her fulfilment.

'You're afraid it will change her,' he said to them, 'and take her away from you. But it will only bring her closer.'

'Such a different way of life,' sighed Dove. 'So strange, almost foreign.'

'Not so strange as May thinks, perhaps. Forgive me for talking about you as if you were not there, May. You see, Grandmama is highly Orthodox. Now I am not, though rather more so than Basil. It would be impossible for me to keep strictly to the rules and be successful. Others have done it, older men brought up to be devout at any price, but for my generation...' He shrugged. 'The more English our race becomes, the more easy in our ways. That's why we have a Reform Synagogue.'

'But I want to be like Mrs Absalom!' May exclaimed. 'She explained...'

'I know, darling, and quite right. But the Gospel according to Grandmama is a difficult one to follow in the world of international banking. I do my best, but ... don't worry. It will work out very well.'

Because he was David, they believed him, in spite of their own reservations. But Dove still could not find the courage to tell Ephraim. He had developed a heavy cold, caught on the journey from Lancaster. It had turned to bronchitis, and he had been in bed for over a week when May made her dramatic declaration. He seemed very ill, occasionally wandering in his mind, to Dove's alarm. When he turned the corner and began to recover she decided to risk his health no further, and made the guest bedroom he occupied into a bed-sitting room, with a large comfortable armchair placed by a fire which was never allowed to go out, and everything to hand that he could possibly want, and the services of young Warburton as attendant, valet and part-time nurse. The old man and the young one got on well; what they talked about nobody knew, but the drone of Warburton's voice could be heard going on and on, Ephraim's sometimes replying.

He seemed to have no wish to go home, perhaps because he knew himself unfit for the journey. Margaret, alone and worried in Lancaster, sent him a parcel of books he had ordered. He glanced at them, then turned away to a pile of *Gentlemen's Magazine*s covering the last century and more, as though only the past held any interest for him. Dove wished guiltily that he had not come to the Lion House when he did, to complicate first the issue of May's engagement and then the arrangements for her wedding.

It was fixed for just after Passover, the festival coinciding with Easter. The young couple were anxious to get married, Esther encouraged them, observing that she intended to see them man and wife before she died — though her abounding good health might have been envied by a woman thirty years her junior — while Dove and Joe felt that the sooner the whole thing was over, the better. Nobody told Ephraim about it. May took David to see him, once, merely saying, 'Grandfather, this is David.' The old man greeted him courteously; May was sure he drew no connection between the elegant, Spanish-featured young man and the cartoon Jew of his imaginings.

The arrangements were complicated. The traditional ceremony made no provision for the bride's father being a Gentile. It was Basil, therefore, who by his own suggestion took over the role, primed as he was with the financial details which must be publicly agreed, and Esther who delightedly put herself in charge of the enormous guest-list and the wedding details — the synagogue, flowers, music, and refreshments for the reception, which was to be held at her home, the centre of that great web of relations. She was helped by her elderly companion, Miss Levy, and David's mother Ruth, who was somewhat nervous and inclined to disapprove of the whole thing. But she was talked down at the first sign of opposition by her husband Louis, David and his brother Victor. The bride's parents were invited to Manchester to meet their in-laws to be. Joe refused to go, saying that he was too unwell. Dove went alone, and found the house and the people strange and intimidating, kind and courteous though they all were to her. She could see nothing in them of Basil's dear familiar face, hear nothing like his flat Lancashire voice. She came back, dispirited. There was no place for her in the preparations for her daughter's wedding, only the one concession she had, the supervising of May's wedding dress. Joe would pay for that, of course. Otherwise the expenses would be put down to the Absalom purse — which, he remarked bitterly, could well afford it.

The wedding was three days away, the dress almost finished, May in a fever of excitement. She was to travel to Manchester the previous day, to spend the night at Esther's house; 'not even married from home,' Dove said to Basil.

'Well, there's good reason for it. The bridesmaids are there, she'll have plenty of help with dressing, and Mama can give her moral support, if she needs any. Better than all that last-night-in-the-old-home business, bride turning up with a red nose and puffy eyes.'

'I dare say. I'm sure your Mama knows best. She seems to know best about everything. I don't know why we're bothering to go at all,' she added with an artificial laugh. 'The Absaloms could manage the whole affair between them, very nicely.'

'Don't be sarcastic, it doesn't suit you. Anyway, what are you complaining about? Your sister's coming, and Laurence, and the folk from Downham, and Edwin. That ought to constitute a quorum.'

Two days to go. Dove had sat alone all evening; Joe had gone to visit the estate, May accompanying him, full of goodwill towards others in the glow of her own happiness. Soon she would be gone. Nobody in the Lion House but her lonely self, Joe, ailing and silent, and the servants. Her father lived so remotely that his presence hardly counted, and in any case he would be going home soon. She felt a sudden urge to talk to him, to be cheered and comforted as she had once been by him. It was Warburton's evening off, and he would be alone. She went upstairs, knocked softly, and entered his room.

The lamp was alight, the fire low. He sat in his armchair, a rug over his knees in spite of the warmth of the spring night, his spectacles as usual halfway down his nose.

'I've come to sit with you for a bit, Father, if you don't mind. Oh dear, your book's on the floor.' She bent to pick it up and offered it to him, but his hands lay idle in his lap and he did not answer.

'Father?' She moved the lamp so that the light fell on his face. His eyes were closed and his expression peaceful. She knew at once that he was dead.

When the first shock of grief had waned, and the three of them were calmer, a dreadful dilemma presented itself.

'The wedding will have to be postponed of course,' Joe said. 'You can't go on with it when there's been a death in the house.'

May turned white. 'But it can't be! Everything's arranged. The guests, the … oh, it's impossible. Grandfather wouldn't want that!'

'Your grandfather wouldn't have wanted this wedding at all. Be thankful he's where he'll never know anything about it. I know you're disappointed, but the decencies have to be observed. I'll send Warburton to Manchester tomorrow to tell them. This means a year of mourning, you know; you can think about it again after that.'

Joe, my dear Joe, Dove mourned inwardly, *how changed you are from the man who would have comforted his daughter and thought of her first, and me, before the decencies… What has disease taken from you, and from us all?*

Aloud she said, 'I'm afraid Father's right, dear. We couldn't go on with it now.'

May's face was aflame, her voice shaking. The obedient Jewess-to-be gave way to the old wayward May, fighting now for her happiness.

'You can do what you like, and say what you like. I'm very very sorry Grandfather's dead, but he was a very old man and he died peacefully, so one can't be sorry about *that*. And I know he wouldn't have wanted to spoil things for me and David, and everyone. Anyway, it's no use your going on about the decencies to me, Father. Whatever you and Mother do, I am the person getting married and I intend to get married on Wednesday. I shall pack up my clothes and collect the dress and drive to Grandmama Esther's in the morning, and there's nothing you can do to stop me.'

She rose and swept out of the room, banging the door. They heard her noisy weeping as she ran upstairs.

'Good God,' Joe said. 'That any daughter of mine should be so wicked.'

So it was left to Dove to find some solution. She lay awake all night in the room she had not shared with Joe for so long. Joe was right in principle, of course, and what May had said was deeply shocking. But, being May, she would do exactly as she intended and there would be an awful scandal, not least among the Absaloms, who reverenced their elderly relations.

She confronted Joe at the breakfast table. 'I've thought it out, Joe. Please don't say anything until I've finished. I know how you feel, and how I feel too, but we must be sensible, for everyone's sake. Mrs Skerritt laid Father out last night, and everything is decent for the undertaker to find when he comes this morning. He should be here soon. I shall ask him to take Father's body to his private chapel and keep it there until the funeral. Nothing will be said about his death — *nothing* — until after the wedding. Our guests will arrive tomorrow, and we shall just tell them he's very ill. David's family must be told nothing, either. Can you understand? This is the only way.'

Joe regarded her bleakly. He was weary from sleeplessness, distressed for the loss of the man who had been a father to him, disillusioned with his womenfolk's heartless attitude. 'Do what you please. I shall stay out of it.'

'You won't come to the wedding?'

'No.'

She had sided with May against him; he would side against them both. All that had been built up again after her discovery of his illness was demolished. Into her mind, unbidden, came a rueful memory of themselves, young sweethearts, strolling entwined by the Lancaster canal at Aldcliffe, talking of their children and their wedding, and Joe putting a bunch of wild red campion into her hand. A million years ago; two other people. The man who had made their marriage possible was dead. With his death, another wedge had been driven between them. She looked down at the tablecloth, spread for the breakfast neither wanted; it seemed like an ocean, Joe on the far side of it. Mechanically she poured tea from the urn, then made a last attempt to bridge the ocean.

'I could stop the others coming. If I sent telegrams this morning Belle and the Bradshaws would get them in time. Would that make you feel happier?'

'Don't bother,' he said.

No shadow darkened the cheerfulness of the bride's relations as they entered the synagogue. The four ladies (for Jesse was prevented by parliamentary business from attending) wore their best and brightest clothes. Many eyes were drawn to the shining handsomeness of Lucy and the beguiling beauty of Bertha, a vision in pink. Belle was in her best looks, drinking in admiration. Eleanor beamed on the crowd of strangers as though she had known them all her life; and indeed, many faces she saw recalled her old love, Ben Disraeli, now a leading light in the political world, lately Chancellor of the Exchequer and leader of the House. Dear Ben ... if only these people knew that there had already been a Jewish alliance — of a sort — in the bride's family.

Dove was torn between the excitement of the occasion and her oppressive guilt. She had dressed in the quietest colours she could find. Tomorrow the mourning she had put on for Marigold would be her dress for a year. She tried to forget her trouble, looking round the crowded synagogue, the resplendently dressed ladies, the sombrely suited men all wearing black skull-caps. She smiled at Edwin, also wearing a skull-cap, sitting on the other side of the aisle — for the sexes were segregated. He looked impressively noble in his odd headgear, like a young Florentine. She noticed that his gaze often wandered towards the pew where Lucy sat.

The beautiful singing of unseen choristers in the gallery was forgotten as the bride entered. May, serene and stately in her wide-skirted gown of Honiton lace, its demi-train carried by two pretty dark-eyed girls. Dove's eyes filled as her daughter, on Basil's arm, mounted the rostrum where David waited with his father, mother, Esther, and the rabbi. Once Basil had said something about a canopy of flowers; now May stood there, among spring blossoms and buds. She would not speak during the ceremony, which was conducted entirely by the men. The meaning of it passed Dove by; she wept, as she had not yet been allowed to weep for her father.

It was over, the radiant bride and smiling top-hatted bridegroom moving down the aisle towards the waiting carriage. The wedding breakfast, held at Esther's house, was a sumptuous affair of abundant food and flowing wine, flowers and high spirits. For quite half an hour bride and bridegroom stood by the door of the dining room, shaking hands and receiving good wishes, before they were free to drink and eat themselves. May went straight to Dove and kissed her.

'Thank you, Mother. Thank you for everything. Don't cry any more.'

'No, I won't, dear. You look very beautiful, and I'm very happy for you.'

Edwin found Lucy. 'Well? I hope you enjoyed that splendid ceremony.'

'Very much.'

'Encouraged to go in for something of the kind yourself?'

'When I am, I'll let you know.'

'Is that a promise, Lucy?'

She smiled enigmatically, and moved away from him to talk to Laurence, who had been embarrassed by the extremely un-Anglican nature of the wedding, and was looking unhappy. His mother was surrounded by a group of gentlemen, flashing her eyes and chattering; she had hardly spoken to him. He slipped away, unnoticed, unable to face the hours of merrymaking that would follow.

Late in the afternoon the bride and bridegroom disappeared to change into day-clothes. They were to spend their honeymoon at a Cheshire country house lent to them by David's Uncle Elias. The kisses, embraces, congratulations and exhortations behind them, they found themselves with relief in the carriage, alone.

May said, 'I've something to tell you. It's a bad beginning, but I can't keep it from you any longer.' David listened, impassive, to the story.

'Well? Are you very angry? I expect you despise me.'

'No. I understand why you did it, perfectly.'

'But you wouldn't have done it yourself?'

'That would have been impossible. Our laws say that we must mourn the dead for thirty-seven days. For the first seven, the *Shiva,* we don't leave the house, or do any work, only receive calls of condolence. For the next thirty, the *Shloshim,* we may work but not pursue pleasure or entertainment.'

May was thoughtful. 'I see. Well, I can understand the last part of it, but just sitting at home doing nothing sounds very boring. I don't think I could do that. What use is it?'

David laughed. 'My dear wife, I knew you would never make an Orthodox Jewess. The minute one of the rules fails to please you, you'll break it. I've married a rebel, and I know it. At least it betokens strong-mindedness, and I like that; the children won't be spoilt.' He drew her head to his shoulder. They watched the landscape turn from town to country, and the sunset crown their day with a glory of rose and purple, violet and gold.

The ladies of the Bradshaw family were back home, still discussing the wedding. 'I really thought we would be having another Jewish marriage in the family,' Eleanor said, 'with all the attention that young man Cohen paid to you, Bertha. When the dancing began he hardly let you go for a single dance. Such a good-looking boy. You could do worse, you know.'

Bertha smiled. 'Oh, it wouldn't do at all, Aunt Eleanor. I may have left the convent but I'm still a Catholic. There would be too many obstacles.'

'You're not a remarkably *good* Catholic,' Lucy pointed out. 'I haven't noticed you going to Mass except in fine weather or when you have a new bonnet.'

'Lucy, how unkind!' Eleanor exclaimed, but Bertha said, 'It's quite true. I don't go as often as I should — but it *is* quite a drive to the chapel, and I know Father Andrew doesn't mind. Well, not very much. Perhaps we should ask him to dinner again. Could he come this Saturday? Then we could tell him about the wedding. Poor man, he doesn't hear much news, in that lonely place.'

'But,' Eleanor said, 'have you forgotten that Mr Sherston is invited for Saturday? I *think* it's Saturday, but it might be Friday — I shall have to consult my engagement diary.'

Lucy looked up sharply. 'Mr Sherston?'

'Yes, Billy Sherston. Haven't you met him, my dear? No, perhaps not. He called to see your father, on some political business or other, but now he calls on us ladies. I don't know whose company he finds so agreeable — but I could make a good guess.'

Bertha looked modestly down at her hands. 'Really, Aunt.'

'Quite the old style of country gentleman,' Eleanor continued, 'with a very fine place at Creston. We've only dined there once, but we were most impressed.'

'I believe Mr Sherston is famous for his dinner parties,' Lucy said grimly. So no whisper had reached Eagle Hall of the details of Magnolia's flight and recovery. Lucy knew instinctively that Magnolia had talked about Sir Jesse and his family, and that Sherston had called out of curiosity or some other reason. Evidently he had found an attraction; Bertha, perhaps. An interesting idea took root in her mind.

'Would you like to ask me to dinner with Mr Sherston, Mama? I think I've heard of him. One should get to know one's neighbours.'

'My dear, how ridiculous. This is your home, wherever you choose to keep those animals of yours. Come when you like. I only wish you would come back and behave as the daughter of the house.'

'I'm sure Bertha does that very capably,' said Lucy with a sweet smile.

As it proved, the weekend dinner did not take place. The morning after the return to Eagle Hall Dove's letter arrived, telling them of Ephraim's death.

I cannot suppose you will forgive me. I shall never forgive myself but at the time the dreadful concealment seemed necessary. I tell myself that my father would have wished it for May's sake. Per-haps you will understand now why Joe was not at the wedding. Father's body has been dispatched to Lancaster. The funeral will take place on Friday at the Priory Church, as he would have wished, since he was married there and our mother is buried near the South Door. I beg you to be there with me and others of our family.

Eleanor's grief was great. She retired to her room for a day, then emerged, red-eyed, and sent for the dressmaker to put them all into mourning. Lucy wore hers at the funeral with the mental proviso that it would be packed away as soon as she reached Halton. When the simple service was over they took themselves to St Leonard's Gate. No ceremonial funeral meal, only tea and cakes with Margaret as hostess, sad, resigned, dry-eyed.

'I knew he would never come back from your house, Dove; I knew it when I let him go. Don't weep any more, my dear. His life was becoming a burden to him, and he is happy now. What a fine young man he was. I remember him at his wedding, such a well-set-up figure — though I was very bored and naughty, and misbehaved in some way at the wedding breakfast. Strange, how the old memories are the happiest ones. Yet I remember, as well as though it were yesterday, the night I ran away to join the players, and I was not at all happy then. Ah, well. How fortunate you are in your two girls, Eleanor.'

'Bertha is not —' Eleanor began.

'No, of course. But she seems so much one of your family. Do not you feel like one, my dear?'

'Yes, indeed, ma'am. I am so very happy at Eagle Hall. I never, never want to live anywhere else.' There was an intensity in the girl's tone which struck Margaret's sharpened hearing. She had not said that it was the Bradshaw family which caused her happiness. So the old Hall was stretching out its tentacles to another woman, having captured Eleanor long ago. The idea struck Margaret as an interesting one for a Gothic tale. Perhaps she would experiment with it when the young lady who acted as her amanuensis next called.

A few weeks of mourning, sincere though it was, were enough for Eleanor. 'I really think we might begin to offer hospitality again,' she said to Bertha. 'Goodness knows there's very little chance of indulging in frivolity, living here. But I think a few quiet little parties … yes, because Ephraim was only a brother-in-law, after all, not a blood relation. Yes, I'm sure that would be in order. Shall we renew our invitation to Mr Sherston? And perhaps Father Andrew at the same time. Three ladies and one man is such an awkward number — Lucy must come, of course. I thought she seemed quite interested in meeting Mr Sherston, didn't you?'

The dinner was perfect, the company well matched. Little Father Andrew's cheerful gossip assorted neatly with Sherston's tales of the lighter side of farming. Lucy saw that he paid Bertha assiduous attention, yet glanced often at herself, with something of a puzzled air, and addressed her with admiring respect. She was sure that he knew nothing of her finding of Magnolia; he had probably not given the girl a second thought after that night. It was her inspired guess that he had been told of the existence of a Bradshaw daughter, had at first taken Bertha for one, then discovered his mistake but continued to pay court to her. Now he was confronted with the real heiress of Eagle Hall, also an attractive and nubile young woman. Lucy sensed a divided interest, and played up to it. Bertha was gentle and modest, even coy, hiding behind her long lashes, arranging herself in deliberately pretty positions. Lucy, therefore, used her intelligence as a weapon, talking to Sherston on his own level, yet with feminine deference. She knew a lot about farming, about the life of the countryside, even about the history of Creston Hall. He listened, responded, and was charmed. Lucy was silently gleeful.

Father Andrew enjoyed their account of the Jewish wedding, while tut-tutting over the heathenness of it all. 'Time we had a good Catholic marriage to rival it, eh, Miss Bertha? Very few, there are, in a scattered parish like mine. Come now, what a fine time we'd have of it! Won't you persuade her to put one of her swains out of his misery, Lady Bradshaw?'

Eleanor laughed. 'It's for her to decide, Father. There are enough of them, goodness knows.'

'But very few Catholics, alas,' Bertha said, closing and unclosing her little fan with charming coquetry. Lucy saw the calculation in Sherston's gaze. A Catholic bride would be no disadvantage in these days of broad-mindedness, particularly if she were the well-dowered adopted daughter of a rich man. Not that he had need to marry for money, but it was an advantage. Yet — his eyes slewed round to Lucy — the real daughter was a beauty too, with a wit that promised plenty of entertainment, and a high spirit that might be amusing to break.

'Won't you play for us, Lucy?' Eleanor asked as they were taking tea after the conclusion of the meal. 'She plays very prettily, Mr Sherston, though it's a hard pull to get her to the piano. Do oblige, there's a dear girl.'

Lucy obliged, her pale green skirt flowing over and hiding the piano stool, her face calm and pure in the light of the two candles in their brackets. A brilliant flourish on the keys, and she launched into a ballad her mother for one had scarcely expected.

> *'How happy could I be with either.*
> *Were t'other dear charmer away!*
> *But since you both tease me together,*
> *To neither a word will I say,*
> *But tol-de-rol-lol-de-rol-laddy,*
> *But tol-de-rol-lol-de-rol-lay...'*

Her strong contralto voice filled the room. Bertha hid smiles behind her fan, Eleanor looked taken aback, Sherston stared. Lucy switched to a minor key and another ballad.

> *'Man may escape from rope and gun,*
> *Nay, some have outlived the doctor's pill;*
> *Who takes a woman must be undone,*
> *That basilisk is sure to kill.*
> *The fly that sips treacle is lost in the sweets,*

So he that tastes Woman, Woman, Woman,
He that tastes Woman, ruin meets.'

Eleanor broke the silence. 'My dear, what a very odd choice of song. Mr Sherston will wonder ... such an old-fashioned piece, *The Beggar's Opera*. I thought you might give us something pretty and modern — a tune from *Merrie England*, perhaps.'

'I was always fond of *The Beggar*, Mama,' Lucy said innocently. 'Don't you remember how Papa used to call me Lucy Lockit? It came into my mind, somehow — I don't know why.' She looked straight at Sherston.

He left with a courteous farewell, holding her hand rather longer than was usual. She let it lie, limp and cool, in his.

When he and Father Andrew had gone Lucy followed Bertha upstairs and into her bedroom.

'I want to ask you something. Does that man attract you?'

'Mr Sherston?'

'Well, I didn't mean Father Andrew.'

Bertha slowly let down her hair, admiring herself in the mirror. 'I quite like him. That is, I don't dislike him.'

'How overpoweringly enthusiastic. You were flirting with him quite openly. Has he said anything to you that sounded as if he meant marriage?'

'He's been very civil ... I think he admires me a little.'

Lucy exploded. 'Oh, for pity's sake, Bertha, stop it! Do you mean to marry him, if he asks you? That's a straight question and I want a straight answer. You were mucking out pigs and scrubbing kitchen floors not long before you came to us, so don't play the coy maiden with me.'

Bertha shrugged one dimpled shoulder out of her corsage and glanced at it approvingly. 'Well, then yes, I suppose I would marry him. Though I don't care for him all that much.'

'Then why?'

Bertha lifted limpid forget-me-not eyes that were for once completely truthful. 'Because he's rich. Because he has a fine house. Because he could give me beautiful things.

'Well, you mercenary little wretch!' Lucy sat down abruptly. 'Aren't you ashamed of yourself? Don't Mama and Papa give you everything you could possibly want and keep you in style? You've done jolly well for yourself since you left that convent, and you may thank Aunt Dove and my parents for it. Goodness me, you've had I don't know how many proposals already, none of them from men I'd call actually poor. Who are you waiting for? The Prince of Wales is married, you know.'

'You don't understand,' Bertha answered. 'It's all quite different for you. I never had anything beautiful until I came here. I never even saw anything beautiful until I went to your aunt's to nurse, and then I knew what I was missing and what I must have. That's why I gave up the convent and my vows. No, I don't love Billy Sherston if that's what you were asking me. I love this house — that's what I love.' She put her arms round one of the posts of the Jacobean bed, laying her cheek against the carved wood. 'But I can't have it, because I'm only here by charity. *You'll* have it, and you won't care for it at all, only fill it with messy animals, not love it and look after it, as I should. So that's why I must marry someone who can give me a beautiful house of my own and all the right things to put in it. Creston Hall isn't anything like this, but it would do.'

Lucy said nothing, her breath snatched away from her.

'You think I'm awful, don't you?' Bertha said, 'I'm sorry. I don't mean to sound ungrateful, it's just that I must … that I need…'

'Yes, I see. I didn't understand. Oh, Bertha, you mustn't marry that man. I don't care how rich he is or what he could give you. Trust me, and say no to him.'

'I shall do as I please.' Bertha turned her back and began to undress. Lucy went to her own room, and sat for a long time, thinking.

She had not long to wait for the next encounter with Sherston. She was determined that it should be a fateful one.

The invitation came to Eleanor. Would Lady Bradshaw do him the honour of dining with him the following week, bringing the charming young ladies of the family? Sir Jesse would be most welcome, if at home.

As it happened, Jesse was at home. Eleanor was told that she might accept for him, but he was less than enthusiastic.

'This fellow seems to be cultivating our family very assiduously. At first it was business, now it's pleasure. What's his game, do you suppose?'

'I don't suppose anything, my dear, except neighbourliness. Except that … I believe he is very much attracted to Bertha.'

'Bertha, eh? And what do you feel about that?'

'I hardly know. I've given it thought, of course. She must marry one day, and she seems not at all interested in the young men round here — I don't think it's because no suitable Catholic has offered for her. But Mr Sherston is so much older — forty at least, I should think. But there's something about him I don't quite care for. His eyes, perhaps — or is it the mouth? Something rather hard and cruel. I feel he might not be kind to Bertha, and she needs kindness. I may be imagining it, Jesse, but do you know who he reminds me of?'

'No, my dear. Who?'

'Your father.'

A picture of the long-dead Saul Bradshaw, stout, coarse, lustful and vengeful, came into Jesse's mind.

'I can't say I see much resemblance to Sherston,' he said. 'Quite different types of men in every way, I'd have said.'

'Well, it's a long time ago, and my memory isn't what it was, but I do remember him, and I remember that I asked you not to hang that portrait of him in this house.' She sighed. 'Perhaps it's all my fancy. Bertha should marry well, having nothing of her own, and he's said to be very rich. It would be quite a catch for her.'

'Hmm. I'll have to think about it. Not that she needs my consent, but I'd be happier in my mind if she married a man you and I approved. Let's see what impression he makes as a host.'

'Oh, he's a very good one, or at least he was last time. I hope Lucy will behave herself. When we entertained him she chose to sing some very ... well, unsuitable songs.'

Jesse laughed. 'Our Lucy? Don't tell me she's been taking lessons from the sailors, though I wouldn't put it past her. What did she sing — *Ekidumah,* or *Rollin' down the Highway?*'

'Nothing like that, of course. Well, she won't have a chance at Creston Hall — I haven't noticed a piano.'

Lucy took in with keen interest the atmosphere of Sherston's home. The hallway, its walls studded with the masks of foxes, badgers, otters. She paused, making herself meet the glass eyes of the creatures who had died in agony; how calm they looked now, prettily arranged, white teeth bared in a harmless snarl. Around them whips were arranged in a pattern. Sporting prints were the only pictures, here and on the walls of the staircase. The furniture was antique and good, if severe. No splashes of colour or feminine touches: so Sherston kept no mistress, at least not in this house.

Bertha's eyes too were all about her, confirming what she had thought on her first visit, that here was a house she could mould into beauty. Jesse and Eleanor both noted Lucy's pause at the display of trophies.

'She'll start on him about them,' Eleanor whispered. 'How I wish we hadn't brought her.'

But Lucy's conversation during dinner was impeccable. It emerged that Sherston was indeed a keen sportsman, who had shot wild boar in Bavaria and France, deer in Scotland, as well as lesser game in England; and of course he hunted. Bertha had seen him at a hunt ball, though he had not picked her out from a crowd of beautiful young ladies. 'I must have been temporarily out of my wits,' he said, 'or at least they were not about me.'

Lucy said primly, 'A hunt ball must be a splendid affair.'

'The liveliest evening of the winter,' Sherston agreed. 'But you must have attended many, Miss Bradshaw.'

'None at all,' Lucy said simply. In the silence, Eleanor felt impelled to inform him that Lucy ran an animal sanctuary for sick and ill-treated beasts, being so extremely fond of animals. Sherston laughed, uncomprehending.

'Pet poodles and cats, no doubt. Very charming.'

'Not at all,' Lucy said. 'Mongrel dogs, weakling piglets, wounded foxes, abandoned cubs. Otters, badgers, anything you like.'

'*Vermin?*' Sherston stared. 'What a strange pastime for a young lady.'

'And rather wrong-headed? I'm sure you're just going to say that I should be devoting myself to the deserving poor of our own race. People, after all, must be reckoned as far more important. The young, the defenceless, the victims of society. Don't you agree?' She gave him a dazzling smile, her parents and Bertha staring, uncomprehending. Eleanor shot a look at Jesse, who shook his head and applied himself to his plate. Both knew that Lucy was up to something.

Thereafter she was utterly winning in her manner to their host, flirtatious as never before, hanging on his every word until he was half-hypnotised by her gaze. Bertha was nettled. She saw her prize slipping away from her in the toils of the irresistible Lucy, and redoubled her efforts to captivate him. Between the two, Sherston was agreeably bewildered. He was deeply attracted to Bertha, fortune or not, seeing in her just the kind of kittenish ultra-feminine creature he enjoyed having at his mercy. She would make an undemanding wife, a pretty hostess, obedient to his every word, too timid to make a fuss about rivals. He wanted her. But the other, the heiress, was beautiful in a different way, quite a Diana, and he was confident of being able to beat the wrong-headedness out of her. It might be most amusing, in fact. He would tease her with half-dead beasts, take her when she was distressed. If only he could have one of the girls as a wife, the other as a mistress. They were as good as half-sisters, it appeared; his imagination rioted. Perhaps they could be persuaded to share him, turn and turn about. Or even better than that. The fair girl's eyes were flashing messages to him, he was sure of it, and his spirits rose with every speaking glance. He drank rather more wine than he was accustomed to drink.

The moment came for Eleanor to 'collect eyes', and lead the two younger ladies from the room. But Lucy sat where she was, very still, her hands clasped on the table.

'Lucy!' Eleanor hissed. 'Come along.'

'Not yet, Mama.'

327

'Lucy,' Jesse said in a tone she knew well. It meant that even she, his darling, would be in his bad books in a minute.

'No, Papa. Mr Sherston, there's something I think my family should hear. Did you not agree with me, some time ago, when I mentioned the abuse of young, defenceless persons, and how it was our duty to care for them?'

Nonplussed, his wine-lulled brain hardly taking in her words, he answered, 'Of course. I believe you said something of the kind.'

'I was thinking of one defenceless young person in particular. Not exactly a relation of mine, though I called her Cousin. You may remember her as Maggie Dilworth.'

Eleanor started. 'But that's George's b — George's daughter — Magnolia.'

'Exactly, Mama. Uncle George's daughter, Magnolia. A pretty, simple girl. Our host must remember her well — not very long since he ruined her.'

Sherston had gone greyish-white, the wine flush faded. 'Be careful what you say, Miss Bradshaw.'

Lucy smiled sweetly. 'Oh, but I won't, Mr Sherston. I shall tell them just what happened.' She embarked, coolly and precisely, on the story of Magnolia's luring and betrayal, the brutal treatment she had received, the callous abandonment of her to any fate that might befall her. Magnolia had in the end told Lucy everything, as though to tell the details would exorcise them from her mind. Lucy repeated them, sparing her hearers nothing, ignoring Bertha's violent blushes and her parents' shocked faces. Sherston was immobile, seeming hardly to breathe.

'If I hadn't gone riding out looking for her in every hole and corner I could think of, she might be dead by now. Or on the streets, taking sailors back to some hovel in China Lane. As it is, she's gone back home to Haiti with her father. Well, that's all. I thought you might like to hear the story, so that you can all think carefully whether this gentleman is a fitting husband for Bertha. Or for me. Or for any decent woman.'

Jesse was the first to speak. 'Well, Sherston?'

Not looking up, he said dully, 'I had no idea she was a close relative of yours. She said she had never met you. I thought she and her father were just … drifters. And she was…'

'Coloured?' Lucy suggested. 'No better than the slaves your ancestors carted back here in their stinking holds?'

He raised his hand involuntarily, and she knew he itched to strike her. She sat unmoving, her battle won, for Bertha had dissolved into tears and Eleanor's arm was round her shoulders. Jesse stood up.

'Normally I should thank you for your hospitality at this point, Sherston. As things stand, I'm sorry my daughter's story had to be told under your roof. Or at all. The fact that this unsavoury treatment was meted out to a connection of ours is irrelevant; the circumstances are all that matter. I really think there is no more to be said between us.'

Sherston got up and pulled the bell-rope. Only Bertha's sniffs were heard as a servant appeared and conducted the guests downstairs. Lucy did not look back at the man she had foiled. There was no way in which he could hit back at her.

He who tastes Woman, ruin meets.

CHAPTER EIGHTEEN

The grey ramparts of Lancaster Castle station seemed to beckon welcomingly to Edwin, the 'Way Out' sign on the platform to point him to an enchanted gateway. He was not given to airy fancies, but today his spirits were exalted. The night before he had hardly slept, having been engaged in delivering the sixth child of an unemployed weaver whose other children were near starvation point, and whose wife had become so dangerously ill in labour that he had run to the hospital for help. Neither sleeplessness nor the memory of the unhappy family could depress Edwin, for he was going to tell Lucy his news. He had been appointed senior obstetrician of St Aidan's Hospital, on the outskirts of Preston, the youngest man to have held such an office, thanks to a shortage of doctors with as high qualifications as his own, the degrees he had studied for so hard.

He could have telegraphed the news, or written, but only a visit would do. He must see the gladness in her face, hear the warmth in her voice. Outside the station he felt so filled with bounding energy that he could have walked the miles to Halton. Good sense prevailing, he took a cab.

His cheerful knock at the door of Lucy's house went unanswered. Could she be out, or staying with her parents? He knocked again, and stood surveying the neat cottage garden, the spotless sprigged curtains at the windows. After the sights and sounds and smells of the hospital his senses were refreshed, his spirits bounding even higher. If only she were at home!

But it was Joan Butterworth who answered the door, her broad face unsmiling. 'Doctor Edwin. Come in, will you.'

Puzzled, he stepped inside. 'Miss Lucy in, Joan? I've got something to tell her, so I thought I'd take a chance —'

She interrupted him. 'Doctor, I'm glad it's thee. Summat very bad's happened.'

He felt his blood grow chill. 'She's not ill? An accident?'

'No accident about it,' Joan said grimly. 'No, she's not ill, but she's in a right bad way. I can't tell thee. Go in and see.'

He entered the back room that was used as a surgery.

'Lucy! Oh, good God.'

She was sitting on a low chair in the middle of the room; her face was swollen and contorted with the tears that were still streaming down it, while harsh mechanical sobs shook her.

'She's been like it these two hours,' Joan said. 'I can't do owt for her.' Edwin's eyes ranged round the room. Blood was everywhere, and the corpses of slain animals and birds; fowls, a rabbit, two cats, a puppy. From a dark corner two eyes glared. The fox was alive, but badly injured.

'What in God's name happened?'

Lucy seemed not to hear his shocked question.

Joan answered, 'We went into town this morning, in t'trap, like we do twice a week. Miss Lucy wanted to call on Miss Bateman with some things, so she stopped there a while and I went to t'shops. Then we come back, and found this.'

'But who ... *what* ... did it?' He could only think of a mad dog, a savage wild cat, some beast unimaginable in that part of the world.

Lucy said, her voice an unrecognisable croak, 'A man.'

Edwin went to her and gently raised her from the chair. 'Come on. We'll go into the parlour. Joan, I want some hot sweet tea making, and some brandy.' He half-carried Lucy to the sofa in the next room, laid her on it and loosened the collar of her blouse. When the brandy was brought he poured out a generous glassful and held it to her lips. She drank it unresistingly. The sobbing lessened. Edwin wiped her face with his handkerchief dipped in water, and sat by her side, holding her hand and patting it, until Joan brought the tea. Lucy sipped from the cup he held in both his hands. He wished passionately that he had his doctor's bag with him, containing a sedative and sal volatile. But Lucy, strong vital Lucy, had come low enough to do what he told her. When he thought she had taken enough of the tea he laid her head back on a cushion and saw her eyes close.

Joan, who had watched anxiously, breathed a sigh of relief. 'Thank the Lord you came, Doctor. I thought she'd run mad. She seemed to hear nowt I said.'

'Well, tell me about it, Joan.'

Her story was meaningless to him. When they had come home and found the dreadful carnage in the surgery Joan had run across the lane to a neighbour, whose elderly mother spent most of her time sitting at the window. The old lady had seen a tall gentleman, whom she described in detail, ride up to Lucy's house with a couple of foxhounds at his horse's heels, dismount, and go through the gate to the paddock. After some minutes he had reappeared, hurriedly remounted and ridden away. 'Right flustered, he looked, as if he'd been up to summat wrong. Mrs Marten didn't know who he were, but she said she'd soon find out.'

'*I* know,' Lucy said, her eyes still shut.

'Don't try to talk now,' Edwin said. 'I want you to go upstairs with Joan, and she'll put you to bed. You've had quite a lot of brandy and you're very shocked. I'll give you a hand if you like, Joan.' But the big woman gathered Lucy up like a child and took her up the stairs.

Edwin went back to the surgery. The victims appeared to have been killed outright, obviously by dogs. Their cages had been opened, and when they had emerged they had been set on. But inside the cages he found two hens and a brown duck, apparently paralysed with fright, unharmed. The fox still lay in its corner. Edwin examined it carefully, keeping clear of the bared teeth. There were several wounds, ranging from slight to severe, but none of them in vital places. From the way Brushy lay he diagnosed a broken foreleg. If only, if only, he had had his bag, with its phial of chloroform!

Lucy slept for half an hour, waking to find Edwin sitting by her bed. As memory returned her eyes filled.

'Lucy,' he said firmly, 'no more tears, please. They won't do any good, and I need help from you. Do you feel strong enough to get up?'

She nodded. He helped her from the bed and downstairs, talking of nothing in particular, the weather, his journey from Preston. At the door of the surgery she stopped, and he felt her tremble.

'No, we must go in. Look, three of the birds are safe. They were hiding. And Brushy — you can help Brushy. Listen. I want you to kneel on the floor, close to him, and talk to him, comfort him, in your usual voice. He's been hurt and he's terrified and suspicious. You see what you have to do?'

'Yes.' She began to murmur to the fox, pet names, the special sounds he was used to hearing from her, until Edwin saw a relaxation in the pricked ears and the fiery eyes. 'Now, put your hand out. See if he'll let you touch him.'

He watched apprehensively as she advanced her fingers. The pointed muzzle drooped a little towards them, until it rested against her palm.

'Go on talking,' Edwin said. 'Look, I've prepared a splint. His off foreleg's broken. Go closer and hold him, while I put the splint on. Keep away from his mouth.'

'No. I'll put it on myself. I've done it to animals hundreds of times.'

'He'll bite.'

'Not me.'

Edwin watched as she crawled forward, caressed the fox's head, then laid the splint beside the broken leg and put a hand out to the limb. Brushy snarled and snapped at the hand, then, almost incredibly to Edwin, at a soft word from her drew back his head and let her bring the splint and the leg together, binding the stick of firewood on with a length of bandage. Though he whined pitifully, he made no further attempt to bite. When the leg was bound up, Edwin brought Lucy a bowl of warm water and a cloth and told her to wash the wounds.

'Now,' he said to Joan, who had been watching in amazement, 'let's have a shot of that brandy in his drinking bowl. He'll be thirsty, if I'm right.'

The fox sniffed suspiciously at the water, then began to lap, tentatively at first, then eagerly, until it was all gone. The watchers saw the tension go out of him, and his head droop to the ground. Lucy exclaimed anxiously, but Edwin said, 'He's only asleep. The brandy's knocked him out, on top of pain and exhaustion. There's nothing more we can do for the moment. He may be all right — I hope to God he is.'

'You're wonderful,' Lucy said simply.

'No, you are, my dear. I could never have got near him. I mean that you ... listen! Can you hear something?' Small muffled sounds were coming from the cupboard in the window alcove. Edwin opened the door, but could see nothing until he struck a match. On the bottom shelf, lying on a folded blanket, a cat was kittening.

'Oh!' Lucy dropped to her knees beside him. 'It's the little tabby. Oh, the darling, she hid, just in time. Three already. Here's the fourth.' They watched the tiny compact bundle slither out, and the mother attack it with her pink tongue, purring. Edwin marvelled at the ease and grace of it, in contrast to the agonies of human childbirth.

'Let's leave them,' he said. 'She knows best. There are some more lives saved, you see.'

Later, herself again, Lucy told him, 'It was Sherston. It could only have been him. He'd watched us, or sent somebody else to watch us, and then he came with the hounds when he knew we'd be out. He must even have known the surgery door wasn't locked.'

'But who is this person, and why do such a savage thing?'

'Because he owed it to me.' She told the story of Magnolia, and her own public humiliation of Sherston. 'I ought to have known a man like that would have his revenge.'

'Yes, you ought.' Edwin was very grave. 'Lucy, I know you love grand gestures, but you went too far. Couldn't you have told your parents and Bertha, quietly? He'd have been forbidden in the house, but never connected it with you. What happened was terrible enough, but it might have been even more terrible; it might have been you yourself.'

'I wish it had, instead of those poor things.'

'And how would your family have felt, then? How would I have felt? I love you very much, Lucy. Isn't it odd; I never loved you as much as today, when you were in such distress —

and I thought it was your strength I admired. What contradictory creatures we are.'

'I *thought* I was strong,' she said. 'Nobody's ever challenged me, all my life, and my parents let me do exactly what I wanted, so I grew up with all kinds of grand ideas about myself. I thought I could do anything and manage anybody. Well, I was quite wrong; what a way to learn, though. I'm glad you love me. You never said so before.'

'Of course I did!'

'No, Eddie. There was quite a lot about marriage, nothing about love. I love you, too, and I only found that out today, too. When I saw you come into the surgery I thought there was nobody else I could have borne to see come through that door just then. I know I seemed to be off my head — but I did think so in a muddled kind of way. And again, when you told me what to do for Brushy. Yes, I do love you, Eddie, and if you still want me to marry you, I will.'

'That's just as well, in view of what I came here to tell you.'

When Joan came in from her merciful errand of disposing of the poor corpses and cleaning up the surgery, the two were seated on the sofa, Lucy's head on Edwin's shoulder. She looked tired, tear-stained and plainer than Joan had ever seen her look, yet far happier. Joan surveyed them shrewdly.

'I reckon I'll be out of a job soon,' she said.

'Oh no, Joan!' Lucy cried. 'We'll take you with us to Preston — won't we, Eddie? when Edwin's found a house. If you'll come, that is.'

'Oh, I'll come. Happen you'll be starting another surgery there?'

Lucy looked up at Edwin. 'I don't know. I'll have to get over this, first. Just now I don't feel I trust myself any more.'

He took her hands between his own. 'We'll work something out. I'll have plenty of surgical instruments, remember, and all the books you could want. We'll look for a place just outside town, a house with a bit of land, where you can have a paddock and a stable yard. Who knows, one day we might see Mrs Edwin Atkinson's name in the rolls of the Royal Veterinary College. You would like that, wouldn't you?'

She shook her head, her lips trembling. Edwin pulled her to her feet. 'Come on, we must carry Brushy in here and make him comfortable before I go back.' Between them they conveyed the suspicious animal to the parlour hearth-rug with a clean blanket under him. 'Thank heaven he's more of a dog than a fox,' Edwin said. 'We'd never have got near a wild animal. Keep him nourished and reassured, and it's my guess he'll soon mend.'

'I'll sleep in here with him, tonight at least. Oh, Eddie, must you go? I wish you could stay.'

'A most improper suggestion, Miss Bradshaw. Seriously, I have to go on duty.' He kissed her, a long kiss which she returned passionately. His goddess had stepped down from her pedestal at last, and he liked her even better as a woman.

The fox's broken leg healed swiftly, with Lucy's nursing and care. Within a month he was limping about, always avoiding the room in which he had been attacked. The tabby cat and he formed a curious alliance, sleeping in the same basket and sharing meals, as though they knew themselves joint survivors of a disaster. He nosed the kittens inquisitively, was patient under their pestering, and formed an attachment to two of them, a ginger tom and a tortoiseshell female, perhaps taking to their foxy colours. Lucy kept them back, when the others went to farms. She was going to have a considerable menagerie to take with her to Preston, to the pretty old half-timbered house Edwin had taken at a very reasonable rent, so little it fitted in with modern tastes. They were to be married in September.

Dreadfully hasty, Eleanor said. She had wanted an elaborate wedding for Lucy, perhaps in Manchester Cathedral, with a wedding dress modelled on the Princess of Wales's and a professional choir. But Lucy cared nothing for such splendours, preferring to order for herself a simple dress of creamy satin, on the lines favoured by Pre-Raphaelite painters, with a headdress of roses. Eleanor watched the fitting of it, delighted by Lucy's radiance and the smiles which kept breaking out on her face.

'Happy, my dear? Yes, I can see that. Goodness, what wonders Edwin has performed.'

Lucy looked up from observing the fall of a mediaeval sleeve. 'In fact, Mama, it's not Edwin making me so cheerful. Though of course he does, always. I heard some news today, collected in Lancaster by Joan. Would it interest you to know that Mr Billy Sherston is laid up, seriously injured, with a poisoned wound in the leg? It seems that the bite of an animal's teeth set up an inflammation, and it's turned gangrenous. You know what that means.'

Eleanor was shocked. 'Not amputation?'

Lucy shrugged. 'Who knows? I don't, nor care. But I know whose teeth did it, my Brushy's, and I think it serves that man jolly well right for everything. Poetic justice, I call it. He may never hunt again.'

Eleanor shook her head. She hoped Lucy's future would be quite free from any more such unpleasant incidents.

That evening, at home, Lucy was intent on something else. 'I want to talk to you both alone,' she said. 'Bertha, could you find something to do for a little while, there's a dear? It's family matters, very important.' Bertha smiled and effaced herself. She had quite forgiven Lucy for the dreadful scene at Creston Hall. Had it not saved her from marriage to a wicked, cruel man, one of whom Father Andrew had confided to her that he did not really approve?

'My dear,' Lucy began, 'I want to ask you something. It sounds shocking, to mention your deaths. But we must be realistic. You're both so much older than me, I mean as generations go, because you were middle-aged when I was born. So one day the question of inheritance will come up. I feel ... it's very presumptuous of me. But — would you consider leaving Eagle Hall to Bertha, and enough money to run it? You see, she simply adores it, it's all she wants. She only thought of marrying Sherston because he could give her a handsome house not very far from here — but this is what she loves. She needs it so much, Papa. I used to think she was mercenary; I don't, now. She's somebody who's been starved all her life of what she finds here. I know that she'd make a wonderful mistress of it, just as you've done, Mama. And if she *were* mistress of it she could take her pick of suitors, and not marry just anyone.'

Eleanor looked questioningly at Jesse. 'Well ... Bertha is no blood relation of ours. We don't know...'

'You know enough about her, surely,' Lucy put in quickly. 'She's fitted in here as though she were a daughter. She's very simple, but quite clever too, when you think of the way she's turned herself from the frightened little mouse she was when she came here to a very passable young lady. And she's quite alone in the world except for a very old grandmother and an aunt, who wrote to tell her they wanted no more to do with her when she ran away from the convent. Oh, and there's a sister who's a nun.'

Eleanor said, 'But Eagle Hall should be kept in the family. I don't like the idea of its going outside.'

'Quite, Mama. But none of us is going to live in it. May's settled in Manchester with that rich husband of hers and about ten thousand relatives by marriage. Edwin won't want it — we shall always have to live in a town or near one, when he goes into practice for himself. Laurence is going to be living in vicarages — one hopes. Who else is there? And don't forget, it isn't everyone's house. People think such ancient places very old-fashioned these days when everything's spiky with Gothic turrets and the smart thing to build is another imitation of Balmoral. Somebody will buy it, knock it down, and create a perfectly awful house in its place.'

'That would have happened before our time here,' Jesse said, 'if my brother Shem hadn't come to the rescue. No, I wouldn't like to think of it.' He got up and began to pace the carpet. 'It's very noble and unselfish of you, my darling. Because the sale of the house, even if you didn't want to live in it, would bring you in a good deal of money.'

'I shall have a good deal already,' Lucy said placidly. 'Edwin is going to have a great name one day. I shouldn't be surprised if he didn't bring another title into the family.'

'Married to you, I shouldn't either,' Jesse said, smiling. 'But — to be serious — this decision is not one to be taken lightly. It would have to be discussed with lawyers and trustees. I can't promise anything until I've talked it over. I'm not sure that I am in favour of it, any more than your mother is. I had thought of you here, carrying on the name...'

'It won't be your name when I'm married,' Lucy pointed out.

'No, no. I mean, rather, the ... Eleanor, may I tell her?'

'If you wish.' Eleanor did not look at him. She had cherished her proxy motherhood; to relinquish it would be a wrench.

'Well, then.' Jesse stopped pacing. 'We always told you that you were adopted, Lucy; the child of friends who were dead. Everybody believes that. But — my dear, it's not true. I think the time has come to tell you that you are my own daughter.'

'I know,' Lucy said. 'I've known for years and years.' Jesse gasped, and Eleanor put her hand to her heart.

'You know? But how? Nobody could have told you. It was our secret.'

'I'll show you how.' Lucy put her arm through his and led him to the fireplace. Their two faces, close together, were reflected in the overmantel mirror. 'There. Anybody could see with half an eye that we're father and daughter. You're a good deal fatter than me, of course, and quite a bit pinker, but I expect that will come with time. And there was something else, the way we understand each other. Now sit down. It's been a little shock, hasn't it.' She went to kneel by Eleanor's side, putting an arm round her shoulders. 'Don't think I want to hear all about my real mother, though it would be interesting, if you felt like telling me, because you're my real mother, dearest, in everything that matters. Darling Mama. Don't cry. It won't make any difference at all. I only told you I knew to make you see that I understand why you hesitate about leaving the house to Bertha. Whatever you think is right, you must do. I merely recommended it.'

Lengthy discussions with Jesse's lawyers led to a final settlement apportioning Eagle Hall to Bertha for her lifetime, with an entail reversion of it and its lands to Lucy, if her lifetime exceeded Bertha's, or her heirs if she died first. When the last of the papers was signed Lucy and Edwin had been married almost a year, and she was pregnant with her first child. He was born in Preston, his two succeeding brothers in London, where Edwin was establishing a reputation as a specialist in gynaecology. Lucy's prophecy was correct. An appointment to the confinement of a Royal Personage led in due course to a title. Thanks to Sir Edwin Atkinson, thousands of women in generations to come would neither die nor lose their babies in childbirth, and his somewhat eccentric, strong-minded wife produced seven outstandingly healthy babies of her own. When other unusual ladies were campaigning for Women's Rights, Lucy continued her work for animals, with strong support from a public which was beginning to care for such causes. Her name was never to appear in the rolls of the Royal Veterinary College in London's Camden Town, but she was given the distinction of becoming an Honorary Member. As a very old lady she appeared in a newspaper photograph, proudly brandishing the cane with which she had floored a carter for ill-treating his horse.

Eleanor had fought for the retention of Eagle Hall for a time, only giving way when she saw how convinced Jesse was by his daughter's wishes. On the day the settlement was finalised she was unable to sleep. Stealing from Jesse's side, she went quietly downstairs, as she had done so long, long ago, to the old panelled room. The scent of roses was strong, as it had been on that night; but she sat for almost an hour in the dark, only the starlight faintly lighting the room through the diamond-paned windows.

Then she saw it, in the corner where the doll's house had been: a shimmer of colour, no form visible. At last a part of it became clear, a whitish blur that became a face. Although her sight had begun to fail, and she had brought no spectacles, she saw it sharply — a charmingly pretty pointed face, bright-eyed, with a political patch near the corner of the mouth, and the vague shape of piled hair above it. It was the face of her recurrent vision, she knew, though as she had never seen it before, much younger and happy, neither warning nor pleading. She smiled, saying, 'I hope you're satisfied, madam,' and saw the face smile in return, and felt a cold touch on her hand. The guardian of Eagle Hall had signified that all was to be well with it, the rightful owner chosen.

They found Eleanor there next morning, slumped in a chair. She had suffered a mild stroke, from which she recovered, only to have another, and a third, from which she died peacefully, holding Bertha's hand.

Bertha remained with Jesse, dutiful, devoted, everything a true daughter could have been. When he died, quite suddenly, in London, after a late-night sitting in the House, she became the mistress of Eagle Hall. She was only thirty, and in the height of her beauty. From her many suitors, she picked out Ralph Ashton, young, handsome, with a comfortable fortune, and Roman Catholic. There was no question of the young couple living anywhere but at Eagle Hall. For the rest of her life Bertha was supremely happy and fulfilled. She cared nothing that the house would not fall to her children, so long as she could live in it and care for it herself. She was not fifty when she died; and Ralph re-married, a comfortable lady who became a second mother to his four young ones, while Eagle Hall passed into trust for Lucy's eldest son. When the twentieth century dawned it would still stand, strong, ancient and wise. But never again haunted, after the electric light came to seek out dark corners and mysterious shadows. In the old graveyard Lucetta Bradshaw's stone grew thick with lichen, its inscription soon to be quite illegible.

'Yet shall thy grave with rising flow'rs be dressed,
And the green turf lie lightly on thy breast.

Some two years after George and Magnolia had sailed for Haiti, Belle received a letter in an unfamiliar, dashing handwriting.

Madam,
I must tell you that my father died on May 30th, last. He became suddenly ill with a return of his old fever, and within a week was dead. In his Will all his furniture and possessions in England are left to you. His lawyers will be informing you of this in time. My husband and I send you our commiserations on the loss of your husband.
Faithfully yours,
Magnolia de Serrano.

Sarcastic cat, thought Belle, folding the letter. Commiserations, indeed. So she had caught a husband, in spite of the mysterious scandal which had been spread about before George's sudden decision to take her back to the island of her birth.

She looked round at the furniture. Hers, now, but shabby and old-fashioned. She had lived in the narrow house by the quays all her married life, yet spent scarcely a happy day in it, only moments and hours of fleeting pleasure; and now even those had passed. The times were gone when men, married or otherwise, had been drawn to her beauty, for the beauty, too, was gone.

She was tired of life — or of the life she had led for so long. Since George had left she had gone through many nights of torment, regretting the folly of her behaviour to him, her crazy jealousy that had driven him away. There had been love behind it, but a love that killed. Often she would have given anything to have had him back, handsome and warm and passionate as he had once been. Well, she had paid for her conduct, and for the allowance she had taken from him, cheating on the clause which stipulated her chastity. Perhaps that money would now cease, and she would have nothing to live on. Somehow that seemed the least of her troubles.

For now she was quite alone. Of all her one-time friends and her family there was no one who wanted her. Her father dead, Aunt Margaret almost blind, dependent upon a companion, Laurence living far away, happy in his first curacy, writing dutifully to his mother but never suggesting she should travel south to join him. From Dove she had become estranged, shrinking away from her sister's domestic troubles and conscious of the disapproval she had earned at the Lion House. There was nobody.

How the thought came to her she did not know. But, in her solitude, a voice from the past spoke to her in her mind as clearly as though the speaker were in the room. 'Belle, my lass.'

'Yes,' she said aloud. 'Yes, of course.'

She had not been back to Kendal since her precipitate flight there in her girlhood, when her mare had gone lame. She had not found a welcome then, and there was no reason to suppose that she would now, or that her old lover would even be still alive, but she would go, if only as a kind of pilgrimage.

From Kendal station she took a cab. She would have liked to walk through the familiar streets, reviving memories; but nowadays there was rheumatism in her back and legs, making the steep cobbled slopes daunting to her.

'Stop here, please.' The cab drew up outside the antique shop, its bow window unchanged; even the muddle of contents looked the same, and the name was still Raven.

The shop-bell clanged loudly as she went in. The man who had been mending a piece of china got to his feet. He was old, his white hair and beard sharply contrasted to the country brown of his face, but the dark eyes were still bright and the broad shoulders hardly stooped. He surveyed the woman whose fashionably flowing coat and crinoline could not conceal the thinness of her figure, and whose saucy pork-pie hat was perched upon hair from which the yellow dye was fading, unflatteringly to her haggard face.

'Come on in, Belle,' said Will Raven. 'I've been half expecting you.'

She went into his outstretched arms, where she should have been thirty years before, and knew, as they closed comfortingly round her, that she would never leave him again.

The cotton famine was over, Atkinson and Absalom's mill itself again. David had insisted on setting up a trust, financed by himself to maintain the estate and its inhabitants until the end of the American blockade. Some of his relatives and colleagues thought it odd that he should support a non-Jewish charity; but after all, it was in the family, which made it acceptable. He was rich enough to afford such gestures.

Once the anxiety over his workers ended, Joe began to improve in health and spirits, though he would never be quite his old self again. There had been a time when Dove had wondered — not hoped, for that would have been wicked — whether his illness would be fatal. Could it be, in time, that she and Basil would be together, before the last remnants of her youth faded?

But it was not to be. Friendship was all that was left to them, and that must be enough; and the memory they shared of an evening by flickering firelight.

And there was no time to brood on the past and what might have been, for every year brought new excitements; the birth of May's children, all beautiful in their different ways, dark and fair; much visiting between Deansbury and Manchester taking place; and the more leisured arrival of Edwin's and Lucy's. The quiet, brooding house became disorderly and cheerful, loud with young voices and the stamping of boys' boots on the stairs. Ponies were in the stables, to be ridden in the holidays, kittens, firmly deposited there by Lucy, in the kitchens. The Queen herself had never had such over-flowing nurseries, said Dove, when Laurence's well-behaved twin boys came with their mother, Agnes, to join the holiday throng.

Dove, in the summer-flowering garden, turned and looked at the plain face of the grey house that had seen so much sorrow, and longing, and anxiety, and now held only calm and laughter. The two lions which gave it its name were a little more weather-beaten and chipped, their features a trifle blurred.

'Thank you for guarding my nest so long,' she said. 'It was so empty, and now it's full. I hope you'll see many, many more children in your house, when ours are grown and gone.'

She stooped and stroked the rough curls of their manes, sun-warmed, and fancied that the stern whiskered mouths faintly smiled.

A NOTE TO THE READER

If you have enjoyed this novel enough to leave a review on **Amazon** and **Goodreads**, then we would be truly grateful.
Sapere Books

Sapere Books is an exciting new publisher of brilliant fiction and popular history.

To find out more about our latest releases and our monthly bargain books visit our website: **saperebooks.com**